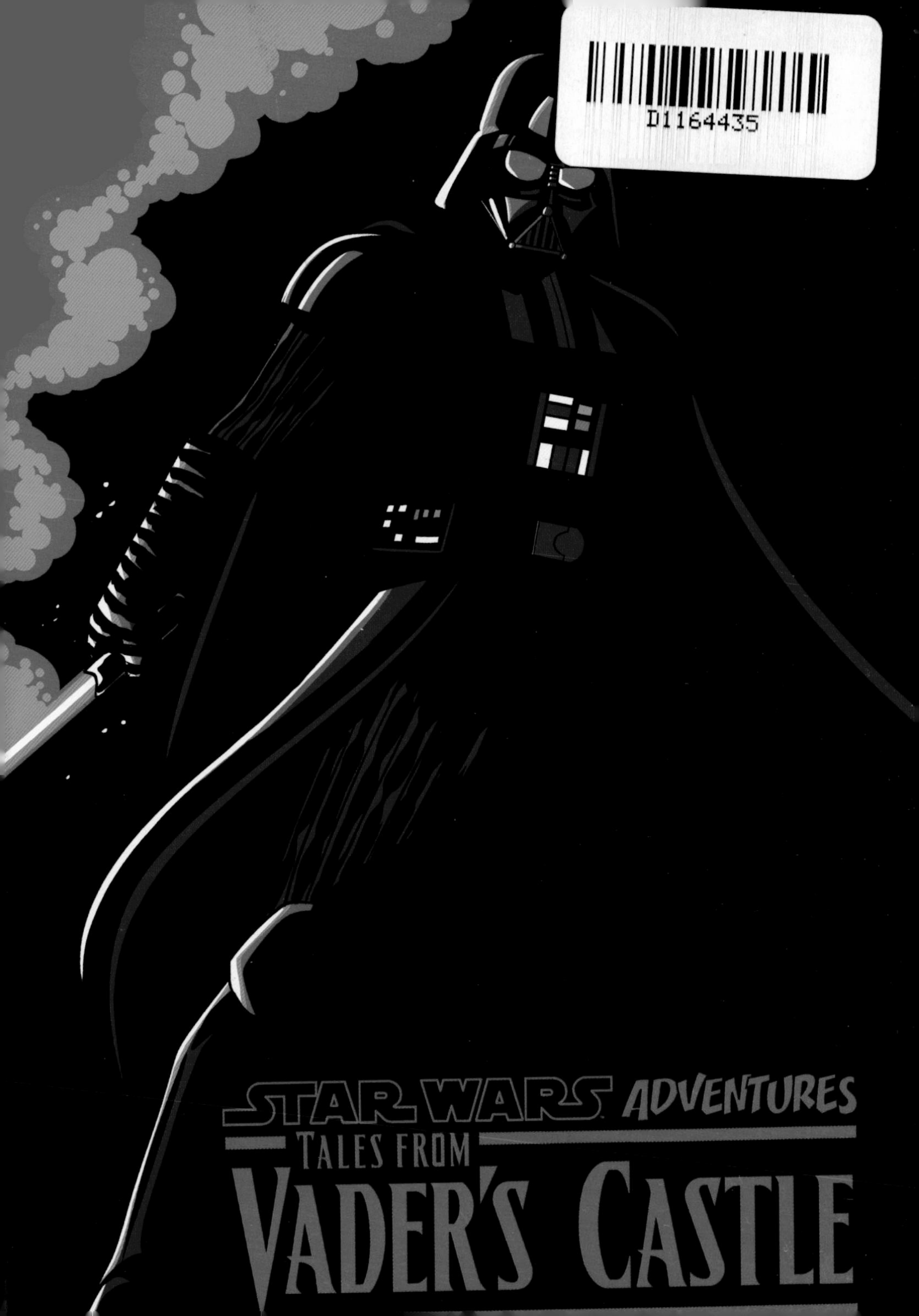
STAR WARS ADVENTURES
TALES FROM
VADER'S CASTLE

Facebook: **facebook.com/idwpublishing**
Twitter: **@idwpublishing**
YouTube: **youtube.com/idwpublishing**
Tumblr: **tumblr.idwpublishing.com**
Instagram: **instagram.com/idwpublishing**

ISBN: 978-1-68405-407-7   22 21 20 19   1 2 3 4

LETTERERS
ROBBIE ROBBINS
& TOM B. LONG

SERIES ASSISTANT EDITOR
ELIZABETH BREI

SERIES EDITOR
DENTON J. TIPTON

COLLECTION EDITORS
JUSTIN EISINGER
& ALONZO SIMON

COLLECTION DESIGNER
CLYDE GRAPA

PUBLISHER
CHRIS RYALL

Originally published as STAR WARS ADVENTURES: TALES
FROM VADER'S CASTLE issues #1–5.

Chris Ryall, President, Publisher, and CCO
John Barber, Editor-In-Chief
Robbie Robbins, EVP/Sr. Art Director
Cara Morrison, Chief Financial Officer
Matt Ruzicka, Chief Accounting Officer
Anita Frazier, SVP of Sales and Marketing
David Hedgecock, Associate Publisher
Jerry Bennington, VP of New Product Development
Lorelei Bunjes, VP of Digital Services
Justin Eisinger, Editorial Director, Graphic Novels & Collections
Eric Moss, Senior Director, Licensing and Business Development

Ted Adams, IDW Founder

Lucasfilm Credits:
Senior Editor: Robert Simpson
Creative Director: Michael Siglain
Story Group: James Waugh, Leland Chee,

Written by: **Cavan Scott**

Issue #1: Art and Colors by **Derek Charm** [1-5, 19-20] & **Chris Fenoglio** [4-18]

Issue #2: Art by **Derek Charm** [1-3, 19-20] & **Kelley Jones** [4-18], with colors by **Derek Charm** [1-3, 19-20] & **Michelle Madsen** [4-18]

Issue #3: Art by **Derek Charm** [1-3, 19-20] & **Corin Howell** [4-18], with colors by **Derek Charm** [1-3, 19-20] & **Valentina Pinto** [4-18]

Issue #4: Art by **Derek Charm** [1-2, 17-20] & **Robert Hack** [3-16], with colors by **Derek Charm** [1-2, 17-20] & **Charlie Kirchoff** [3-16]

Issue #5: Art by **Derek Charm** [1-2, 7-20] & **Charles Paul Wilson III** [3-6], with colors by **Derek Charm** [1-2, 7-20] & **Michael Devito** [3-6]

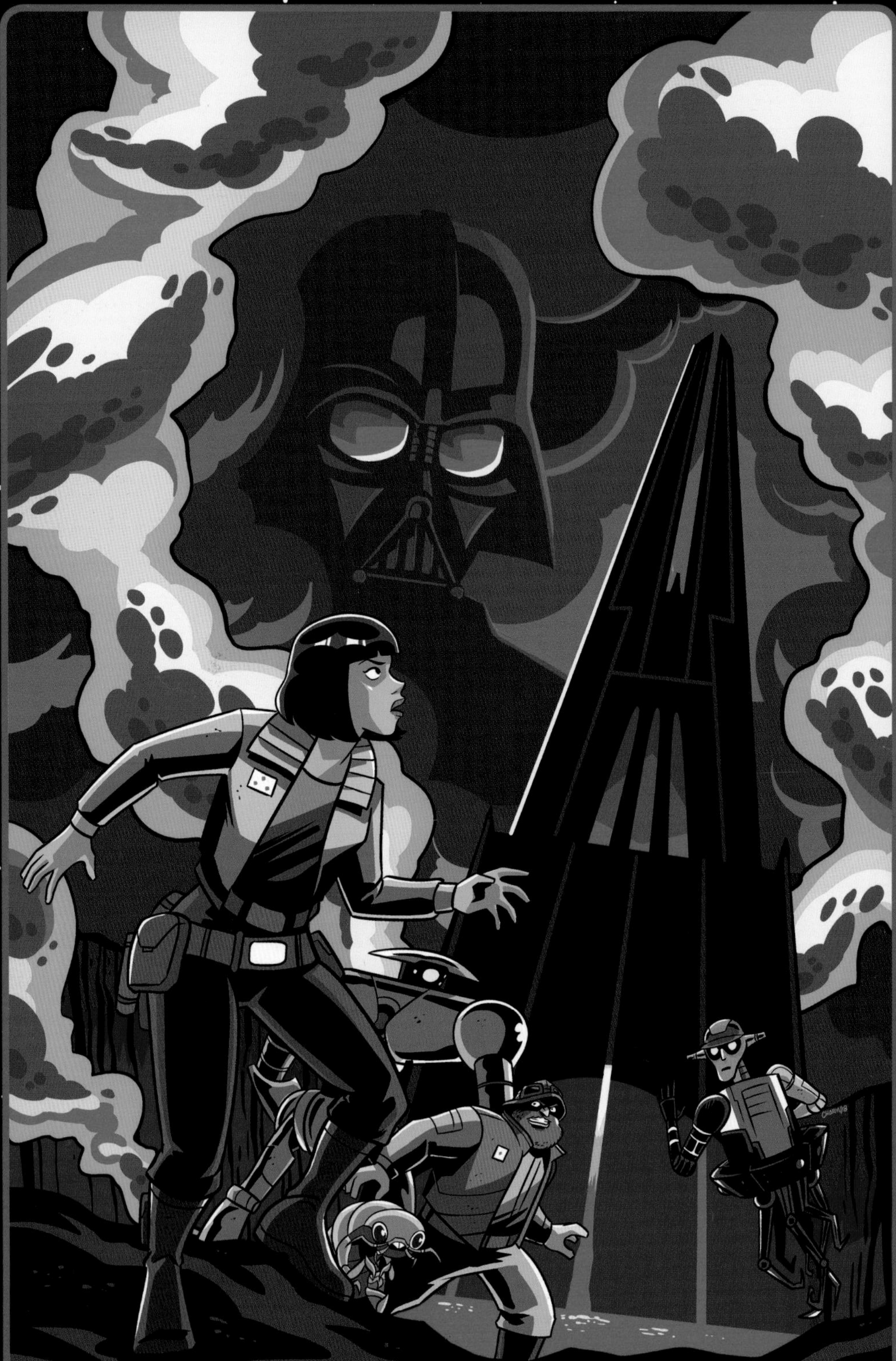

Art by Derek Charm

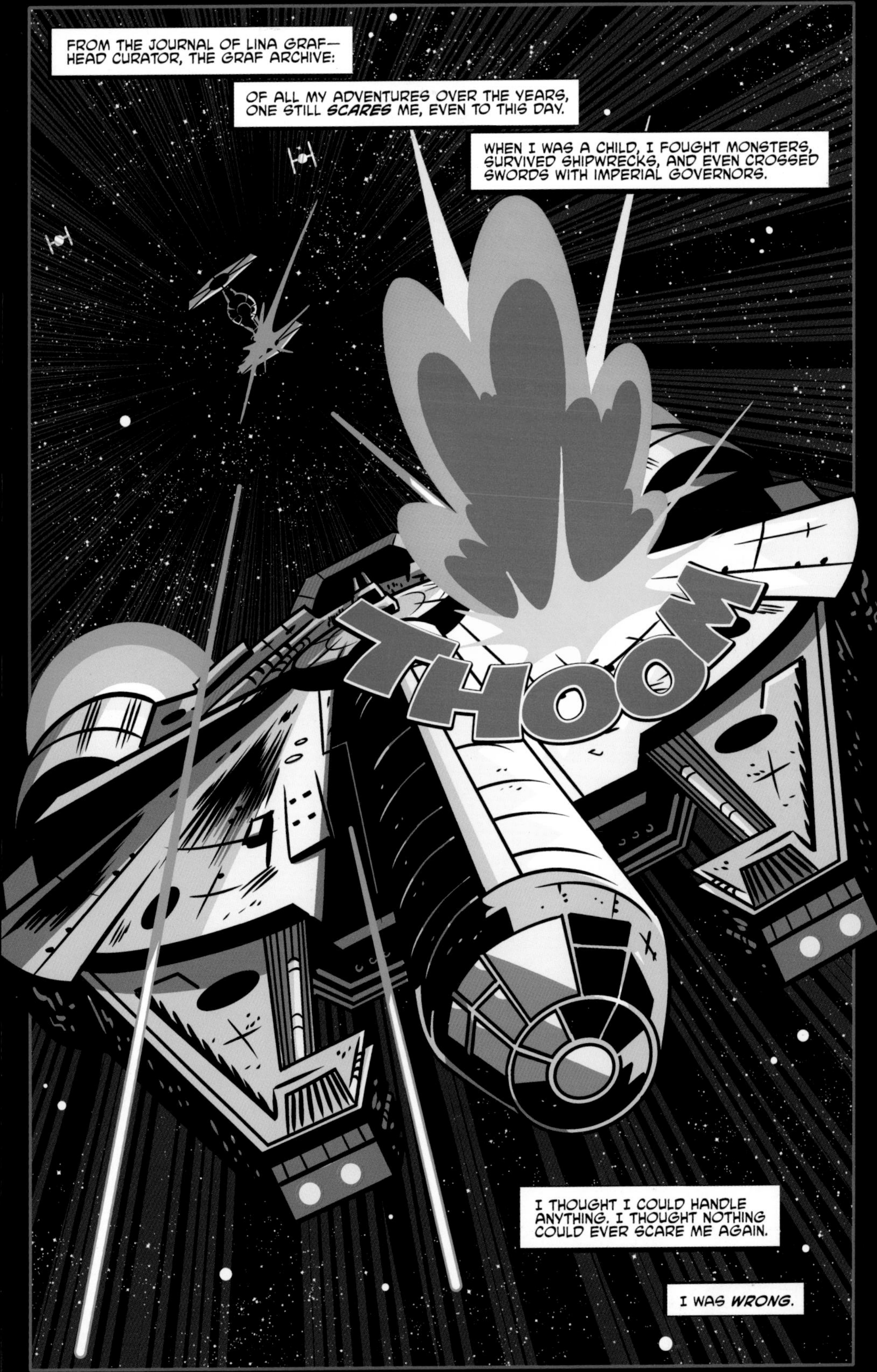
FROM THE JOURNAL OF LINA GRAF—
HEAD CURATOR, THE GRAF ARCHIVE:
OF ALL MY ADVENTURES OVER THE YEARS, ONE STILL *SCARES* ME, EVEN TO THIS DAY.
WHEN I WAS A CHILD, I FOUGHT MONSTERS, SURVIVED SHIPWRECKS, AND EVEN CROSSED SWORDS WITH IMPERIAL GOVERNORS.
THOOM
I THOUGHT I COULD HANDLE ANYTHING. I THOUGHT NOTHING COULD EVER SCARE ME AGAIN.
I WAS *WRONG*.

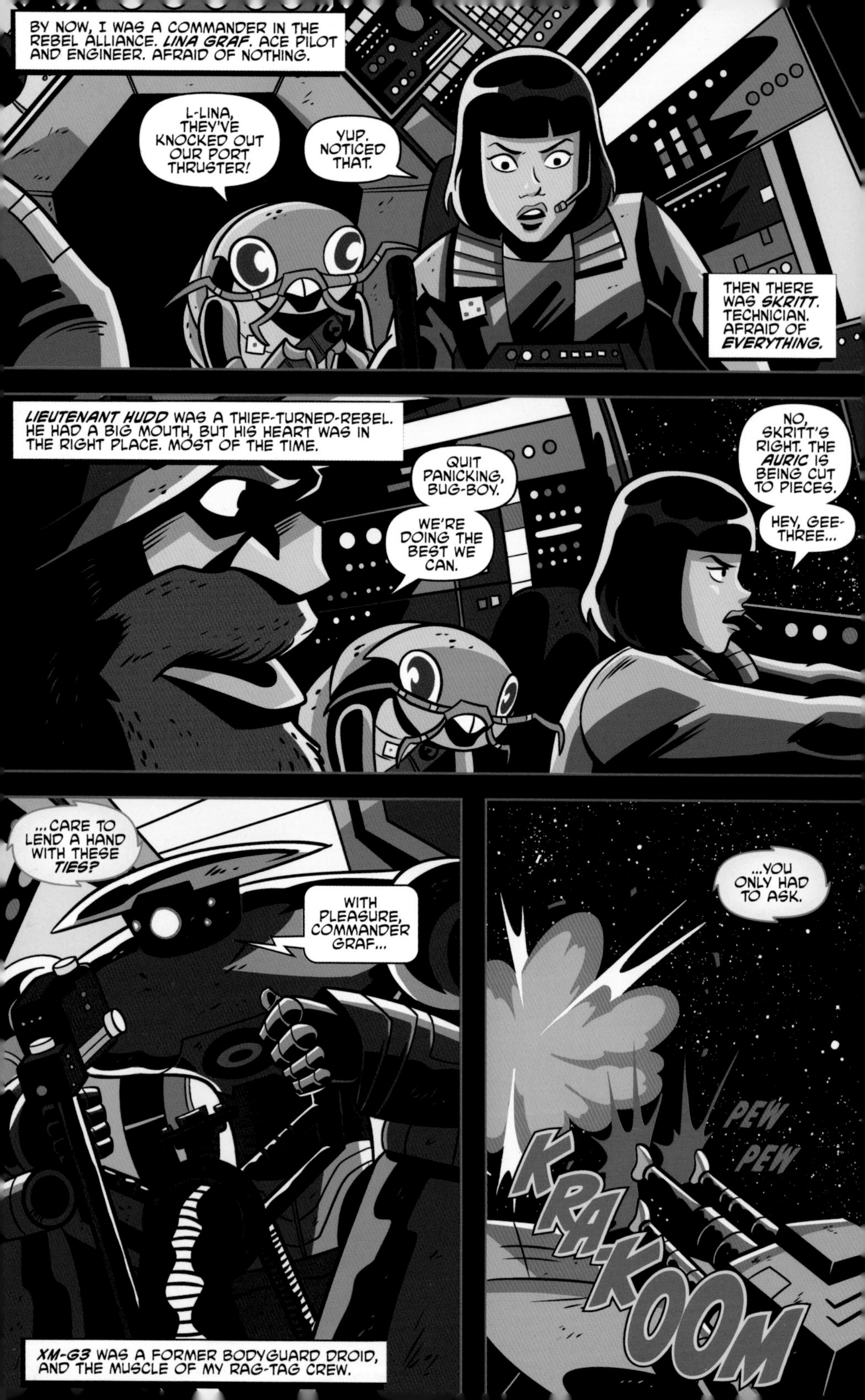
BY NOW, I WAS A COMMANDER IN THE REBEL ALLIANCE. *LINA GRAF*. ACE PILOT AND ENGINEER. AFRAID OF NOTHING.
L-LINA, THEY'VE KNOCKED OUT OUR PORT THRUSTER!
YUP. NOTICED THAT.
THEN THERE WAS *SKRITT*. TECHNICIAN. AFRAID OF *EVERYTHING.*
LIEUTENANT HUDD WAS A THIEF-TURNED-REBEL. HE HAD A BIG MOUTH, BUT HIS HEART WAS IN THE RIGHT PLACE. MOST OF THE TIME.
QUIT PANICKING, BUG-BOY.
WE'RE DOING THE BEST WE CAN.
NO, SKRITT'S RIGHT. THE *AURIC* IS BEING CUT TO PIECES.
HEY, GEE-THREE...
...CARE TO LEND A HAND WITH THESE *TIES?*
WITH PLEASURE, COMMANDER GRAF...
XM-G3 WAS A FORMER BODYGUARD DROID, AND THE MUSCLE OF MY RAG-TAG CREW.
...YOU ONLY HAD TO ASK.
PEW
PEW
KRA-KOOM

HA HA! NOT A BAD SHOT FOR A *TIN-CAN*.

NEVER CALL HIM THAT TO HIS FACE, HUDD.

GEE-THREE'S SEEN MORE ACTION THAN ALL OF US PUT TOGETHER.

AND WE'RE NOT OUT OF THE WOODS YET. SHIELDS ARE DOWN AND THE POWER CORE'S ABOUT TO BLOW.

WE NEED SOMEWHERE TO LAND, AND FAST. ANY IDEAS, CRATER?

THERE IS ONE PLANET THAT MIGHT BE SUITABLE. A FORMER MINING WORLD, NOW HEAVILY GUARDED BY *IMPERIAL FORCES*.

CR-8R WAS THERE AS WELL. MY CONSTANT COMPANION SINCE I WAS A KID... AND AS CRANKY AS THE DAY HE WAS ACTIVATED.

WHY? WHAT'S DOWN THERE?

HOW EXACTLY AM I SUPPOSED TO KNOW *THAT?*

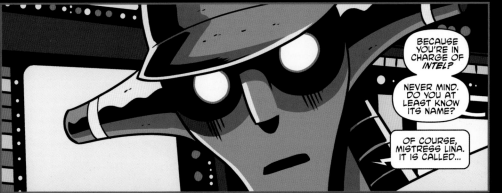

BECAUSE YOU'RE IN CHARGE OF *INTEL?*

NEVER MIND. DO YOU AT LEAST KNOW ITS NAME?

OF COURSE, MISTRESS LINA. IT IS CALLED...

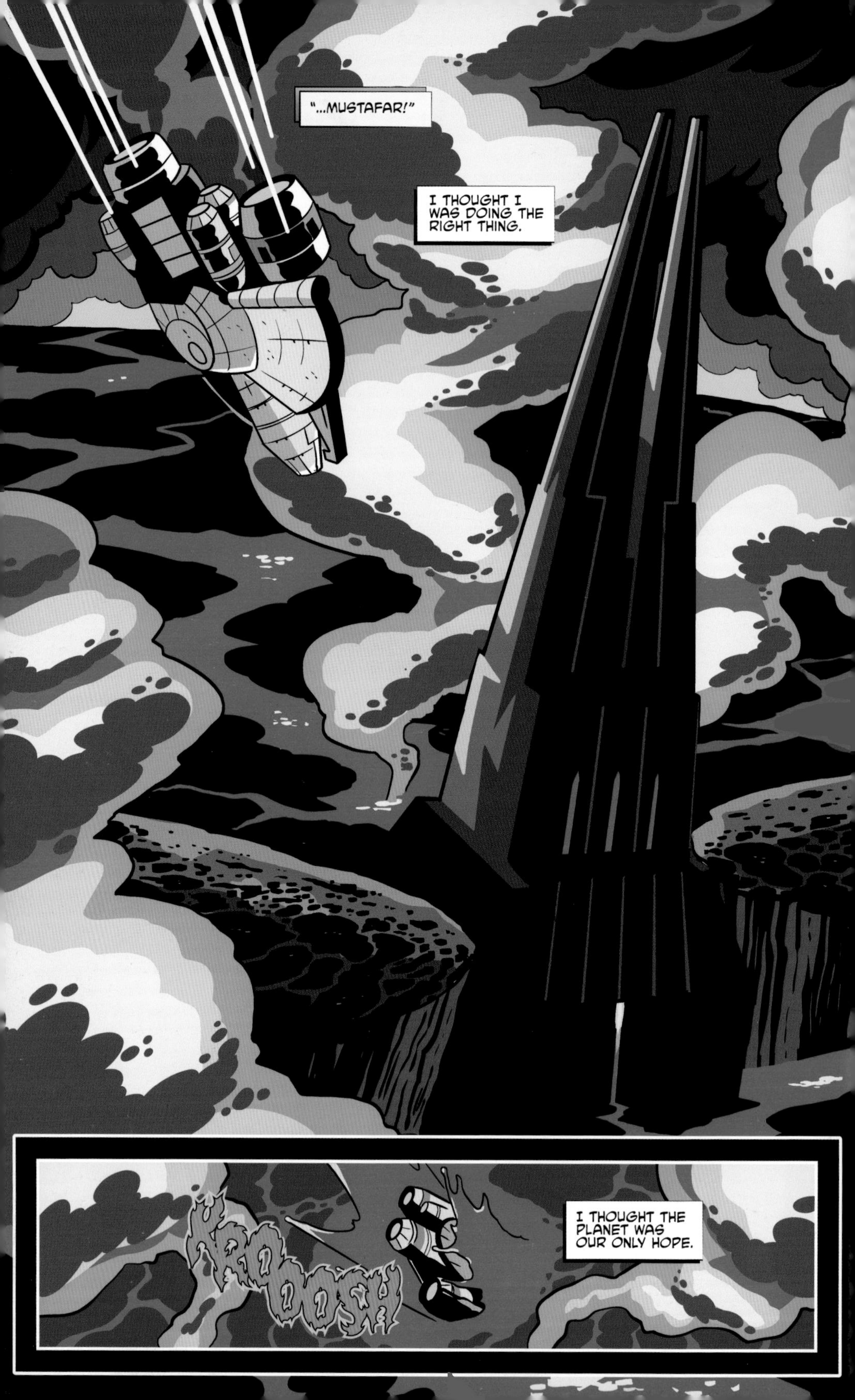
"...MUSTAFAR!"
I THOUGHT I WAS DOING THE RIGHT THING.
I THOUGHT THE PLANET WAS OUR ONLY HOPE.

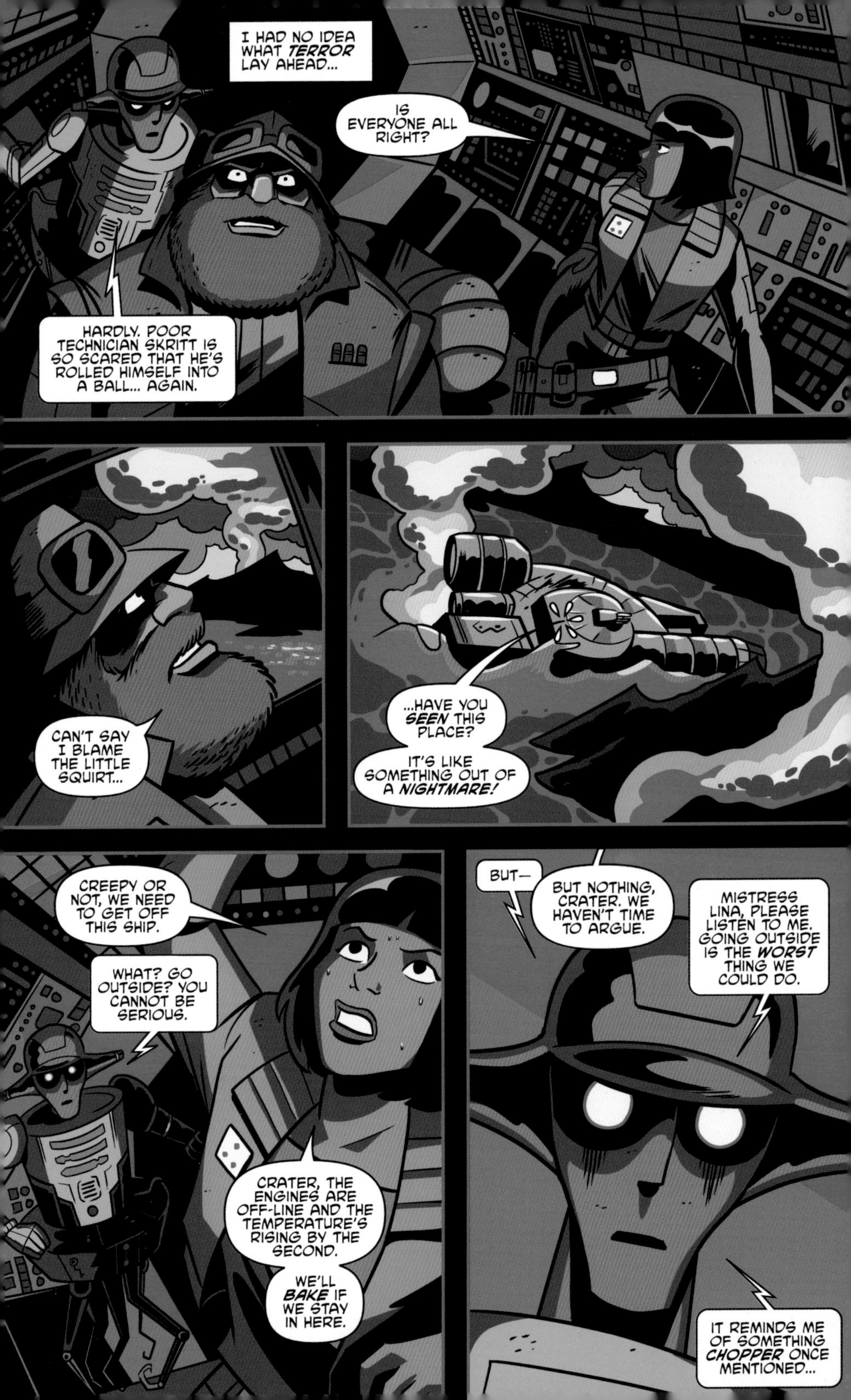
I HAD NO IDEA WHAT TERROR LAY AHEAD...
IS EVERYONE ALL RIGHT?
HARDLY. POOR TECHNICIAN SKRITT IS SO SCARED THAT HE'S ROLLED HIMSELF INTO A BALL... AGAIN.
CAN'T SAY I BLAME THE LITTLE SQUIRT...
...HAVE YOU SEEN THIS PLACE?
IT'S LIKE SOMETHING OUT OF A NIGHTMARE!
CREEPY OR NOT, WE NEED TO GET OFF THIS SHIP.
WHAT? GO OUTSIDE? YOU CANNOT BE SERIOUS.
CRATER, THE ENGINES ARE OFF-LINE AND THE TEMPERATURE'S RISING BY THE SECOND.
WE'LL BAKE IF WE STAY IN HERE.
BUT—
BUT NOTHING, CRATER. WE HAVEN'T TIME TO ARGUE.
MISTRESS LINA, PLEASE LISTEN TO ME. GOING OUTSIDE IS THE WORST THING WE COULD DO.
IT REMINDS ME OF SOMETHING CHOPPER ONCE MENTIONED...

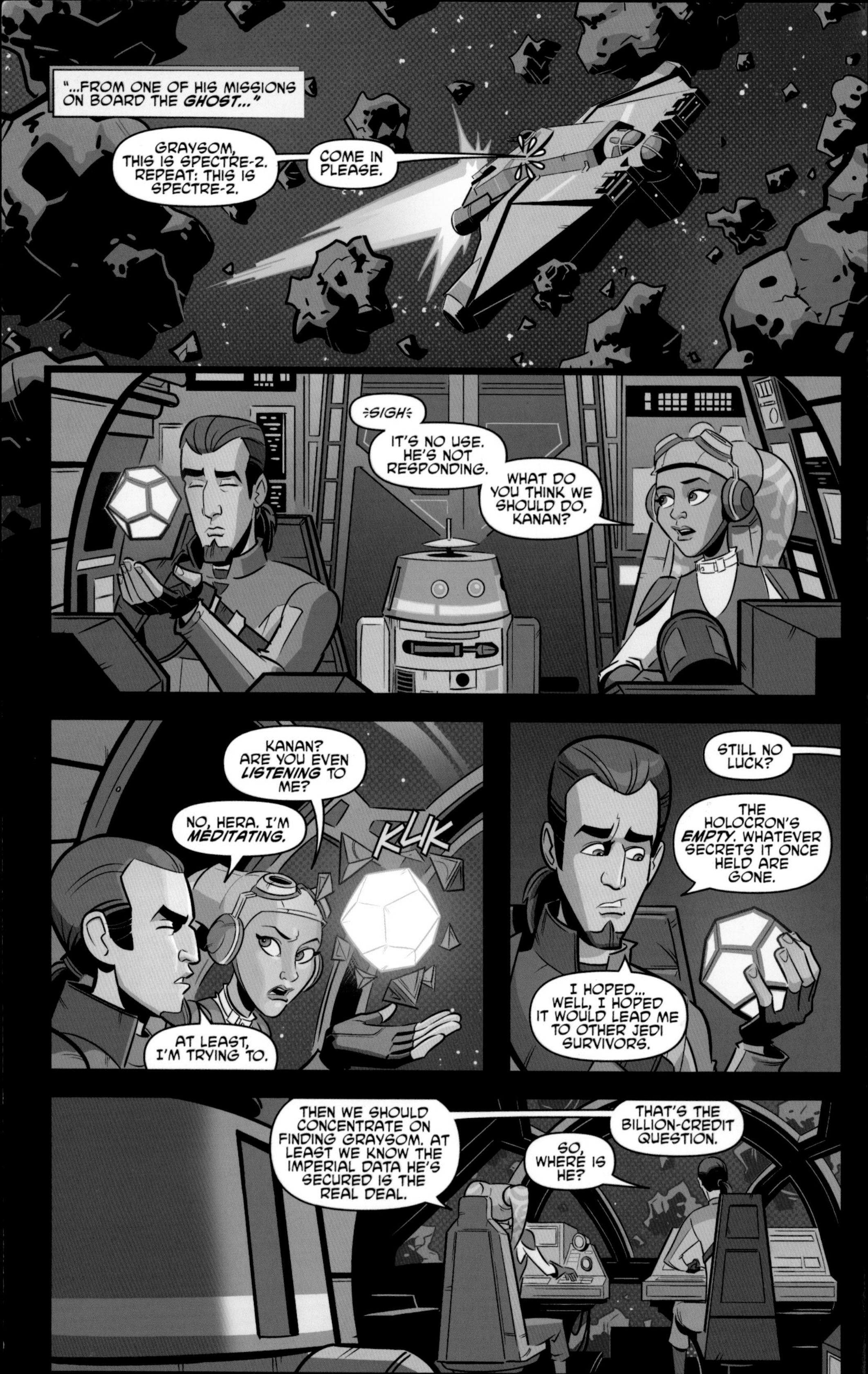

"...FROM ONE OF HIS MISSIONS ON BOARD THE *GHOST*..."
GRAYSOM, THIS IS SPECTRE-2. REPEAT: THIS IS SPECTRE-2.
COME IN PLEASE.
SIGH
IT'S NO USE. HE'S NOT RESPONDING.
WHAT DO YOU THINK WE SHOULD DO, KANAN?
KANAN? ARE YOU EVEN *LISTENING* TO ME?
NO, HERA. I'M *MEDITATING.*
KLIK
AT LEAST, I'M TRYING TO.
STILL NO LUCK?
THE HOLOCRON'S *EMPTY*. WHATEVER SECRETS IT ONCE HELD ARE GONE.
I HOPED... WELL, I HOPED IT WOULD LEAD ME TO OTHER JEDI SURVIVORS.
THEN WE SHOULD CONCENTRATE ON FINDING GRAYSOM. AT LEAST WE KNOW THE IMPERIAL DATA HE'S SECURED IS THE REAL DEAL.
SO, WHERE IS HE?
THAT'S THE BILLION-CREDIT QUESTION.

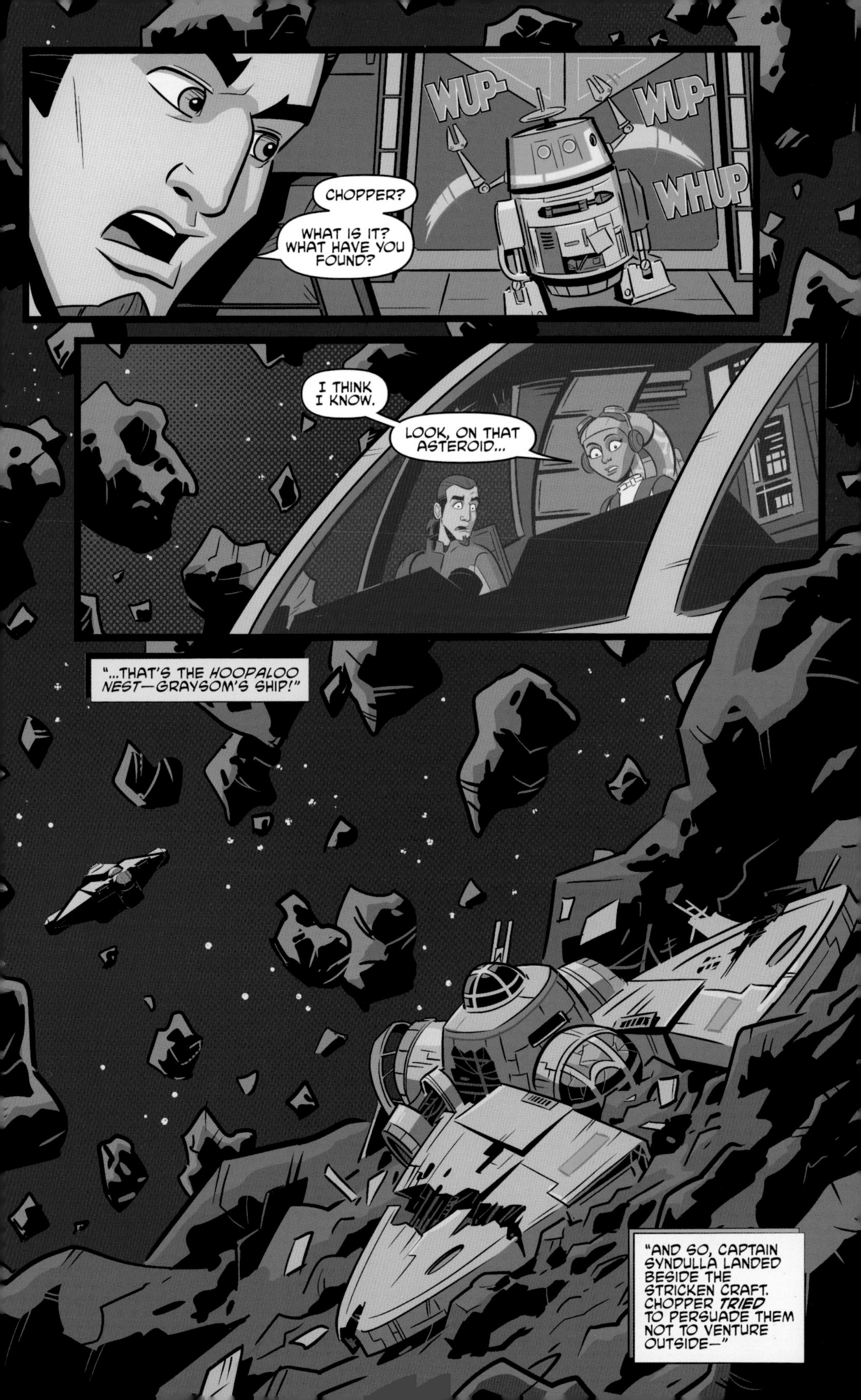
WUP-
WUP-
WHUP
CHOPPER?
WHAT IS IT? WHAT HAVE YOU FOUND?
I THINK I KNOW.
LOOK, ON THAT ASTEROID...
"...THAT'S THE *HOOPALOO NEST*—GRAYSOM'S SHIP!"
"AND SO, CAPTAIN SYNDULLA LANDED BESIDE THE STRICKEN CRAFT. CHOPPER *TRIED* TO PERSUADE THEM NOT TO VENTURE OUTSIDE—"

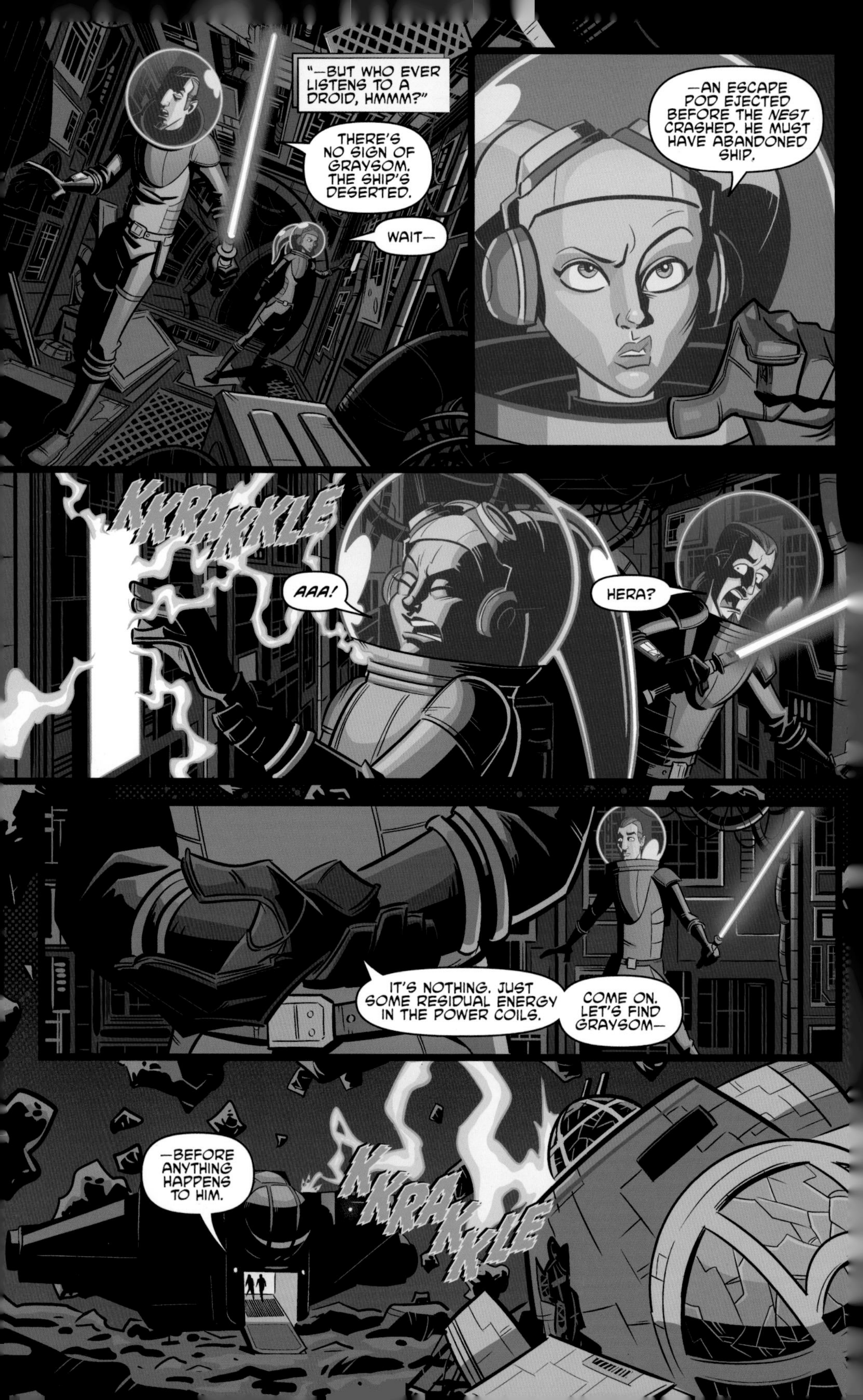
"—BUT WHO EVER LISTENS TO A DROID, HMMM?"
THERE'S NO SIGN OF GRAYSOM. THE SHIP'S DESERTED.
WAIT—
—AN ESCAPE POD EJECTED BEFORE THE *NEST* CRASHED. HE MUST HAVE ABANDONED SHIP.
KKRAKKLE
AAA!
HERA?
IT'S NOTHING. JUST SOME RESIDUAL ENERGY IN THE POWER COILS.
COME ON. LET'S FIND GRAYSOM—
—BEFORE ANYTHING HAPPENS TO HIM.
KKRAKKLE

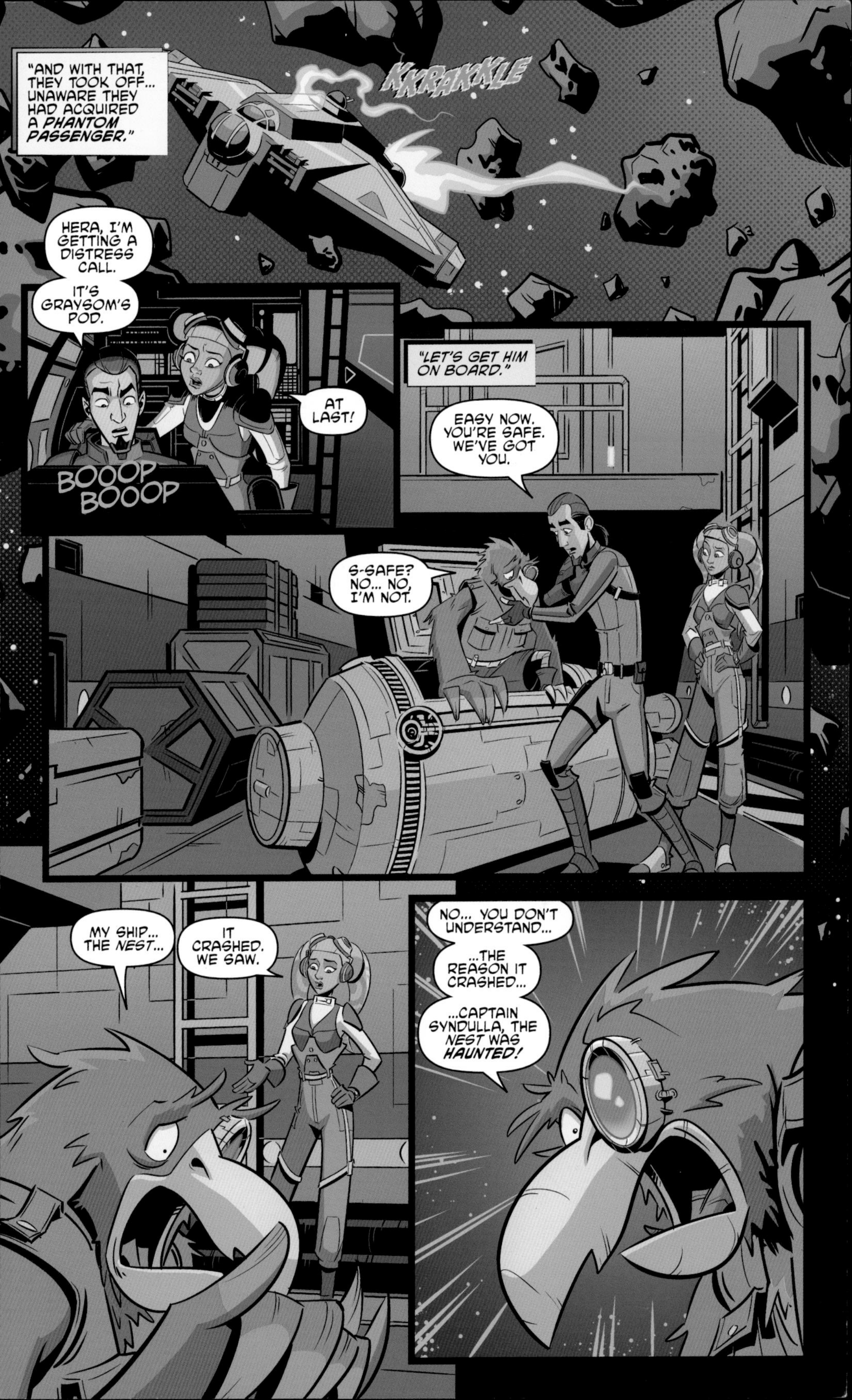
"AND WITH THAT, THEY TOOK OFF... UNAWARE THEY HAD ACQUIRED A *PHANTOM PASSENGER.*"
KKRAKKLE
HERA, I'M GETTING A DISTRESS CALL.
IT'S GRAYSOM'S POD.
AT LAST!
BOOOP BOOOP
"LET'S GET HIM ON BOARD."
EASY NOW. YOU'RE SAFE. WE'VE GOT YOU.
S-SAFE? NO... NO, I'M NOT.
MY SHIP... THE *NEST*...
IT CRASHED. WE SAW.
NO... YOU DON'T UNDERSTAND...
...THE REASON IT CRASHED...
...CAPTAIN SYNDULLA, THE *NEST* WAS ***HAUNTED!***

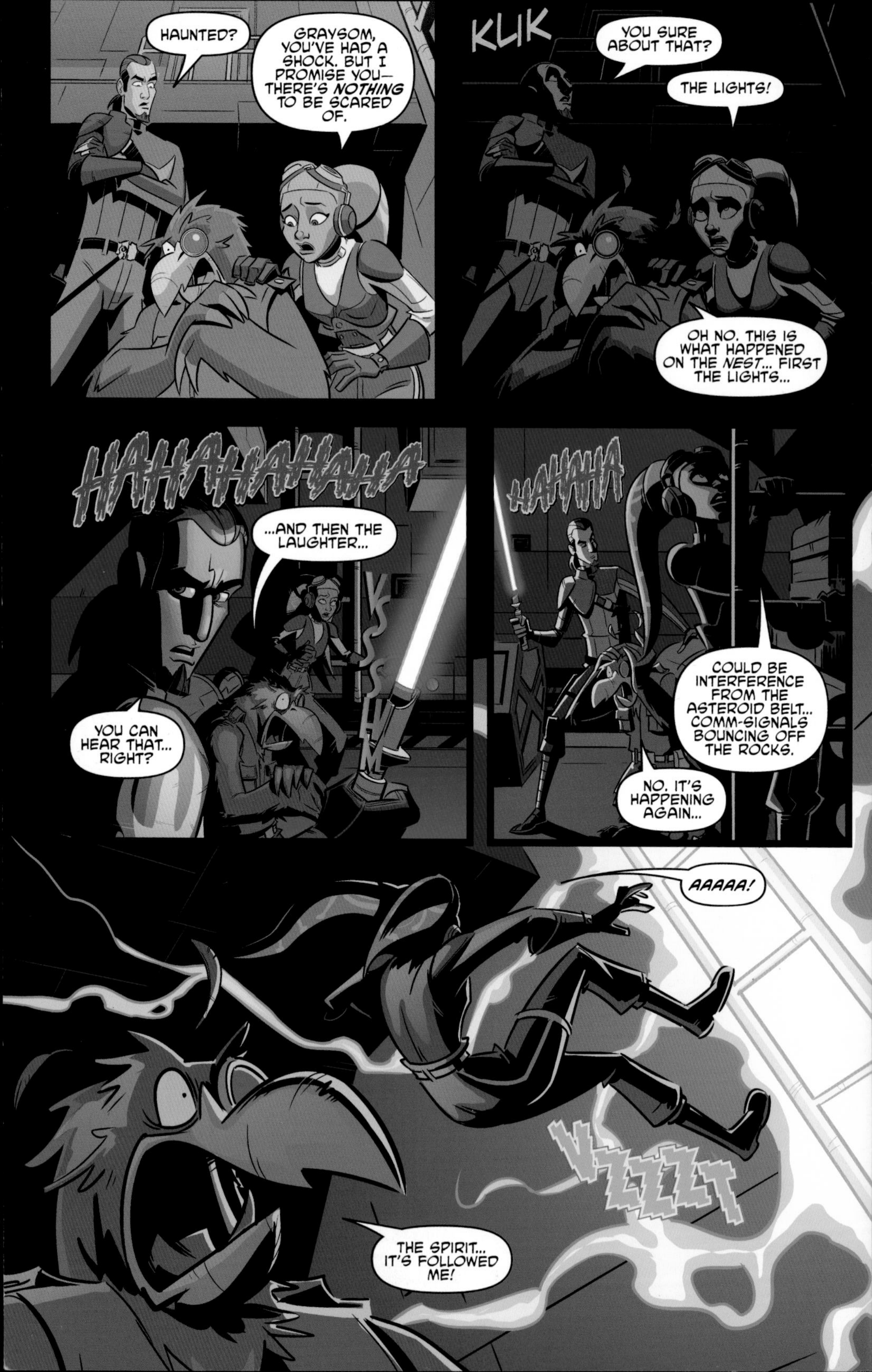
HAUNTED?
GRAYSOM, YOU'VE HAD A SHOCK. BUT I PROMISE YOU— THERE'S *NOTHING* TO BE SCARED OF.
KLIK
YOU SURE ABOUT THAT?
THE LIGHTS!
OH NO. THIS IS WHAT HAPPENED ON THE *NEST*... FIRST THE LIGHTS...
HAHAHAHAHAHAHA
...AND THEN THE LAUGHTER...
YOU CAN HEAR THAT... RIGHT?
VSSHMM
HAHAHA
COULD BE INTERFERENCE FROM THE ASTEROID BELT... COMM-SIGNALS BOUNCING OFF THE ROCKS.
NO. IT'S HAPPENING AGAIN...
AAAAA!
VZZZZT
THE SPIRIT... IT'S FOLLOWED ME!

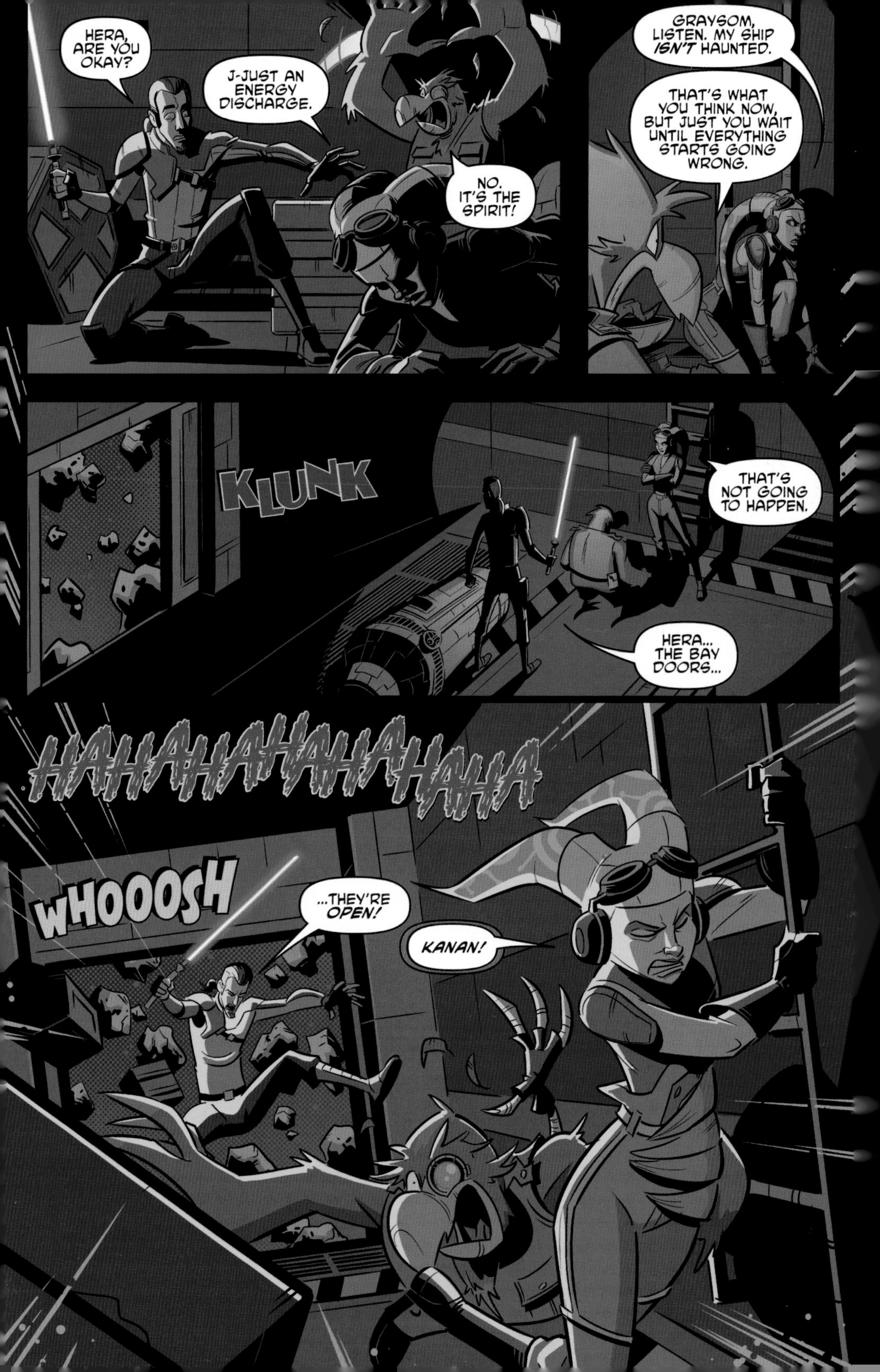
HERA, ARE YOU OKAY?
J-JUST AN ENERGY DISCHARGE.
NO. IT'S THE SPIRIT!
GRAYSOM, LISTEN. MY SHIP *ISN'T* HAUNTED.
THAT'S WHAT YOU THINK NOW, BUT JUST YOU WAIT UNTIL EVERYTHING STARTS GOING WRONG.
KLUNK
THAT'S NOT GOING TO HAPPEN.
HERA... THE BAY DOORS...
HAHAHAHAHAHAHAHA
WHOOOSH
...THEY'RE *OPEN!*
KANAN!

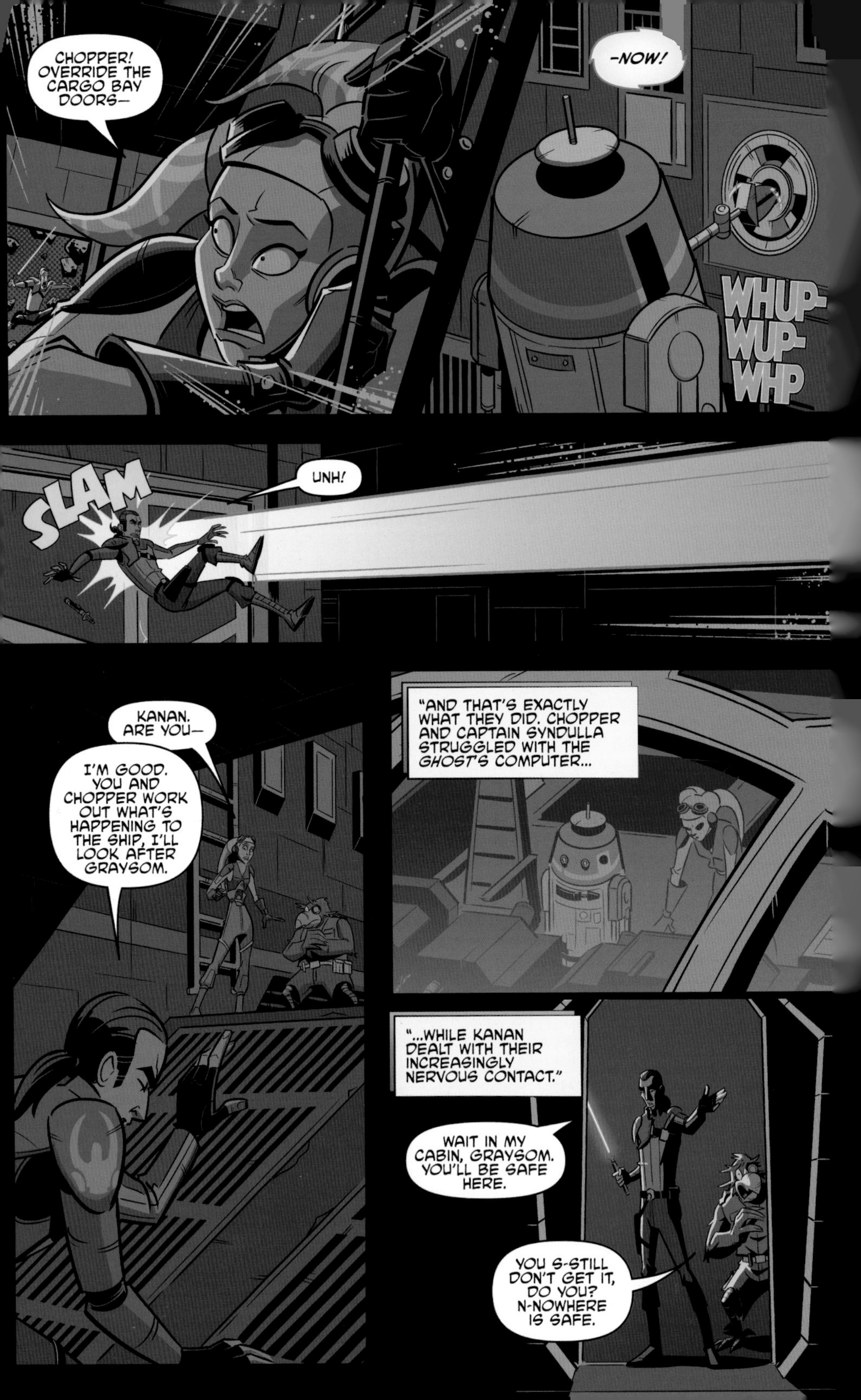
CHOPPER! OVERRIDE THE CARGO BAY DOORS—
—NOW!
WHUP-WUP-WHP
SLAM
UNH!
KANAN. ARE YOU—
I'M GOOD. YOU AND CHOPPER WORK OUT WHAT'S HAPPENING TO THE SHIP, I'LL LOOK AFTER GRAYSOM.
"AND THAT'S EXACTLY WHAT THEY DID. CHOPPER AND CAPTAIN SYNDULLA STRUGGLED WITH THE GHOST'S COMPUTER...
"...WHILE KANAN DEALT WITH THEIR INCREASINGLY NERVOUS CONTACT."
WAIT IN MY CABIN, GRAYSOM. YOU'LL BE SAFE HERE.
YOU S-STILL DON'T GET IT, DO YOU? N-NOWHERE IS SAFE.

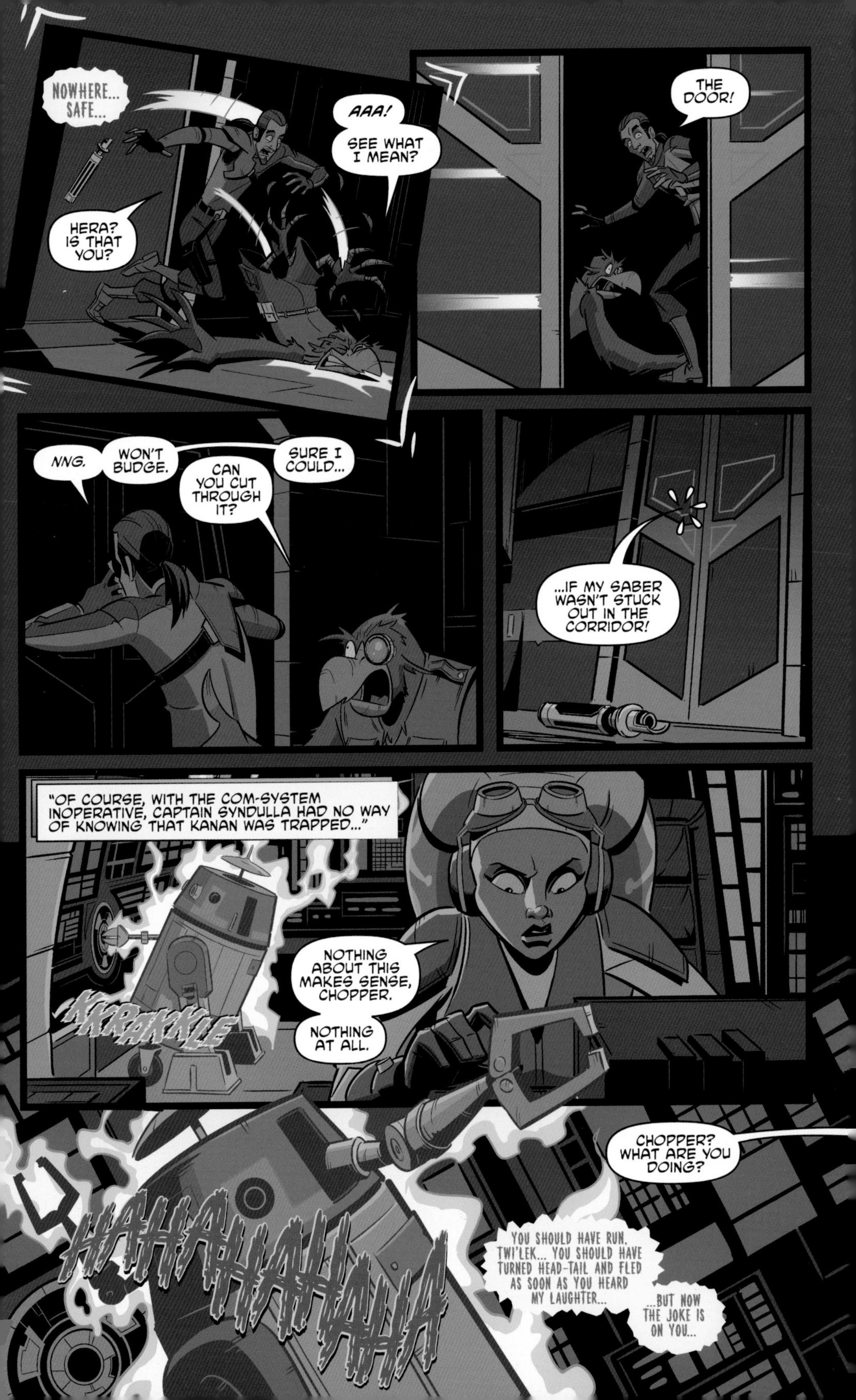
NOWHERE... SAFE...
AAA!
SEE WHAT I MEAN?
HERA? IS THAT YOU?
THE DOOR!
NNG.
WON'T BUDGE.
CAN YOU CUT THROUGH IT?
SURE I COULD...
...IF MY SABER WASN'T STUCK OUT IN THE CORRIDOR!
"OF COURSE, WITH THE COM-SYSTEM INOPERATIVE, CAPTAIN SYNDULLA HAD NO WAY OF KNOWING THAT KANAN WAS TRAPPED..."
KKRAKKLE
NOTHING ABOUT THIS MAKES SENSE, CHOPPER.
NOTHING AT ALL.
CHOPPER? WHAT ARE YOU DOING?
HAHAHAHAHAHAHA
YOU SHOULD HAVE RUN, TWI'LEK... YOU SHOULD HAVE TURNED HEAD-TAIL AND FLED AS SOON AS YOU HEARD MY LAUGHTER...
...BUT NOW THE JOKE IS ON YOU...

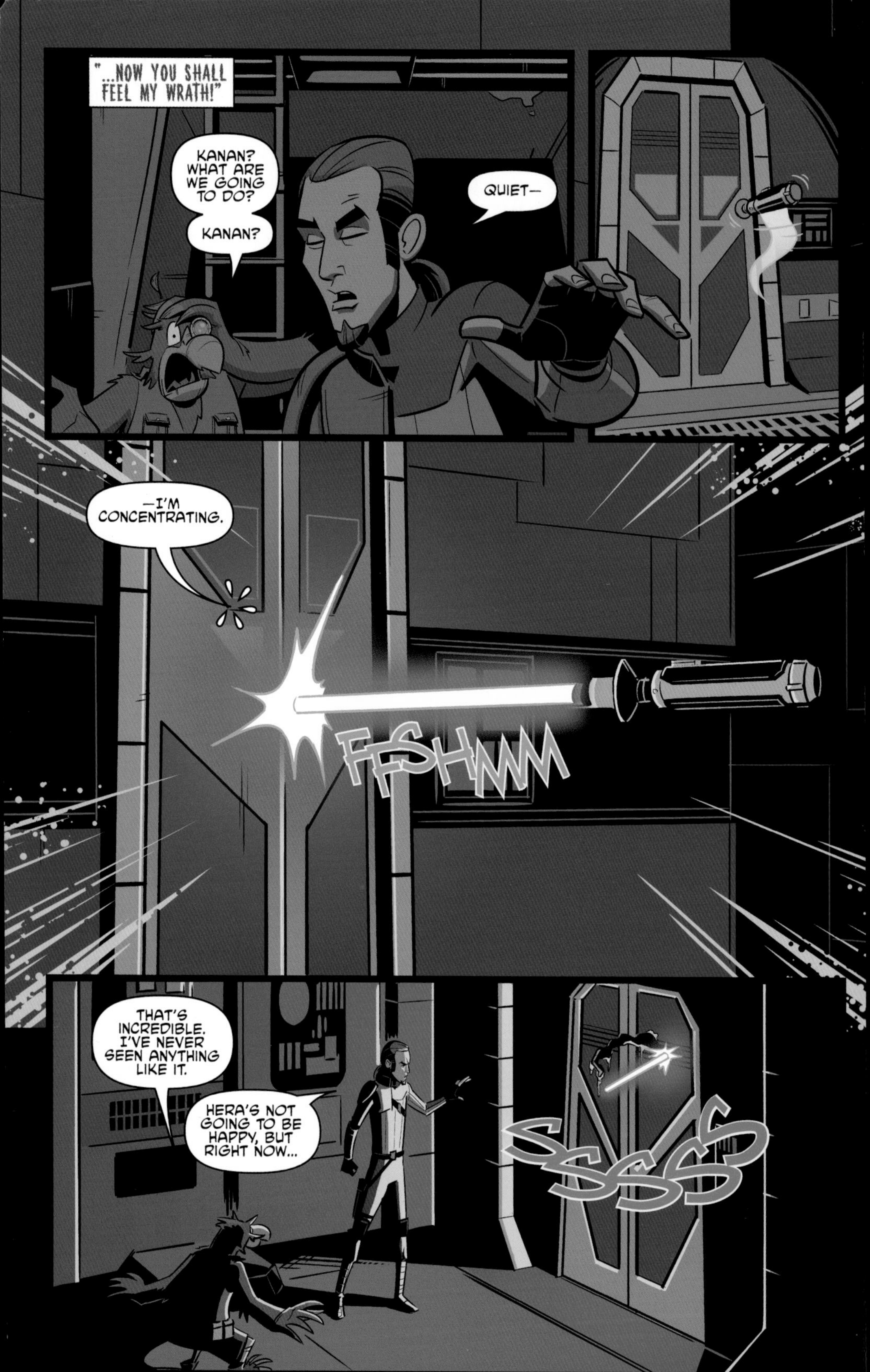
"...NOW YOU SHALL FEEL MY WRATH!"
KANAN? WHAT ARE WE GOING TO DO?
KANAN?
QUIET—
—I'M CONCENTRATING.
FFSHMMM
THAT'S INCREDIBLE. I'VE NEVER SEEN ANYTHING LIKE IT.
HERA'S NOT GOING TO BE HAPPY, BUT RIGHT NOW...
SSSSS

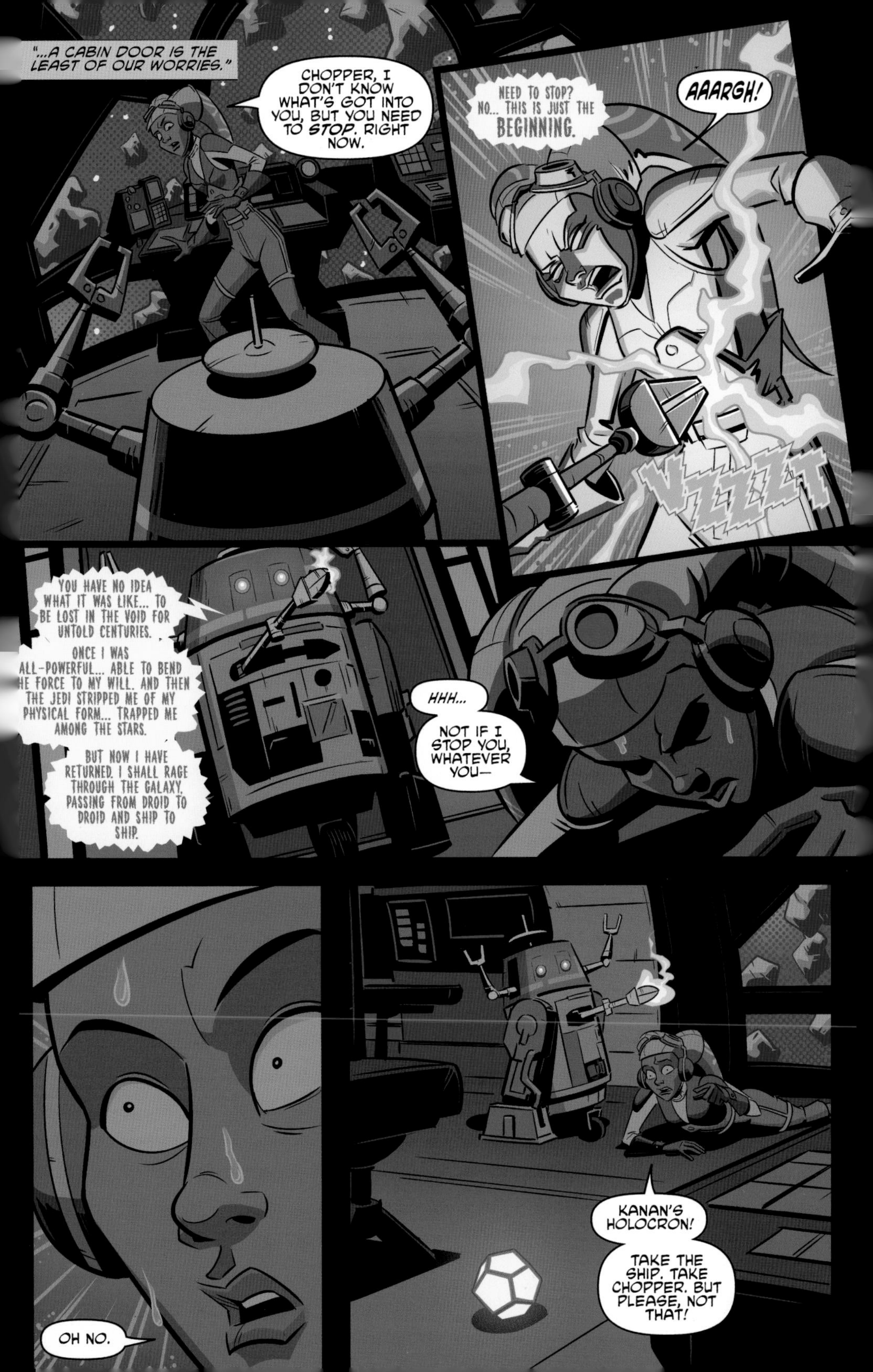
"...A CABIN DOOR IS THE LEAST OF OUR WORRIES."
CHOPPER, I DON'T KNOW WHAT'S GOT INTO YOU, BUT YOU NEED TO STOP. RIGHT NOW.
NEED TO STOP? NO... THIS IS JUST THE BEGINNING.
AAARGH!
VZZZZT
YOU HAVE NO IDEA WHAT IT WAS LIKE... TO BE LOST IN THE VOID FOR UNTOLD CENTURIES.
ONCE I WAS ALL-POWERFUL... ABLE TO BEND THE FORCE TO MY WILL. AND THEN THE JEDI STRIPPED ME OF MY PHYSICAL FORM... TRAPPED ME AMONG THE STARS.
BUT NOW I HAVE RETURNED. I SHALL RAGE THROUGH THE GALAXY, PASSING FROM DROID TO DROID AND SHIP TO SHIP.
HHH...
NOT IF I STOP YOU, WHATEVER YOU—
OH NO.
KANAN'S HOLOCRON!
TAKE THE SHIP. TAKE CHOPPER. BUT PLEASE, NOT THAT!

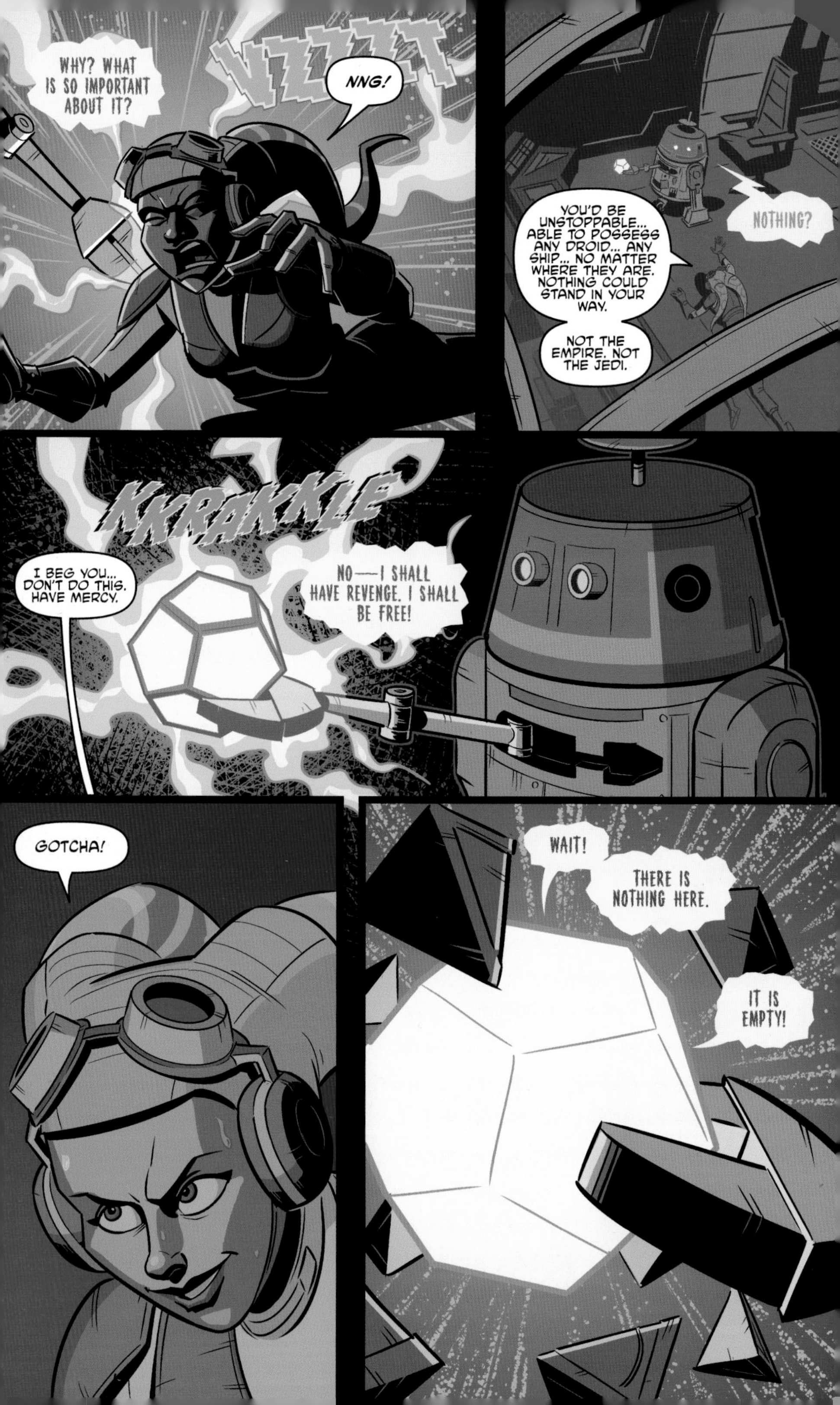
WHY? WHAT IS SO IMPORTANT ABOUT IT?
VZZZZT
NNG!
YOU'D BE UNSTOPPABLE... ABLE TO POSSESS ANY DROID... ANY SHIP... NO MATTER WHERE THEY ARE. NOTHING COULD STAND IN YOUR WAY.
NOT THE EMPIRE. NOT THE JEDI.
NOTHING?
KKRAKKLE
I BEG YOU... DON'T DO THIS. HAVE MERCY.
NO—I SHALL HAVE REVENGE. I SHALL BE FREE!
GOTCHA!
WAIT!
THERE IS NOTHING HERE.
IT IS EMPTY!

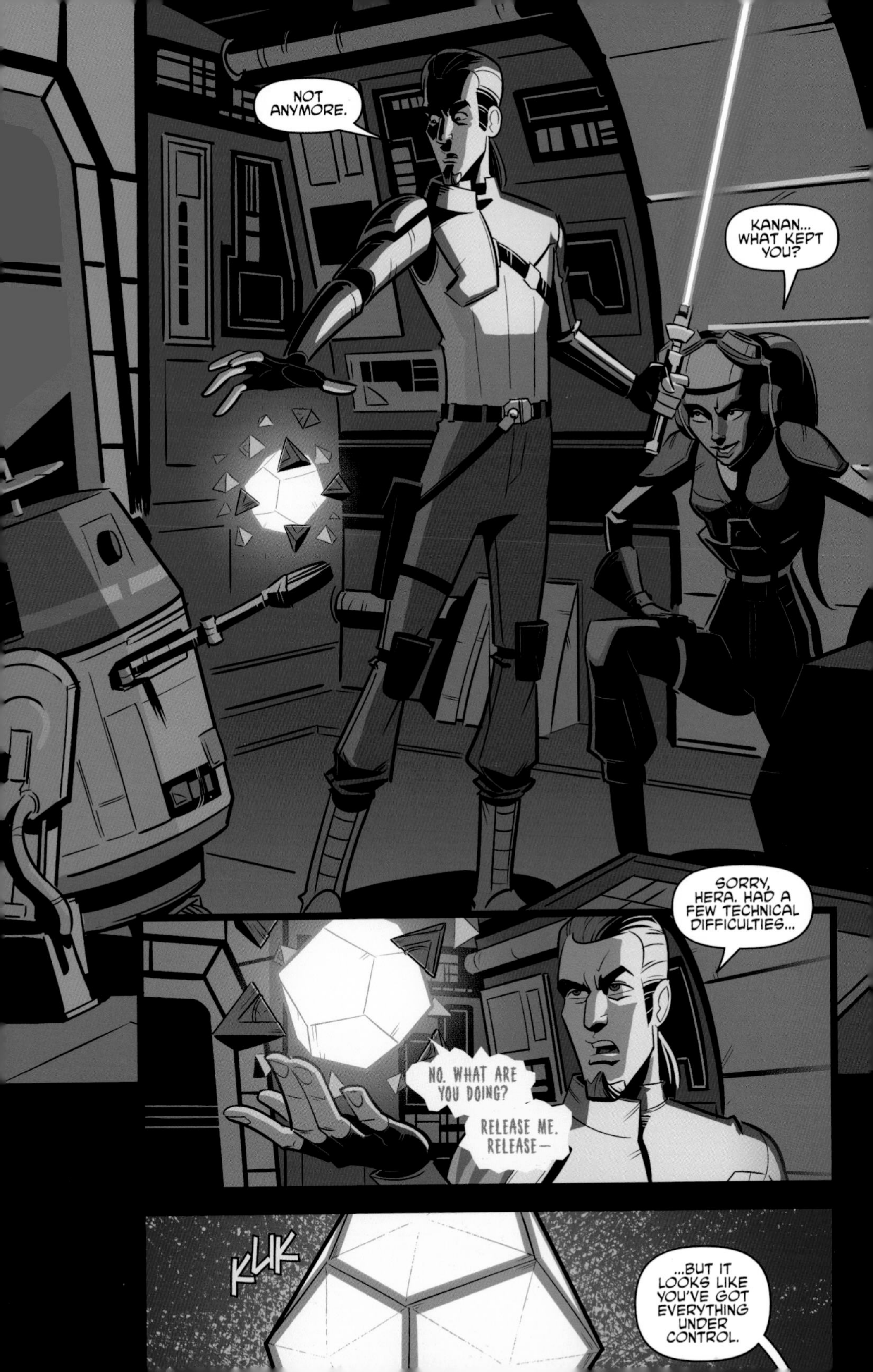
NOT ANYMORE.
KANAN... WHAT KEPT YOU?
SORRY, HERA. HAD A FEW TECHNICAL DIFFICULTIES...
NO. WHAT ARE YOU DOING?
RELEASE ME. RELEASE—
KLIK
...BUT IT LOOKS LIKE YOU'VE GOT EVERYTHING UNDER CONTROL.

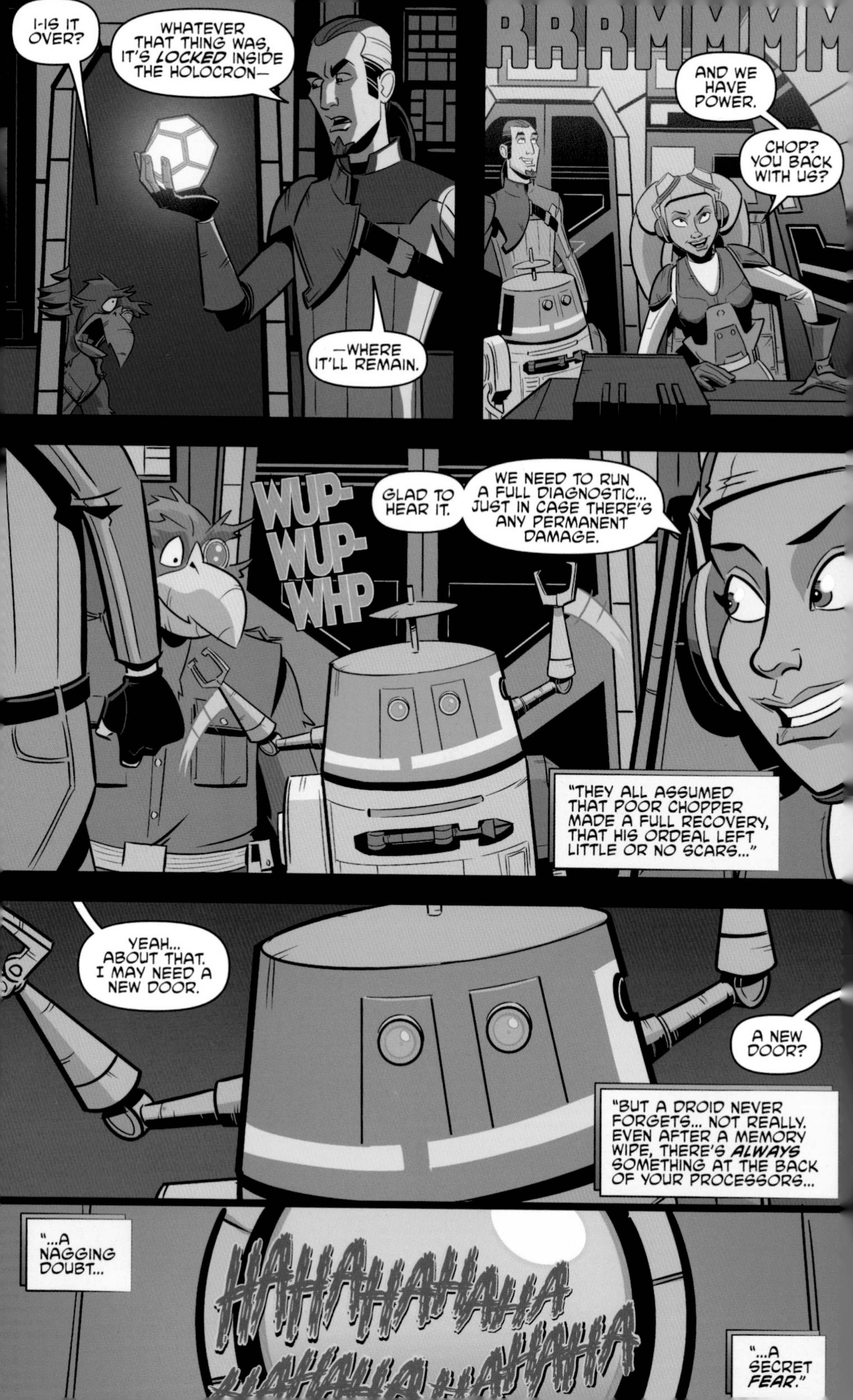
I-IS IT OVER?
WHATEVER THAT THING WAS, IT'S LOCKED INSIDE THE HOLOCRON—
—WHERE IT'LL REMAIN.
RRRMMMMM
AND WE HAVE POWER.
CHOP? YOU BACK WITH US?
WUP-WUP-WHP
GLAD TO HEAR IT.
WE NEED TO RUN A FULL DIAGNOSTIC... JUST IN CASE THERE'S ANY PERMANENT DAMAGE.
"THEY ALL ASSUMED THAT POOR CHOPPER MADE A FULL RECOVERY, THAT HIS ORDEAL LEFT LITTLE OR NO SCARS..."
YEAH... ABOUT THAT. I MAY NEED A NEW DOOR.
A NEW DOOR?
"BUT A DROID NEVER FORGETS... NOT REALLY. EVEN AFTER A MEMORY WIPE, THERE'S ALWAYS SOMETHING AT THE BACK OF YOUR PROCESSORS...
"...A NAGGING DOUBT...
HAHAHAHAHA
"...A SECRET FEAR."

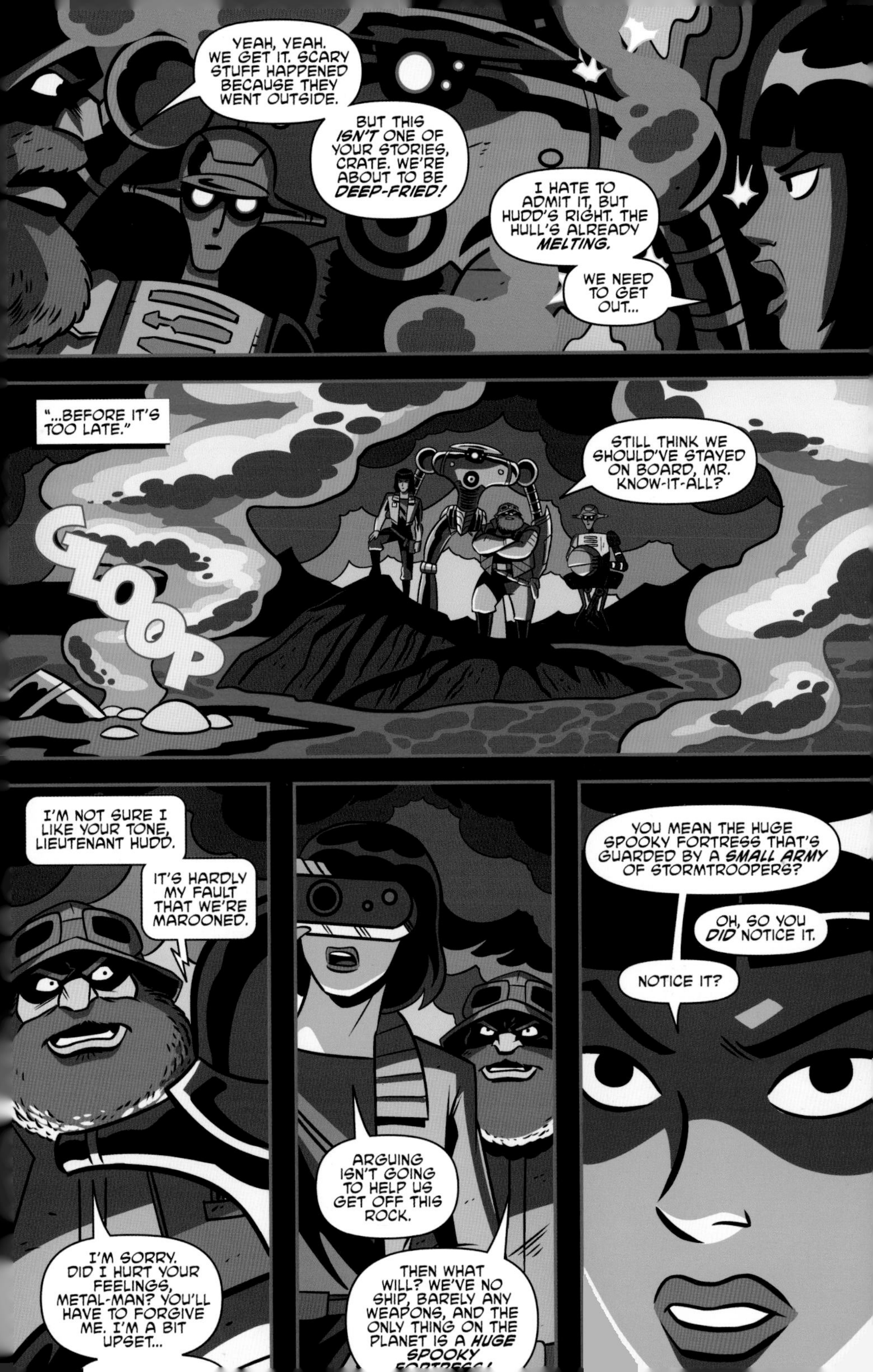

YEAH, YEAH. WE GET IT. SCARY STUFF HAPPENED BECAUSE THEY WENT OUTSIDE.
BUT THIS *ISN'T* ONE OF YOUR STORIES, CRATE. WE'RE ABOUT TO BE *DEEP-FRIED!*
I HATE TO ADMIT IT, BUT HUDD'S RIGHT. THE HULL'S ALREADY *MELTING.*
WE NEED TO GET OUT...
"...BEFORE IT'S TOO LATE."
STILL THINK WE SHOULD'VE STAYED ON BOARD, MR. KNOW-IT-ALL?
GLOOP
I'M NOT SURE I LIKE YOUR TONE, LIEUTENANT HUDD.
IT'S HARDLY MY FAULT THAT WE'RE MAROONED.
I'M SORRY. DID I HURT YOUR FEELINGS, METAL-MAN? YOU'LL HAVE TO FORGIVE ME. I'M A BIT UPSET...
ARGUING ISN'T GOING TO HELP US GET OFF THIS ROCK.
THEN WHAT WILL? WE'VE NO SHIP, BARELY ANY WEAPONS, AND THE ONLY THING ON THE PLANET IS A *HUGE SPOOKY*
YOU MEAN THE HUGE SPOOKY FORTRESS THAT'S GUARDED BY A *SMALL ARMY* OF STORMTROOPERS?
OH, SO YOU *DID* NOTICE IT.
NOTICE IT?

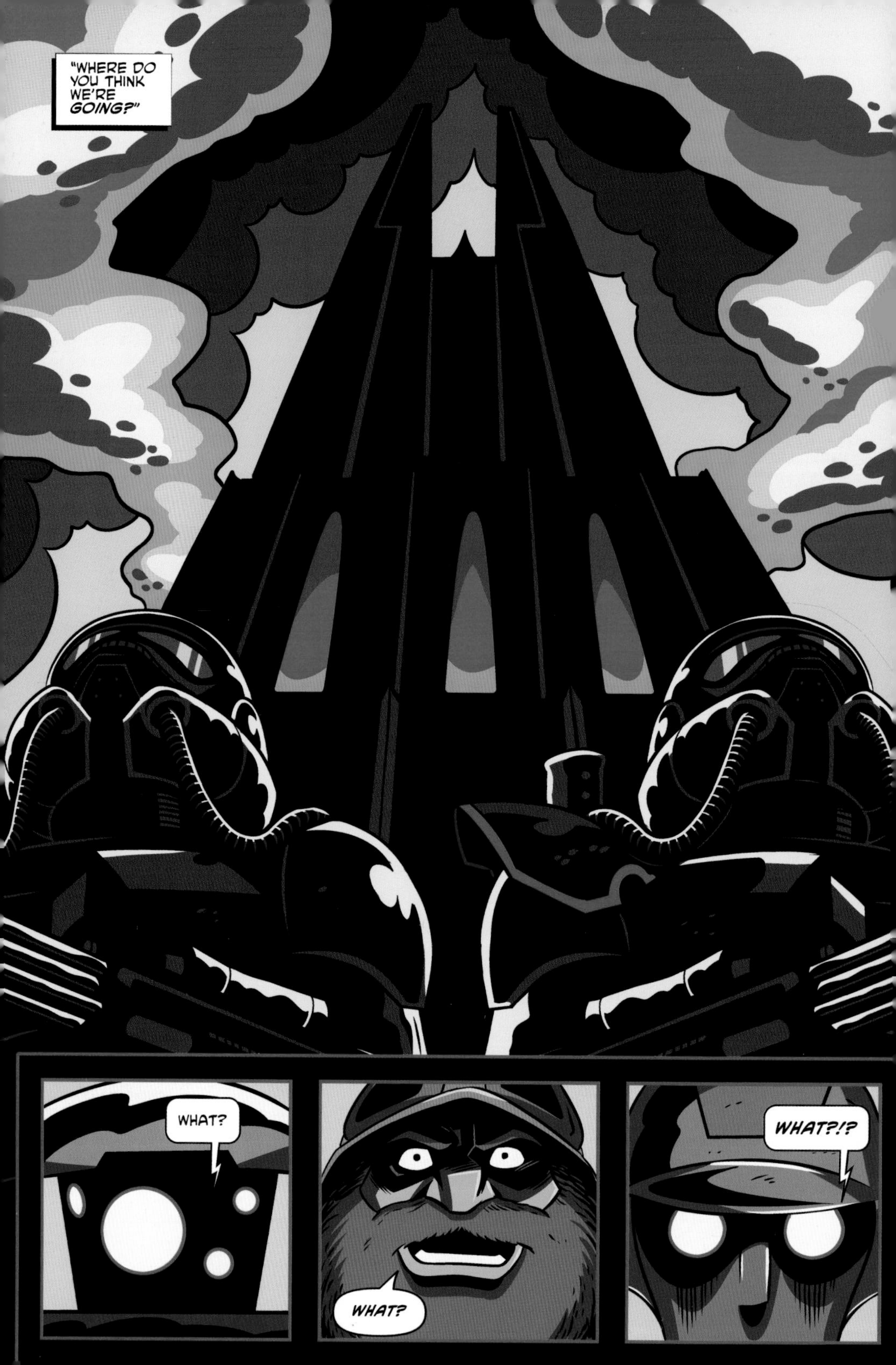
"WHERE DO YOU THINK WE'RE *GOING?*"
WHAT?
WHAT?
WHAT?!?

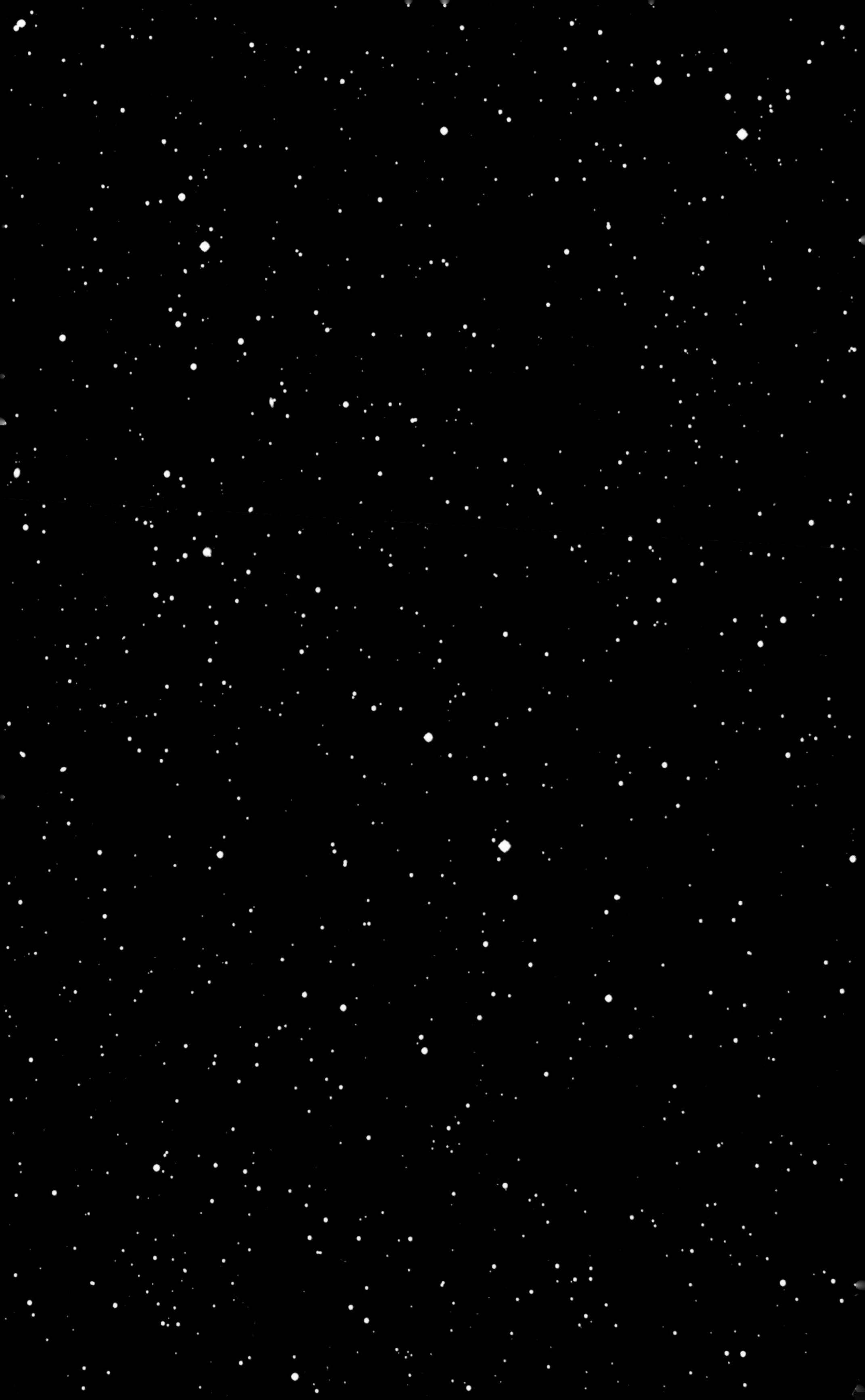

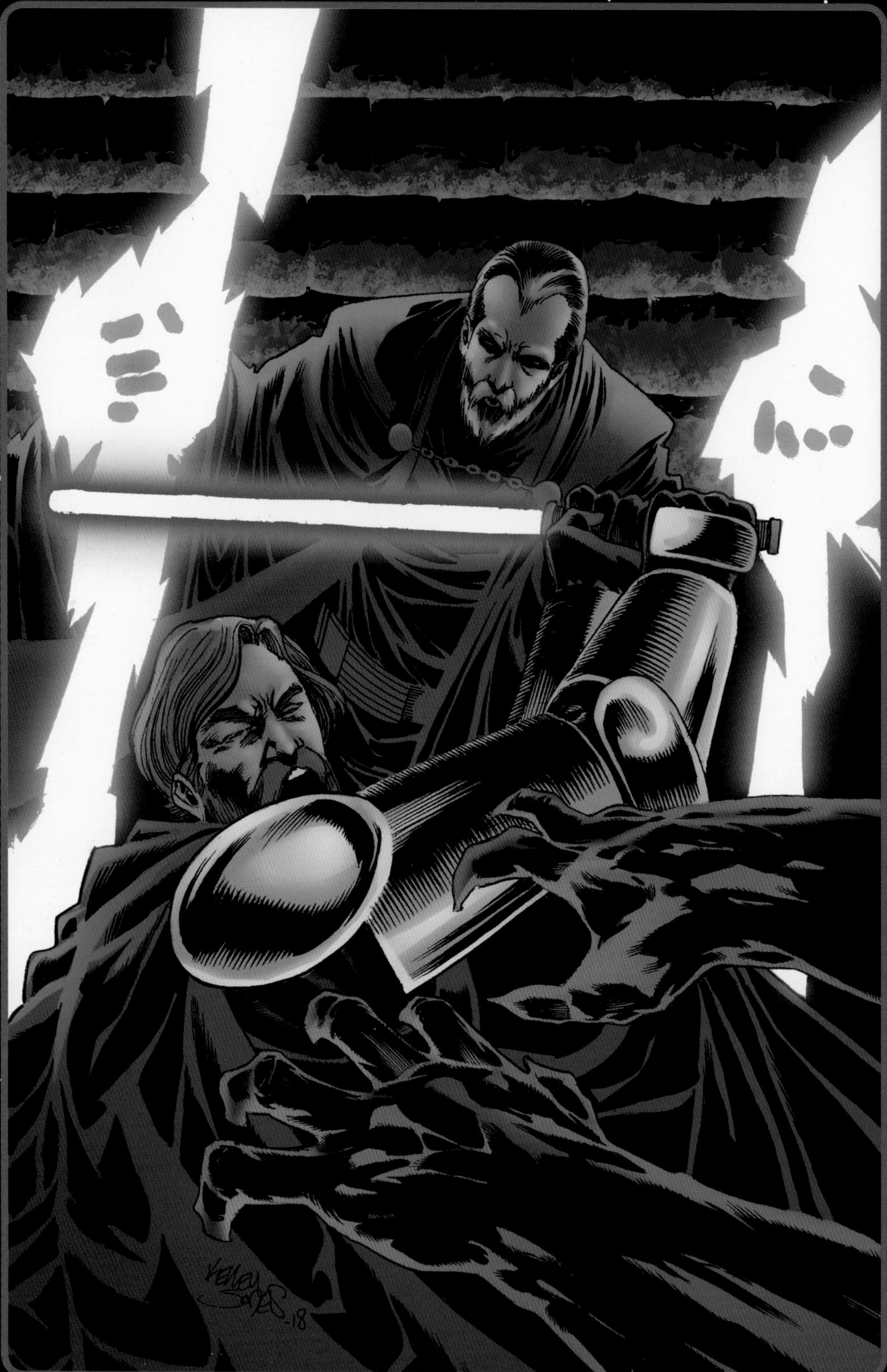
Kelley Jones '18
Art by Kelley Jones, Colors by Michelle Madsen

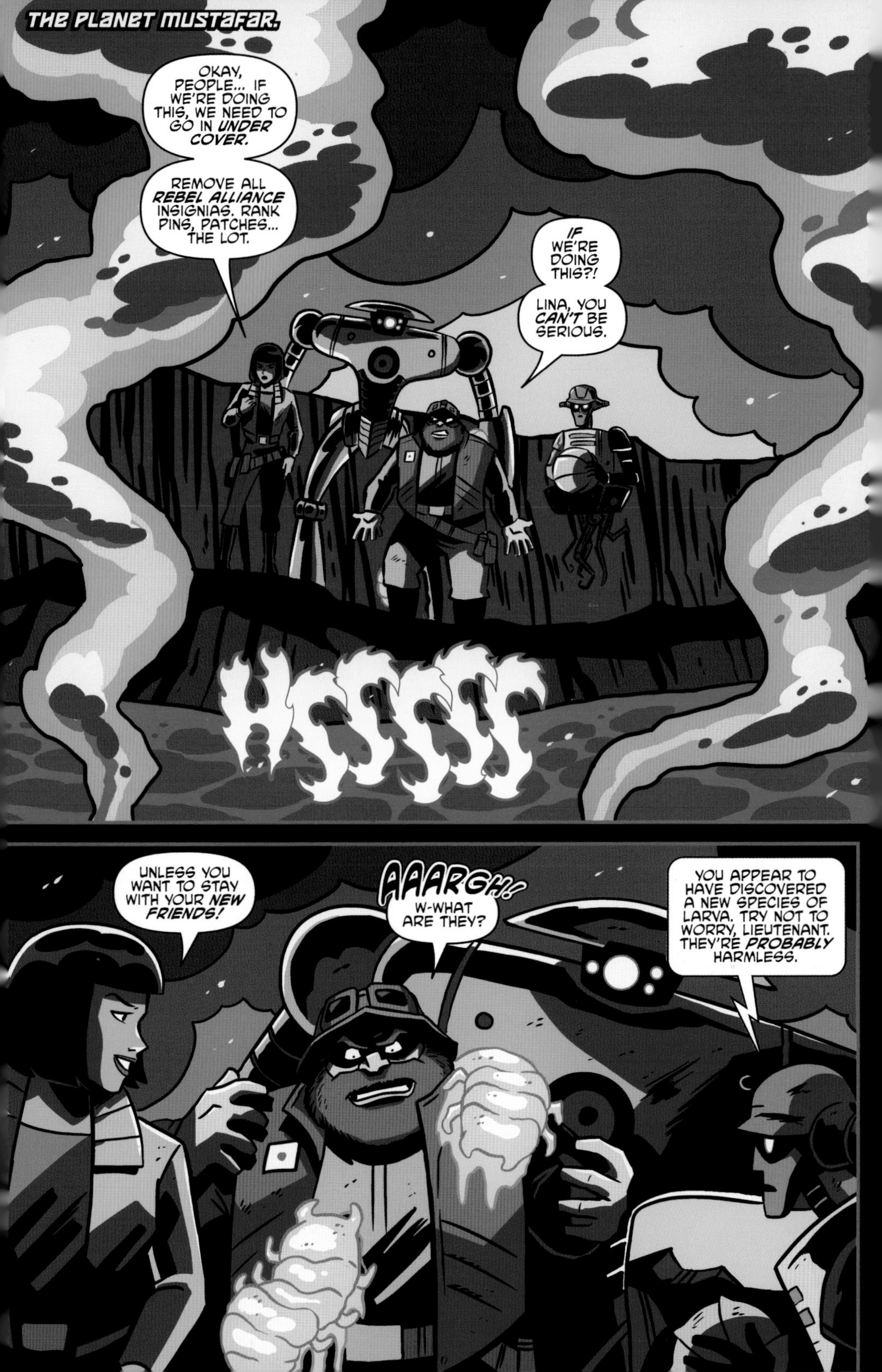
THE PLANET MUSTAFAR.
OKAY, PEOPLE... IF WE'RE DOING THIS, WE NEED TO GO IN *UNDER COVER.*
REMOVE ALL *REBEL ALLIANCE* INSIGNIAS. RANK PINS, PATCHES... THE LOT.
IF WE'RE DOING THIS?!
LINA, YOU *CAN'T* BE SERIOUS.
HSSSSS
UNLESS YOU WANT TO STAY WITH YOUR *NEW FRIENDS!*
AAARGH!
W-WHAT ARE THEY?
YOU APPEAR TO HAVE DISCOVERED A NEW SPECIES OF LARVA. TRY NOT TO WORRY, LIEUTENANT. THEY'RE *PROBABLY* HARMLESS.

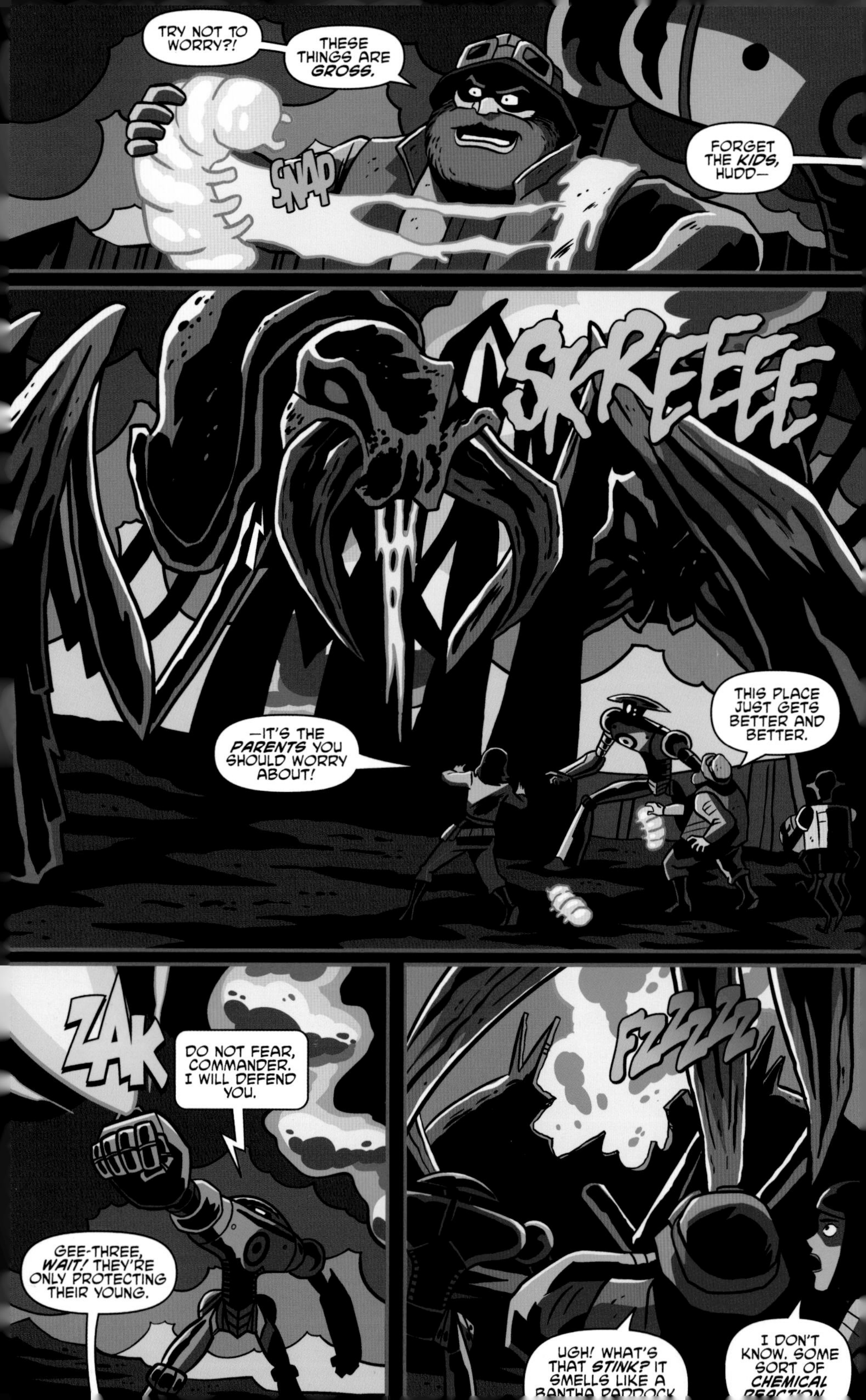
TRY NOT TO WORRY?!
THESE THINGS ARE *GROSS.*
SNAP
FORGET THE *KIDS,* HUDD—
SKREEEE
—IT'S THE *PARENTS* YOU SHOULD WORRY ABOUT!
THIS PLACE JUST GETS BETTER AND BETTER.
ZAK
DO NOT FEAR, COMMANDER. I WILL DEFEND YOU.
GEE-THREE, *WAIT!* THEY'RE ONLY PROTECTING THEIR YOUNG.
FZZZZ
UGH! WHAT'S THAT *STINK?* IT SMELLS LIKE A
I DON'T KNOW. SOME SORT OF *CHEMICAL*

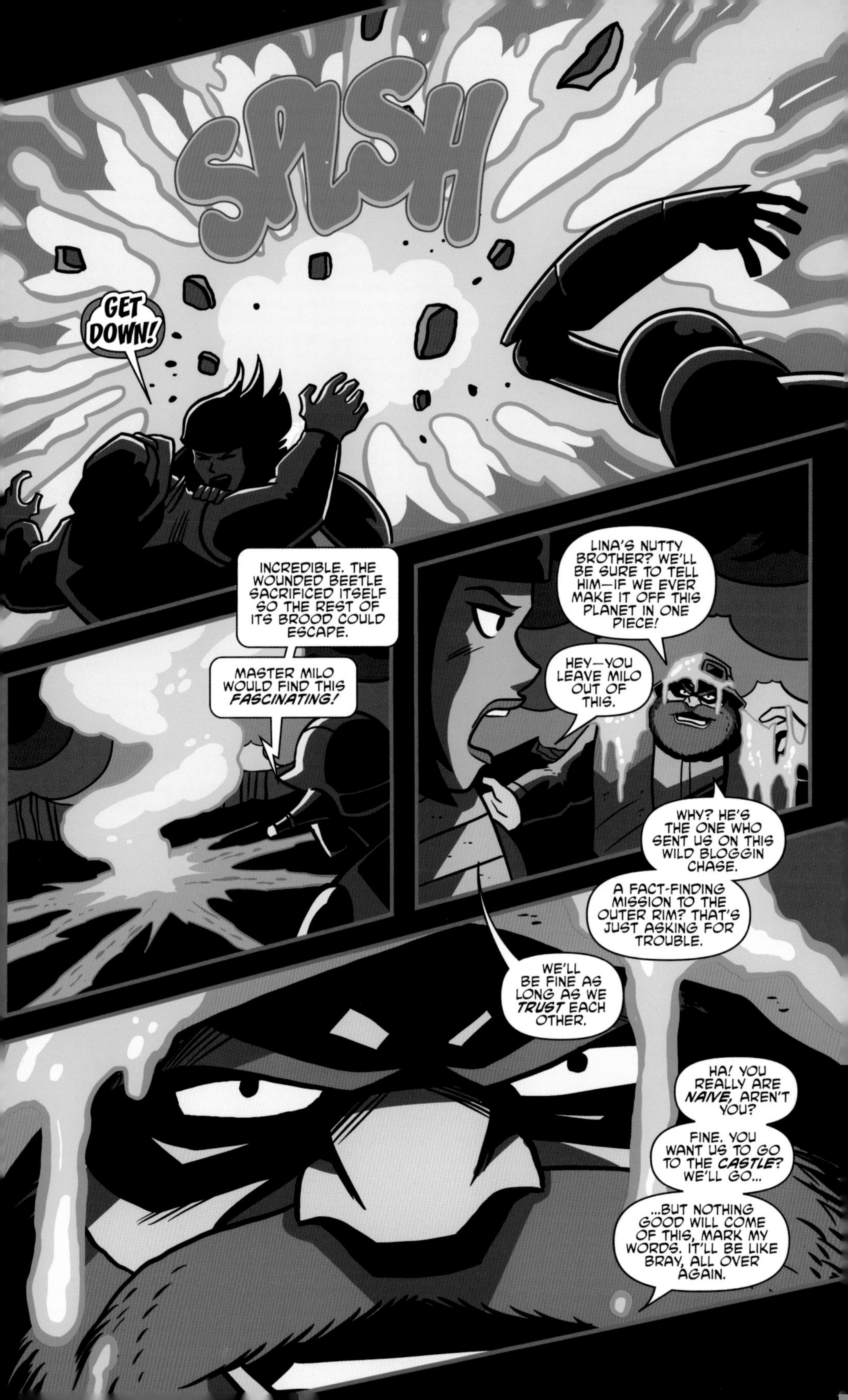
SPLSH
GET DOWN!
INCREDIBLE. THE WOUNDED BEETLE SACRIFICED ITSELF SO THE REST OF ITS BROOD COULD ESCAPE.
MASTER MILO WOULD FIND THIS *FASCINATING!*
LINA'S NUTTY BROTHER? WE'LL BE SURE TO TELL HIM—IF WE EVER MAKE IT OFF THIS PLANET IN ONE PIECE!
HEY—YOU LEAVE MILO OUT OF THIS.
WHY? HE'S THE ONE WHO SENT US ON THIS WILD BLOGGIN CHASE.
A FACT-FINDING MISSION TO THE OUTER RIM? THAT'S JUST ASKING FOR TROUBLE.
WE'LL BE FINE AS LONG AS WE *TRUST* EACH OTHER.
HA! YOU REALLY ARE *NAIVE,* AREN'T YOU?
FINE. YOU WANT US TO GO TO THE *CASTLE?* WE'LL GO...
...BUT NOTHING GOOD WILL COME OF THIS, MARK MY WORDS. IT'LL BE LIKE BRAY, ALL OVER AGAIN.

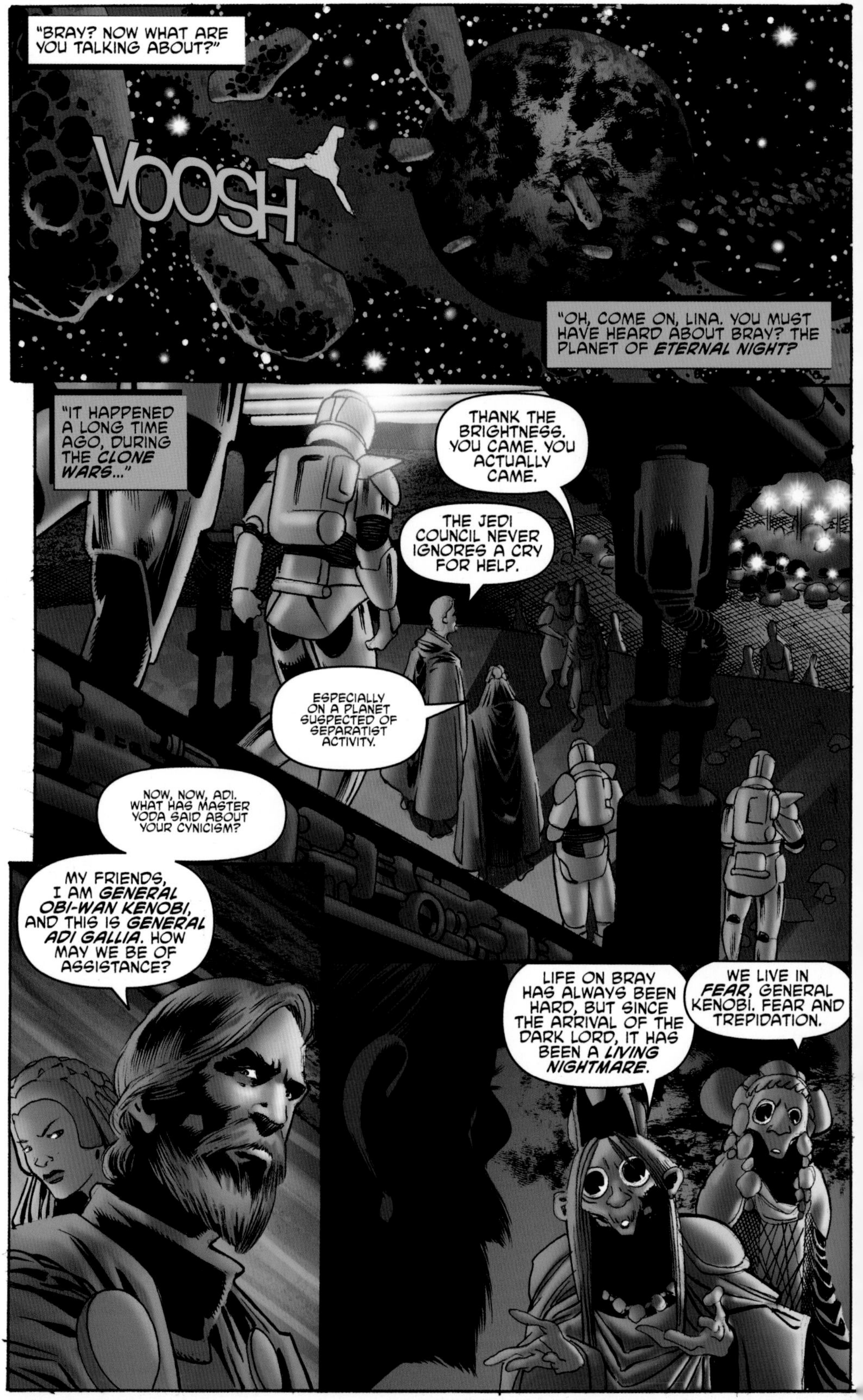
"BRAY? NOW WHAT ARE YOU TALKING ABOUT?"
VOOSH
"OH, COME ON, LINA. YOU MUST HAVE HEARD ABOUT BRAY? THE PLANET OF ETERNAL NIGHT?
"IT HAPPENED A LONG TIME AGO, DURING THE CLONE WARS..."
THANK THE BRIGHTNESS. YOU CAME. YOU ACTUALLY CAME.
THE JEDI COUNCIL NEVER IGNORES A CRY FOR HELP.
ESPECIALLY ON A PLANET SUSPECTED OF SEPARATIST ACTIVITY.
NOW, NOW, ADI. WHAT HAS MASTER YODA SAID ABOUT YOUR CYNICISM?
MY FRIENDS, I AM GENERAL OBI-WAN KENOBI, AND THIS IS GENERAL ADI GALLIA. HOW MAY WE BE OF ASSISTANCE?
LIFE ON BRAY HAS ALWAYS BEEN HARD, BUT SINCE THE ARRIVAL OF THE DARK LORD, IT HAS BEEN A LIVING NIGHTMARE.
WE LIVE IN FEAR, GENERAL KENOBI. FEAR AND TREPIDATION.

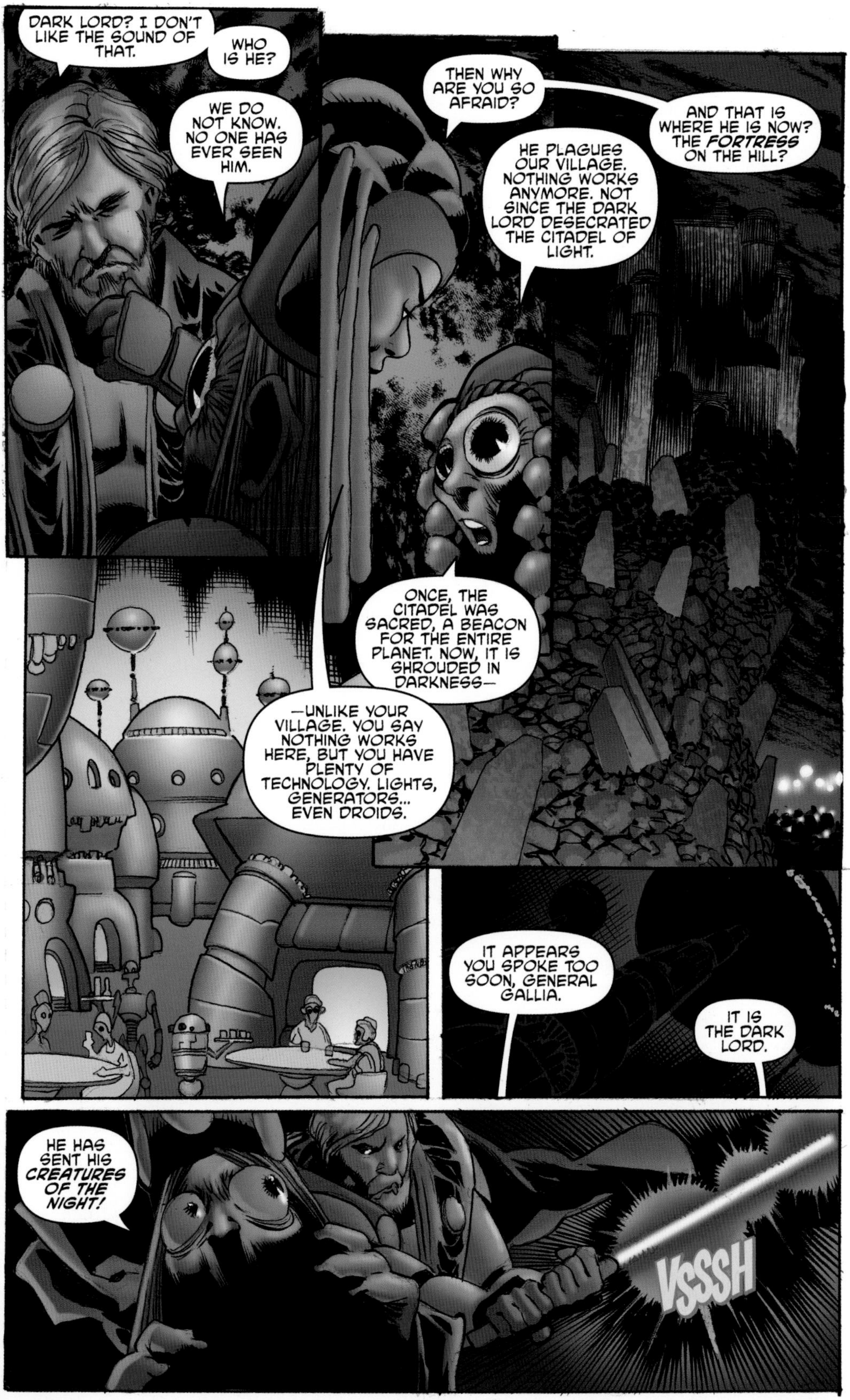
DARK LORD? I DON'T LIKE THE SOUND OF THAT.
WHO IS HE?
WE DO NOT KNOW. NO ONE HAS EVER SEEN HIM.
THEN WHY ARE YOU SO AFRAID?
HE PLAGUES OUR VILLAGE. NOTHING WORKS ANYMORE. NOT SINCE THE DARK LORD DESECRATED THE CITADEL OF LIGHT.
AND THAT IS WHERE HE IS NOW? THE FORTRESS ON THE HILL?
ONCE, THE CITADEL WAS SACRED, A BEACON FOR THE ENTIRE PLANET. NOW, IT IS SHROUDED IN DARKNESS—
—UNLIKE YOUR VILLAGE. YOU SAY NOTHING WORKS HERE, BUT YOU HAVE PLENTY OF TECHNOLOGY. LIGHTS, GENERATORS... EVEN DROIDS.
IT APPEARS YOU SPOKE TOO SOON, GENERAL GALLIA.
IT IS THE DARK LORD.
HE HAS SENT HIS CREATURES OF THE NIGHT!
VSSSH

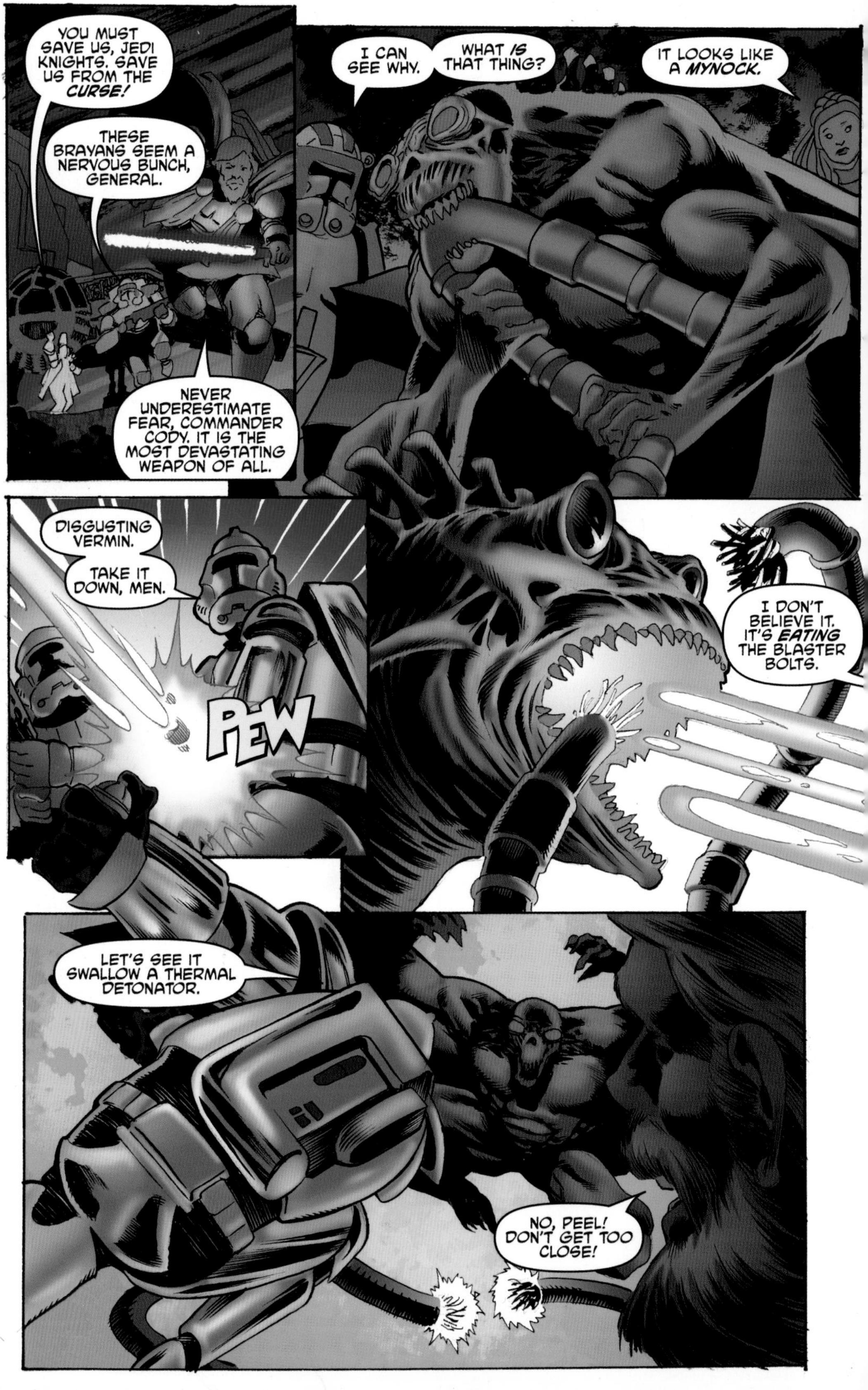
YOU MUST SAVE US, JEDI KNIGHTS. SAVE US FROM THE *CURSE!*
THESE BRAYANS SEEM A NERVOUS BUNCH, GENERAL.
NEVER UNDERESTIMATE FEAR, COMMANDER CODY. IT IS THE MOST DEVASTATING WEAPON OF ALL.
I CAN SEE WHY.
WHAT *IS* THAT THING?
IT LOOKS LIKE A *MYNOCK.*
DISGUSTING VERMIN.
TAKE IT DOWN, MEN.
PEW
I DON'T BELIEVE IT. IT'S *EATING* THE BLASTER BOLTS.
LET'S SEE IT SWALLOW A THERMAL DETONATOR.
NO, PEEL! DON'T GET TOO CLOSE!

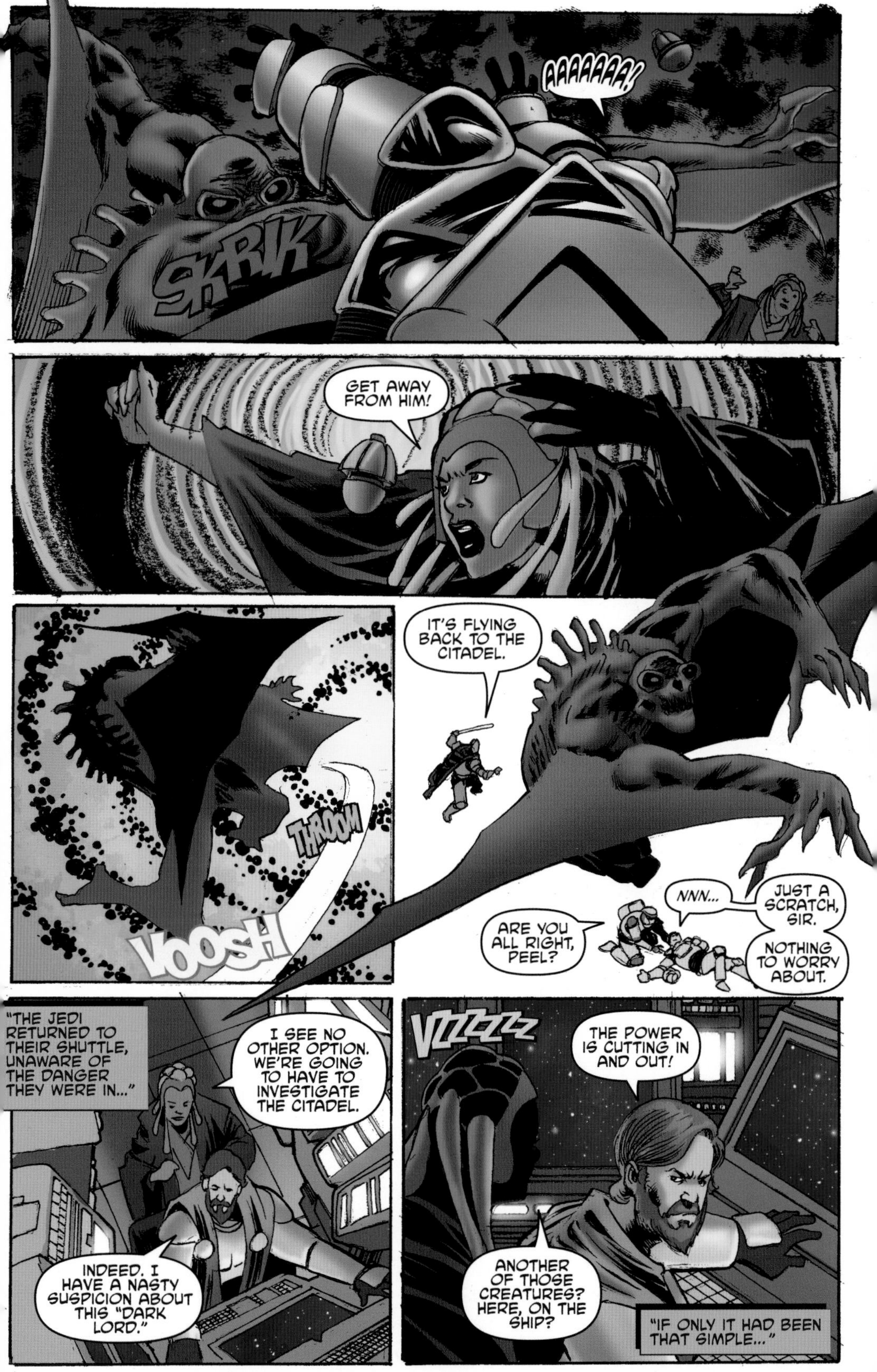
AAAAAAA!
SKRIK
GET AWAY FROM HIM!
IT'S FLYING BACK TO THE CITADEL.
THROOM
VOOSH
ARE YOU ALL RIGHT, PEEL?
NNN...
JUST A SCRATCH, SIR.
NOTHING TO WORRY ABOUT.
"THE JEDI RETURNED TO THEIR SHUTTLE, UNAWARE OF THE DANGER THEY WERE IN..."
I SEE NO OTHER OPTION. WE'RE GOING TO HAVE TO INVESTIGATE THE CITADEL.
INDEED. I HAVE A NASTY SUSPICION ABOUT THIS "DARK LORD."
VZZZZZ
THE POWER IS CUTTING IN AND OUT!
ANOTHER OF THOSE CREATURES? HERE, ON THE SHIP?
"IF ONLY IT HAD BEEN THAT SIMPLE..."

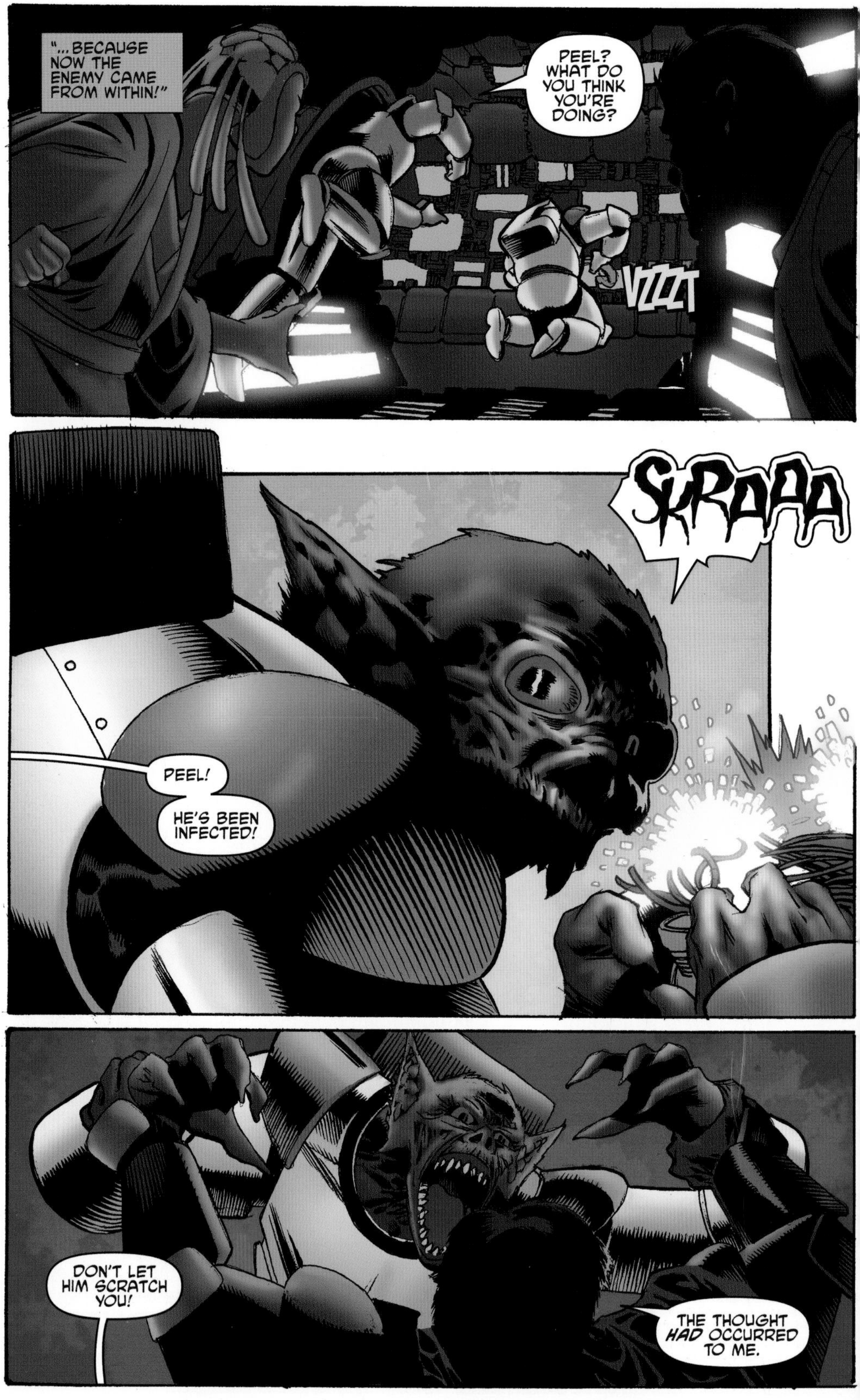
"...BECAUSE NOW THE ENEMY CAME FROM WITHIN!"
PEEL? WHAT DO YOU THINK YOU'RE DOING?
VZZZT
SKRAAA
PEEL!
HE'S BEEN INFECTED!
DON'T LET HIM SCRATCH YOU!
THE THOUGHT *HAD* OCCURRED TO ME.

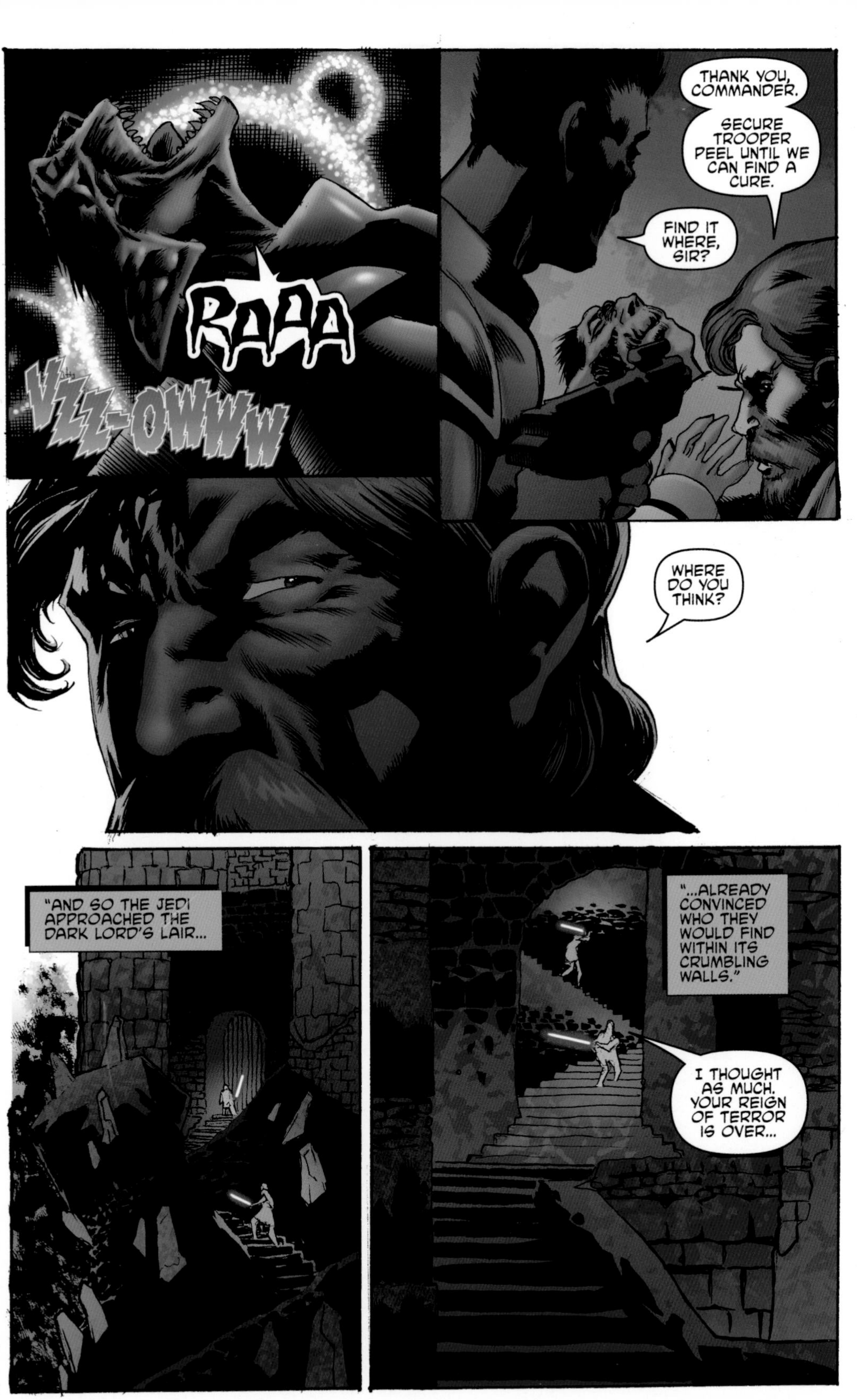
RAAA
VZZ-OWWW
THANK YOU, COMMANDER.
SECURE TROOPER PEEL UNTIL WE CAN FIND A CURE.
FIND IT WHERE, SIR?
WHERE DO YOU THINK?
"AND SO THE JEDI APPROACHED THE DARK LORD'S LAIR...
"...ALREADY CONVINCED WHO THEY WOULD FIND WITHIN ITS CRUMBLING WALLS."
I THOUGHT AS MUCH. YOUR REIGN OF TERROR IS OVER...

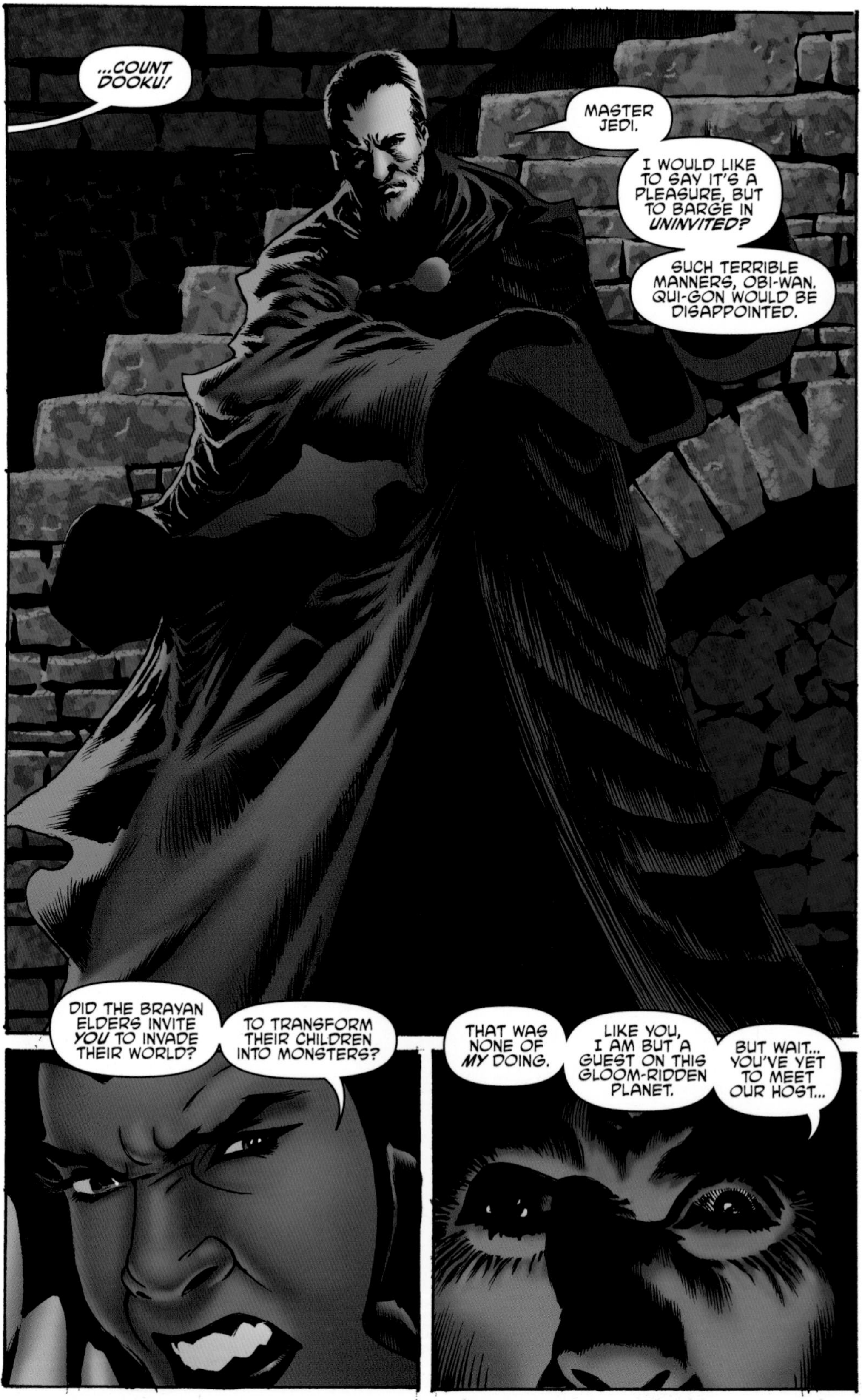

...COUNT DOOKU!
MASTER JEDI.
I WOULD LIKE TO SAY IT'S A PLEASURE, BUT TO BARGE IN *UNINVITED?*
SUCH TERRIBLE MANNERS, OBI-WAN. QUI-GON WOULD BE DISAPPOINTED.
DID THE BRAYAN ELDERS INVITE *YOU* TO INVADE THEIR WORLD?
TO TRANSFORM THEIR CHILDREN INTO MONSTERS?
THAT WAS NONE OF *MY* DOING.
LIKE YOU, I AM BUT A GUEST ON THIS GLOOM-RIDDEN PLANET.
BUT WAIT... YOU'VE YET TO MEET OUR HOST...

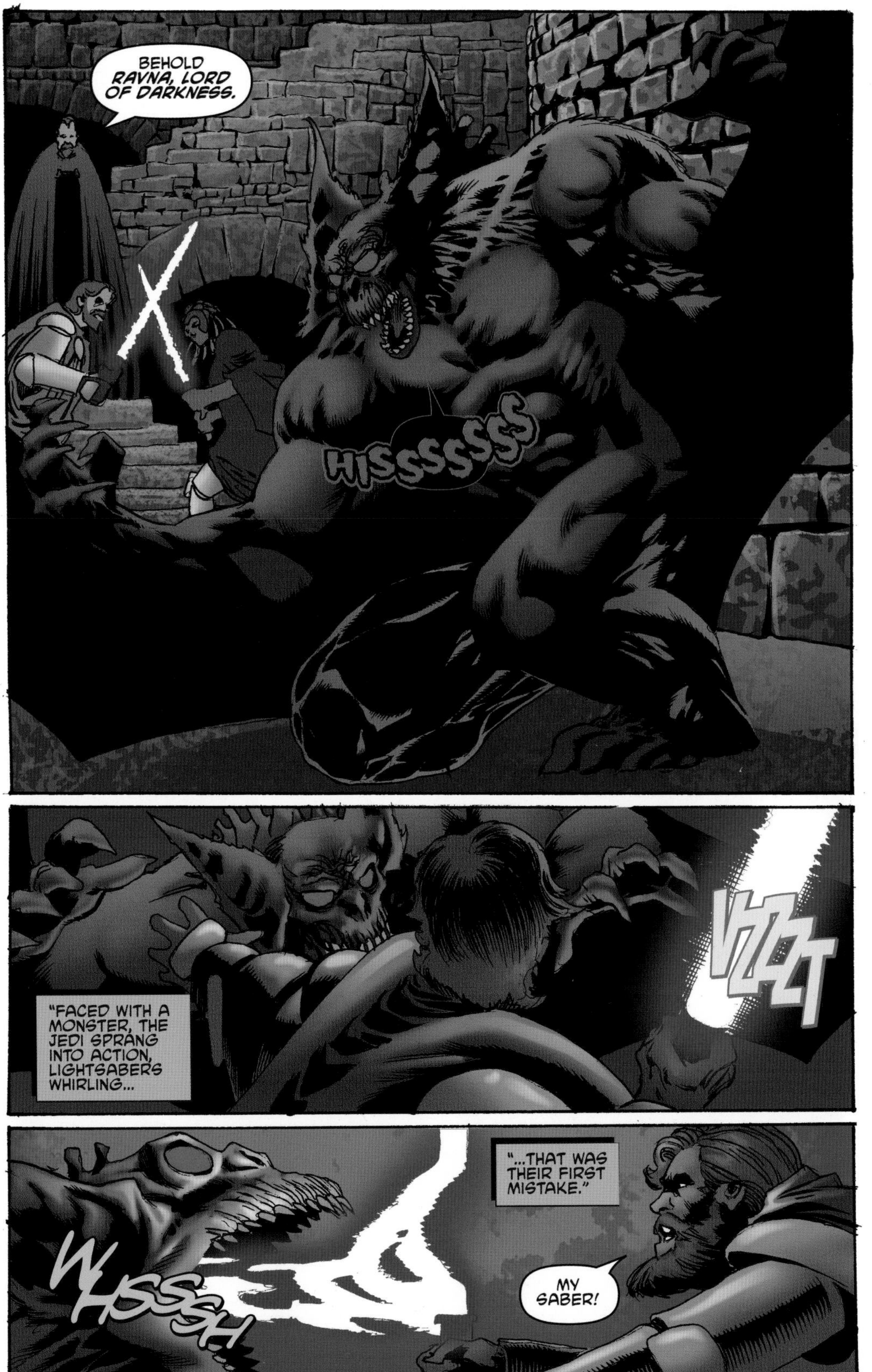
BEHOLD RAVNA, LORD OF DARKNESS.
HISSSSSSS
"FACED WITH A MONSTER, THE JEDI SPRANG INTO ACTION, LIGHTSABERS WHIRLING...
VZZZT
"...THAT WAS THEIR FIRST MISTAKE."
WHSSSH
MY SABER!

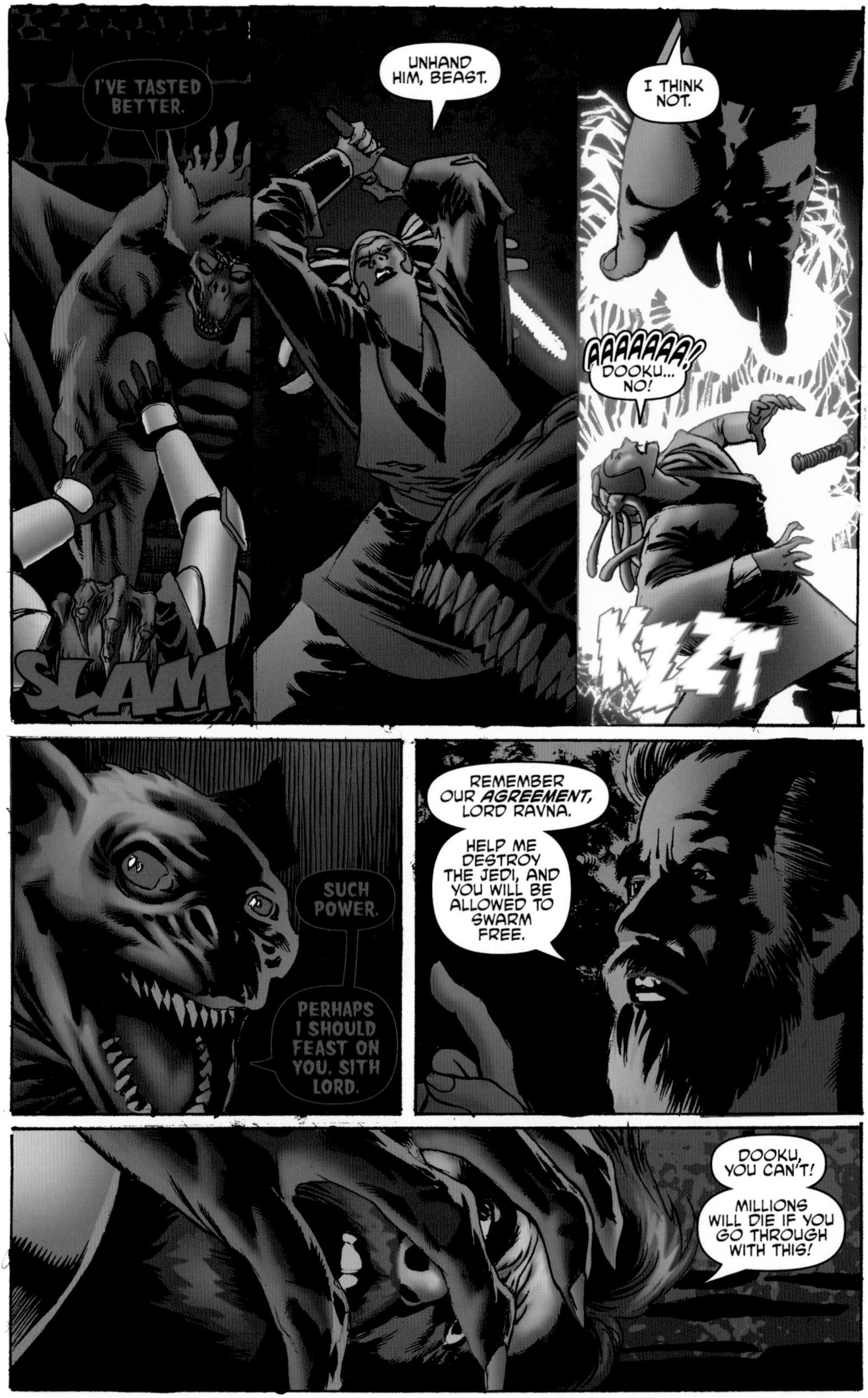
I'VE TASTED BETTER.
SLAM
UNHAND HIM, BEAST.
I THINK NOT.
AAAAAAA! DOOKU... NO!
KZZT
SUCH POWER.
PERHAPS I SHOULD FEAST ON YOU, SITH LORD.
REMEMBER OUR AGREEMENT, LORD RAVNA.
HELP ME DESTROY THE JEDI, AND YOU WILL BE ALLOWED TO SWARM FREE.
DOOKU, YOU CAN'T!
MILLIONS WILL DIE IF YOU GO THROUGH WITH THIS!

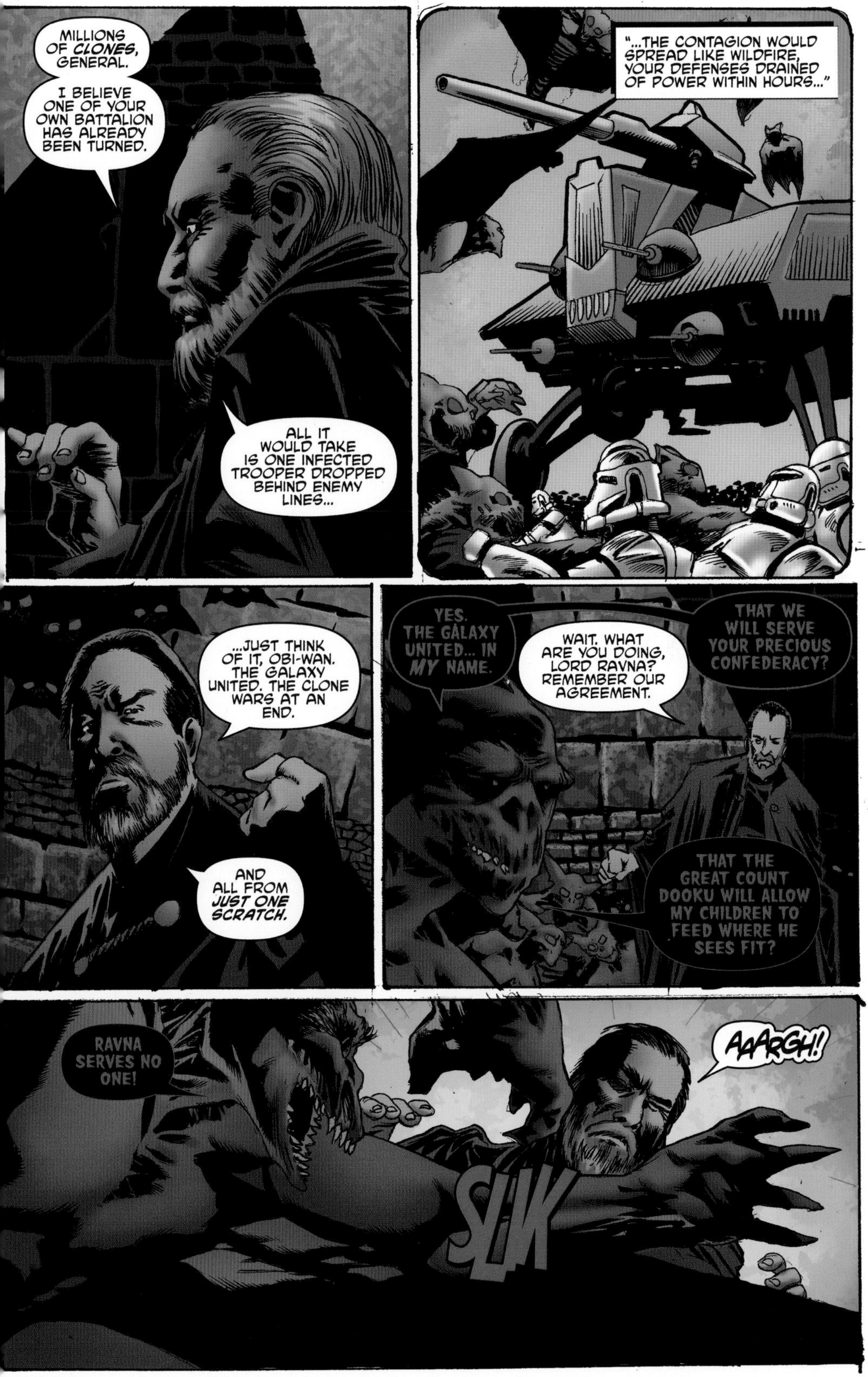
MILLIONS OF CLONES, GENERAL.
I BELIEVE ONE OF YOUR OWN BATTALION HAS ALREADY BEEN TURNED.
ALL IT WOULD TAKE IS ONE INFECTED TROOPER DROPPED BEHIND ENEMY LINES...
"...THE CONTAGION WOULD SPREAD LIKE WILDFIRE, YOUR DEFENSES DRAINED OF POWER WITHIN HOURS..."
...JUST THINK OF IT, OBI-WAN. THE GALAXY UNITED. THE CLONE WARS AT AN END.
AND ALL FROM JUST ONE SCRATCH.
YES. THE GALAXY UNITED... IN MY NAME.
WAIT. WHAT ARE YOU DOING, LORD RAVNA? REMEMBER OUR AGREEMENT.
THAT WE WILL SERVE YOUR PRECIOUS CONFEDERACY?
THAT THE GREAT COUNT DOOKU WILL ALLOW MY CHILDREN TO FEED WHERE HE SEES FIT?
RAVNA SERVES NO ONE!
AAARGH!
SLIK

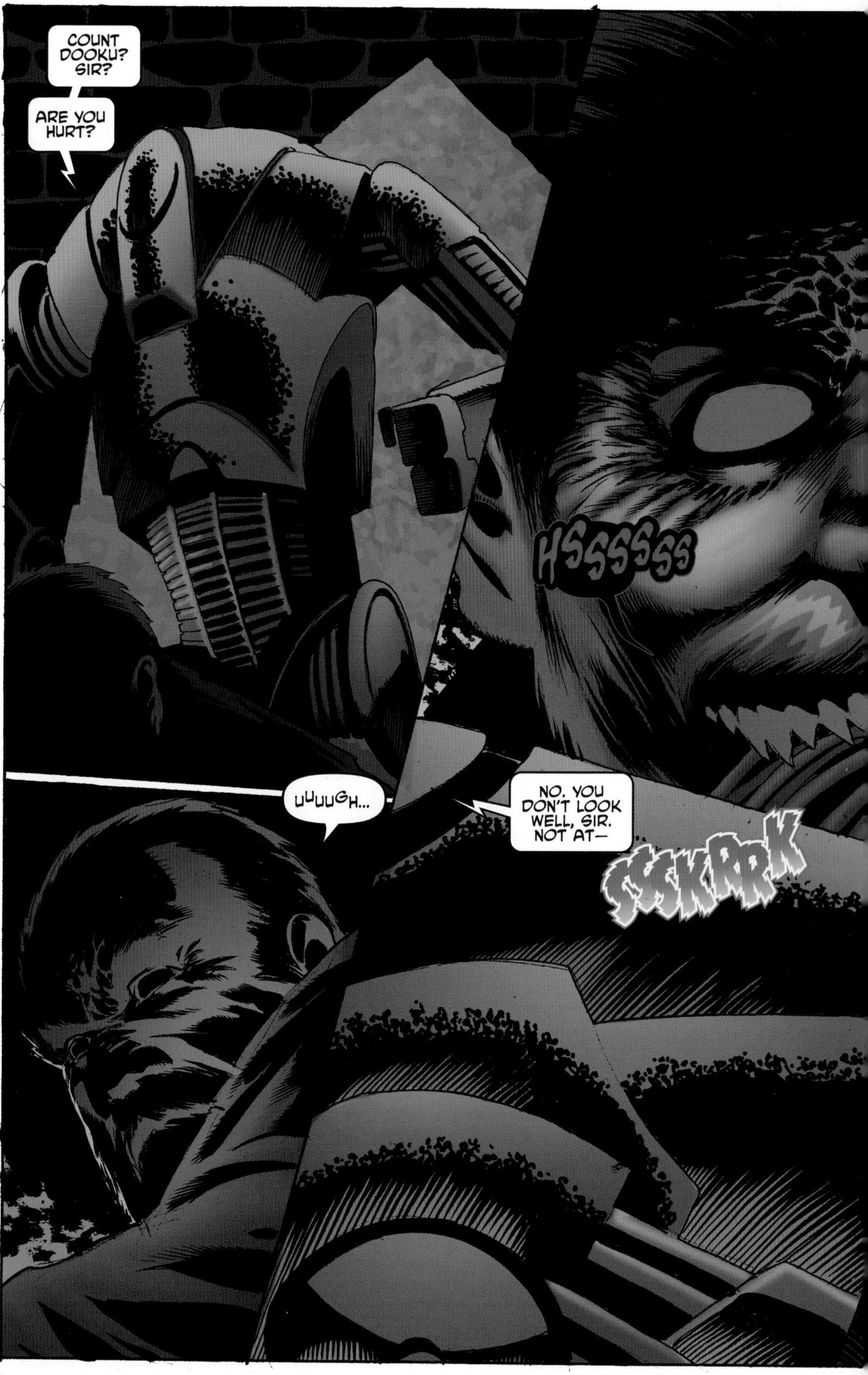
COUNT DOOKU? SIR?
ARE YOU HURT?
HSSSSSS
UUUUGH...
NO. YOU DON'T LOOK WELL, SIR. NOT AT—
SSSKRRK

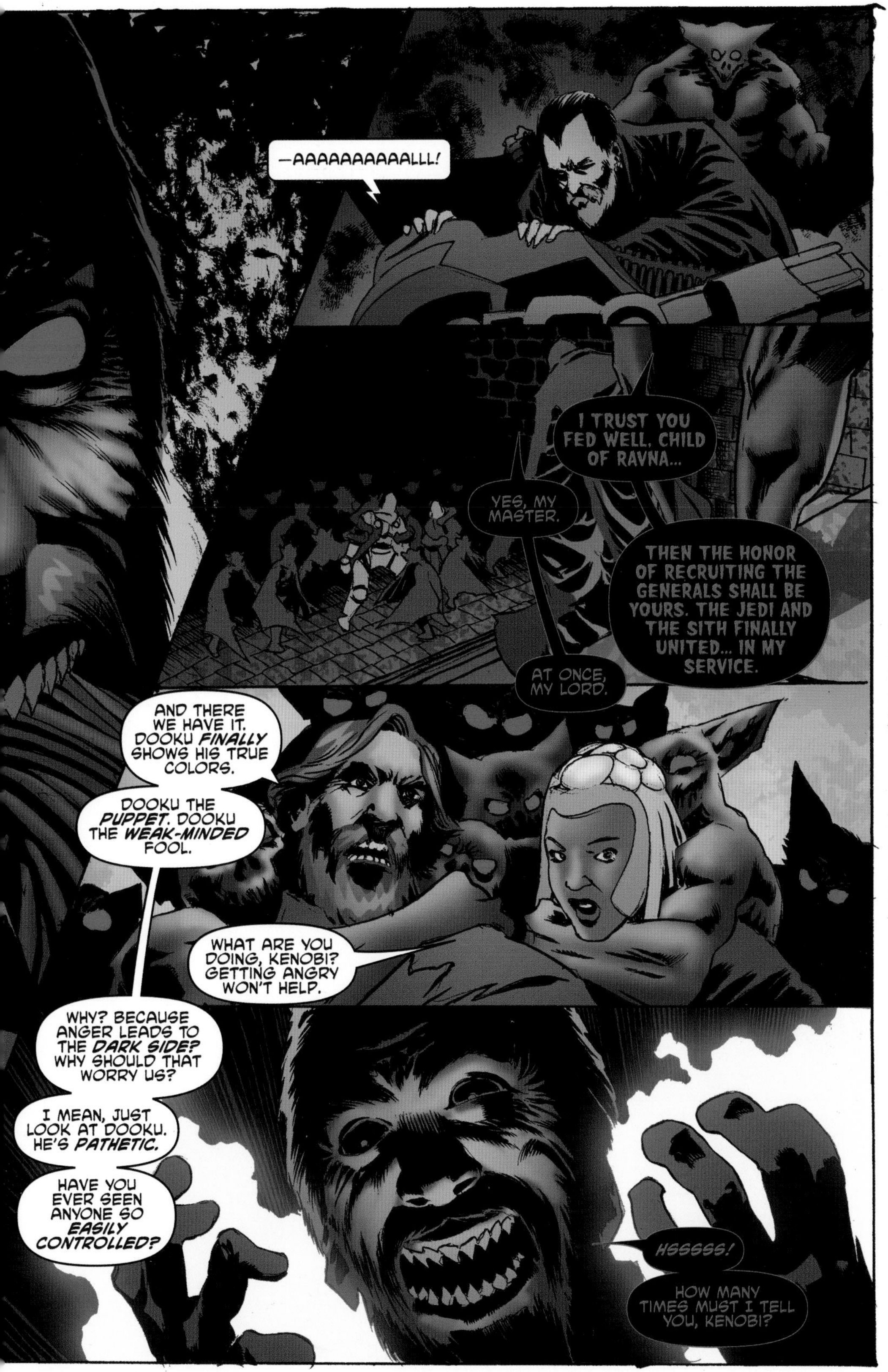

—AAAAAAAAAALLL!
I TRUST YOU FED WELL, CHILD OF RAVNA...
YES, MY MASTER.
THEN THE HONOR OF RECRUITING THE GENERALS SHALL BE YOURS. THE JEDI AND THE SITH FINALLY UNITED... IN MY SERVICE.
AT ONCE, MY LORD.
AND THERE WE HAVE IT. DOOKU *FINALLY* SHOWS HIS TRUE COLORS.
DOOKU THE *PUPPET*. DOOKU THE *WEAK-MINDED* FOOL.
WHAT ARE YOU DOING, KENOBI? GETTING ANGRY WON'T HELP.
WHY? BECAUSE ANGER LEADS TO THE *DARK SIDE?* WHY SHOULD THAT WORRY US?
I MEAN, JUST LOOK AT DOOKU. HE'S *PATHETIC.*
HAVE YOU EVER SEEN ANYONE SO *EASILY CONTROLLED?*
HSSSSS!
HOW MANY TIMES MUST I TELL YOU, KENOBI?

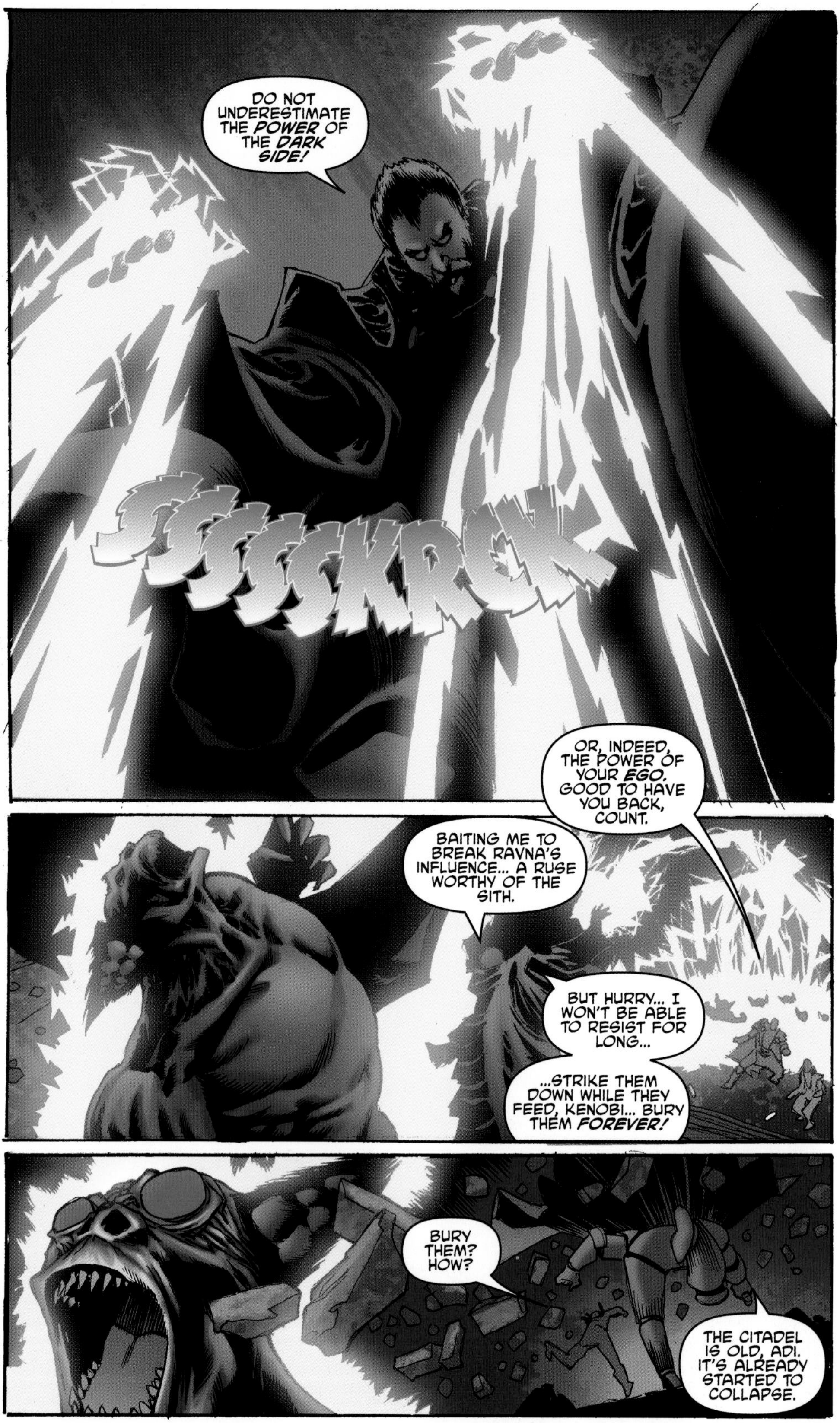
DO NOT UNDERESTIMATE THE *POWER* OF THE *DARK SIDE!*
SSSSSKRCK
OR, INDEED, THE POWER OF YOUR *EGO*. GOOD TO HAVE YOU BACK, COUNT.
BAITING ME TO BREAK RAVNA'S INFLUENCE... A RUSE WORTHY OF THE SITH.
BUT HURRY... I WON'T BE ABLE TO RESIST FOR LONG...
...STRIKE THEM DOWN WHILE THEY FEED, KENOBI... BURY THEM *FOREVER!*
BURY THEM? HOW?
THE CITADEL IS OLD, ADI. IT'S ALREADY STARTED TO COLLAPSE.

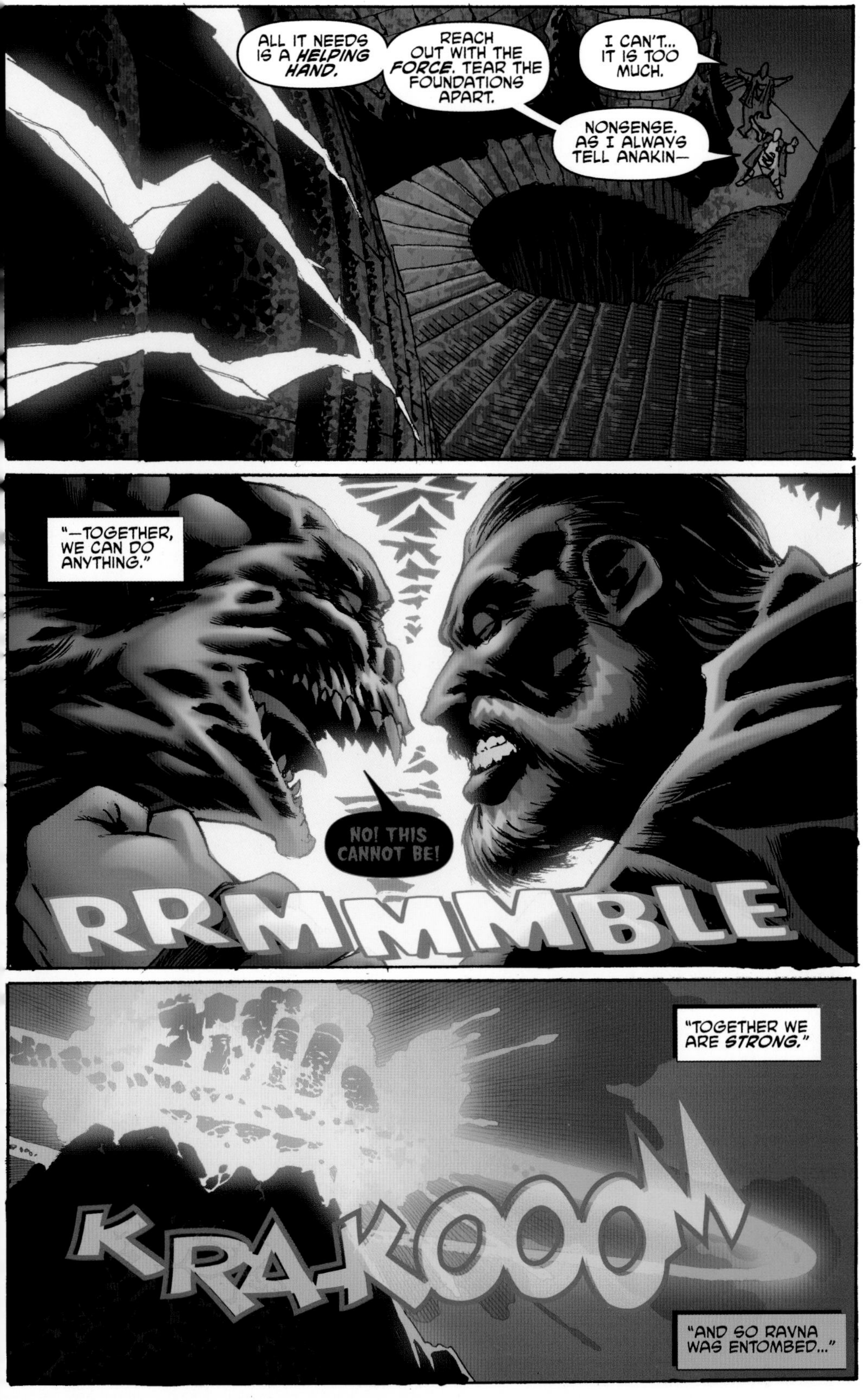
ALL IT NEEDS IS A *HELPING HAND.*
REACH OUT WITH THE *FORCE*. TEAR THE FOUNDATIONS APART.
I CAN'T... IT IS TOO MUCH.
NONSENSE. AS I ALWAYS TELL ANAKIN—
"—TOGETHER, WE CAN DO ANYTHING."
NO! THIS CANNOT BE!
RRMMMBLE
"TOGETHER WE ARE *STRONG.*"
KRA-KOOOM
"AND SO RAVNA WAS ENTOMBED..."

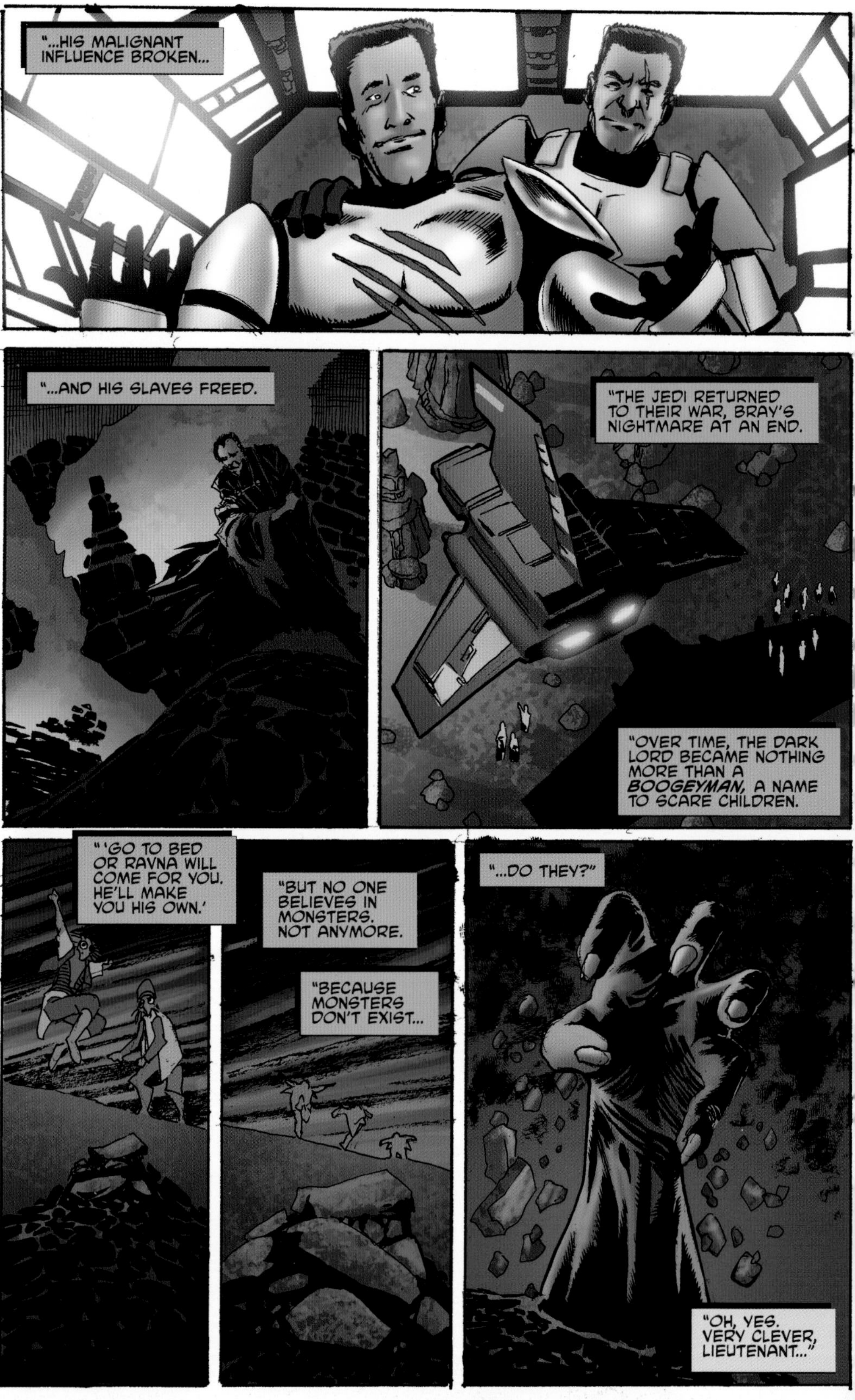
"...HIS MALIGNANT INFLUENCE BROKEN...
"...AND HIS SLAVES FREED.
"THE JEDI RETURNED TO THEIR WAR, BRAY'S NIGHTMARE AT AN END.
"OVER TIME, THE DARK LORD BECAME NOTHING MORE THAN A *BOOGEYMAN,* A NAME TO SCARE CHILDREN.
"'GO TO BED OR RAVNA WILL COME FOR YOU. HE'LL MAKE YOU HIS OWN.'
"BUT NO ONE BELIEVES IN MONSTERS. NOT ANYMORE.
"BECAUSE MONSTERS DON'T EXIST...
"...DO THEY?"
"OH, YES. VERY CLEVER, LIEUTENANT..."

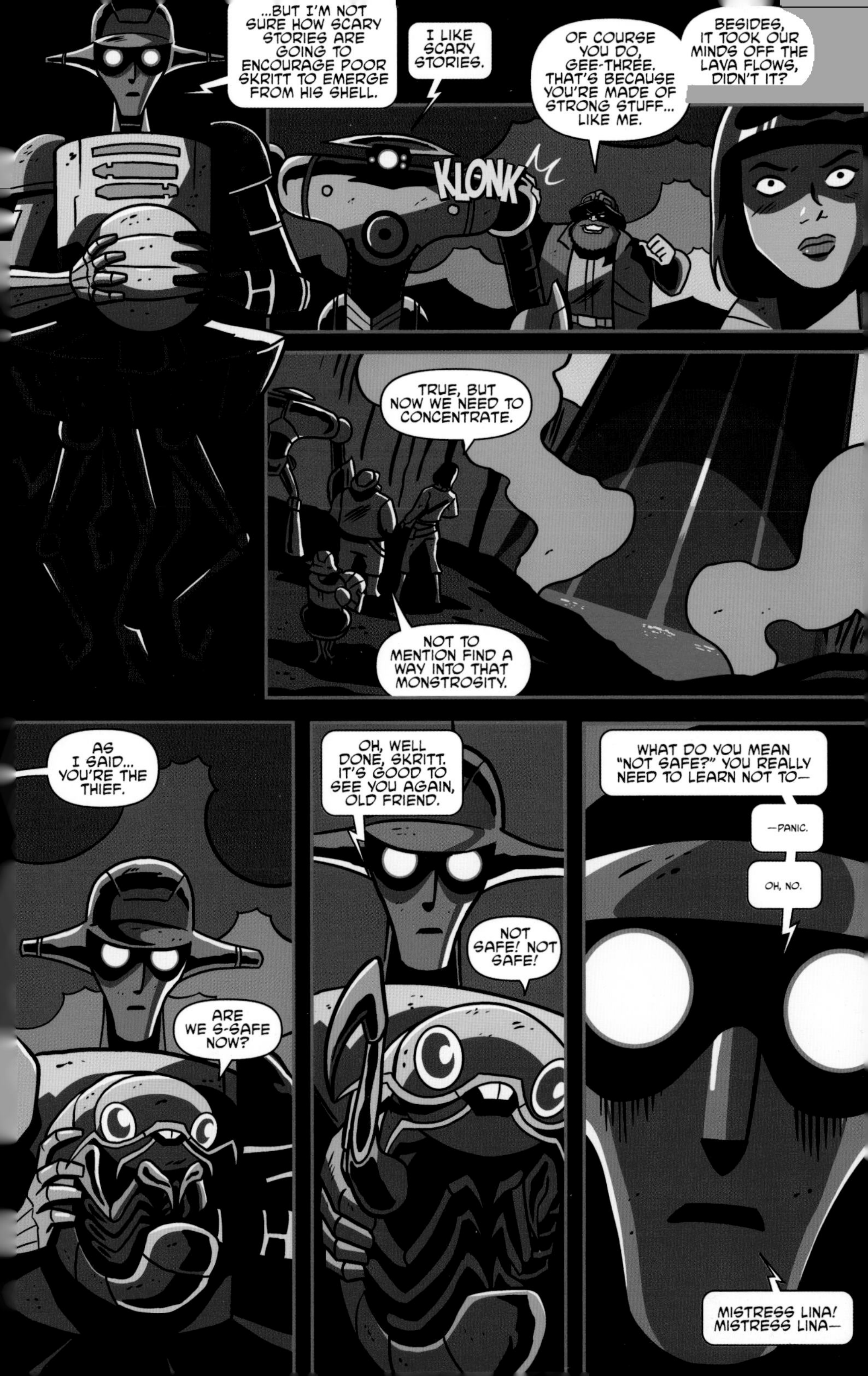
...BUT I'M NOT SURE HOW SCARY STORIES ARE GOING TO ENCOURAGE POOR SKRITT TO EMERGE FROM HIS SHELL.
I LIKE SCARY STORIES.
KLONK
OF COURSE YOU DO, GEE-THREE. THAT'S BECAUSE YOU'RE MADE OF STRONG STUFF... LIKE ME.
BESIDES, IT TOOK OUR MINDS OFF THE LAVA FLOWS, DIDN'T IT?
TRUE, BUT NOW WE NEED TO CONCENTRATE.
NOT TO MENTION FIND A WAY INTO THAT MONSTROSITY.
AS I SAID... YOU'RE THE THIEF.
ARE WE S-SAFE NOW?
OH, WELL DONE, SKRITT. IT'S GOOD TO SEE YOU AGAIN, OLD FRIEND.
NOT SAFE! NOT SAFE!
WHAT DO YOU MEAN "NOT SAFE?" YOU REALLY NEED TO LEARN NOT TO—
—PANIC.
OH, NO.
MISTRESS LINA! MISTRESS LINA—

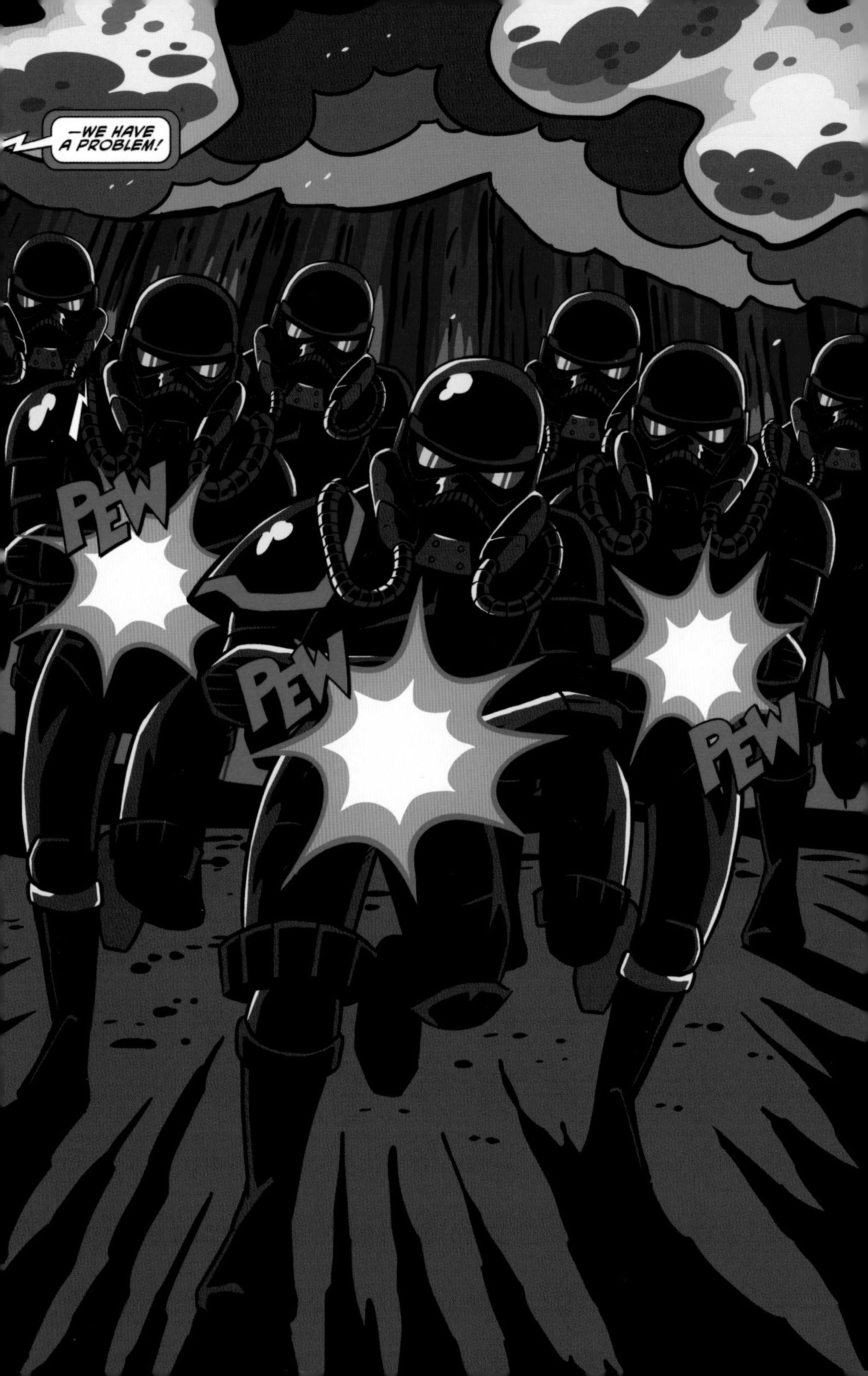
—WE HAVE A PROBLEM!
PEW
PEW
PEW

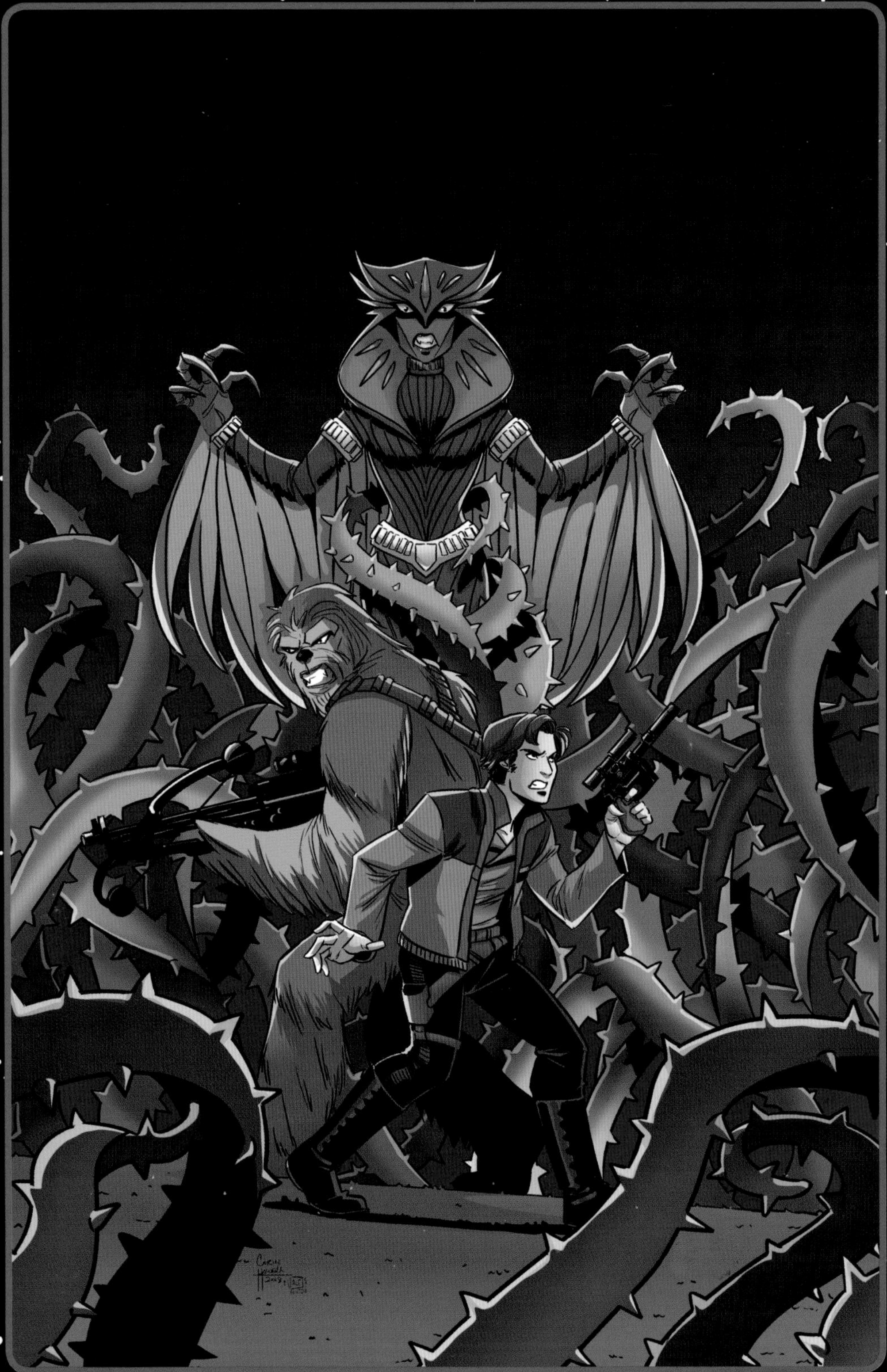

Art by Corin Howell, Colors by Valentina Pinto

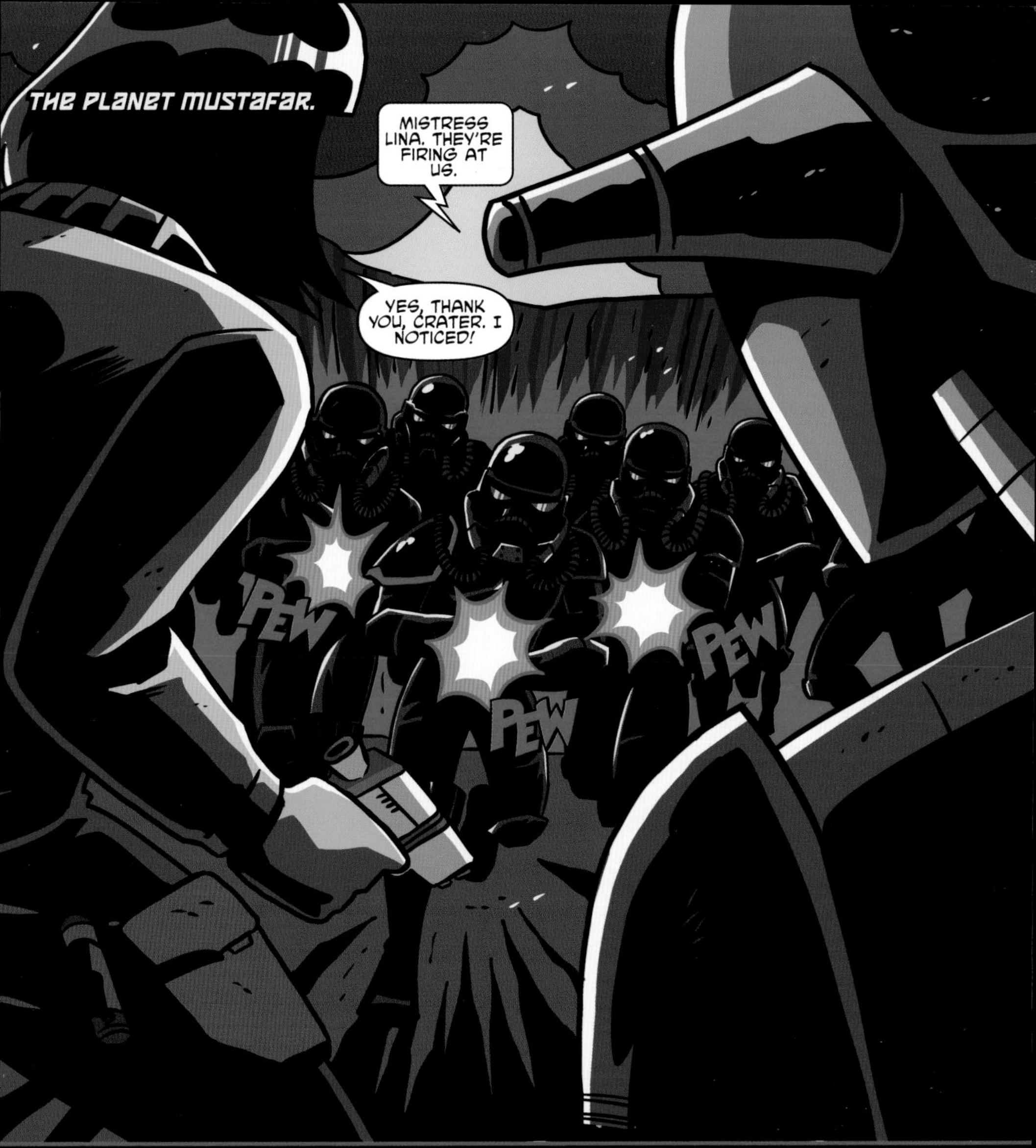
THE PLANET MUSTAFAR.
MISTRESS LINA. THEY'RE FIRING AT US.
YES, THANK YOU, CRATER. I NOTICED!
PEW
PEW
PEW

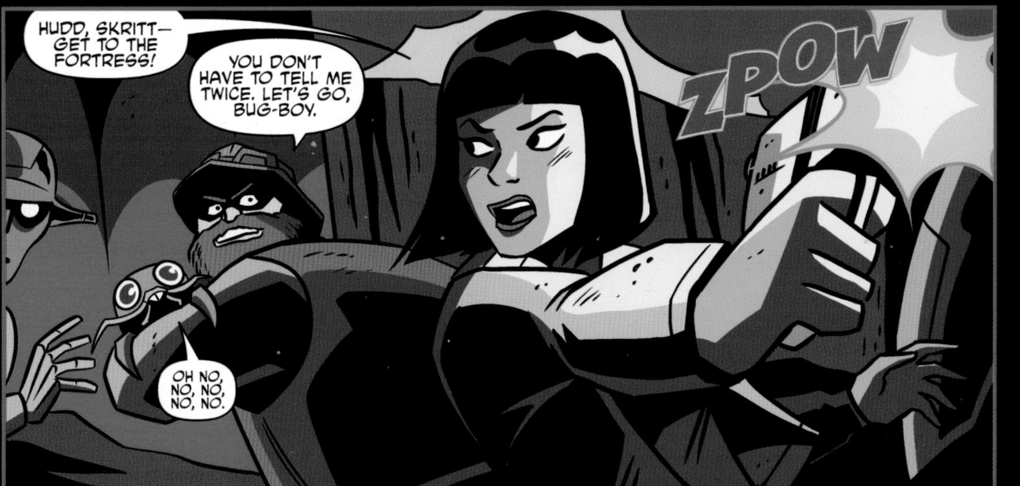
HUDD, SKRITT— GET TO THE FORTRESS!
YOU DON'T HAVE TO TELL ME TWICE. LET'S GO, BUG-BOY.
ZPOW
OH NO, NO, NO, NO, NO.

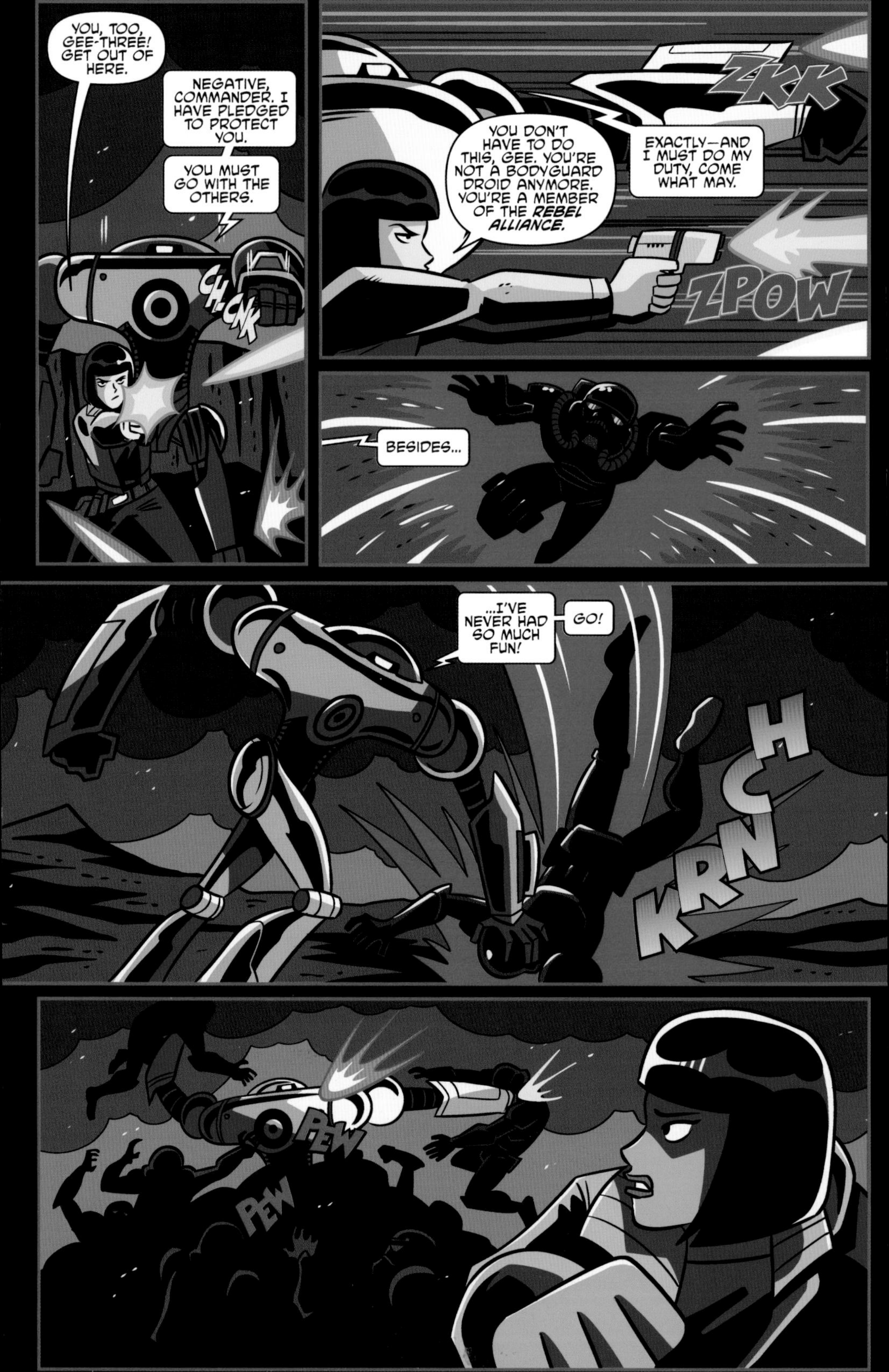

YOU, TOO, GEE-THREE! GET OUT OF HERE.
NEGATIVE, COMMANDER. I HAVE PLEDGED TO PROTECT YOU.
YOU MUST GO WITH THE OTHERS.
CH-CNK
ZKK
YOU DON'T HAVE TO DO THIS, GEE. YOU'RE NOT A BODYGUARD DROID ANYMORE. YOU'RE A MEMBER OF THE *REBEL ALLIANCE.*
EXACTLY—AND I MUST DO MY DUTY, COME WHAT MAY.
ZPOW
BESIDES...
...I'VE NEVER HAD SO MUCH FUN!
GO!
KRNCH
PEW
PEW

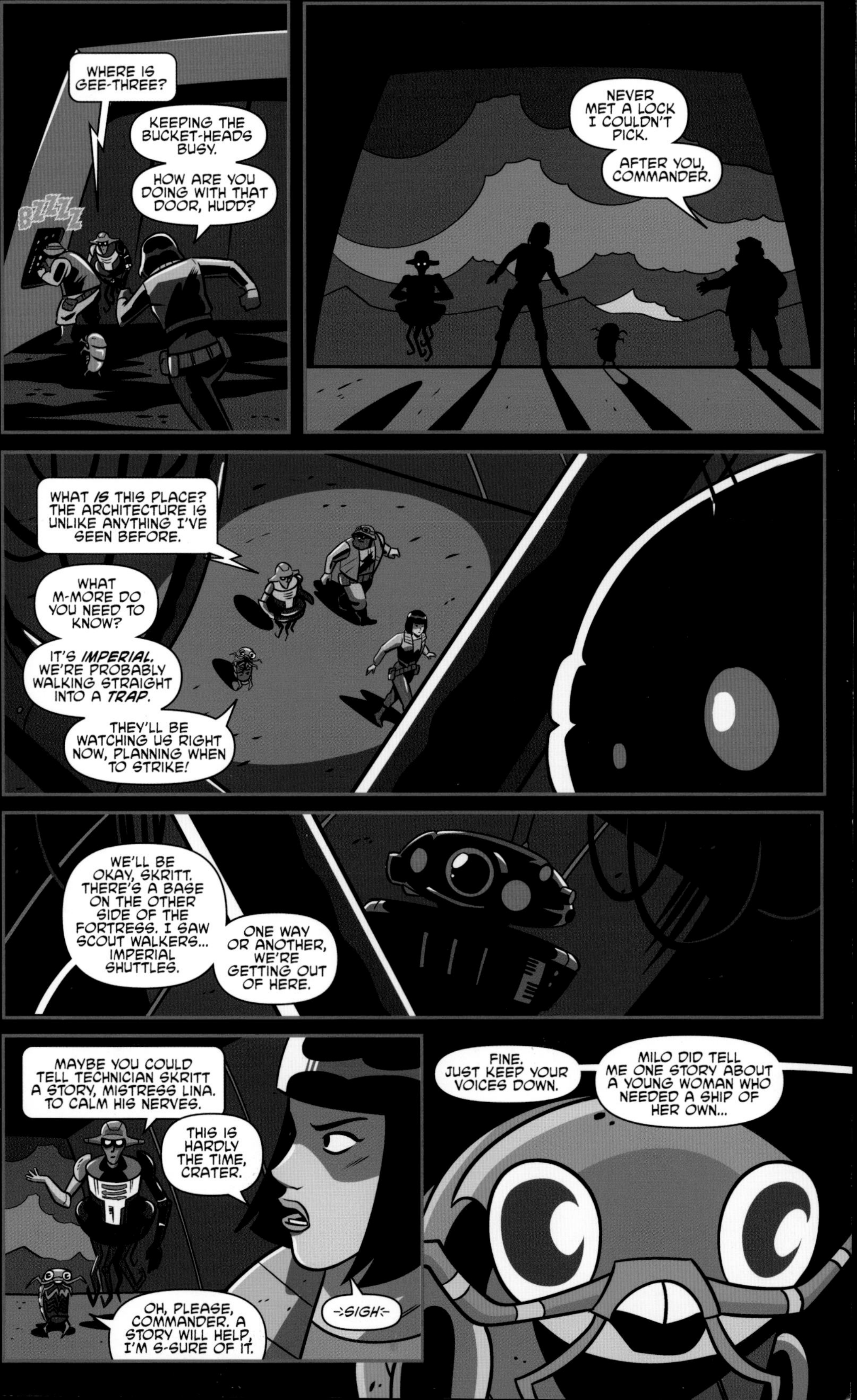
WHERE IS GEE-THREE?
KEEPING THE BUCKET-HEADS BUSY.
HOW ARE YOU DOING WITH THAT DOOR, HUDD?
BZZZZ
NEVER MET A LOCK I COULDN'T PICK.
AFTER YOU, COMMANDER.
WHAT IS THIS PLACE? THE ARCHITECTURE IS UNLIKE ANYTHING I'VE SEEN BEFORE.
WHAT M-MORE DO YOU NEED TO KNOW?
IT'S IMPERIAL. WE'RE PROBABLY WALKING STRAIGHT INTO A TRAP.
THEY'LL BE WATCHING US RIGHT NOW, PLANNING WHEN TO STRIKE!
WE'LL BE OKAY, SKRITT. THERE'S A BASE ON THE OTHER SIDE OF THE FORTRESS. I SAW SCOUT WALKERS... IMPERIAL SHUTTLES.
ONE WAY OR ANOTHER, WE'RE GETTING OUT OF HERE.
MAYBE YOU COULD TELL TECHNICIAN SKRITT A STORY, MISTRESS LINA. TO CALM HIS NERVES.
THIS IS HARDLY THE TIME, CRATER.
OH, PLEASE, COMMANDER. A STORY WILL HELP, I'M S-SURE OF IT.
SIGH
FINE. JUST KEEP YOUR VOICES DOWN.
MILO DID TELL ME ONE STORY ABOUT A YOUNG WOMAN WHO NEEDED A SHIP OF HER OWN...

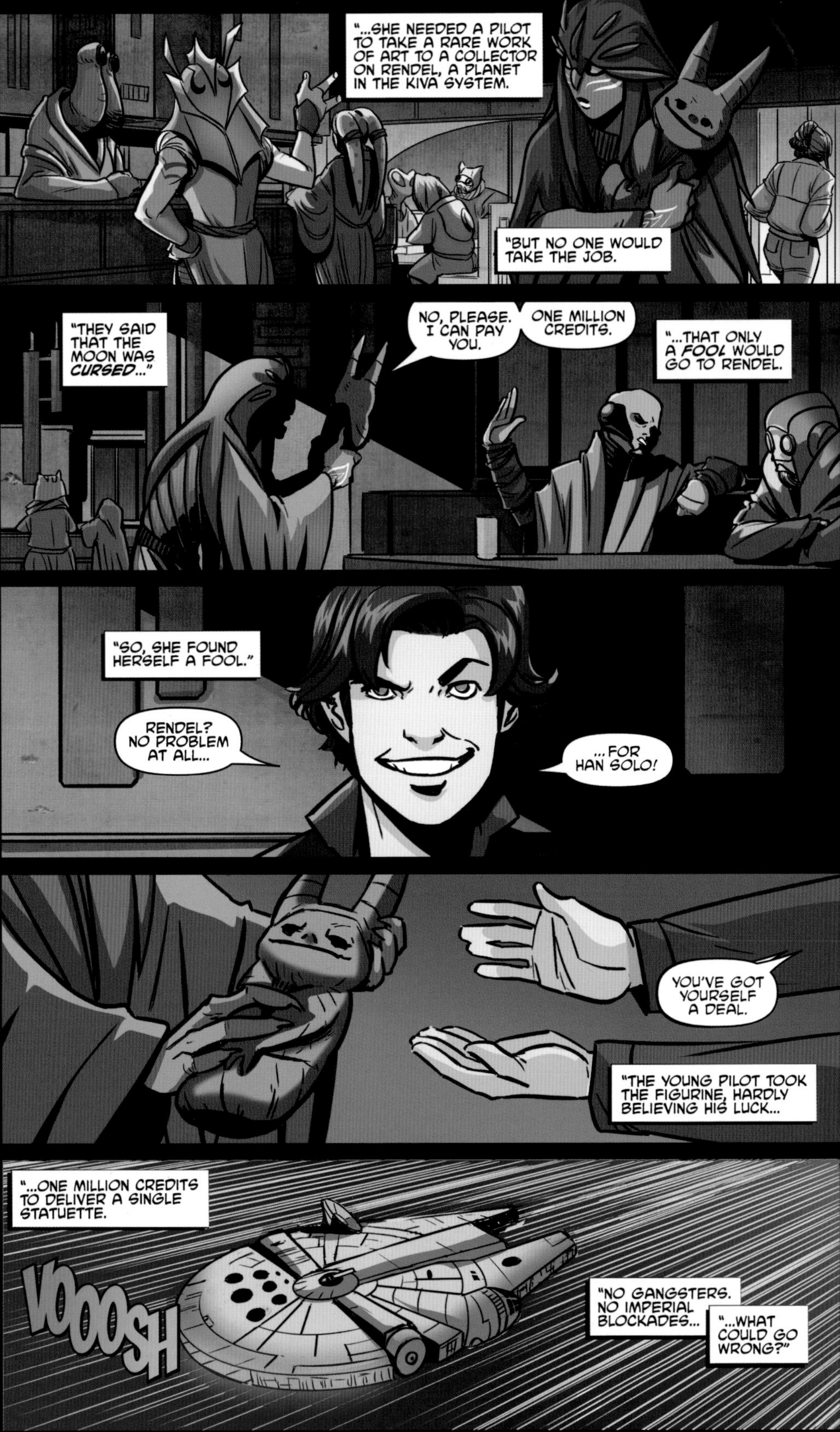
"...SHE NEEDED A PILOT TO TAKE A RARE WORK OF ART TO A COLLECTOR ON RENDEL, A PLANET IN THE KIVA SYSTEM.
"BUT NO ONE WOULD TAKE THE JOB.
"THEY SAID THAT THE MOON WAS *CURSED*..."
NO, PLEASE. I CAN PAY YOU.
ONE MILLION CREDITS.
"...THAT ONLY A *FOOL* WOULD GO TO RENDEL.
"SO, SHE FOUND HERSELF A FOOL."
RENDEL? NO PROBLEM AT ALL...
...FOR HAN SOLO!
YOU'VE GOT YOURSELF A DEAL.
"THE YOUNG PILOT TOOK THE FIGURINE, HARDLY BELIEVING HIS LUCK...
"...ONE MILLION CREDITS TO DELIVER A SINGLE STATUETTE.
VOOOSH
"NO GANGSTERS. NO IMPERIAL BLOCKADES...
"...WHAT COULD GO WRONG?"

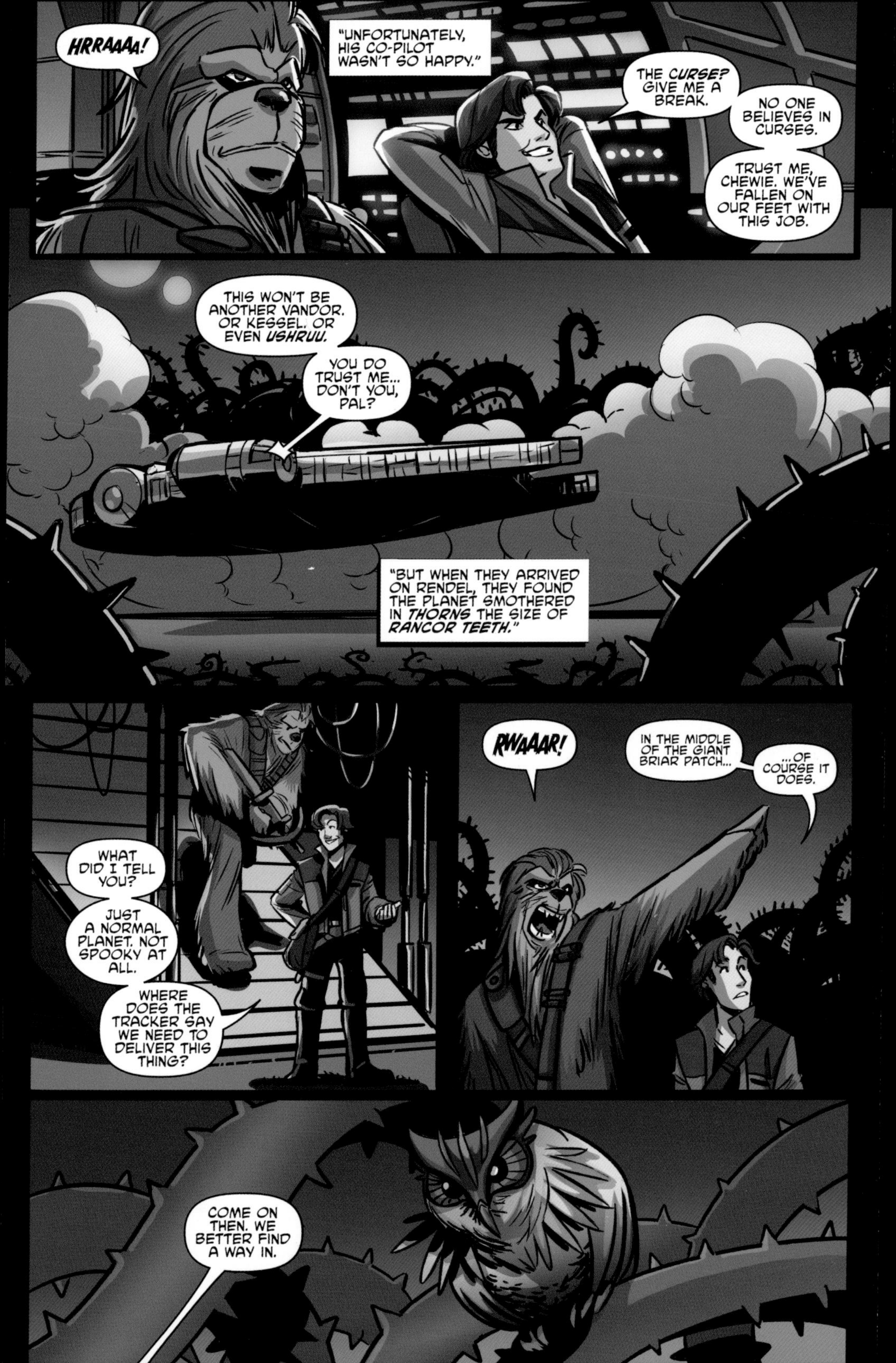
HRRAAAA!
"UNFORTUNATELY, HIS CO-PILOT WASN'T SO HAPPY."
THE *CURSE?* GIVE ME A BREAK.
NO ONE BELIEVES IN CURSES.
TRUST ME, CHEWIE. WE'VE FALLEN ON OUR FEET WITH THIS JOB.
THIS WON'T BE ANOTHER VANDOR. OR KESSEL. OR EVEN *USHRUU.*
YOU DO TRUST ME... DON'T YOU, PAL?
"BUT WHEN THEY ARRIVED ON RENDEL, THEY FOUND THE PLANET SMOTHERED IN *THORNS* THE SIZE OF *RANCOR TEETH.*"
WHAT DID I TELL YOU?
JUST A NORMAL PLANET. NOT SPOOKY AT ALL.
WHERE DOES THE TRACKER SAY WE NEED TO DELIVER THIS THING?
RWAAAR!
IN THE MIDDLE OF THE GIANT BRIAR PATCH...
...OF COURSE IT DOES.
COME ON THEN. WE BETTER FIND A WAY IN.

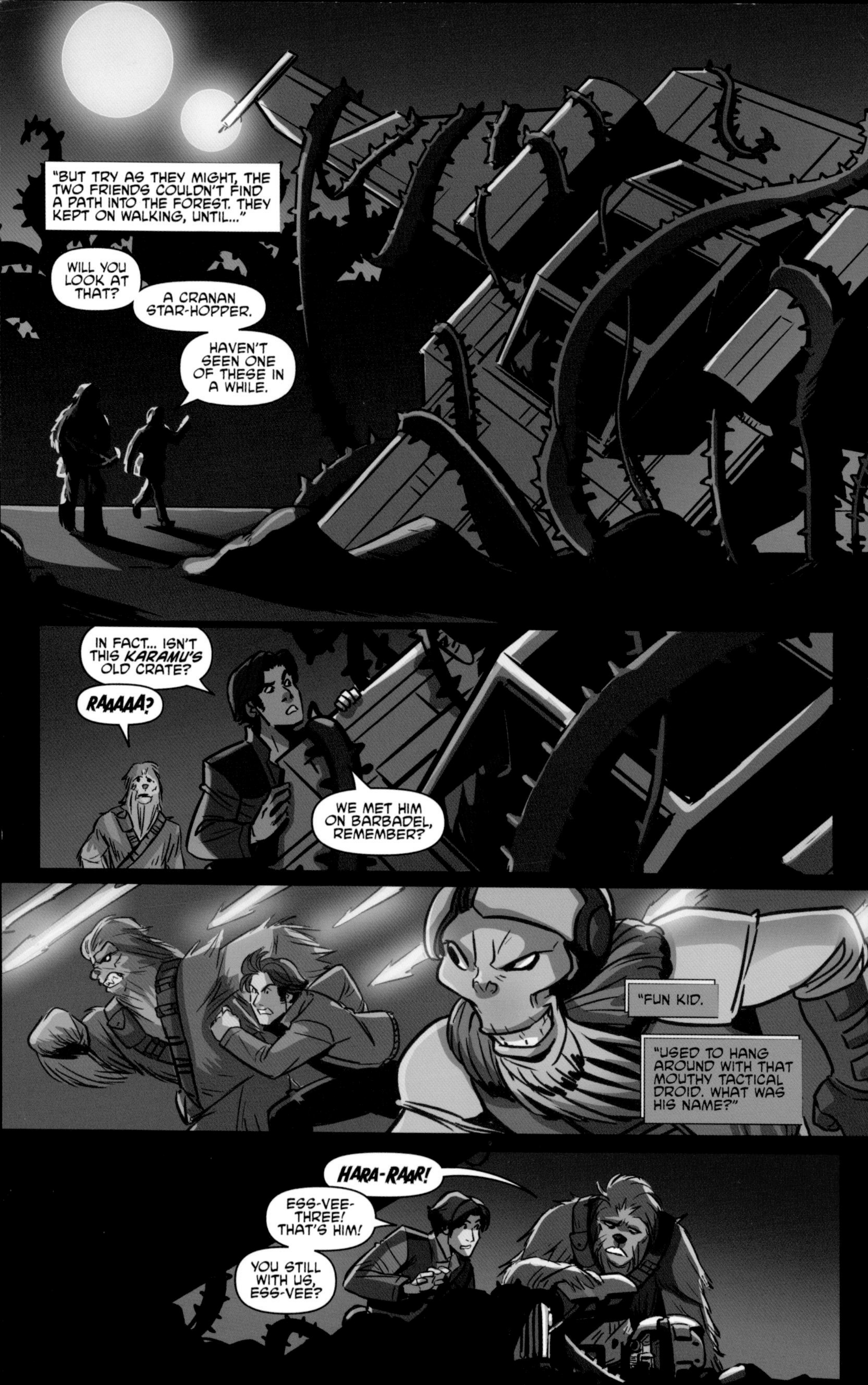
"BUT TRY AS THEY MIGHT, THE TWO FRIENDS COULDN'T FIND A PATH INTO THE FOREST. THEY KEPT ON WALKING, UNTIL..."
WILL YOU LOOK AT THAT?
A CRANAN STAR-HOPPER.
HAVEN'T SEEN ONE OF THESE IN A WHILE.
IN FACT... ISN'T THIS *KARAMU'S* OLD CRATE?
RAAAAA?
WE MET HIM ON BARBADEL, REMEMBER?
"FUN KID.
"USED TO HANG AROUND WITH THAT MOUTHY TACTICAL DROID. WHAT WAS HIS NAME?"
HARA-RAAR!
ESS-VEE-THREE! THAT'S HIM!
YOU STILL WITH US, ESS-VEE?

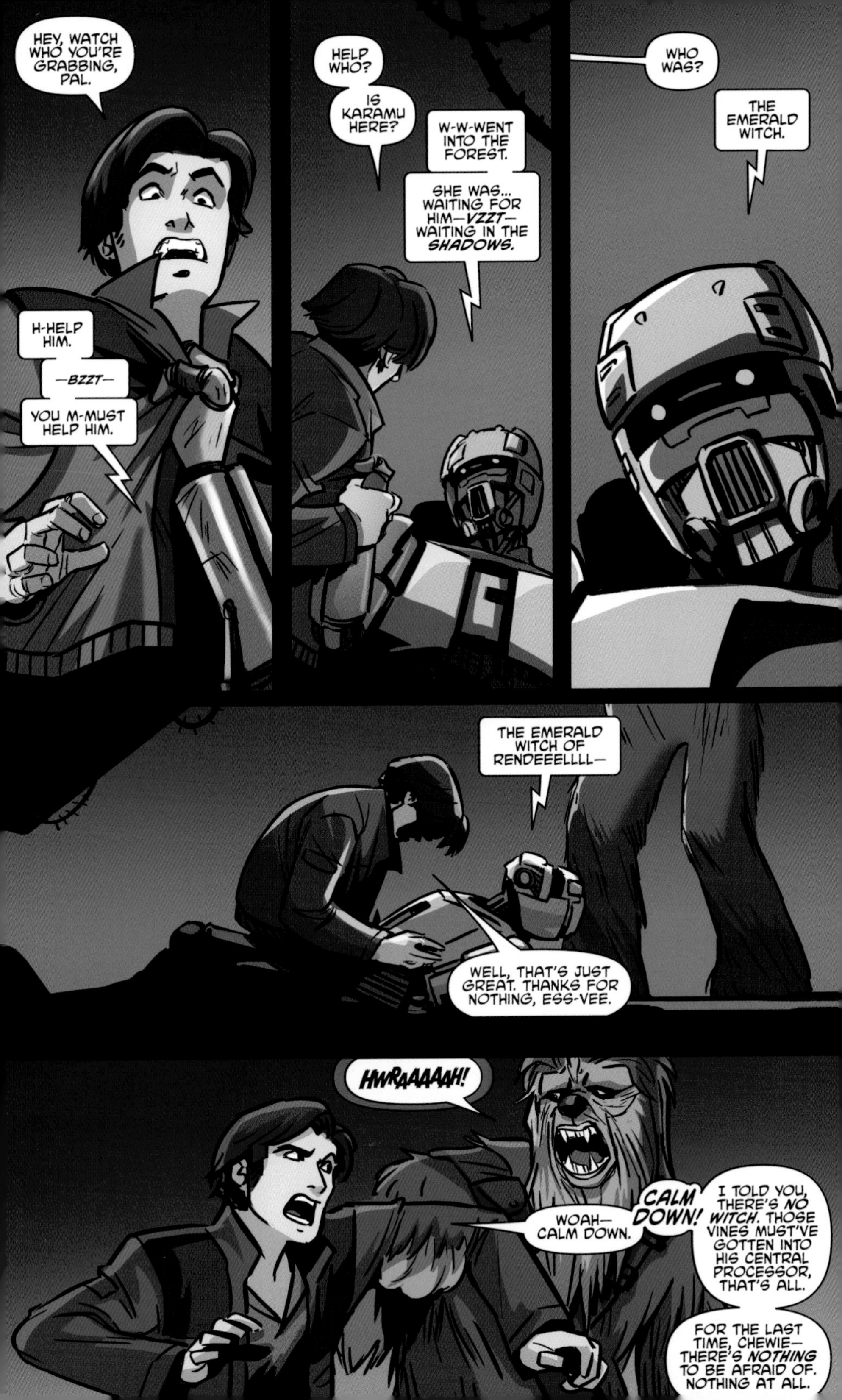
HEY, WATCH WHO YOU'RE GRABBING, PAL.
H-HELP HIM.
—BZZT—
YOU M-MUST HELP HIM.
HELP WHO?
IS KARAMU HERE?
W-W-WENT INTO THE FOREST.
SHE WAS... WAITING FOR HIM—VZZT—WAITING IN THE SHADOWS.
WHO WAS?
THE EMERALD WITCH.
THE EMERALD WITCH OF RENDEEELLLL—
WELL, THAT'S JUST GREAT. THANKS FOR NOTHING, ESS-VEE.
HWRAAAAAH!
WOAH—CALM DOWN.
CALM DOWN!
I TOLD YOU, THERE'S NO WITCH. THOSE VINES MUST'VE GOTTEN INTO HIS CENTRAL PROCESSOR, THAT'S ALL.
FOR THE LAST TIME, CHEWIE—THERE'S NOTHING TO BE AFRAID OF. NOTHING AT ALL.

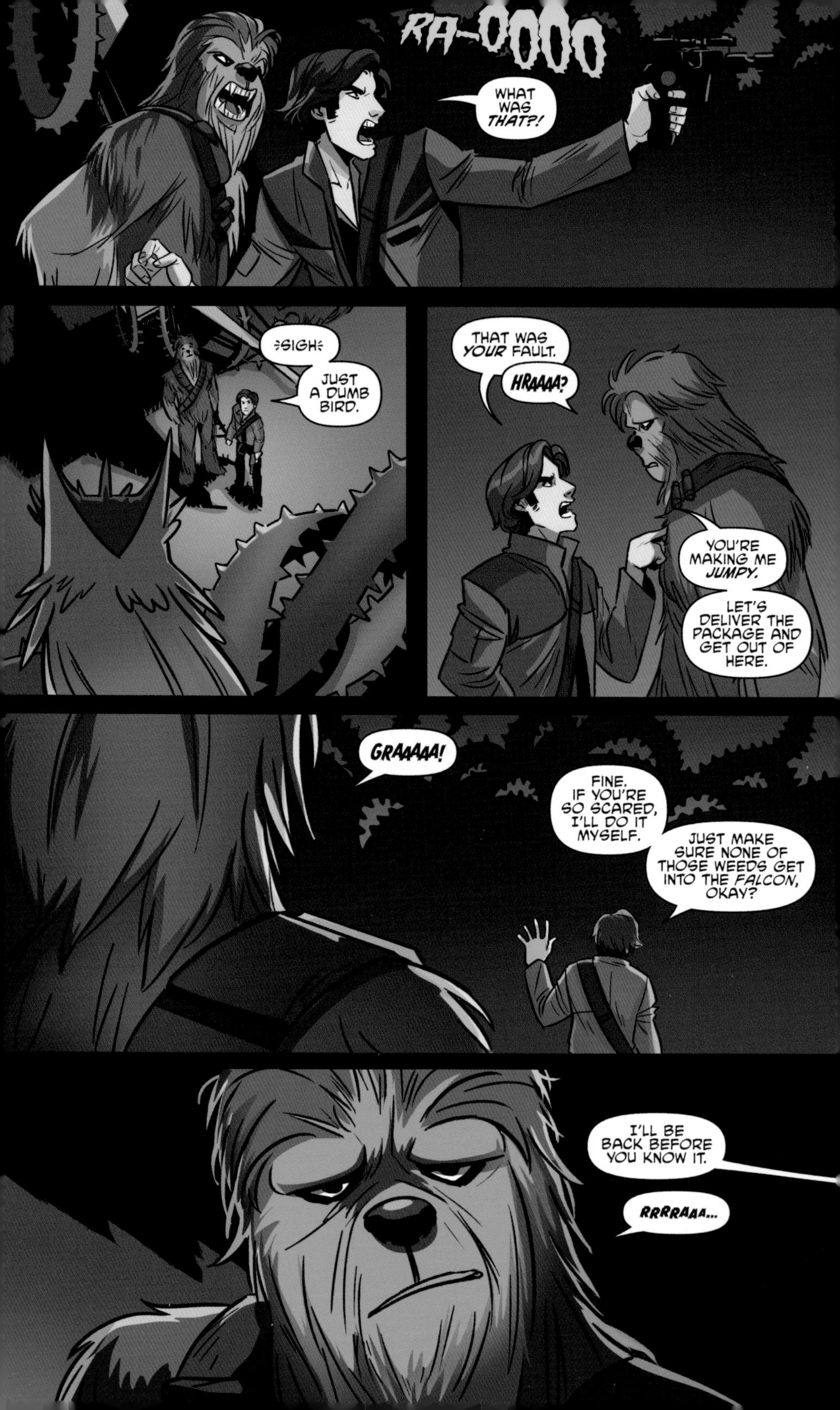
RA-OOOO
WHAT WAS *THAT?!*
⸗SIGH⸗
JUST A DUMB BIRD.
THAT WAS *YOUR* FAULT.
HRAAAA?
YOU'RE MAKING ME *JUMPY.*
LET'S DELIVER THE PACKAGE AND GET OUT OF HERE.
GRAAAAA!
FINE. IF YOU'RE SO SCARED, I'LL DO IT MYSELF.
JUST MAKE SURE NONE OF THOSE WEEDS GET INTO THE *FALCON,* OKAY?
I'LL BE BACK BEFORE YOU KNOW IT.
RRRRAAA...

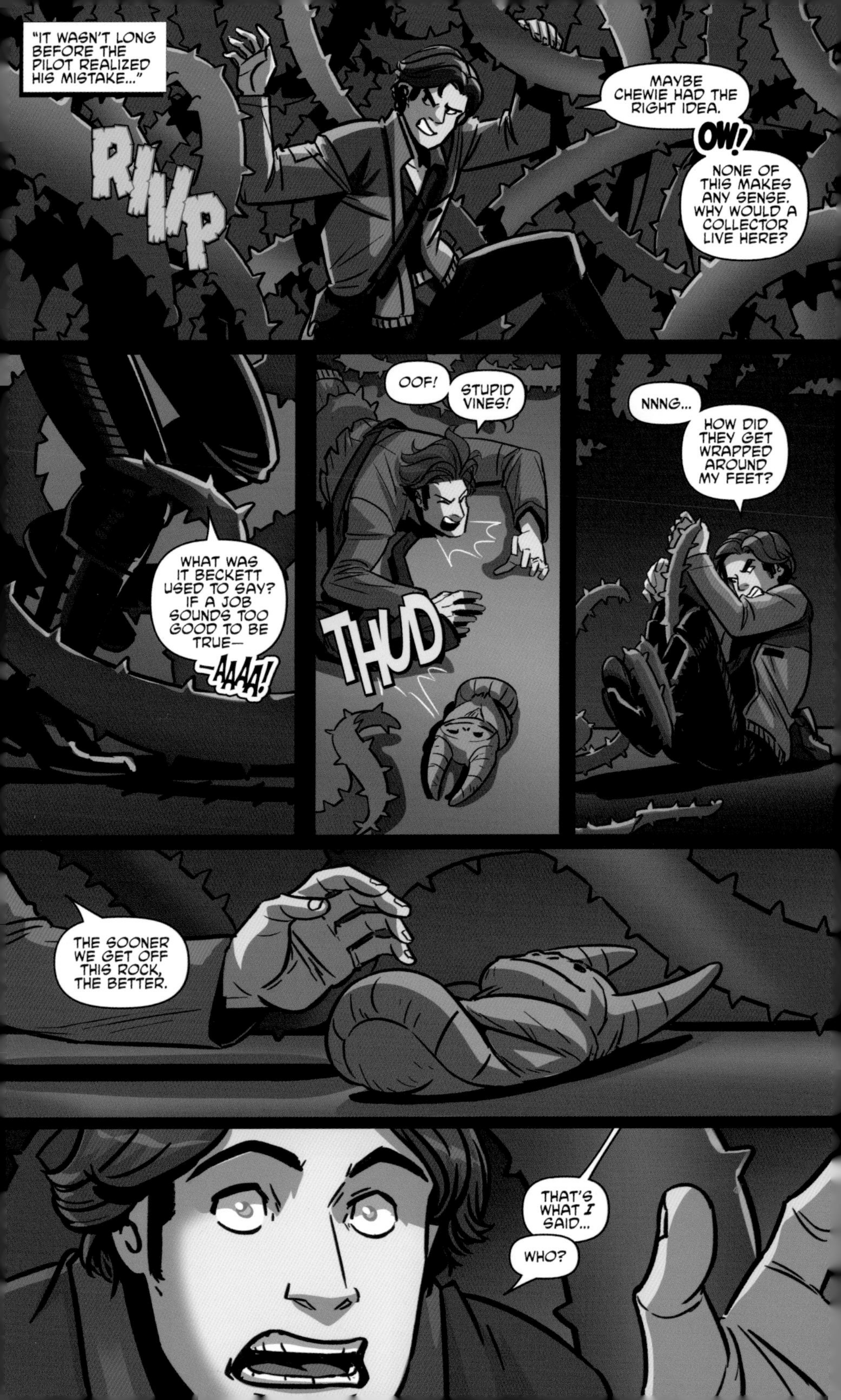
"IT WASN'T LONG BEFORE THE PILOT REALIZED HIS MISTAKE..."
RIIIP
MAYBE CHEWIE HAD THE RIGHT IDEA.
OW!
NONE OF THIS MAKES ANY SENSE. WHY WOULD A COLLECTOR LIVE HERE?
WHAT WAS IT BECKETT USED TO SAY? IF A JOB SOUNDS TOO GOOD TO BE TRUE—
—AAAA!
OOF!
STUPID VINES!
THUD
NNNG...
HOW DID THEY GET WRAPPED AROUND MY FEET?
THE SOONER WE GET OFF THIS ROCK, THE BETTER.
THAT'S WHAT I SAID...
WHO?

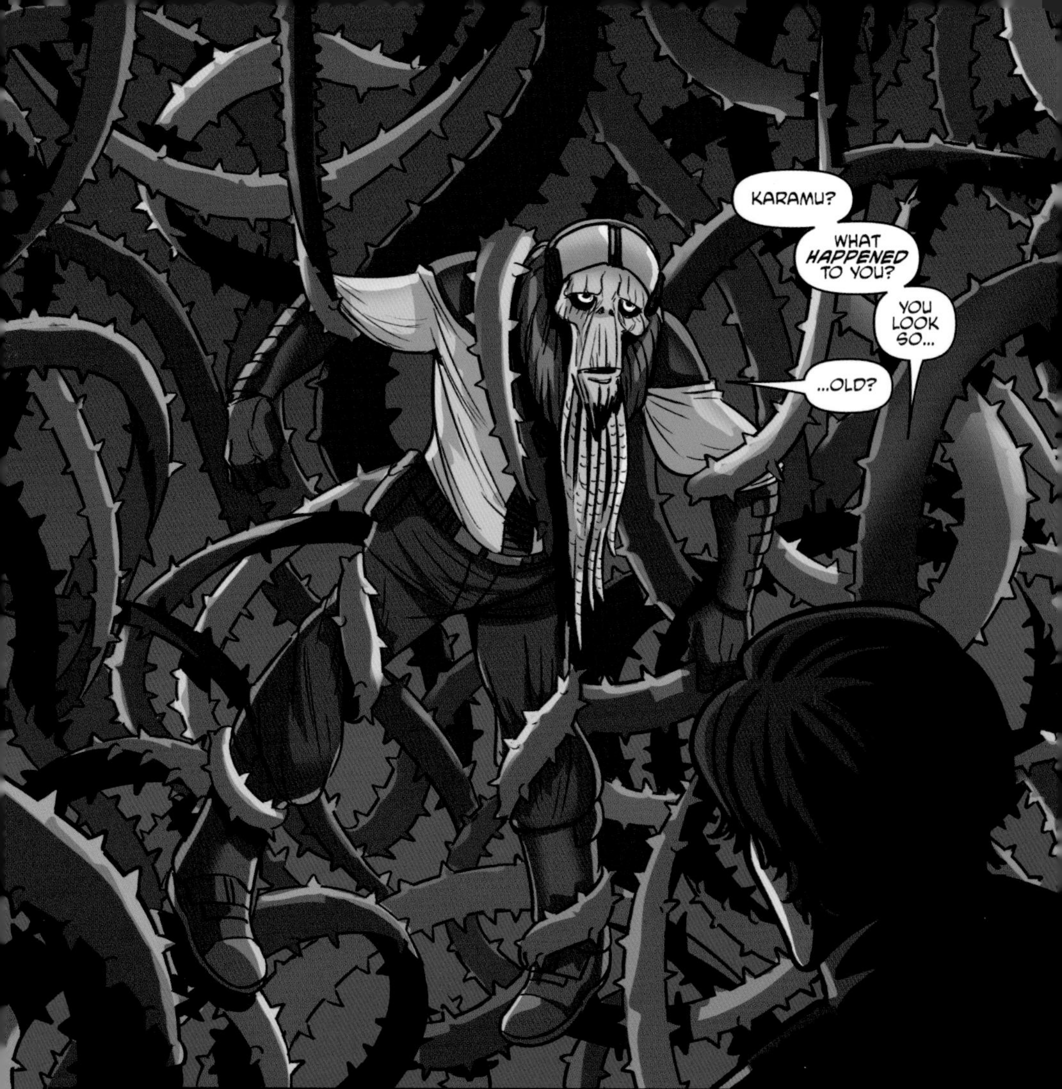
KARAMU?
WHAT *HAPPENED* TO YOU?
YOU LOOK SO...
...OLD?

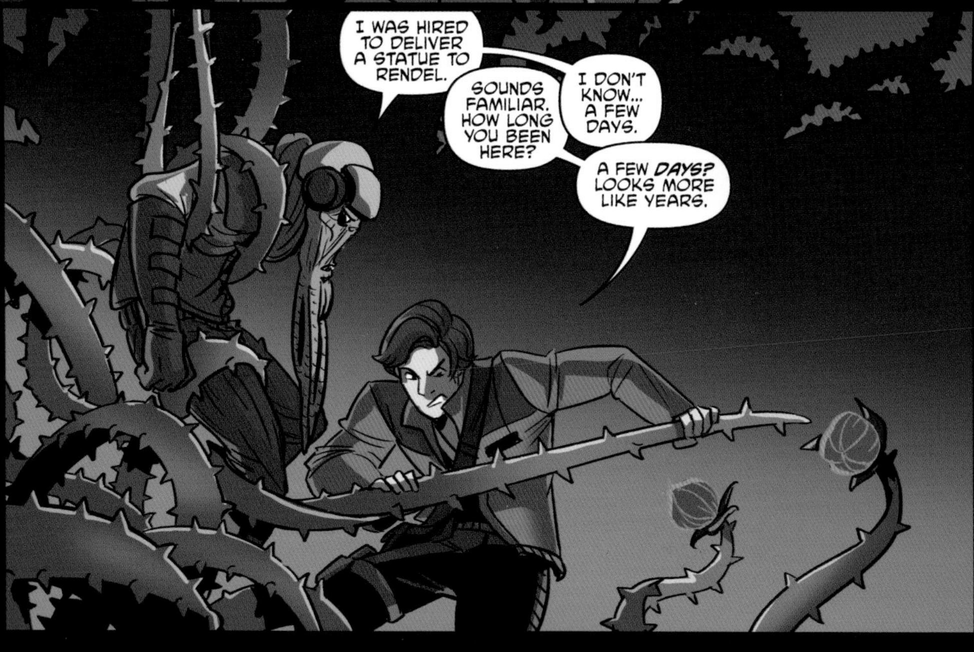
I WAS HIRED TO DELIVER A STATUE TO RENDEL.
I DON'T KNOW... A FEW DAYS.
SOUNDS FAMILIAR. HOW LONG YOU BEEN HERE?
A FEW *DAYS?* LOOKS MORE LIKE YEARS.

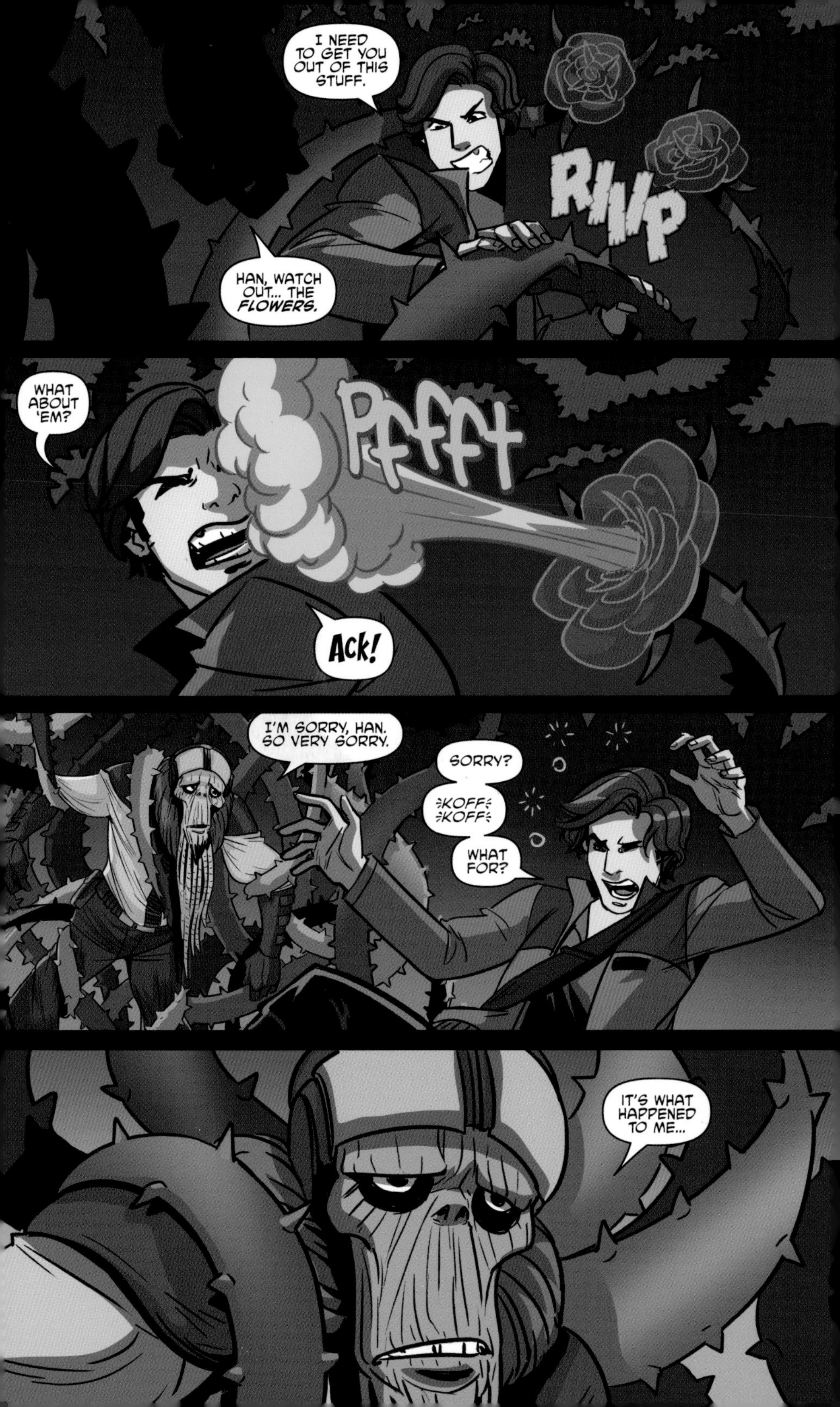
I NEED TO GET YOU OUT OF THIS STUFF.
RIIIP
HAN, WATCH OUT... THE FLOWERS.
WHAT ABOUT 'EM?
Pffft
ACK!
I'M SORRY, HAN. SO VERY SORRY.
SORRY?
KOFF KOFF
WHAT FOR?
IT'S WHAT HAPPENED TO ME...

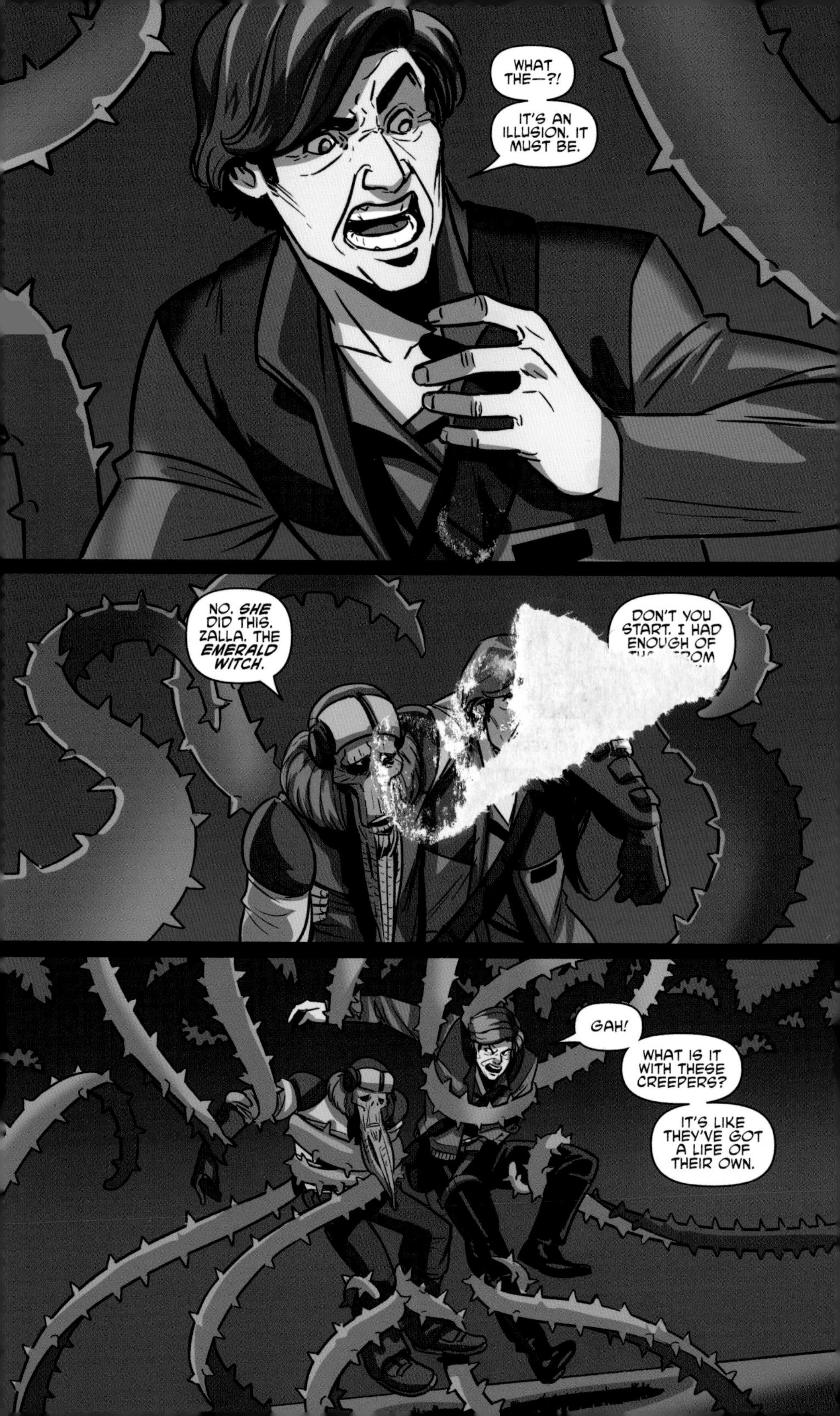
WHAT THE—?!
IT'S AN ILLUSION. IT MUST BE.
NO. SHE DID THIS. ZALLA. THE EMERALD WITCH.
DON'T YOU START. I HAD ENOUGH OF
GAH!
WHAT IS IT WITH THESE CREEPERS?
IT'S LIKE THEY'VE GOT A LIFE OF THEIR OWN.

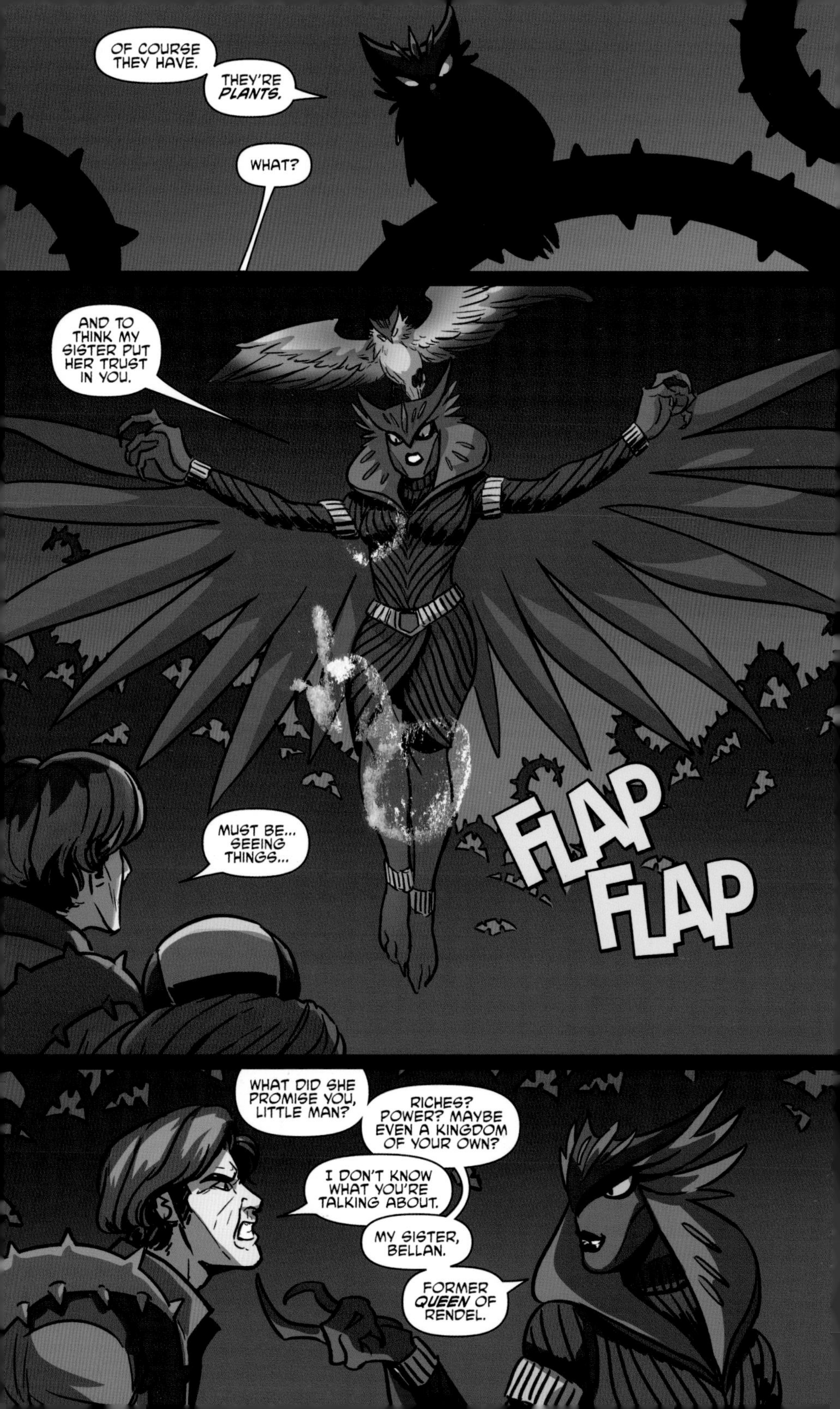

OF COURSE THEY HAVE.
THEY'RE *PLANTS.*
WHAT?
AND TO THINK MY SISTER PUT HER TRUST IN YOU.
MUST BE... SEEING THINGS...
FLAP FLAP
WHAT DID SHE PROMISE YOU, LITTLE MAN?
RICHES? POWER? MAYBE EVEN A KINGDOM OF YOUR OWN?
I DON'T KNOW WHAT YOU'RE TALKING ABOUT.
MY SISTER, BELLAN.
FORMER *QUEEN* OF RENDEL.

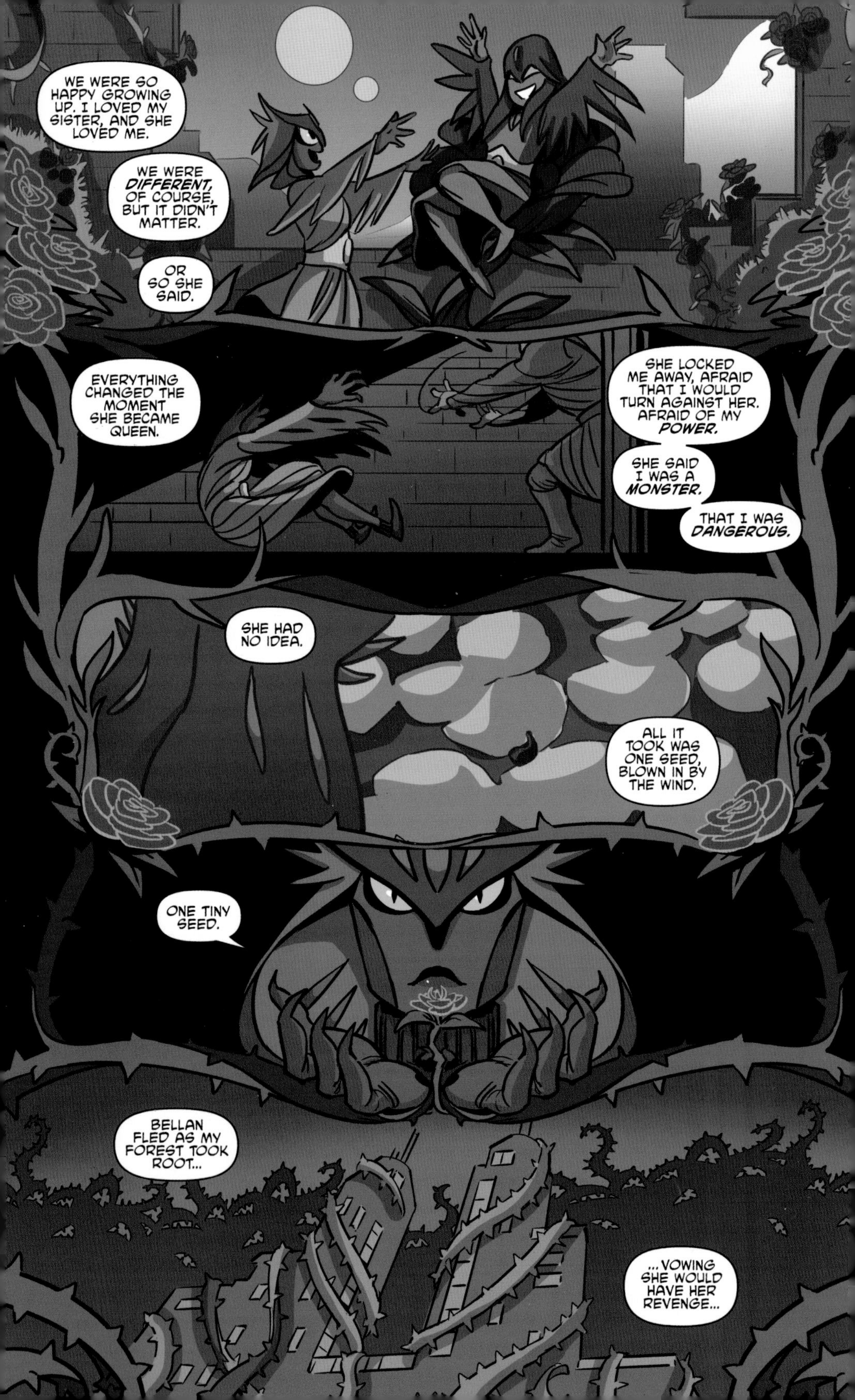
WE WERE SO HAPPY GROWING UP. I LOVED MY SISTER, AND SHE LOVED ME.
WE WERE *DIFFERENT,* OF COURSE, BUT IT DIDN'T MATTER.
OR SO SHE SAID.
EVERYTHING CHANGED THE MOMENT SHE BECAME QUEEN.
SHE LOCKED ME AWAY, AFRAID THAT I WOULD TURN AGAINST HER. AFRAID OF MY *POWER.*
SHE SAID I WAS A *MONSTER.*
THAT I WAS *DANGEROUS.*
SHE HAD NO IDEA.
ALL IT TOOK WAS ONE SEED, BLOWN IN BY THE WIND.
ONE TINY SEED.
BELLAN FLED AS MY FOREST TOOK ROOT...
...VOWING SHE WOULD HAVE HER REVENGE...

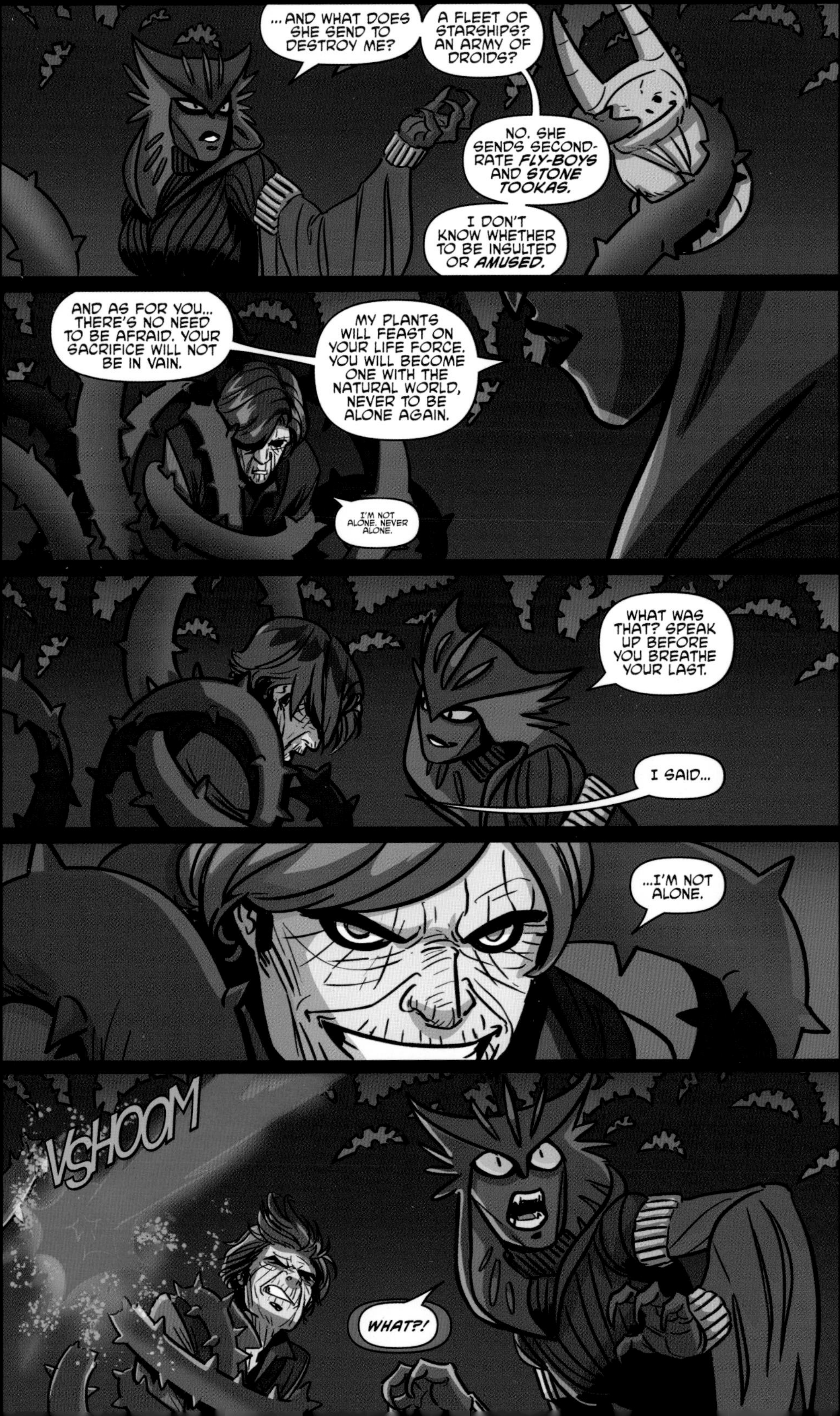
...AND WHAT DOES SHE SEND TO DESTROY ME?
A FLEET OF STARSHIPS? AN ARMY OF DROIDS?
NO. SHE SENDS SECOND-RATE *FLY-BOYS* AND *STONE TOOKAS.*
I DON'T KNOW WHETHER TO BE INSULTED OR *AMUSED.*
AND AS FOR YOU... THERE'S NO NEED TO BE AFRAID. YOUR SACRIFICE WILL NOT BE IN VAIN.
MY PLANTS WILL FEAST ON YOUR LIFE FORCE. YOU WILL BECOME ONE WITH THE NATURAL WORLD, NEVER TO BE ALONE AGAIN.
I'M NOT ALONE. NEVER ALONE.
WHAT WAS THAT? SPEAK UP BEFORE YOU BREATHE YOUR LAST.
I SAID...
...I'M NOT ALONE.
VSHOOM
WHAT?!

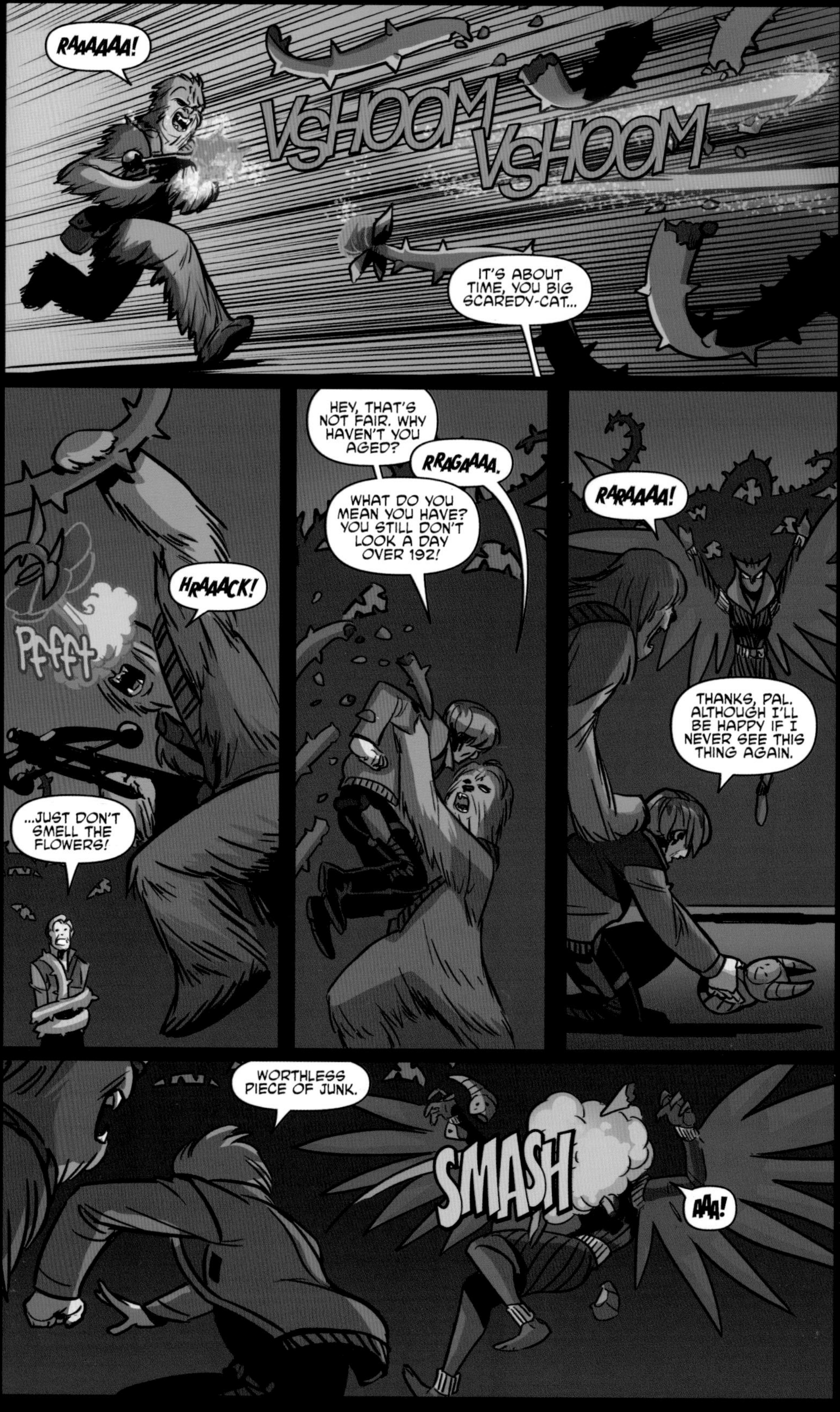
RAAAAAA!
VSHOOM VSHOOM
IT'S ABOUT TIME, YOU BIG SCAREDY-CAT...
HRAAACK!
Pffft
...JUST DON'T SMELL THE FLOWERS!
HEY, THAT'S NOT FAIR. WHY HAVEN'T YOU AGED?
RRAGAAAA.
WHAT DO YOU MEAN YOU HAVE? YOU STILL DON'T LOOK A DAY OVER 192!
RARAAAA!
THANKS, PAL. ALTHOUGH I'LL BE HAPPY IF I NEVER SEE THIS THING AGAIN.
WORTHLESS PIECE OF JUNK.
SMASH
AAA!

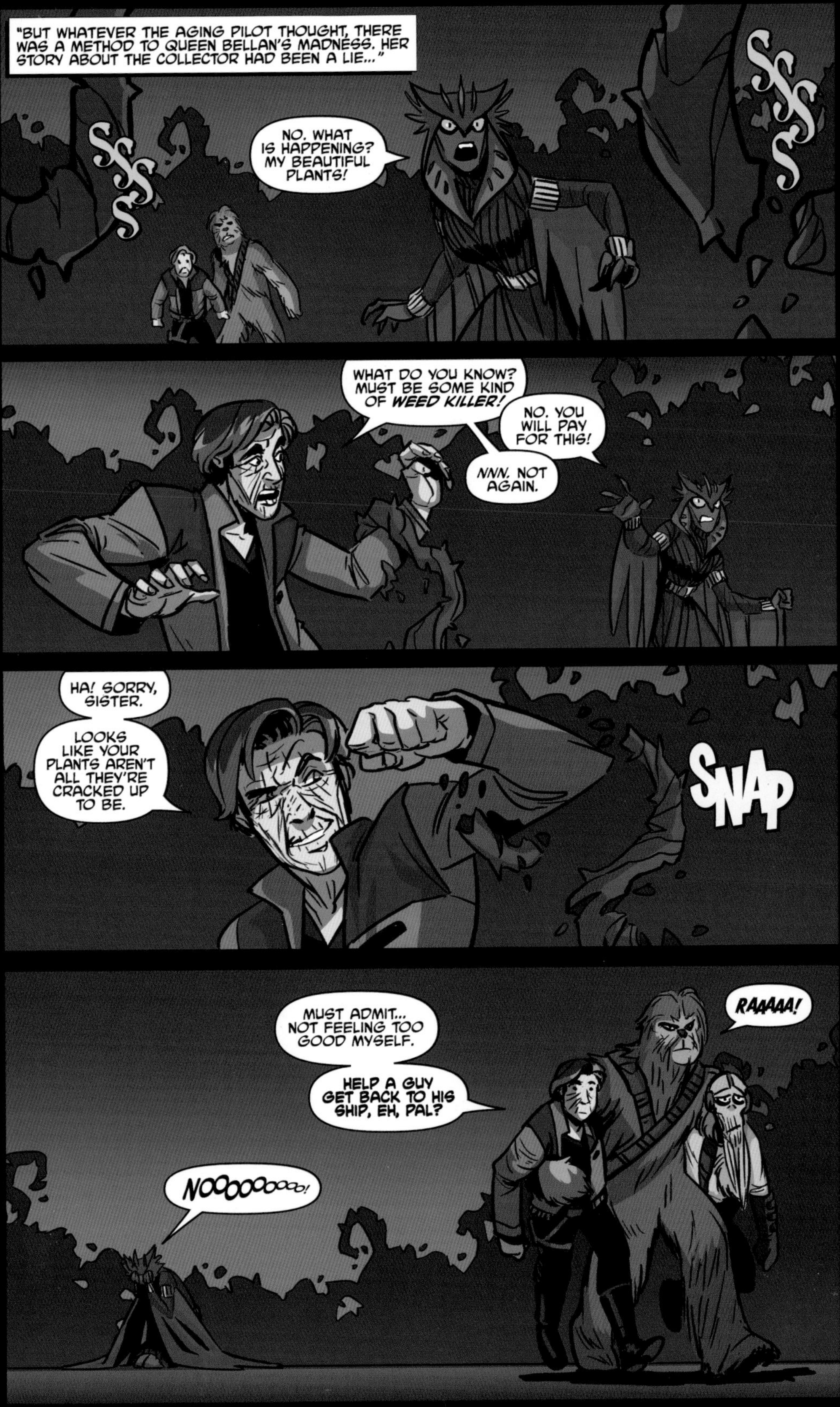
"BUT WHATEVER THE AGING PILOT THOUGHT, THERE WAS A METHOD TO QUEEN BELLAN'S MADNESS. HER STORY ABOUT THE COLLECTOR HAD BEEN A LIE..."
SSSS
NO. WHAT IS HAPPENING? MY BEAUTIFUL PLANTS!
SSSS
WHAT DO YOU KNOW? MUST BE SOME KIND OF WEED KILLER!
NNN. NOT AGAIN.
NO. YOU WILL PAY FOR THIS!
HA! SORRY, SISTER.
LOOKS LIKE YOUR PLANTS AREN'T ALL THEY'RE CRACKED UP TO BE.
SNAP
MUST ADMIT... NOT FEELING TOO GOOD MYSELF.
HELP A GUY GET BACK TO HIS SHIP, EH, PAL?
RAAAAA!
NOOOOOOOOO!

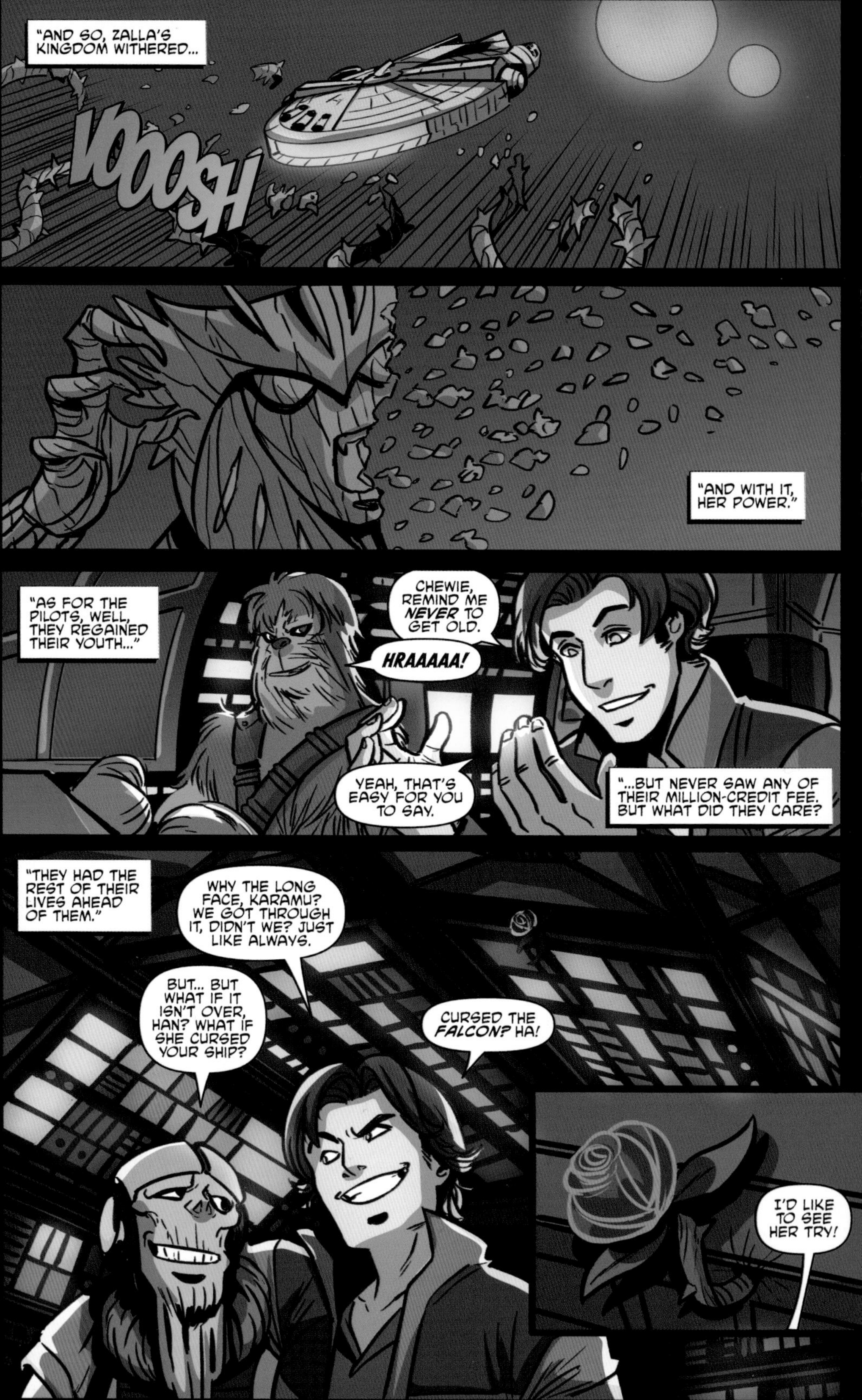
"AND SO, ZALLA'S KINGDOM WITHERED...
VOOOSH
"AND WITH IT, HER POWER."
"AS FOR THE PILOTS, WELL, THEY REGAINED THEIR YOUTH..."
CHEWIE, REMIND ME NEVER TO GET OLD.
HRAAAAA!
YEAH, THAT'S EASY FOR YOU TO SAY.
"...BUT NEVER SAW ANY OF THEIR MILLION-CREDIT FEE. BUT WHAT DID THEY CARE?
"THEY HAD THE REST OF THEIR LIVES AHEAD OF THEM."
WHY THE LONG FACE, KARAMU? WE GOT THROUGH IT, DIDN'T WE? JUST LIKE ALWAYS.
BUT... BUT WHAT IF IT ISN'T OVER, HAN? WHAT IF SHE CURSED YOUR SHIP?
CURSED THE FALCON? HA!
I'D LIKE TO SEE HER TRY!

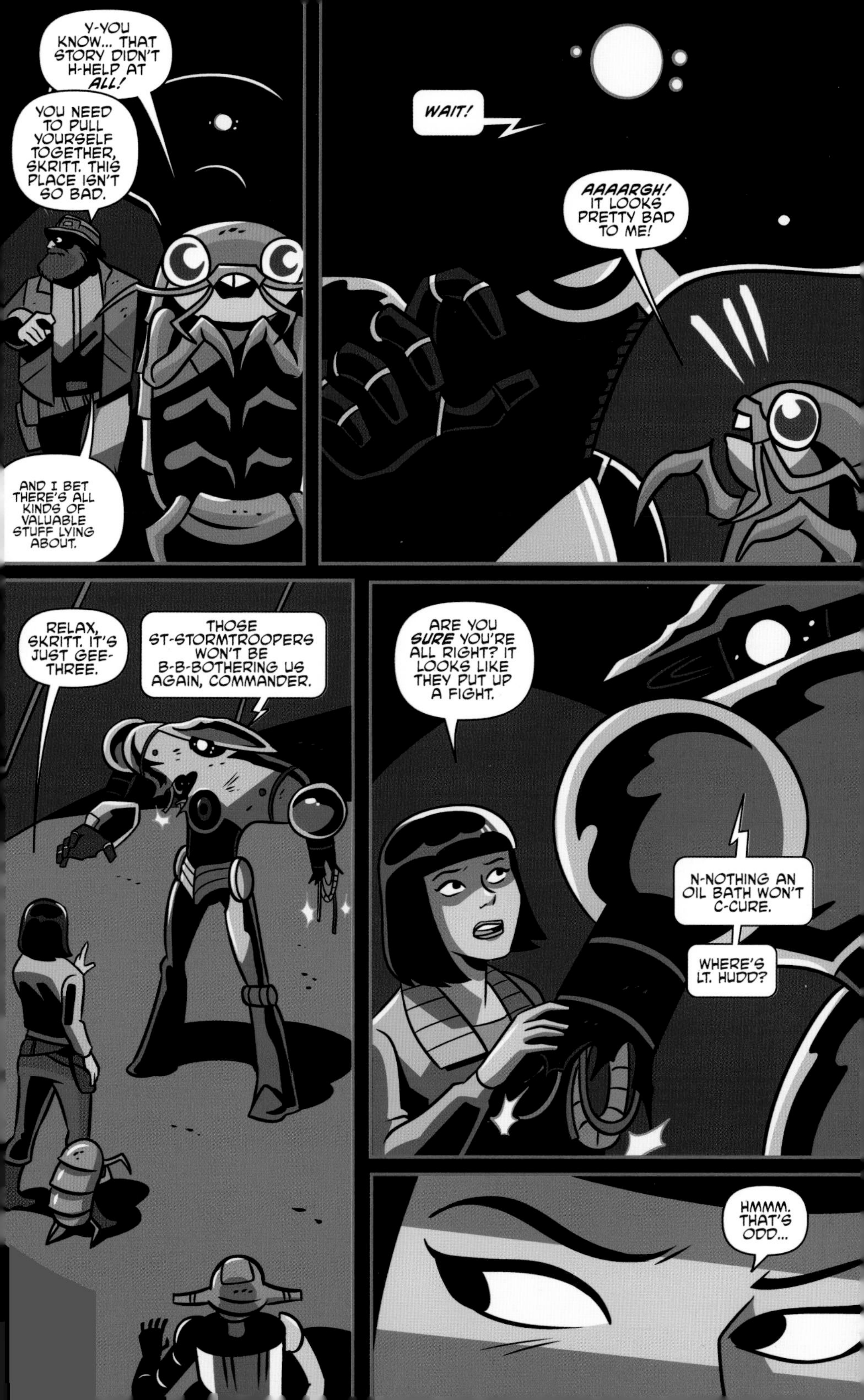
Y-YOU KNOW... THAT STORY DIDN'T H-HELP AT ALL!
YOU NEED TO PULL YOURSELF TOGETHER, SKRITT. THIS PLACE ISN'T SO BAD.
AND I BET THERE'S ALL KINDS OF VALUABLE STUFF LYING ABOUT.
WAIT!
AAAARGH! IT LOOKS PRETTY BAD TO ME!
RELAX, SKRITT. IT'S JUST GEE-THREE.
THOSE ST-STORMTROOPERS WON'T BE B-B-BOTHERING US AGAIN, COMMANDER.
ARE YOU SURE YOU'RE ALL RIGHT? IT LOOKS LIKE THEY PUT UP A FIGHT.
N-NOTHING AN OIL BATH WON'T C-CURE.
WHERE'S LT. HUDD?
HMMM. THAT'S ODD...

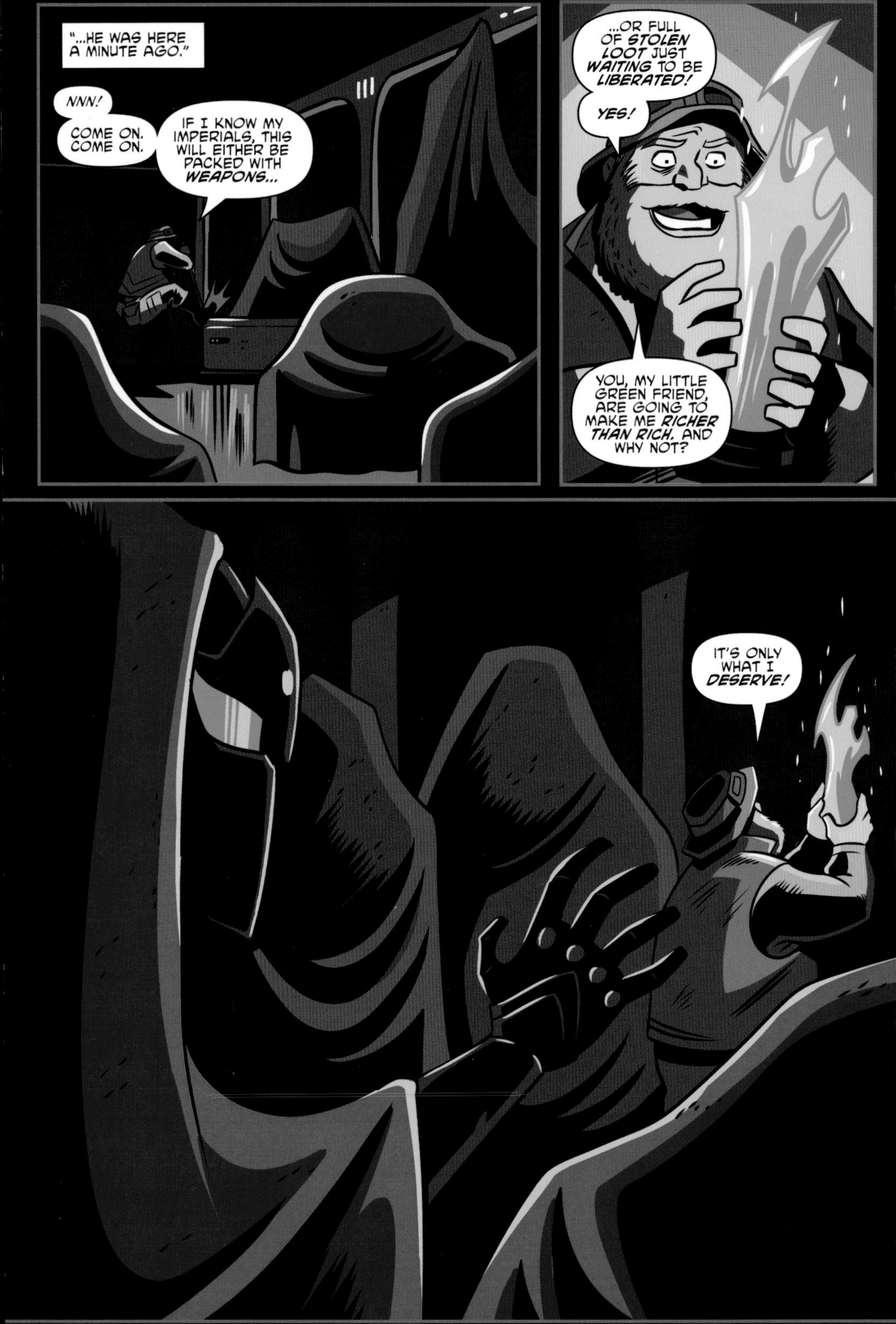
"...HE WAS HERE A MINUTE AGO."
NNN!
COME ON. COME ON.
IF I KNOW MY IMPERIALS, THIS WILL EITHER BE PACKED WITH WEAPONS...
...OR FULL OF STOLEN LOOT JUST WAITING TO BE LIBERATED!
YES!
YOU, MY LITTLE GREEN FRIEND, ARE GOING TO MAKE ME RICHER THAN RICH. AND WHY NOT?
IT'S ONLY WHAT I DESERVE!

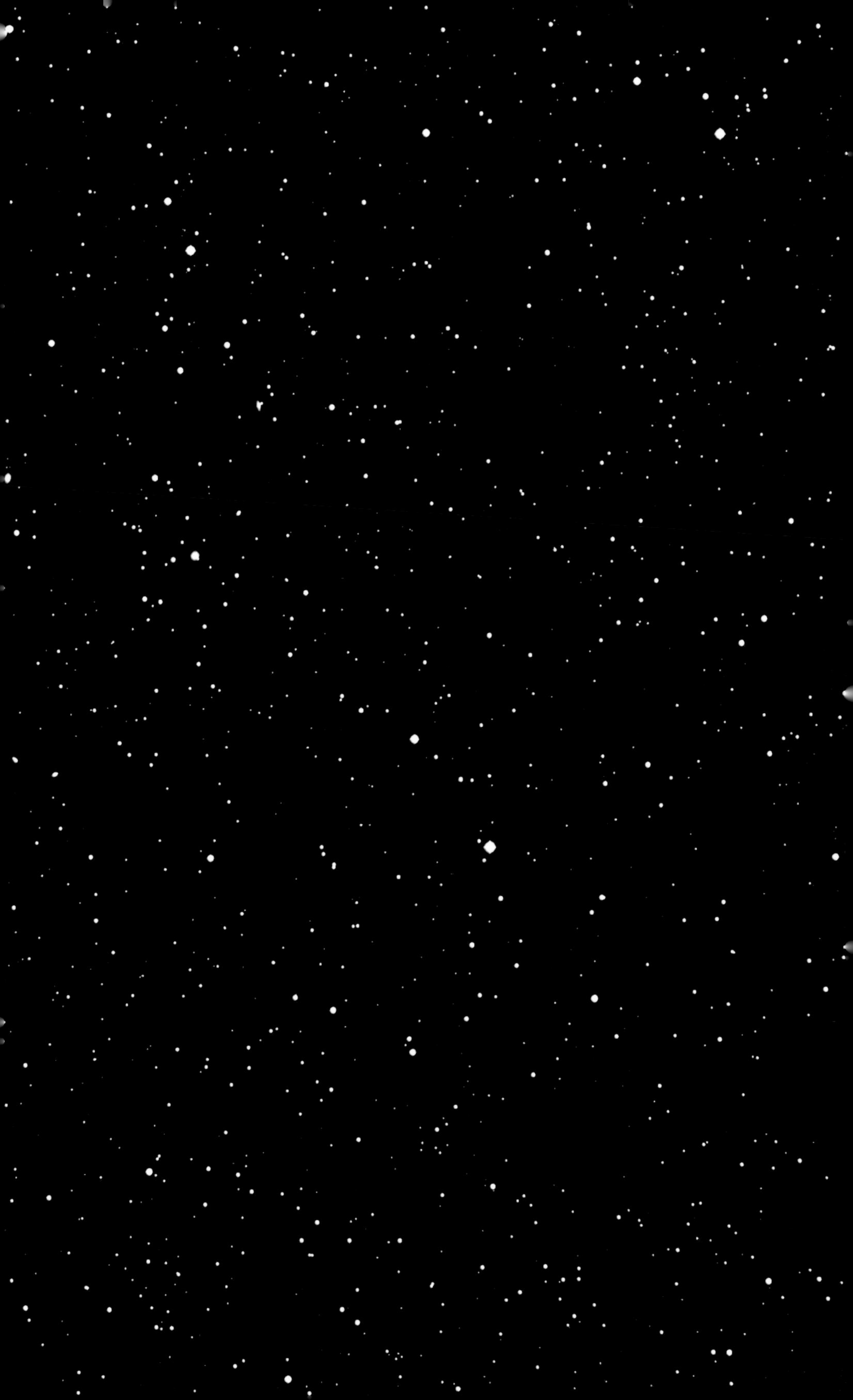

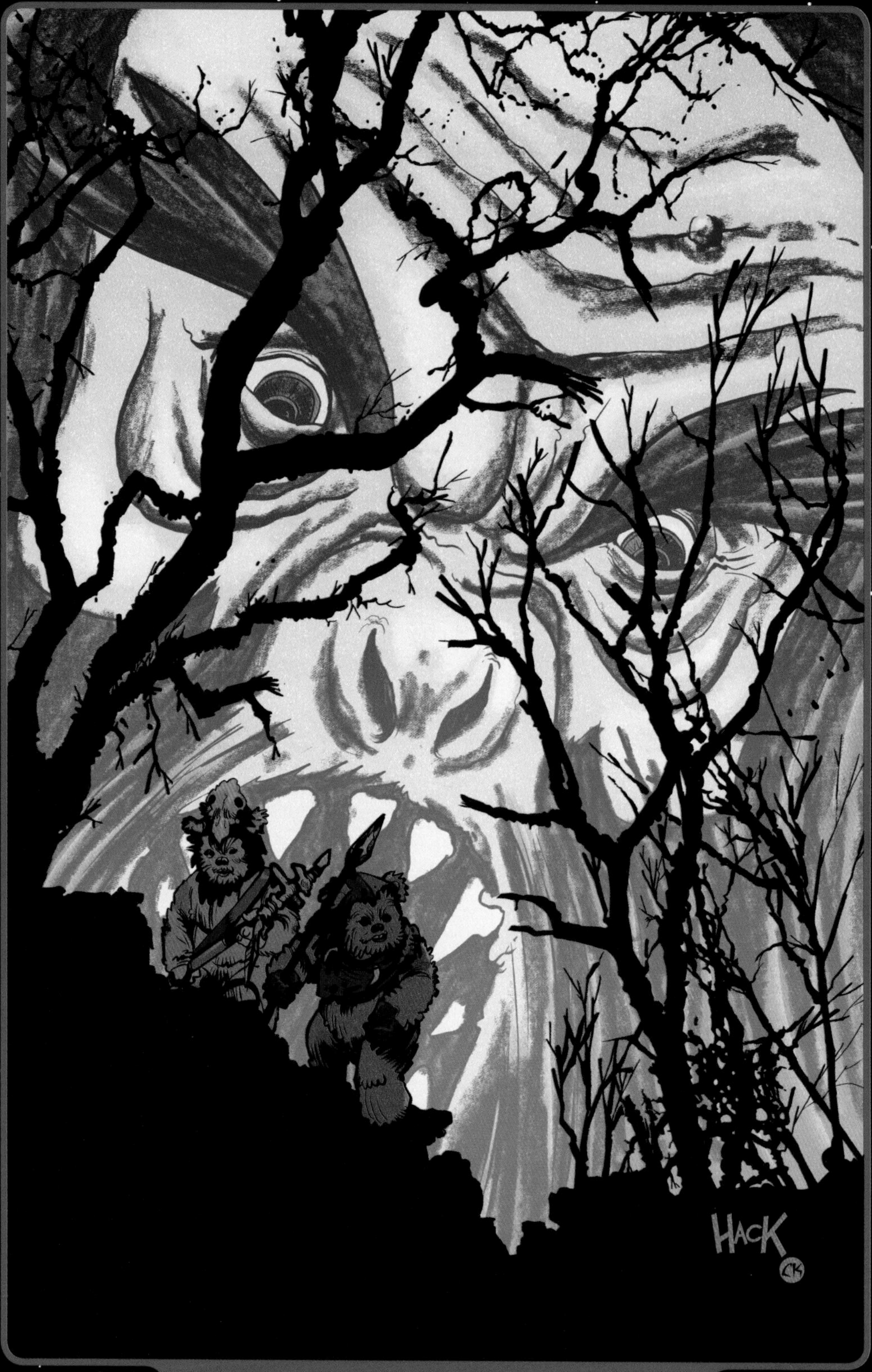
HACK
CK

Art by Robert Hack, Colors by Charlie Kirchoff

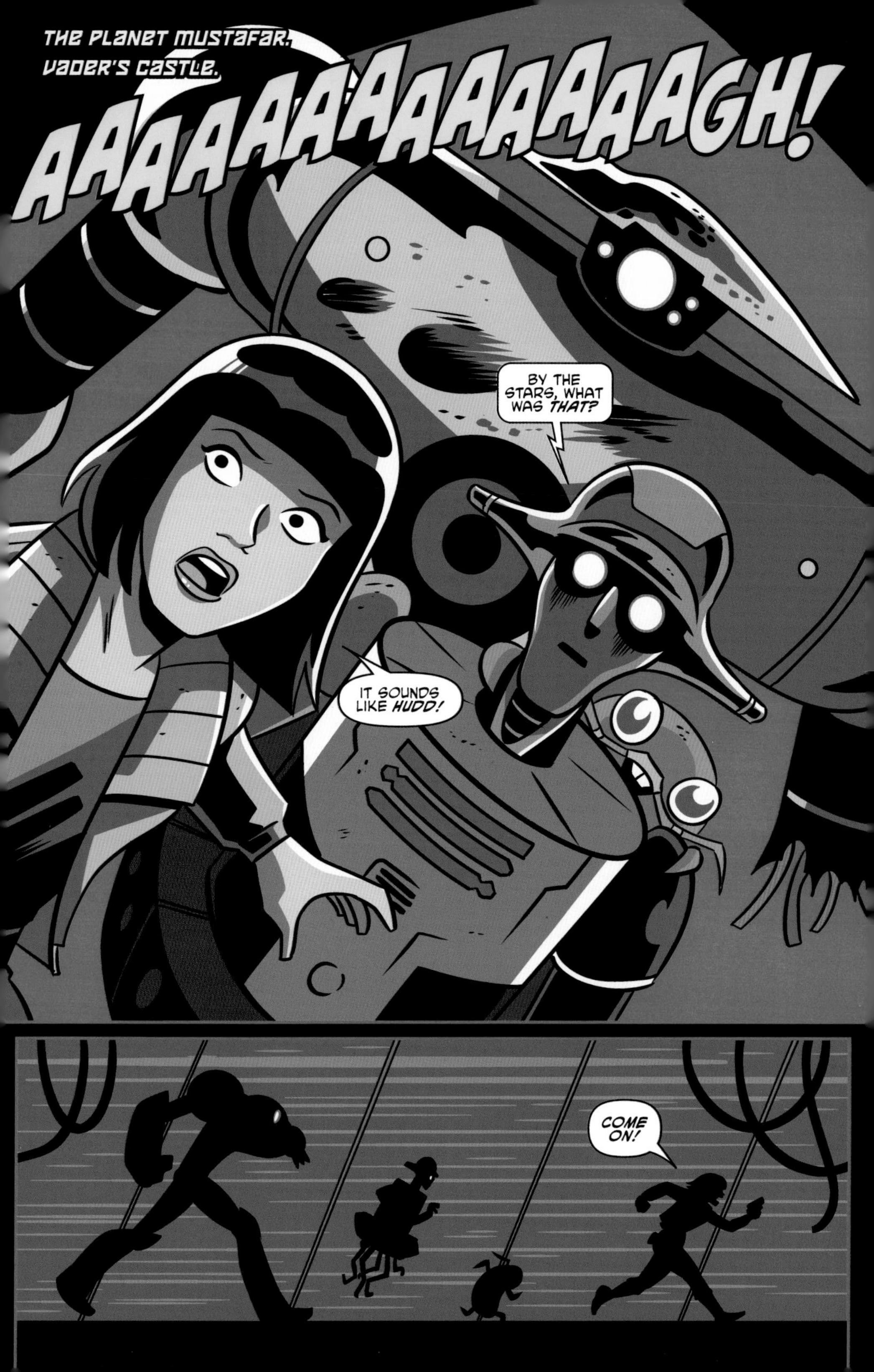
THE PLANET MUSTAFAR.
VADER'S CASTLE.
AAAAAAAAAAAAAAAAGH!
BY THE STARS, WHAT WAS *THAT?*
IT SOUNDS LIKE *HUDD!*
COME ON!

LIEUTENANT HUDD IS NOT HERE.

GREAT. NOW WE NEED TO FIND HIM *AS WELL* AS A NEW SHIP.

ODD. I'M SURE THESE SUITS OF ARMOR WEREN'T HERE A MINUTE AGO.

IT'LL BE QUICKER IF WE SPLIT UP.

SKRITT, YOU GO WITH GEE-THREE. CRATER CAN STAY WITH ME.

REPORT BACK THE MINUTE YOU FIND HUDD.

OH, D-DEAR. I'M JUST NOT SUITED FOR ALL THIS CREEPING ABOUT.

YOU NEED TO ENGAGE YOUR *BRAVERY CIRCUITS,* TECHNICIAN SKRITT.

IF ONLY I C-COULD. IT'S ALL RIGHT FOR YOU, GEE-THREE. YOU'RE SO BIG AND P-POWERFUL.

LOOK HOW YOU TOOK ON THOSE STORMTROOPERS.

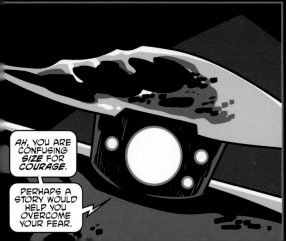

AH, YOU ARE CONFUSING *SIZE* FOR *COURAGE.*

PERHAPS A STORY WOULD HELP YOU OVERCOME YOUR FEAR.

ACTUALLY, NO... I DON'T THINK IT WOULD. NOT AFTER THE LAST ONE.

NONSENSE. A ROUSING TALE IS *JUST* WHAT THE MED-DROID ORDERED...

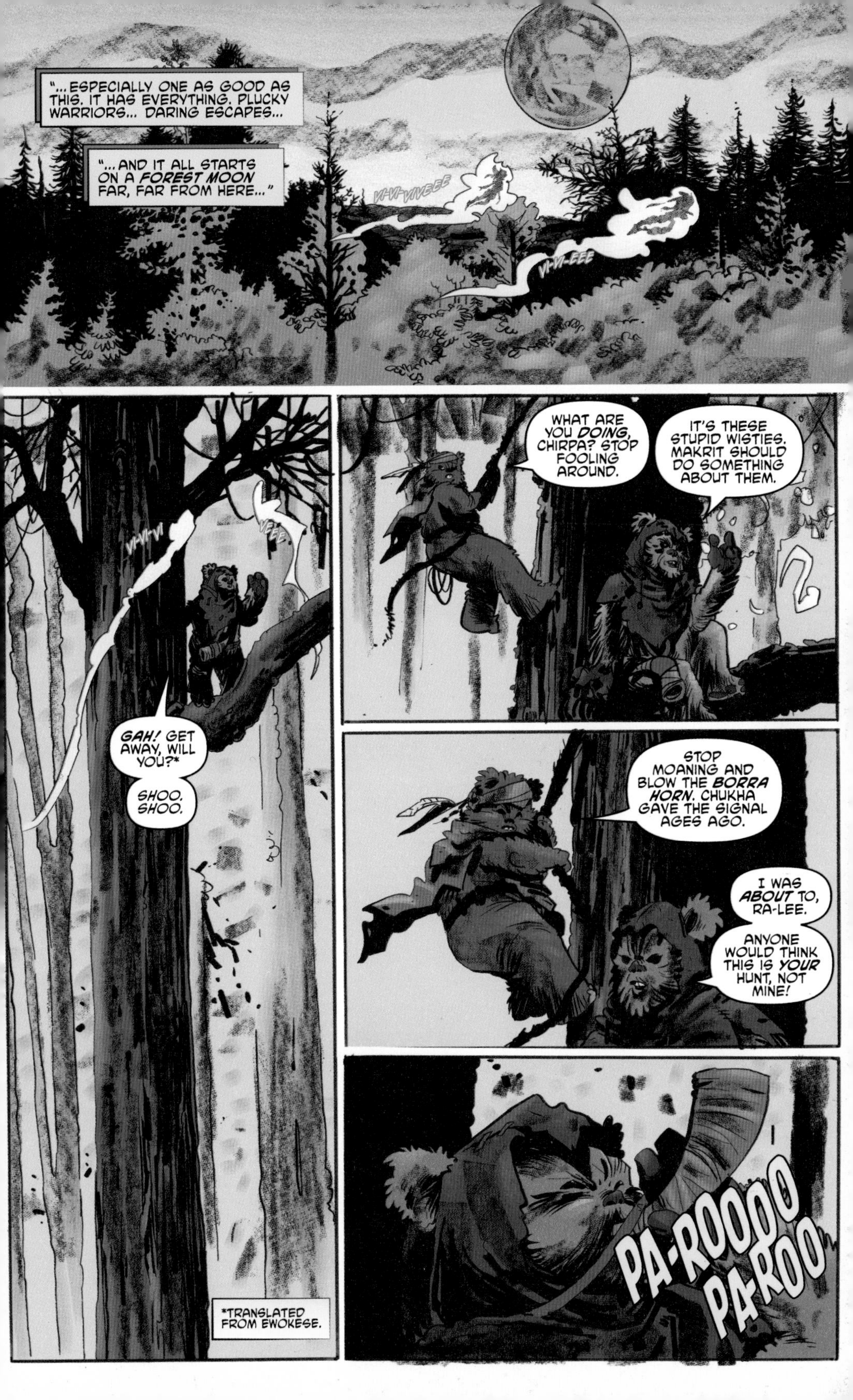
"...ESPECIALLY ONE AS GOOD AS THIS. IT HAS EVERYTHING. PLUCKY WARRIORS... DARING ESCAPES...
"...AND IT ALL STARTS ON A FOREST MOON FAR, FAR FROM HERE..."
VI-VI-VIVEEE
VI-VI-EEE
VI-VI-VI
VEEE
GAH! GET AWAY, WILL YOU?*
SHOO. SHOO.
*TRANSLATED FROM EWOKESE.
WHAT ARE YOU DOING, CHIRPA? STOP FOOLING AROUND.
IT'S THESE STUPID WISTIES. MAKRIT SHOULD DO SOMETHING ABOUT THEM.
STOP MOANING AND BLOW THE BORRA HORN. CHUKHA GAVE THE SIGNAL AGES AGO.
I WAS ABOUT TO, RA-LEE.
ANYONE WOULD THINK THIS IS YOUR HUNT, NOT MINE!
PA-ROOOO PA-ROO

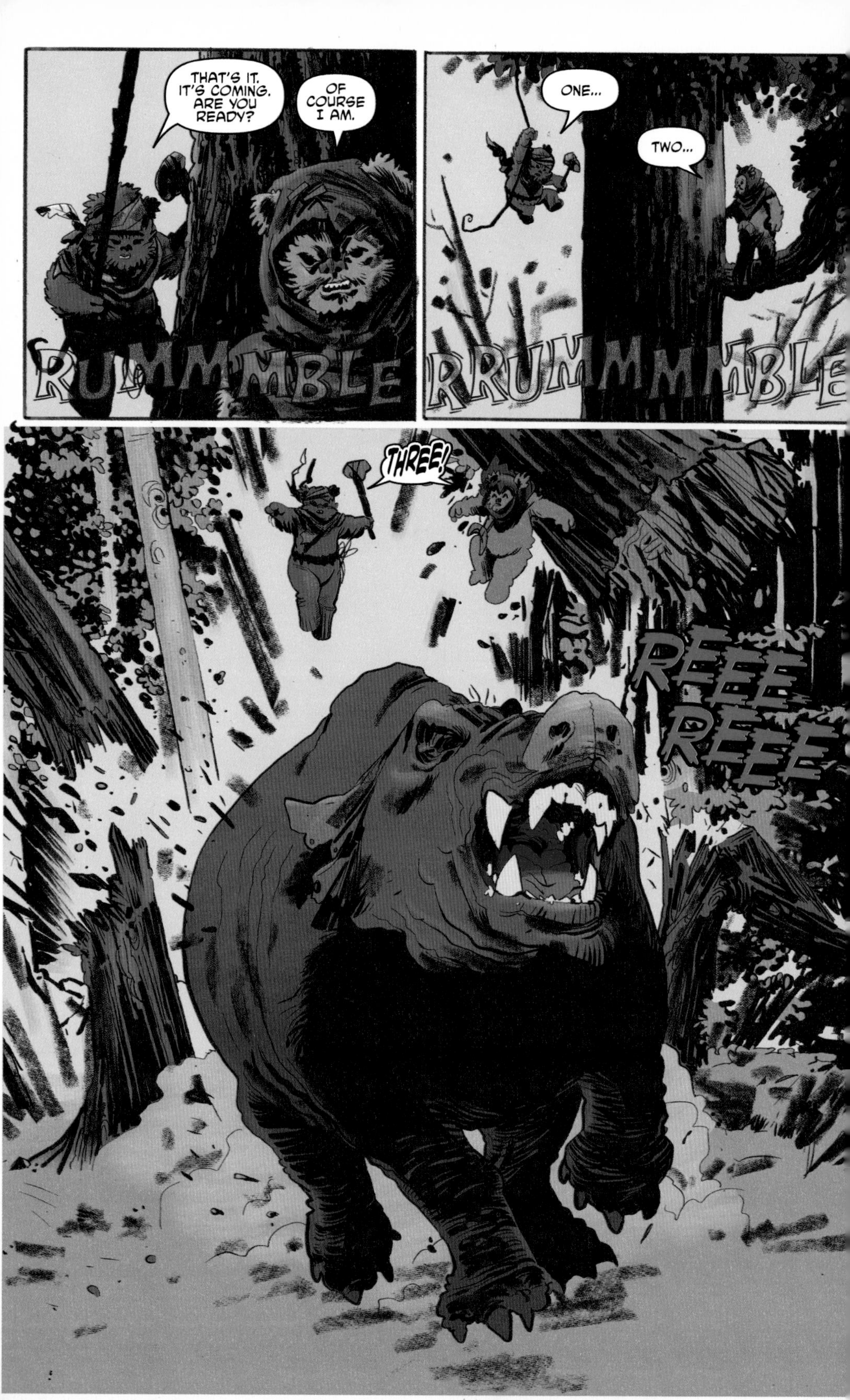
THAT'S IT. IT'S COMING. ARE YOU READY?
OF COURSE I AM.
RUMMMBLE
ONE...
TWO...
RRUMMMMMBLE
THREE!
REEE REEE

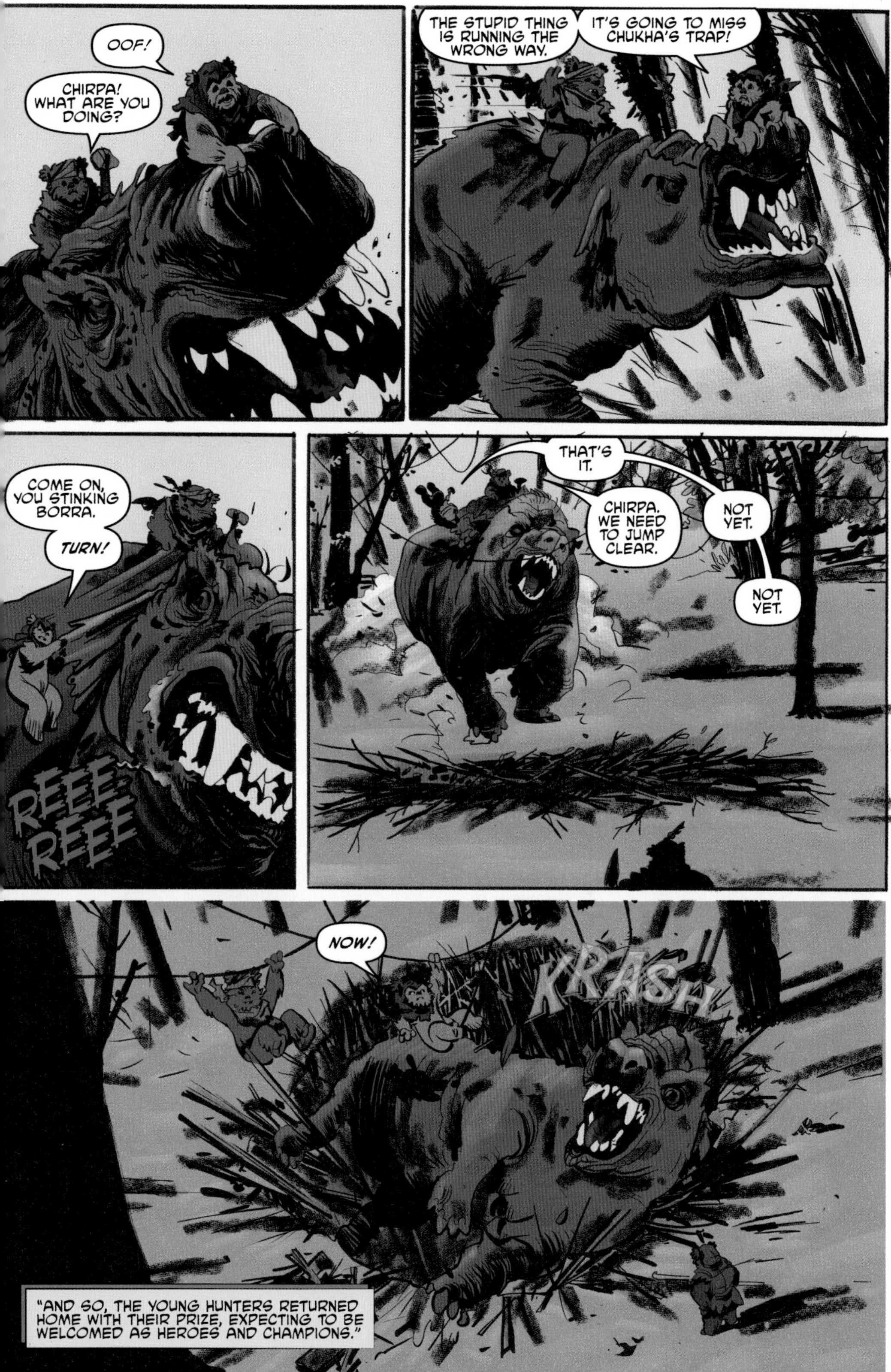

OOF!
CHIRPA! WHAT ARE YOU DOING?
THE STUPID THING IS RUNNING THE WRONG WAY.
IT'S GOING TO MISS CHUKHA'S TRAP!
COME ON, YOU STINKING BORRA.
TURN!
REEEE REEEE
THAT'S IT.
CHIRPA. WE NEED TO JUMP CLEAR.
NOT YET.
NOT YET.
NOW!
KRASH
"AND SO, THE YOUNG HUNTERS RETURNED HOME WITH THEIR PRIZE, EXPECTING TO BE WELCOMED AS HEROES AND CHAMPIONS."

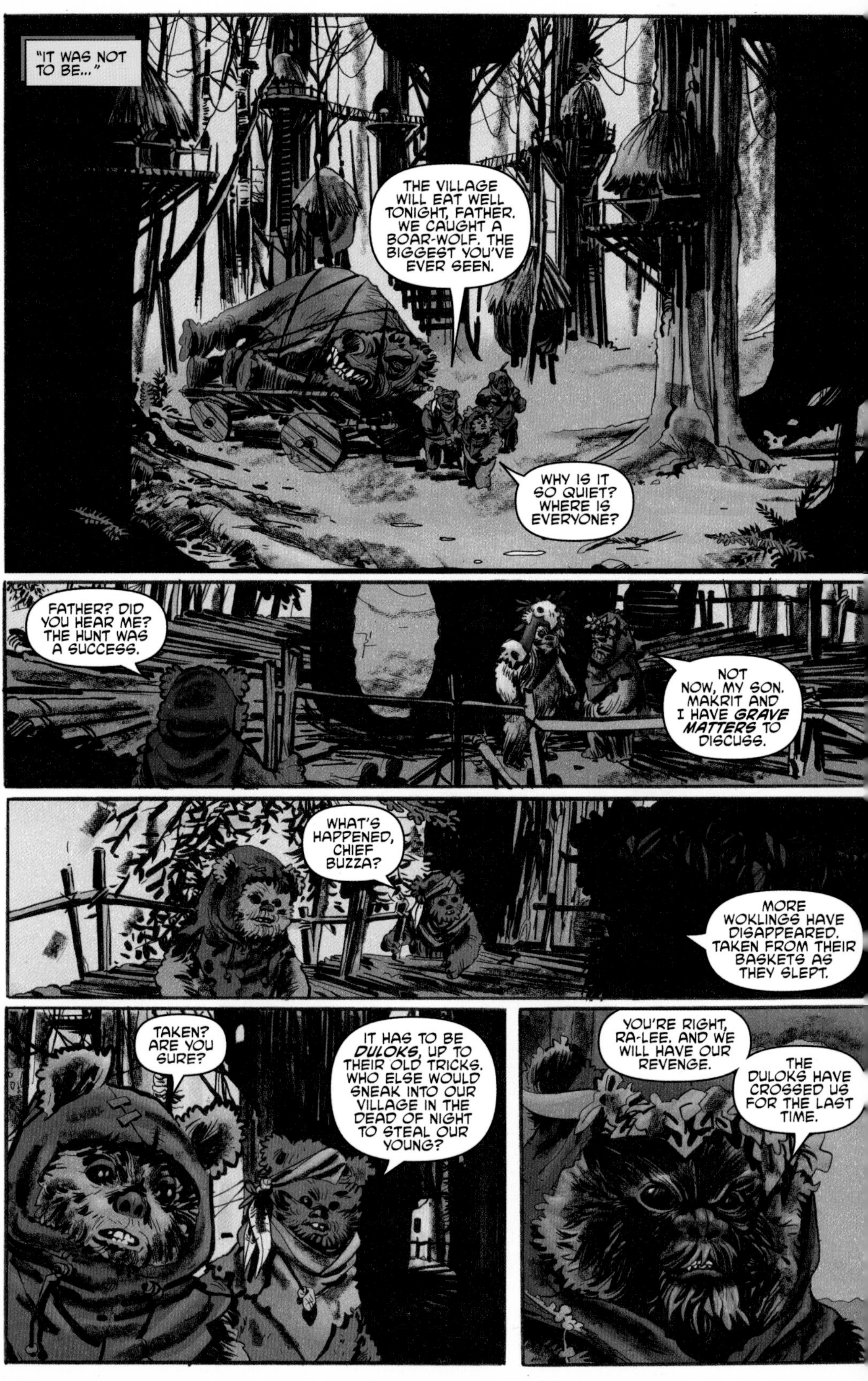
"IT WAS NOT TO BE..."
THE VILLAGE WILL EAT WELL TONIGHT, FATHER. WE CAUGHT A BOAR-WOLF. THE BIGGEST YOU'VE EVER SEEN.
WHY IS IT SO QUIET? WHERE IS EVERYONE?
FATHER? DID YOU HEAR ME? THE HUNT WAS A SUCCESS.
NOT NOW, MY SON. MAKRIT AND I HAVE GRAVE MATTERS TO DISCUSS.
WHAT'S HAPPENED, CHIEF BUZZA?
MORE WOKLINGS HAVE DISAPPEARED. TAKEN FROM THEIR BASKETS AS THEY SLEPT.
TAKEN? ARE YOU SURE?
IT HAS TO BE DULOKS, UP TO THEIR OLD TRICKS. WHO ELSE WOULD SNEAK INTO OUR VILLAGE IN THE DEAD OF NIGHT TO STEAL OUR YOUNG?
YOU'RE RIGHT, RA-LEE. AND WE WILL HAVE OUR REVENGE.
THE DULOKS HAVE CROSSED US FOR THE LAST TIME.

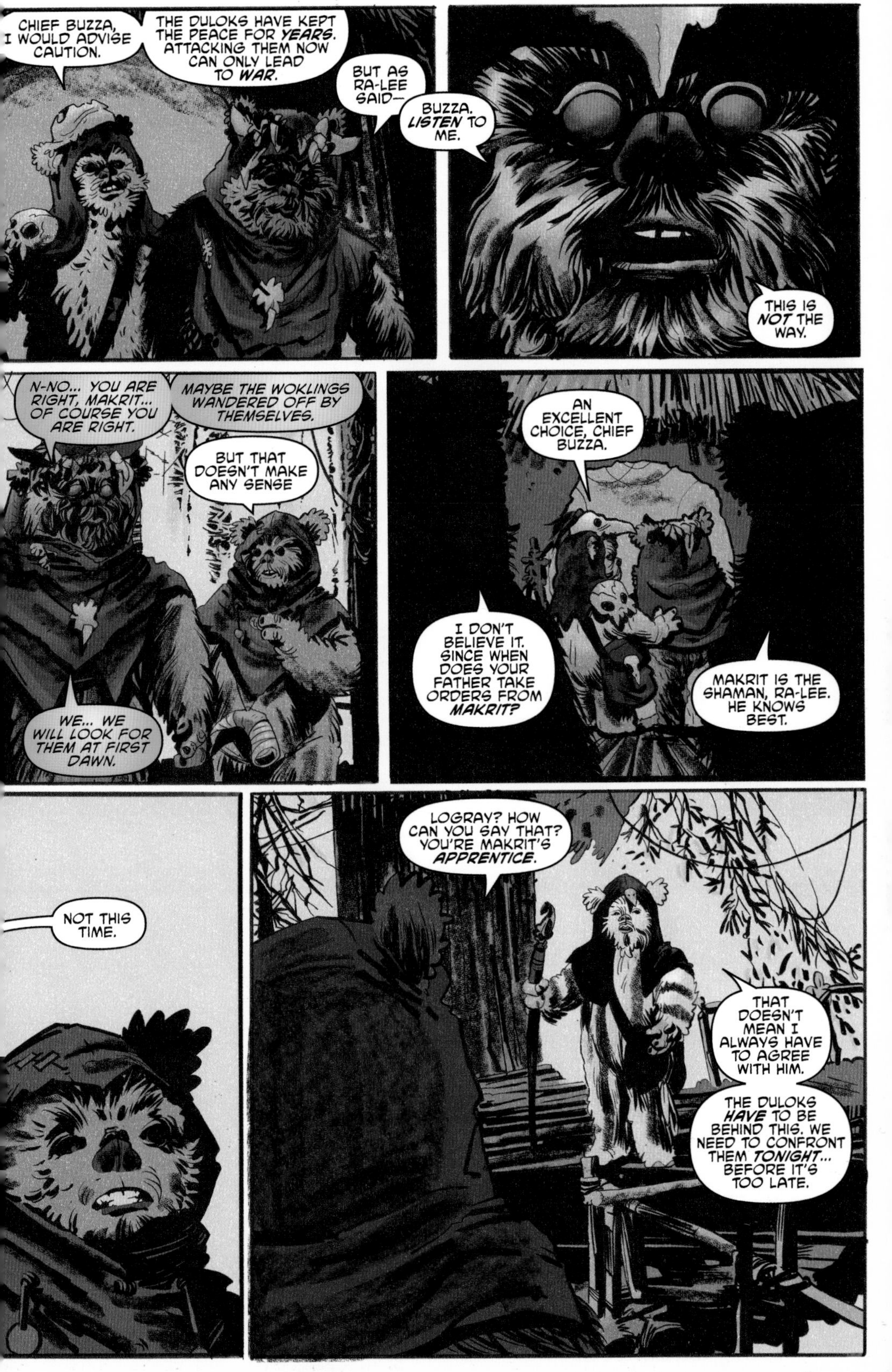
CHIEF BUZZA, I WOULD ADVISE CAUTION.
THE DULOKS HAVE KEPT THE PEACE FOR YEARS. ATTACKING THEM NOW CAN ONLY LEAD TO WAR.
BUT AS RA-LEE SAID—
BUZZA. LISTEN TO ME.
THIS IS NOT THE WAY.
N-NO... YOU ARE RIGHT, MAKRIT... OF COURSE YOU ARE RIGHT.
MAYBE THE WOKLINGS WANDERED OFF BY THEMSELVES.
BUT THAT DOESN'T MAKE ANY SENSE
WE... WE WILL LOOK FOR THEM AT FIRST DAWN.
AN EXCELLENT CHOICE, CHIEF BUZZA.
I DON'T BELIEVE IT. SINCE WHEN DOES YOUR FATHER TAKE ORDERS FROM MAKRIT?
MAKRIT IS THE SHAMAN, RA-LEE. HE KNOWS BEST.
NOT THIS TIME.
LOGRAY? HOW CAN YOU SAY THAT? YOU'RE MAKRIT'S APPRENTICE.
THAT DOESN'T MEAN I ALWAYS HAVE TO AGREE WITH HIM.
THE DULOKS HAVE TO BE BEHIND THIS. WE NEED TO CONFRONT THEM TONIGHT... BEFORE IT'S TOO LATE.

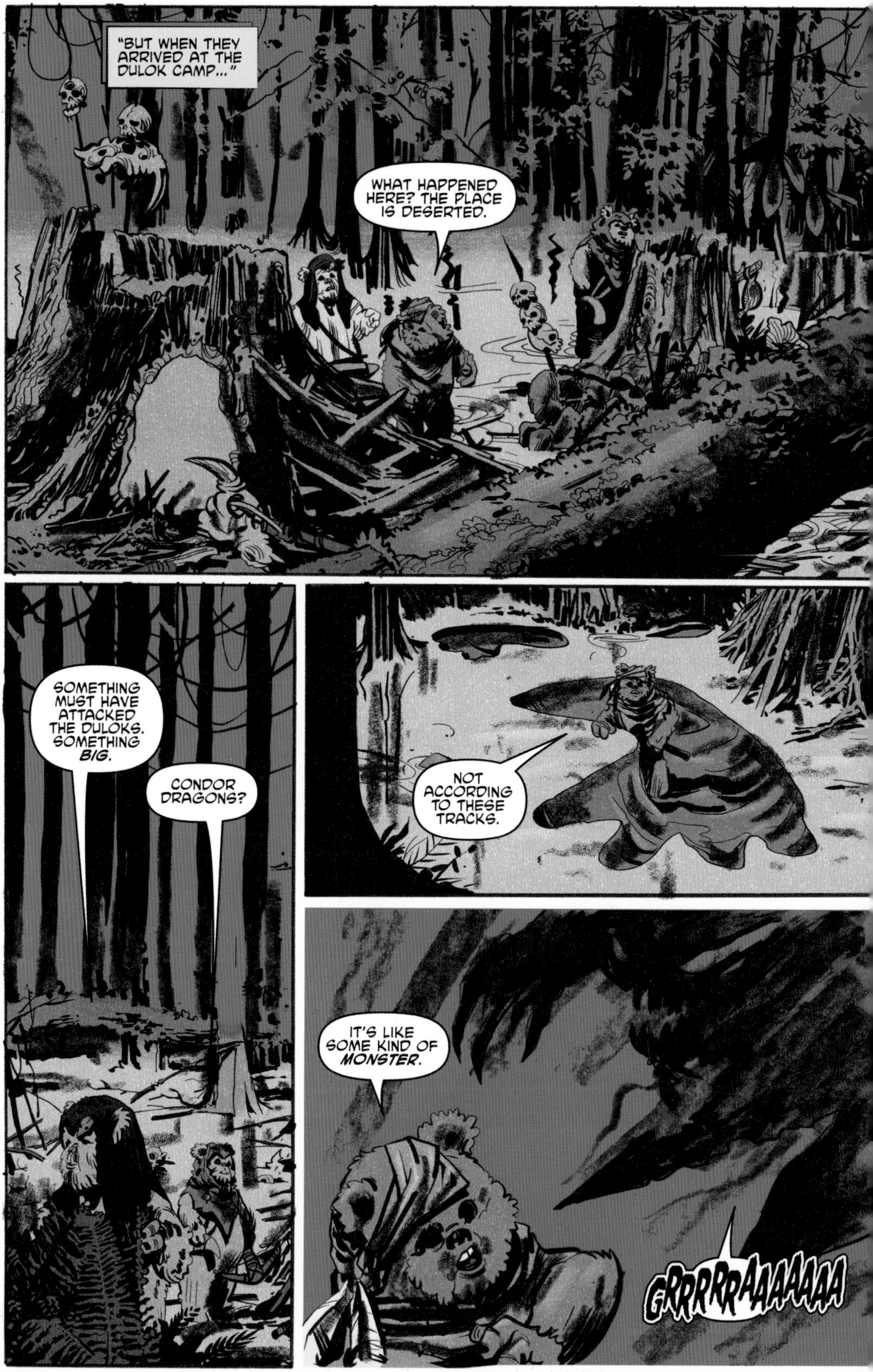
"BUT WHEN THEY ARRIVED AT THE DULOK CAMP..."
WHAT HAPPENED HERE? THE PLACE IS DESERTED.
SOMETHING MUST HAVE ATTACKED THE DULOKS. SOMETHING *BIG*.
CONDOR DRAGONS?
NOT ACCORDING TO THESE TRACKS.
IT'S LIKE SOME KIND OF *MONSTER*.
GRRRRRAAAAAAA

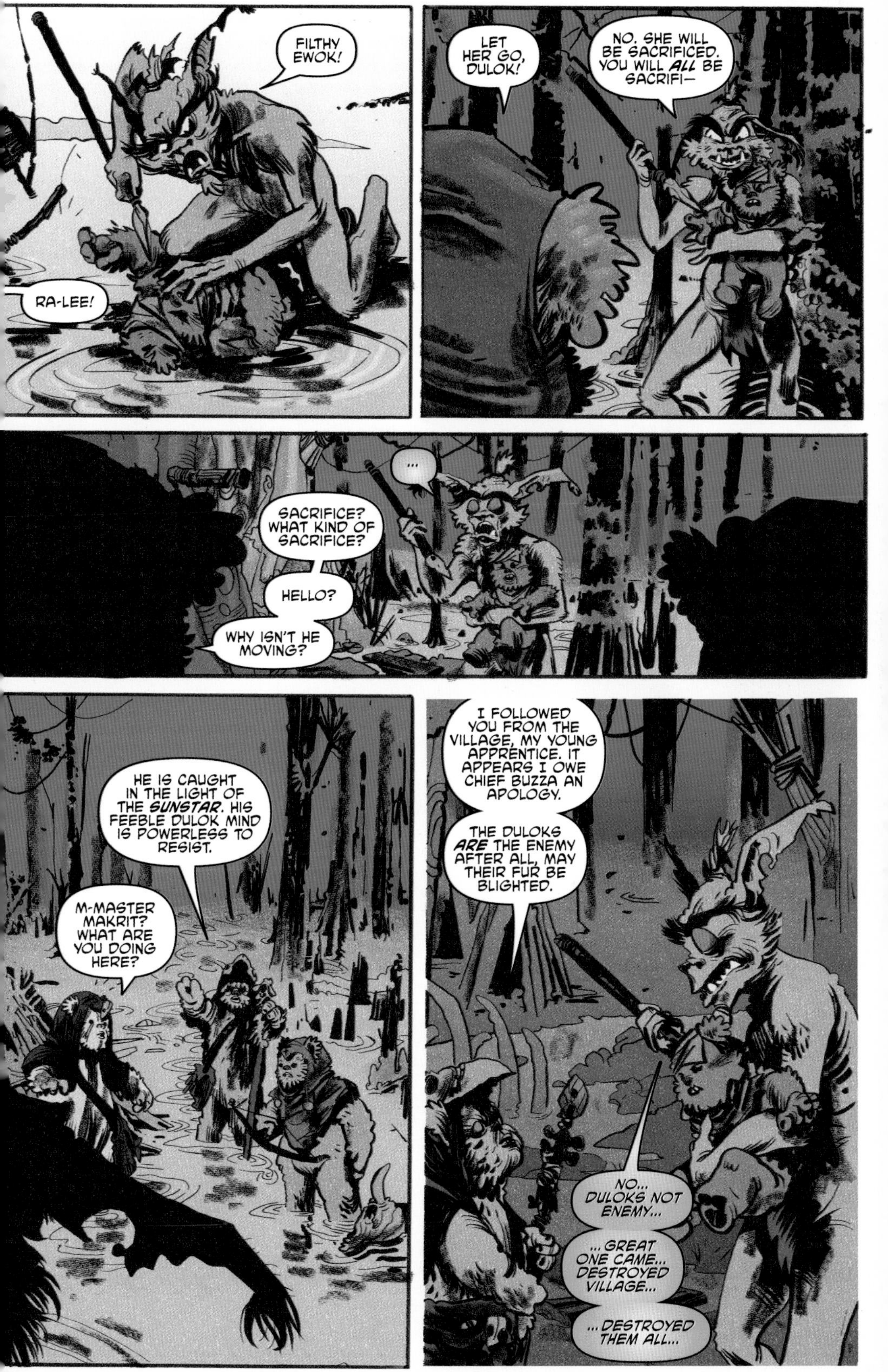
FILTHY EWOK!
RA-LEE!
LET HER GO, DULOK!
NO. SHE WILL BE SACRIFICED. YOU WILL *ALL* BE SACRIFI—
...
SACRIFICE? WHAT KIND OF SACRIFICE?
HELLO?
WHY ISN'T HE MOVING?
HE IS CAUGHT IN THE LIGHT OF THE *SUNSTAR*. HIS FEEBLE DULOK MIND IS POWERLESS TO RESIST.
M-MASTER MAKRIT? WHAT ARE YOU DOING HERE?
I FOLLOWED YOU FROM THE VILLAGE, MY YOUNG APPRENTICE. IT APPEARS I OWE CHIEF BUZZA AN APOLOGY.
THE DULOKS *ARE* THE ENEMY AFTER ALL, MAY THEIR FUR BE BLIGHTED.
NO... DULOKS NOT ENEMY...
... GREAT ONE CAME... DESTROYED VILLAGE...
... DESTROYED THEM ALL...

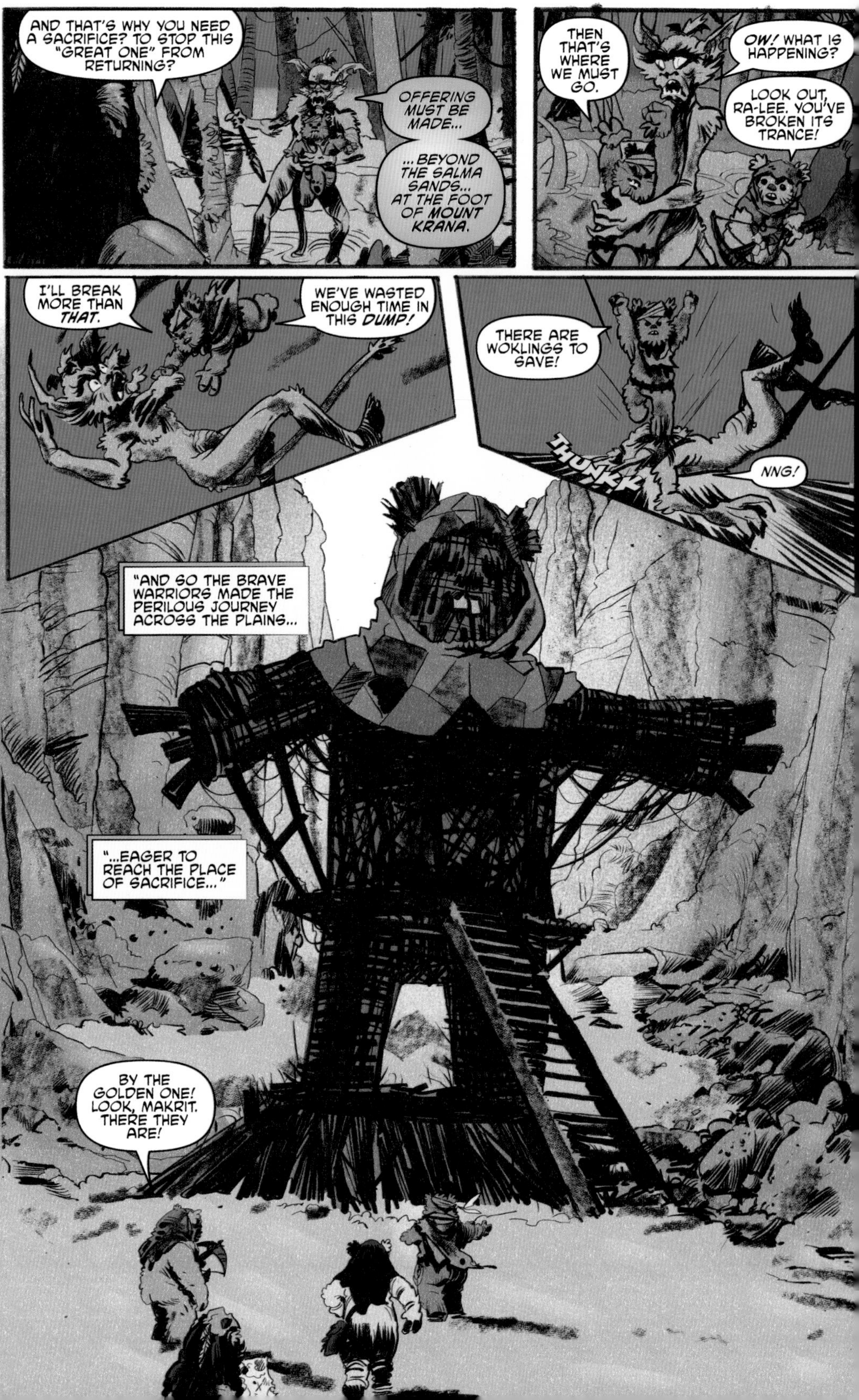
AND THAT'S WHY YOU NEED A SACRIFICE? TO STOP THIS "GREAT ONE" FROM RETURNING?
OFFERING MUST BE MADE...
...BEYOND THE SALMA SANDS... AT THE FOOT OF MOUNT KRANA.
THEN THAT'S WHERE WE MUST GO.
OW! WHAT IS HAPPENING?
LOOK OUT, RA-LEE. YOU'VE BROKEN ITS TRANCE!
I'LL BREAK MORE THAN THAT.
WE'VE WASTED ENOUGH TIME IN THIS DUMP!
THERE ARE WOKLINGS TO SAVE!
THUNK
NNG!
"AND SO THE BRAVE WARRIORS MADE THE PERILOUS JOURNEY ACROSS THE PLAINS...
"...EAGER TO REACH THE PLACE OF SACRIFICE..."
BY THE GOLDEN ONE! LOOK, MAKRIT. THERE THEY ARE!

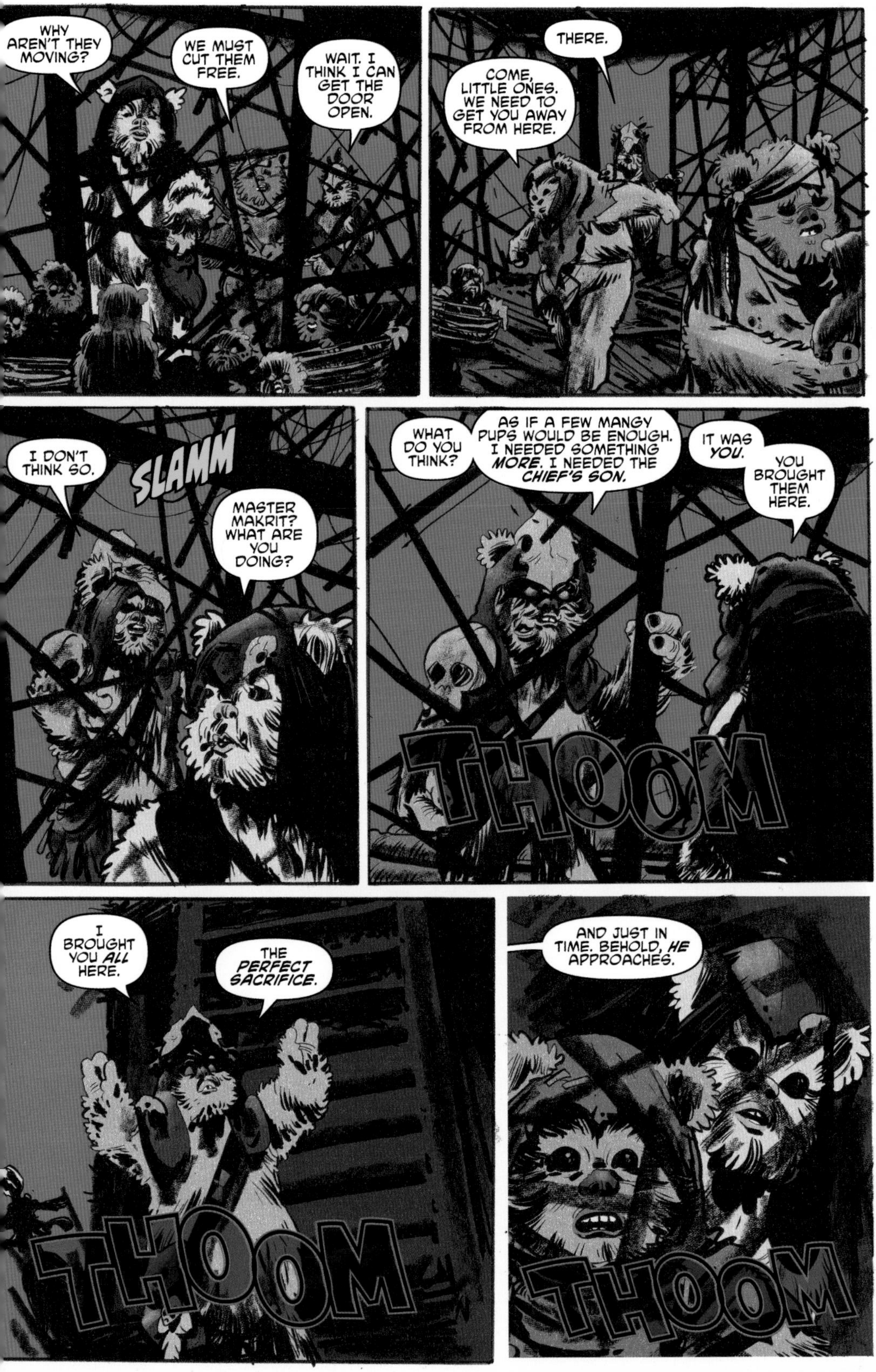
WHY AREN'T THEY MOVING?
WE MUST CUT THEM FREE.
WAIT. I THINK I CAN GET THE DOOR OPEN.
THERE.
COME, LITTLE ONES. WE NEED TO GET YOU AWAY FROM HERE.
I DON'T THINK SO.
SLAMM
MASTER MAKRIT? WHAT ARE YOU DOING?
WHAT DO YOU THINK?
AS IF A FEW MANGY PUPS WOULD BE ENOUGH. I NEEDED SOMETHING *MORE*. I NEEDED THE *CHIEF'S SON.*
IT WAS *YOU.*
YOU BROUGHT THEM HERE.
THOOM
I BROUGHT YOU *ALL* HERE.
THE *PERFECT SACRIFICE.*
THOOM
AND JUST IN TIME. BEHOLD, *HE* APPROACHES.
THOOM

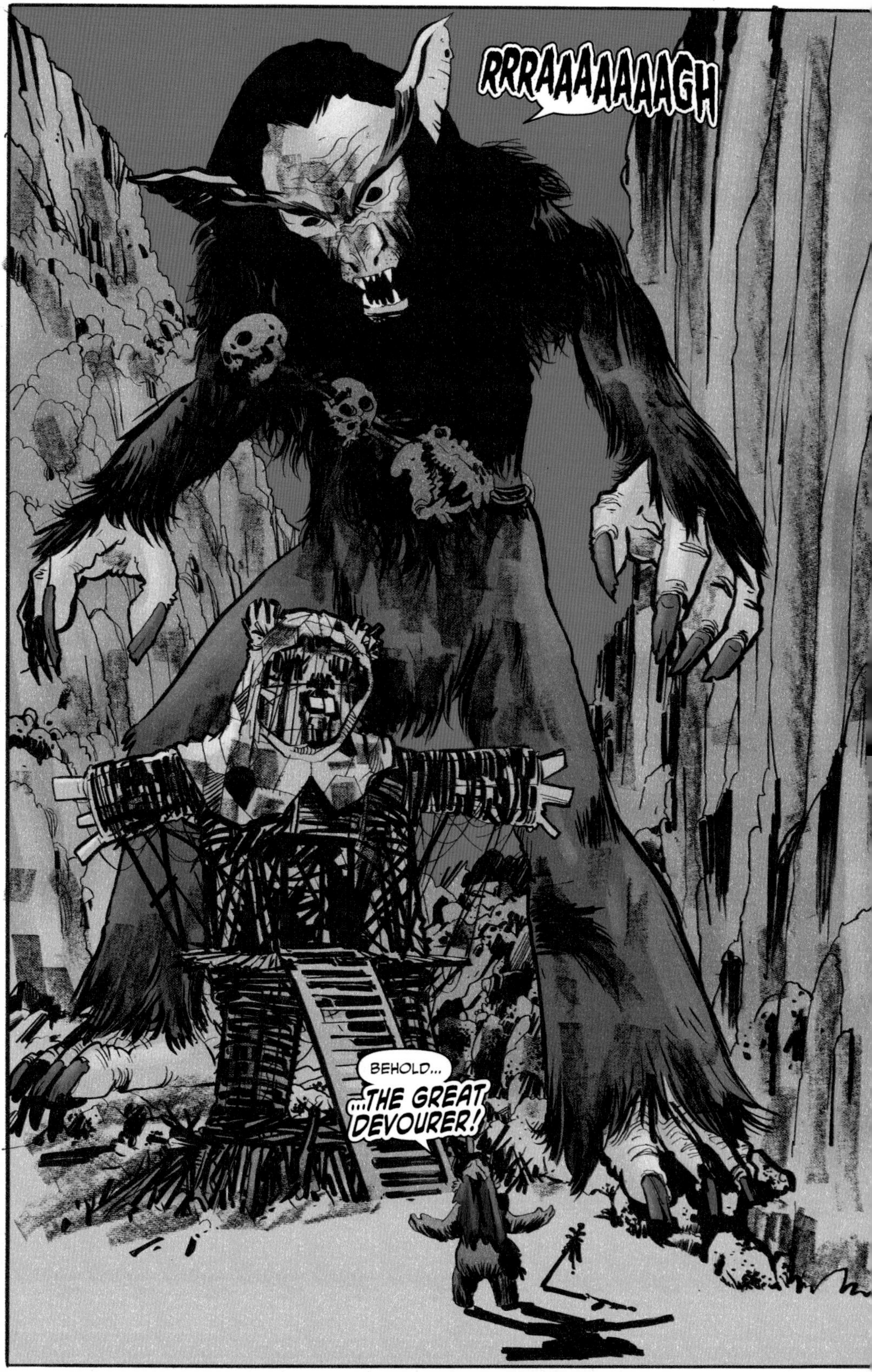
RRRAAAAAAAGH
BEHOLD...
...THE GREAT DEVOURER!

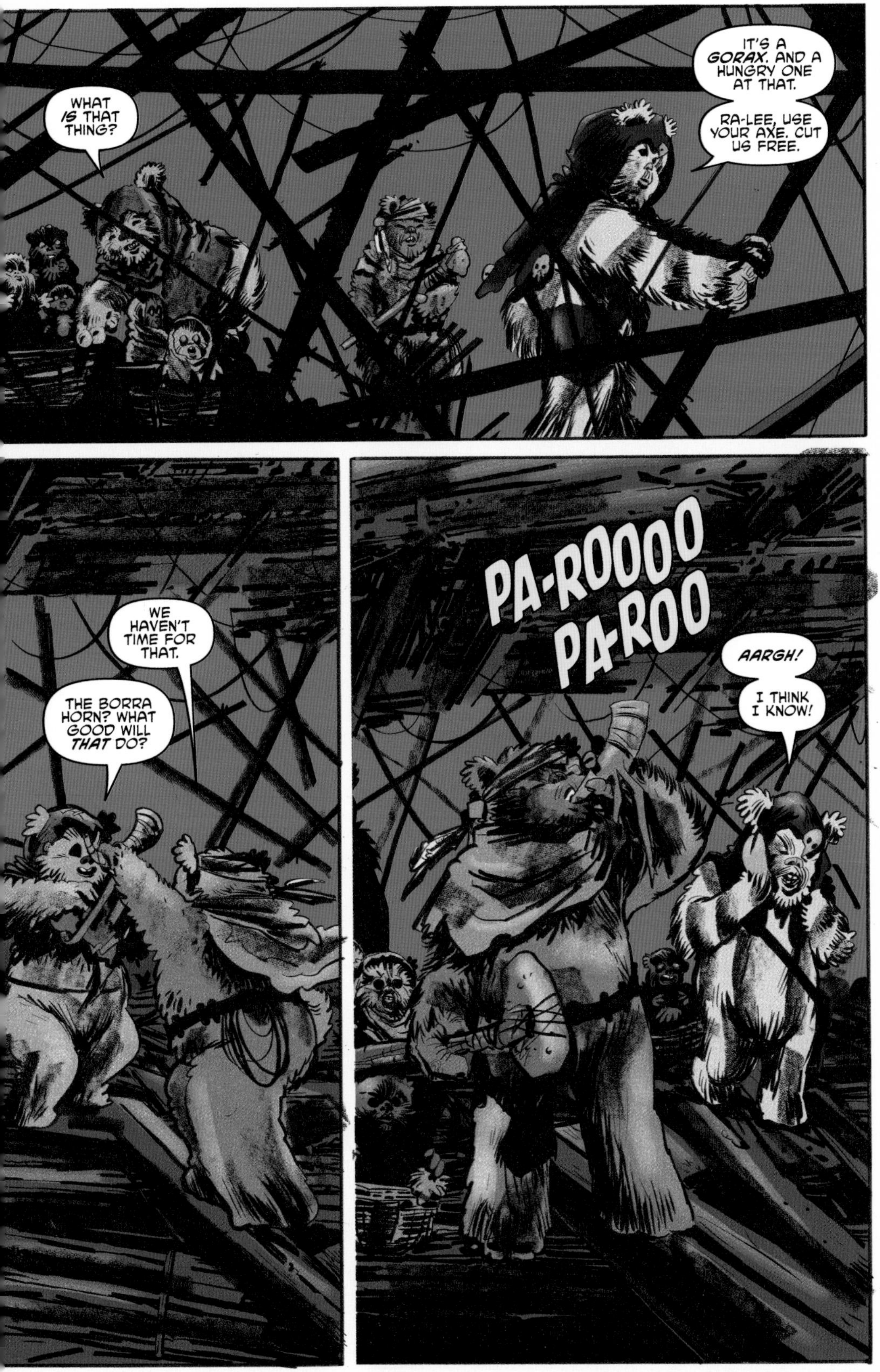
WHAT *IS* THAT THING?
IT'S A *GORAX*. AND A HUNGRY ONE AT THAT.
RA-LEE, USE YOUR AXE. CUT US FREE.
THE BORRA HORN? WHAT GOOD WILL *THAT* DO?
WE HAVEN'T TIME FOR THAT.
PA-ROOOO PA-ROO
AARGH!
I THINK I KNOW!

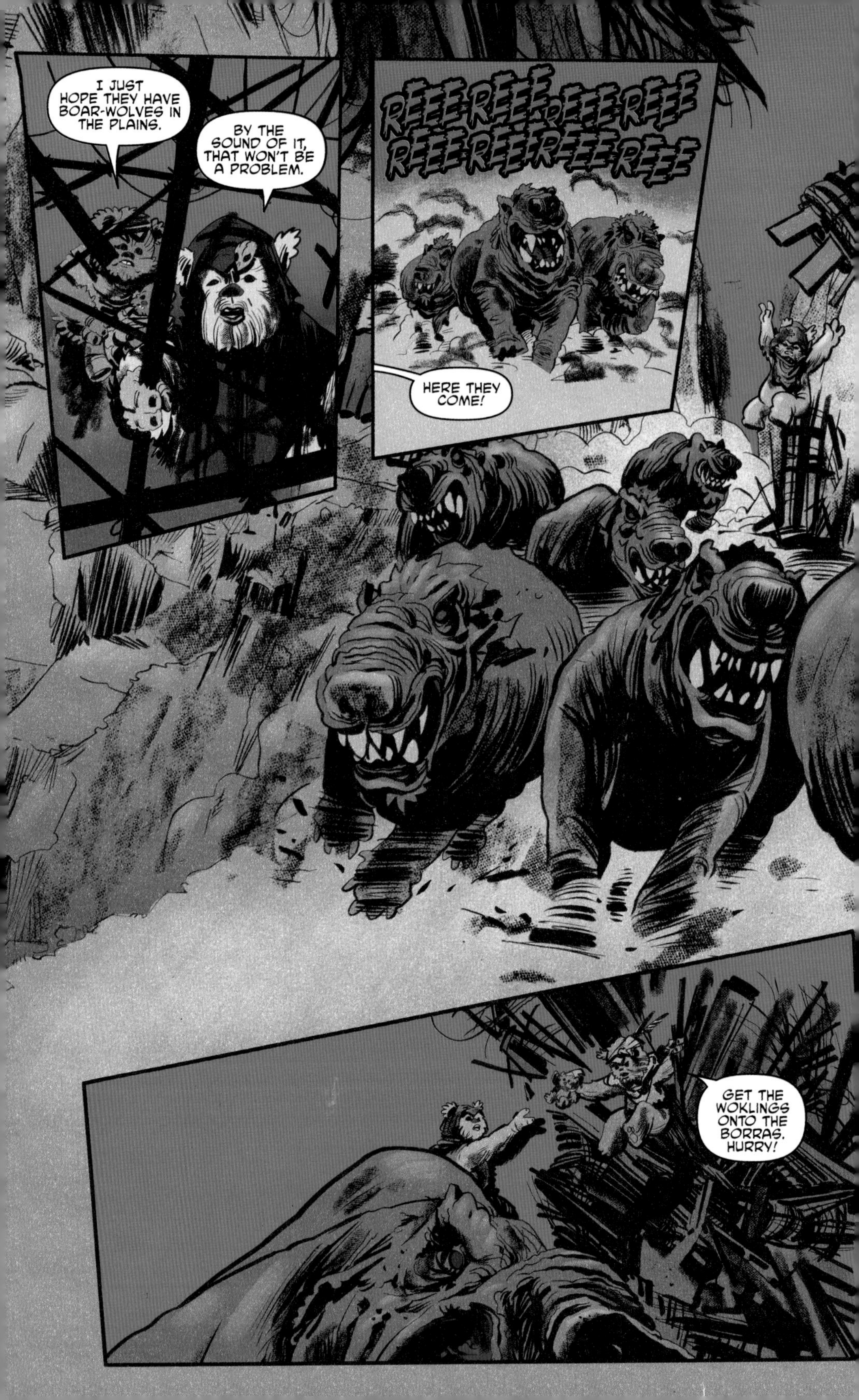
I JUST HOPE THEY HAVE BOAR-WOLVES IN THE PLAINS.
BY THE SOUND OF IT, THAT WON'T BE A PROBLEM.
REEE REEE REEE REEE
REEE REEE R-EEE REEE
HERE THEY COME!
GET THE WOKLINGS ONTO THE BORRAS. HURRY!

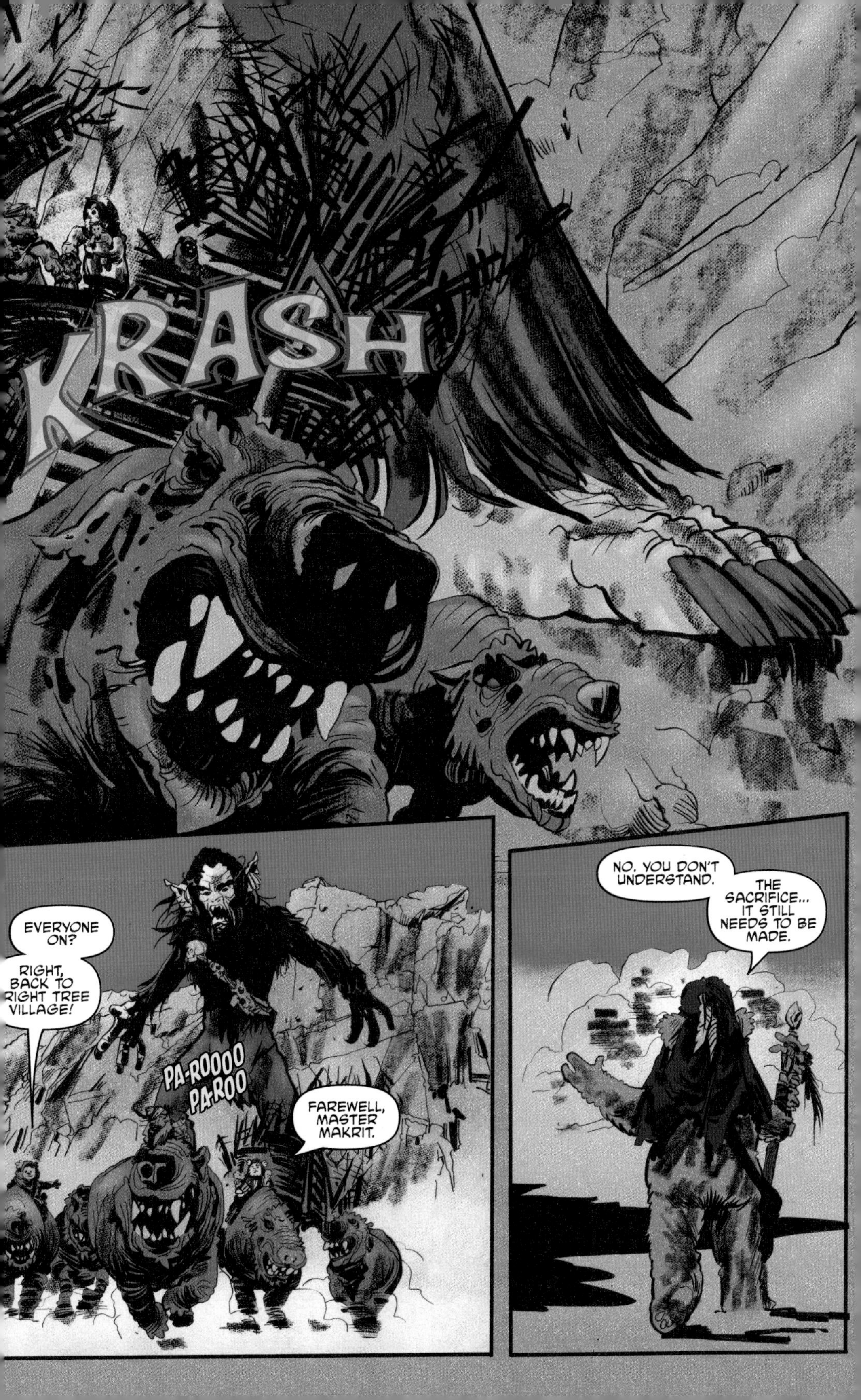
KRASH
EVERYONE ON?
RIGHT, BACK TO RIGHT TREE VILLAGE!
PA-ROOOO PA-ROO
FAREWELL, MASTER MAKRIT.
NO. YOU DON'T UNDERSTAND.
THE SACRIFICE... IT STILL NEEDS TO BE MADE.

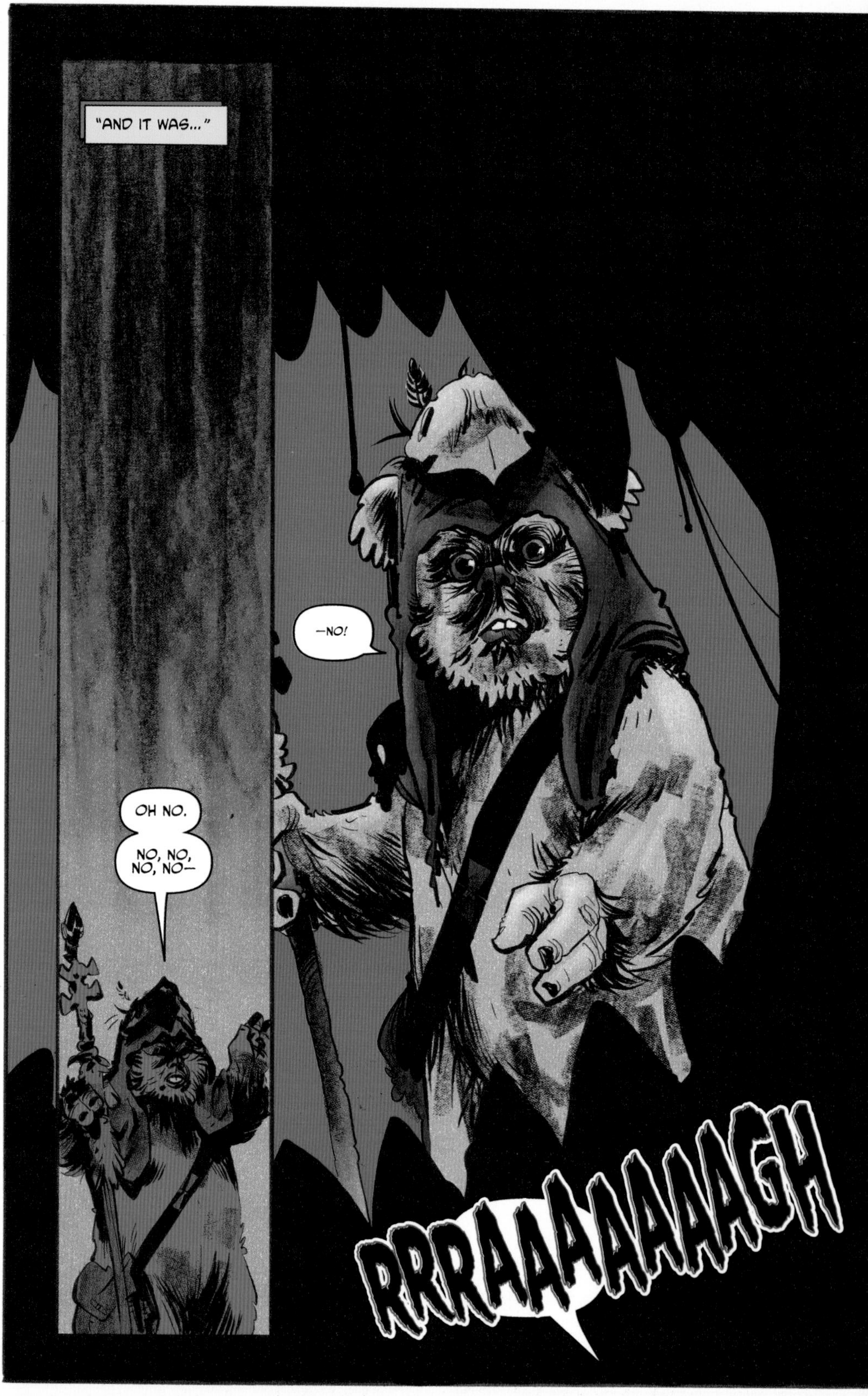
"AND IT WAS..."
OH NO.
NO, NO, NO, NO—
—NO!
RRRAAAAAAAGH

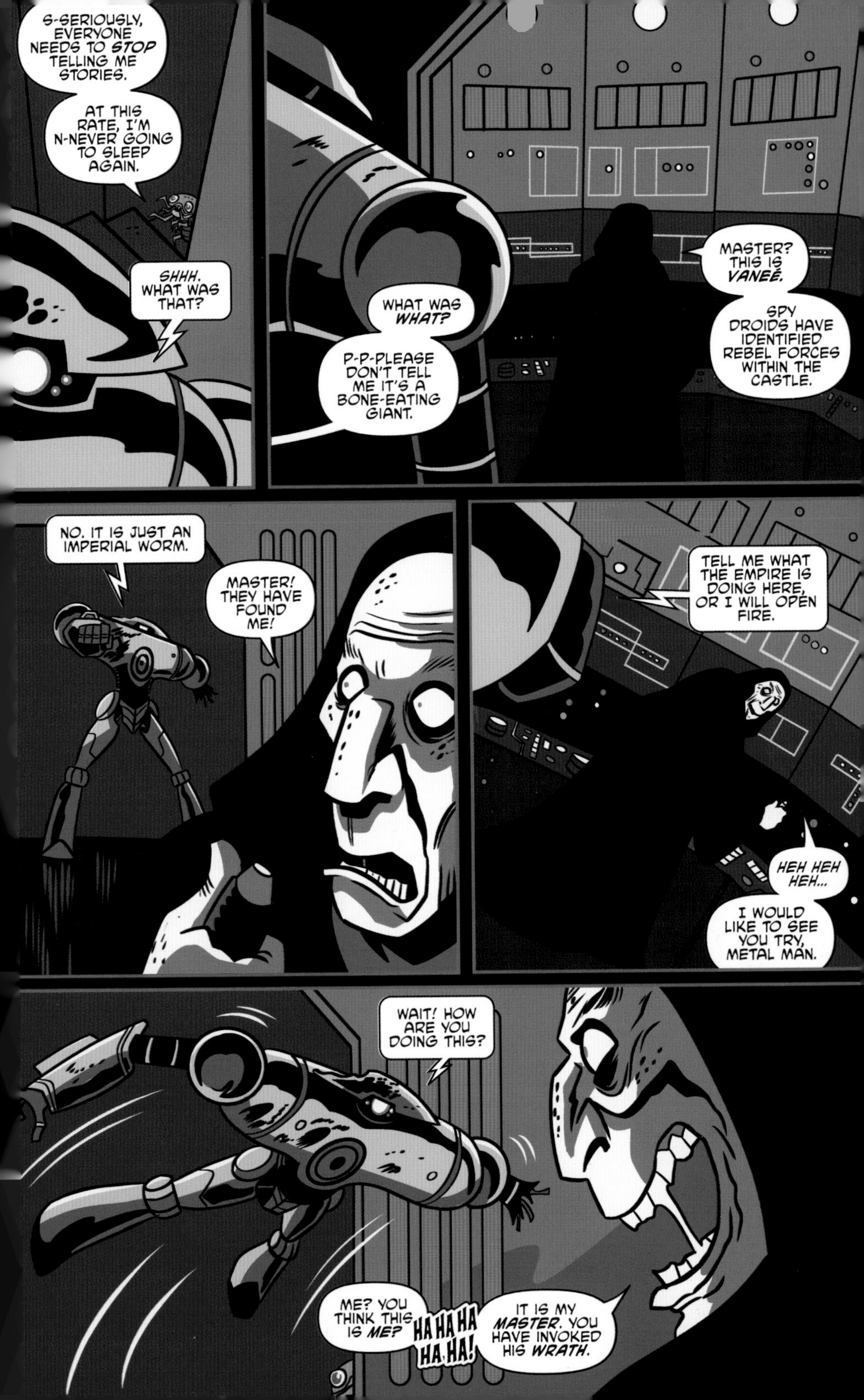
S-SERIOUSLY, EVERYONE NEEDS TO *STOP* TELLING ME STORIES.
AT THIS RATE, I'M N-NEVER GOING TO SLEEP AGAIN.
SHHH. WHAT WAS THAT?
WHAT WAS *WHAT?*
P-P-PLEASE DON'T TELL ME IT'S A BONE-EATING GIANT.
MASTER? THIS IS *VANEÉ.*
SPY DROIDS HAVE IDENTIFIED REBEL FORCES WITHIN THE CASTLE.
NO. IT IS JUST AN IMPERIAL WORM.
MASTER! THEY HAVE FOUND ME!
TELL ME WHAT THE EMPIRE IS DOING HERE, OR I WILL OPEN FIRE.
HEH HEH HEH...
I WOULD LIKE TO SEE YOU TRY, METAL MAN.
WAIT! HOW ARE YOU DOING THIS?
ME? YOU THINK THIS IS *ME?*
HA HA HA HA HA!
IT IS MY *MASTER*. YOU HAVE INVOKED HIS *WRATH*.

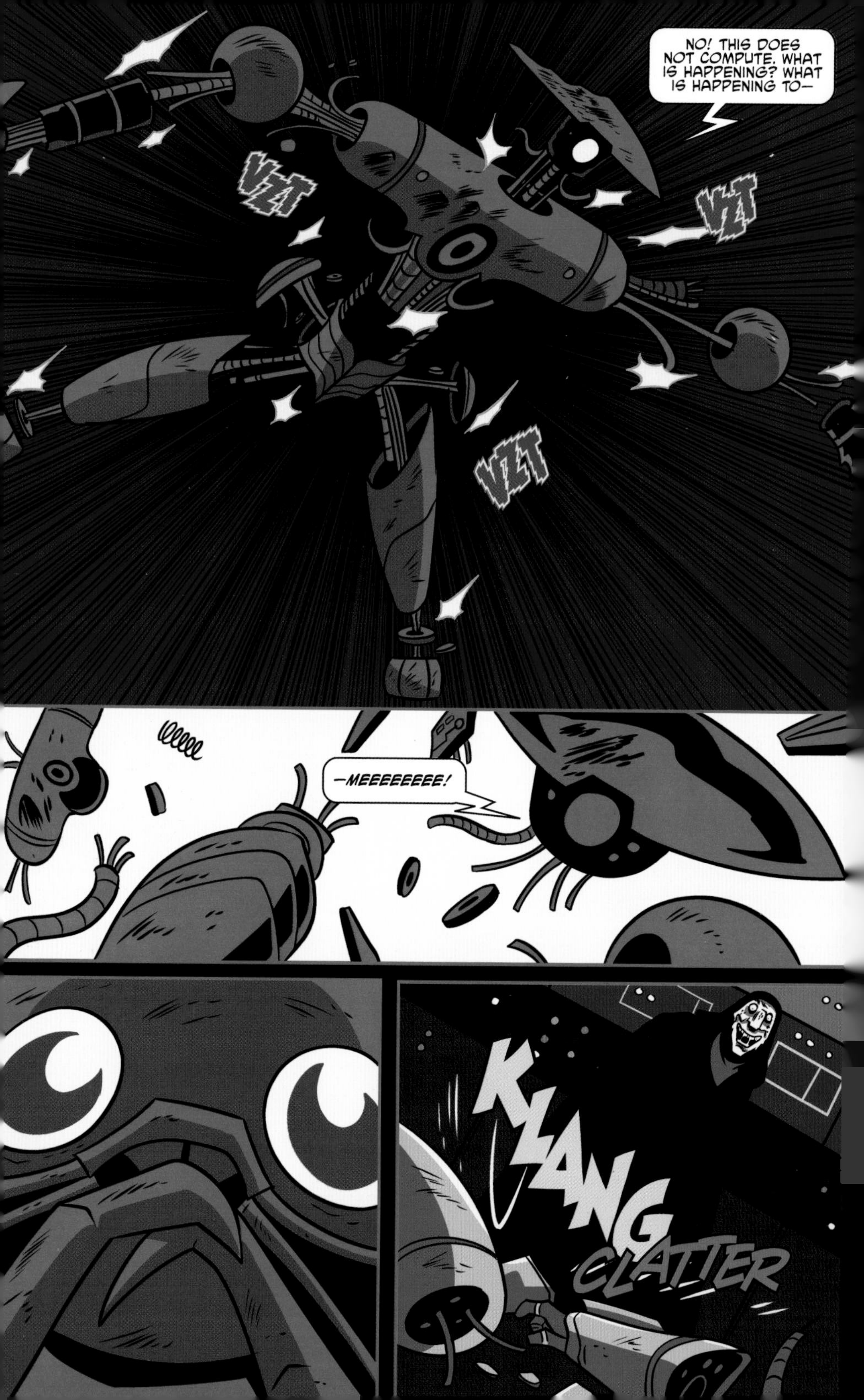
NO! THIS DOES NOT COMPUTE. WHAT IS HAPPENING? WHAT IS HAPPENING TO—
VZT
VZT
VZT
—MEEEEEEEE!
KLANG
CLATTER

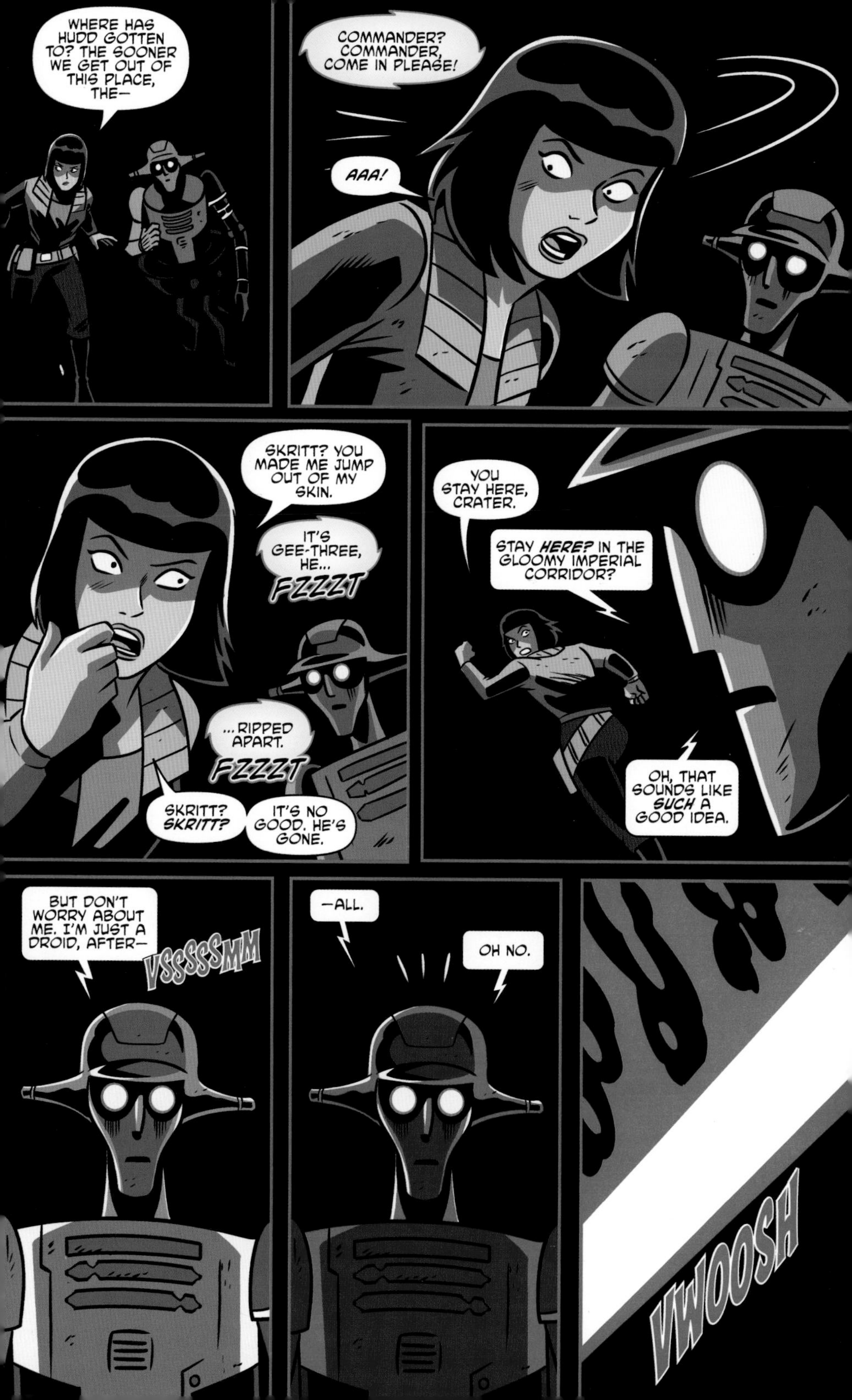
WHERE HAS HUDD GOTTEN TO? THE SOONER WE GET OUT OF THIS PLACE, THE—
COMMANDER? COMMANDER, COME IN PLEASE!
AAA!
SKRITT? YOU MADE ME JUMP OUT OF MY SKIN.
IT'S GEE-THREE, HE...
FZZZT
...RIPPED APART.
FZZZT
SKRITT? SKRITT?
IT'S NO GOOD. HE'S GONE.
YOU STAY HERE, CRATER.
STAY HERE? IN THE GLOOMY IMPERIAL CORRIDOR?
OH, THAT SOUNDS LIKE SUCH A GOOD IDEA.
BUT DON'T WORRY ABOUT ME. I'M JUST A DROID, AFTER—
VSSSSSMM
—ALL.
OH NO.
VWOOSH

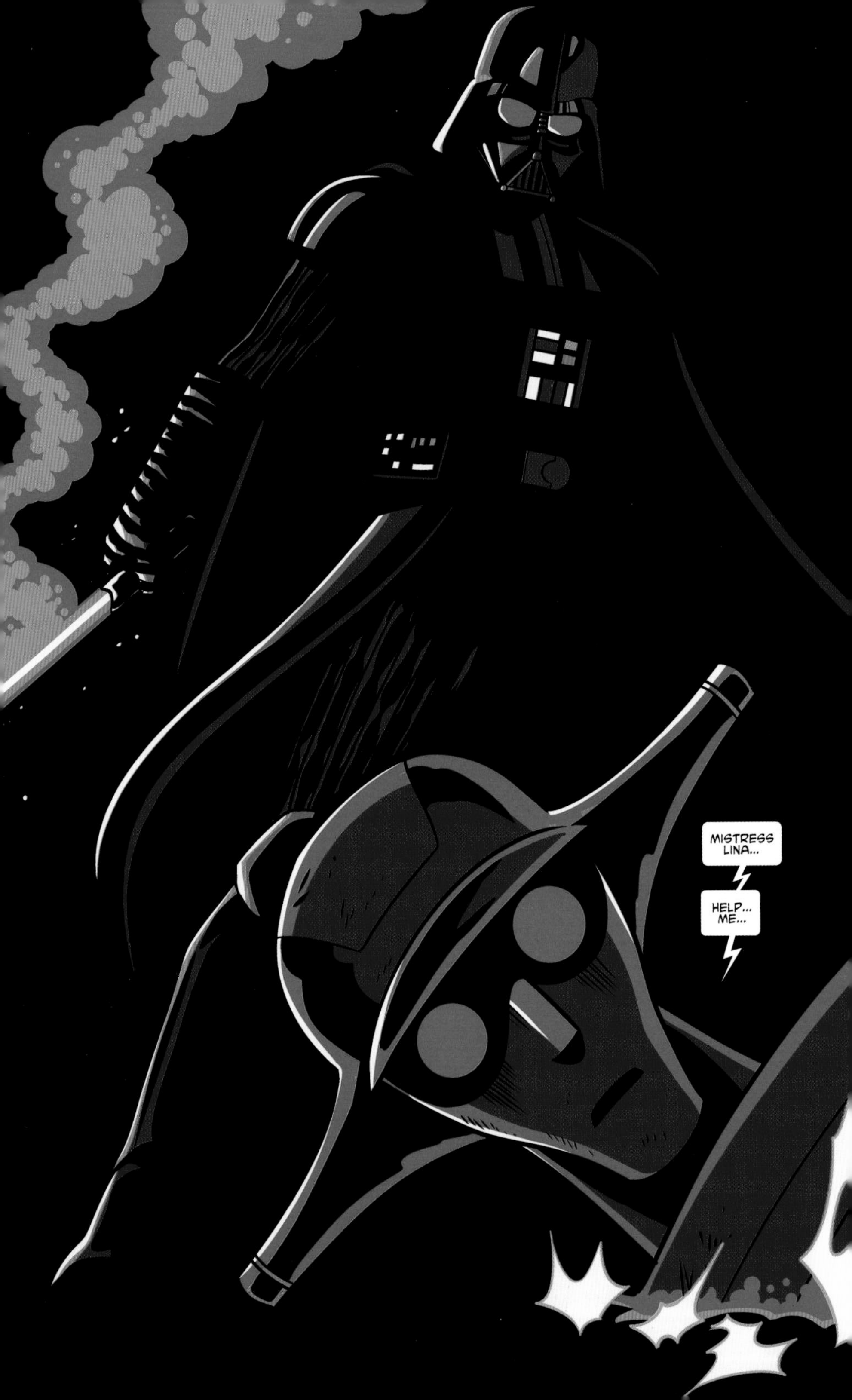
MISTRESS LINA...
HELP... ME...

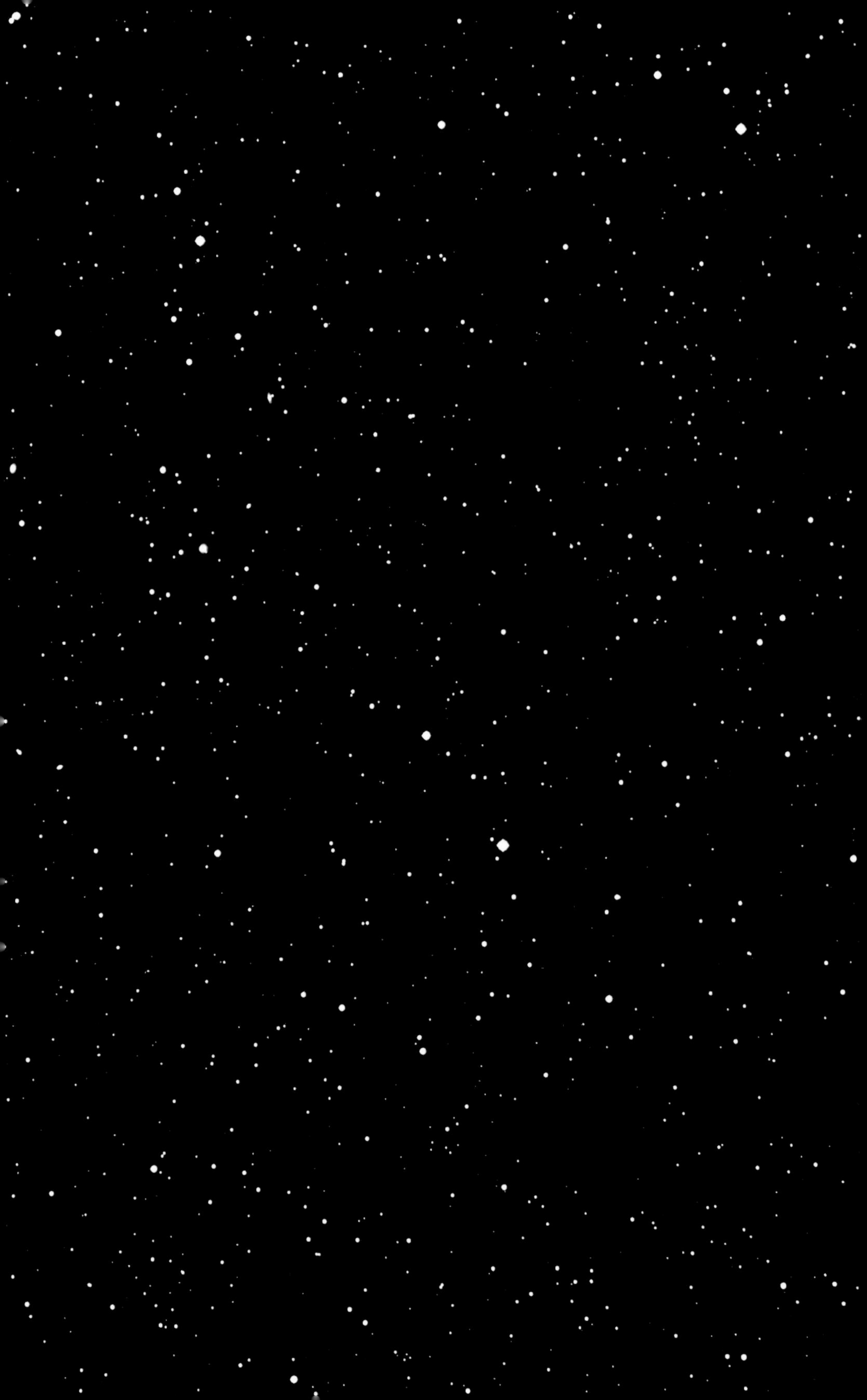

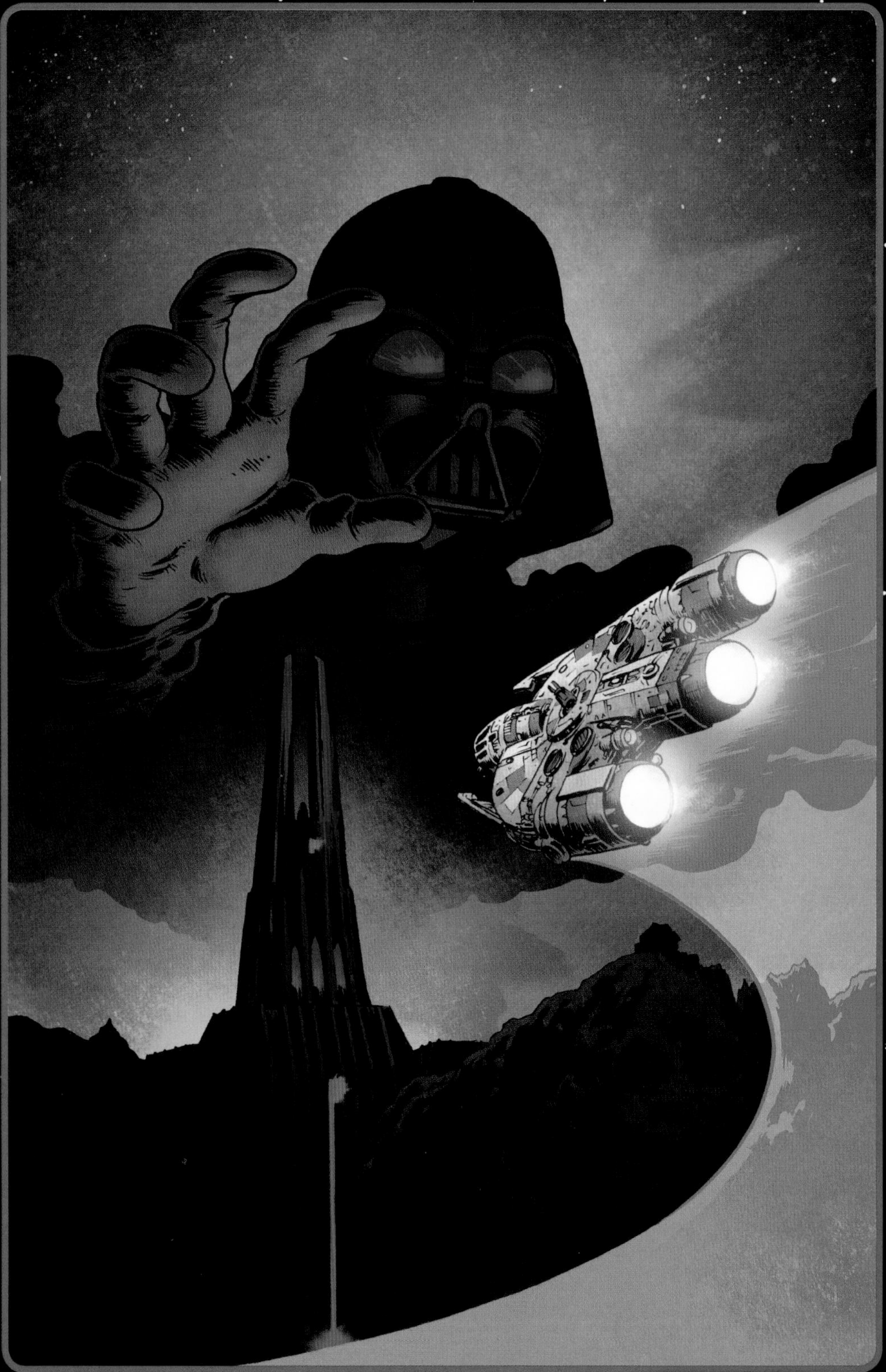

Art by Charles Paul Wilson III

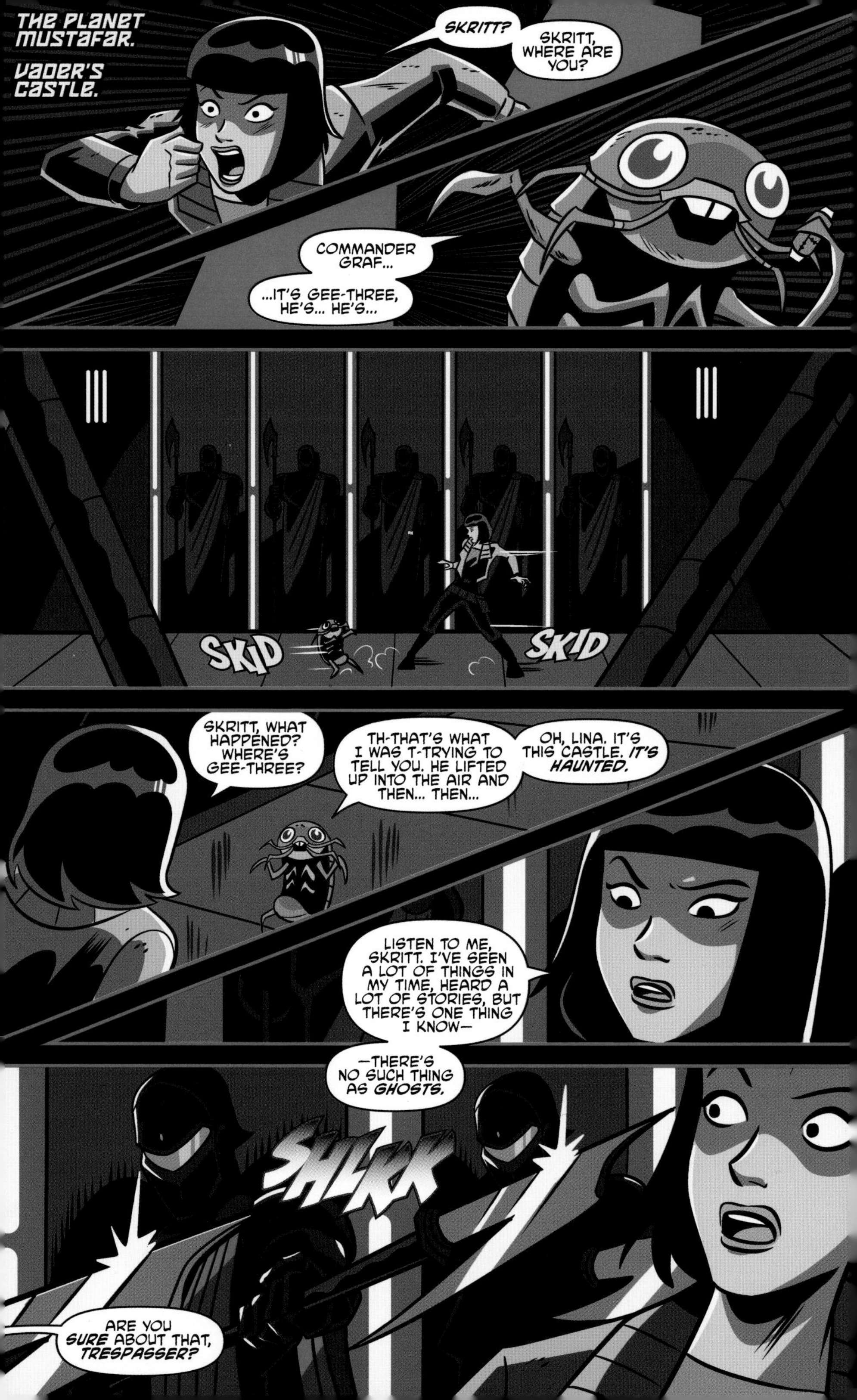
THE PLANET MUSTAFAR.
VADER'S CASTLE.
SKRITT?
SKRITT, WHERE ARE YOU?
COMMANDER GRAF...
...IT'S GEE-THREE, HE'S... HE'S...
SKID
SKID
SKRITT, WHAT HAPPENED? WHERE'S GEE-THREE?
TH-THAT'S WHAT I WAS T-TRYING TO TELL YOU. HE LIFTED UP INTO THE AIR AND THEN... THEN...
OH, LINA. IT'S THIS CASTLE. *IT'S HAUNTED.*
LISTEN TO ME, SKRITT. I'VE SEEN A LOT OF THINGS IN MY TIME, HEARD A LOT OF STORIES, BUT THERE'S ONE THING I KNOW—
—THERE'S NO SUCH THING AS *GHOSTS.*
SHKK
ARE YOU *SURE* ABOUT THAT, *TRESPASSER?*

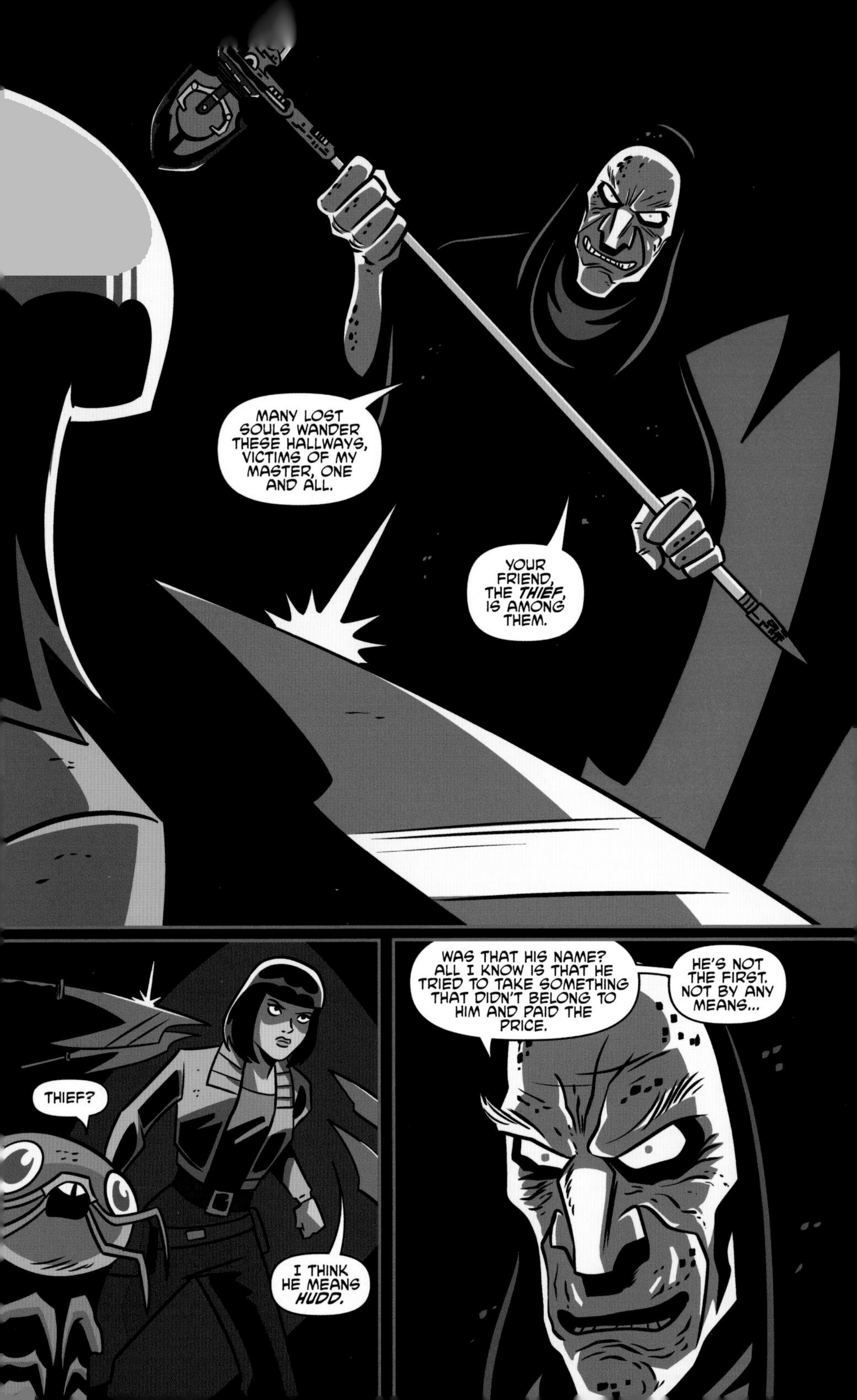
MANY LOST SOULS WANDER THESE HALLWAYS, VICTIMS OF MY MASTER, ONE AND ALL.
YOUR FRIEND, THE *THIEF*, IS AMONG THEM.
THIEF?
I THINK HE MEANS *HUDD*.
WAS THAT HIS NAME? ALL I KNOW IS THAT HE TRIED TO TAKE SOMETHING THAT DIDN'T BELONG TO HIM AND PAID THE PRICE.
HE'S NOT THE FIRST. NOT BY ANY MEANS...

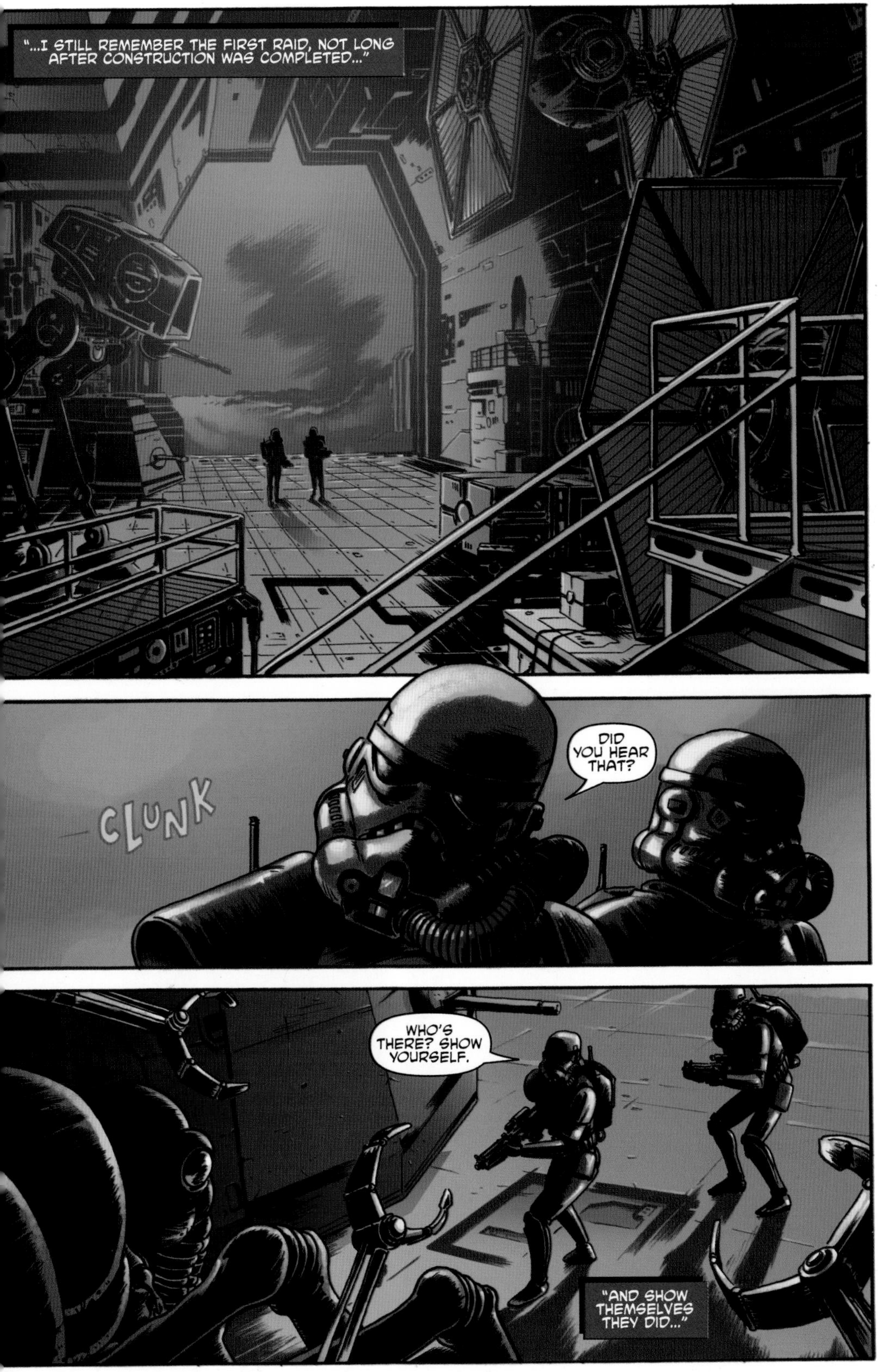
"...I STILL REMEMBER THE FIRST RAID, NOT LONG AFTER CONSTRUCTION WAS COMPLETED..."
DID YOU HEAR THAT?
CLUNK
WHO'S THERE? SHOW YOURSELF.
"AND SHOW THEMSELVES THEY DID..."

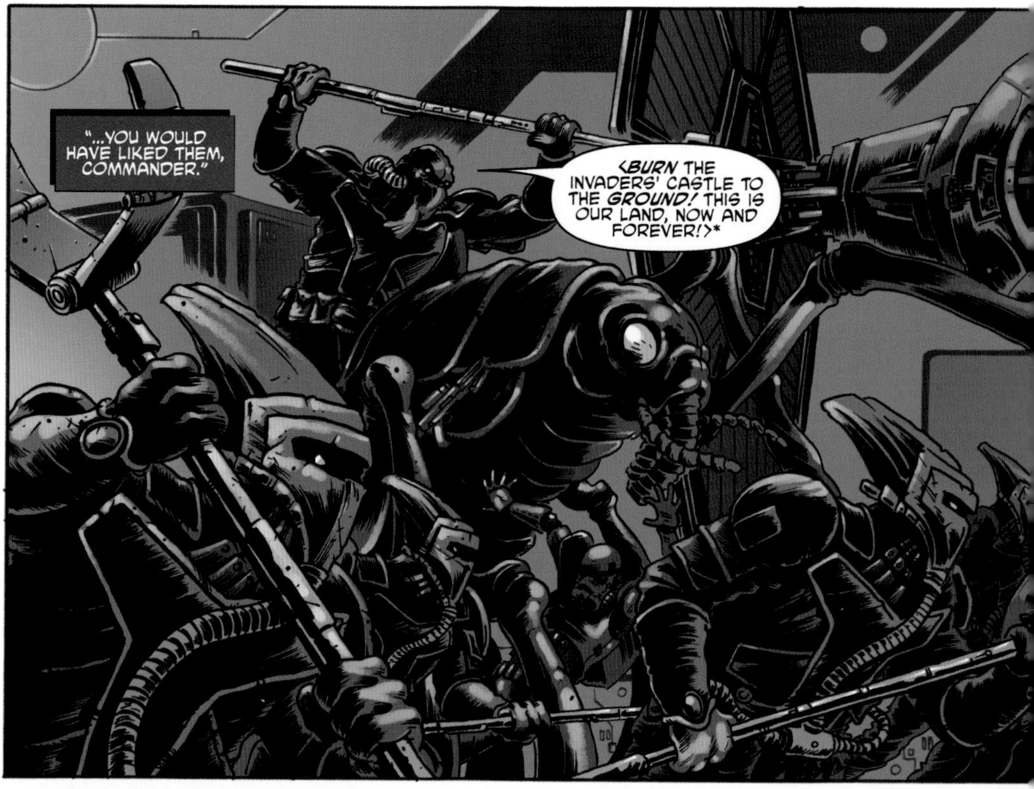
"...YOU WOULD HAVE LIKED THEM, COMMANDER."
<BURN THE INVADERS' CASTLE TO THE GROUND! THIS IS OUR LAND, NOW AND FOREVER!>*

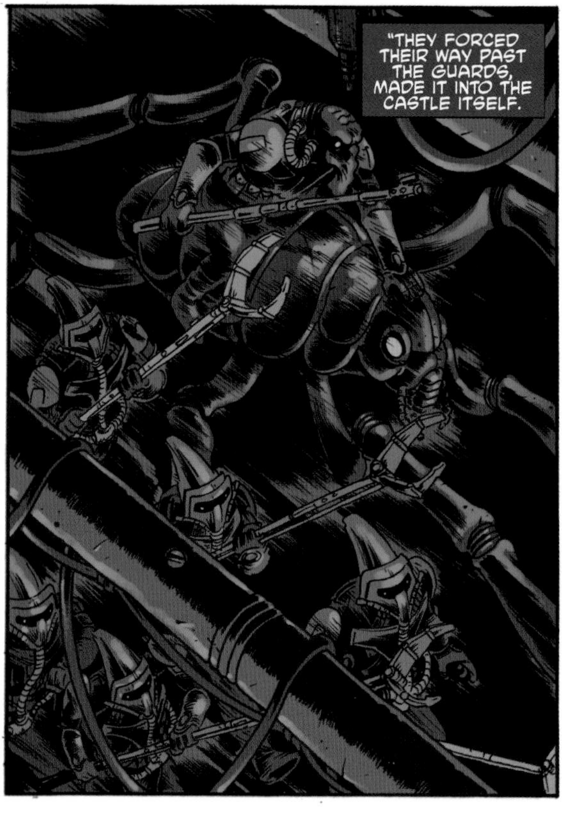
"THEY FORCED THEIR WAY PAST THE GUARDS, MADE IT INTO THE CASTLE ITSELF.

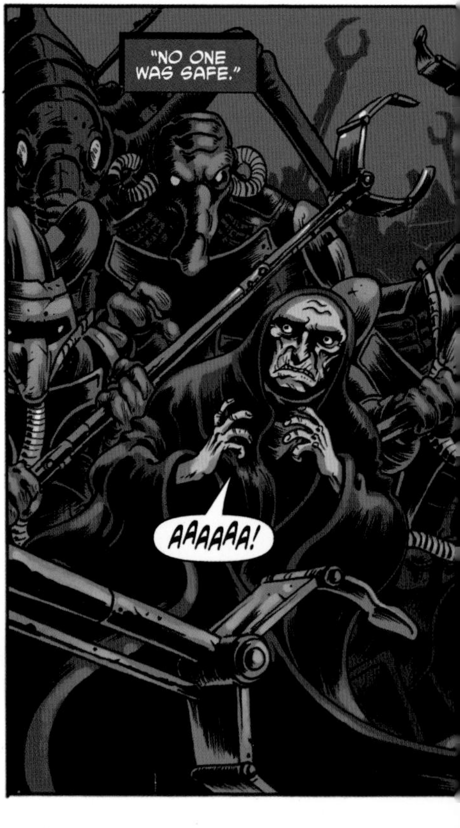
"NO ONE WAS SAFE."
AAAAAA!

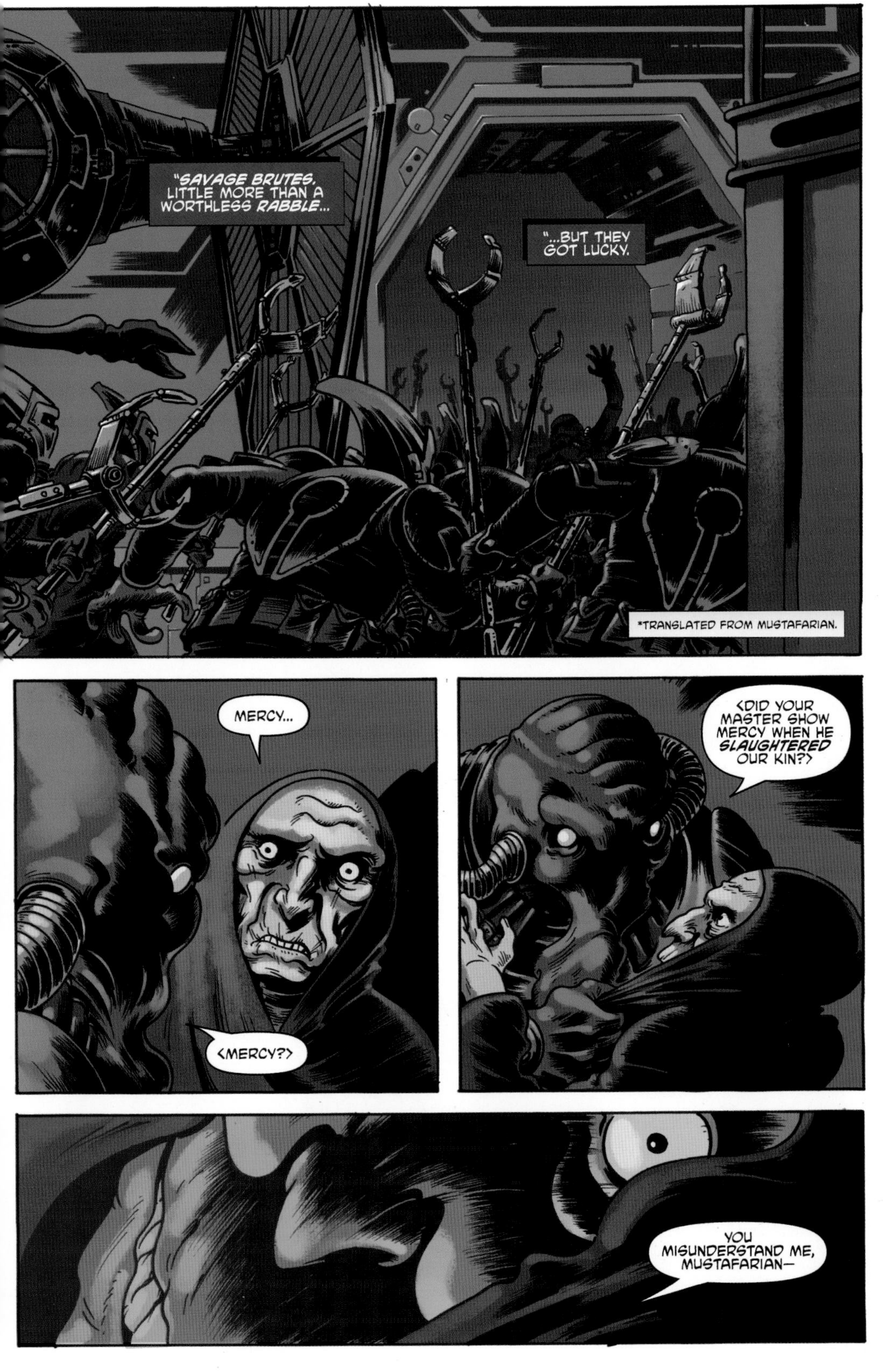
"SAVAGE BRUTES, LITTLE MORE THAN A WORTHLESS RABBLE...
"...BUT THEY GOT LUCKY.
*TRANSLATED FROM MUSTAFARIAN.
MERCY...
<MERCY?>
<DID YOUR MASTER SHOW MERCY WHEN HE SLAUGHTERED OUR KIN?>
YOU MISUNDERSTAND ME, MUSTAFARIAN—

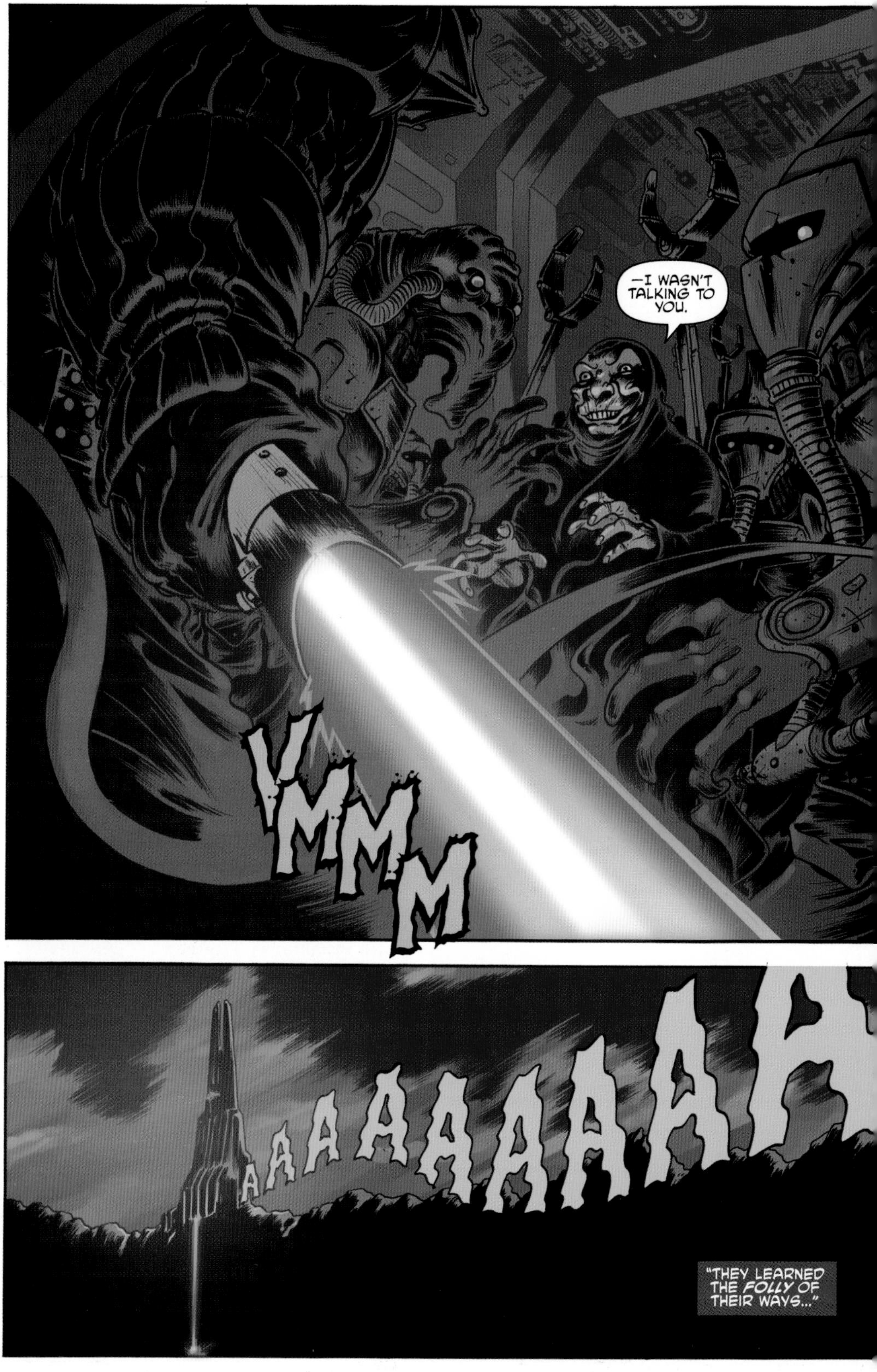
—I WASN'T TALKING TO YOU.
VMMMM
AAAAAAAAAAAA
"THEY LEARNED THE *FOLLY* OF THEIR WAYS..."

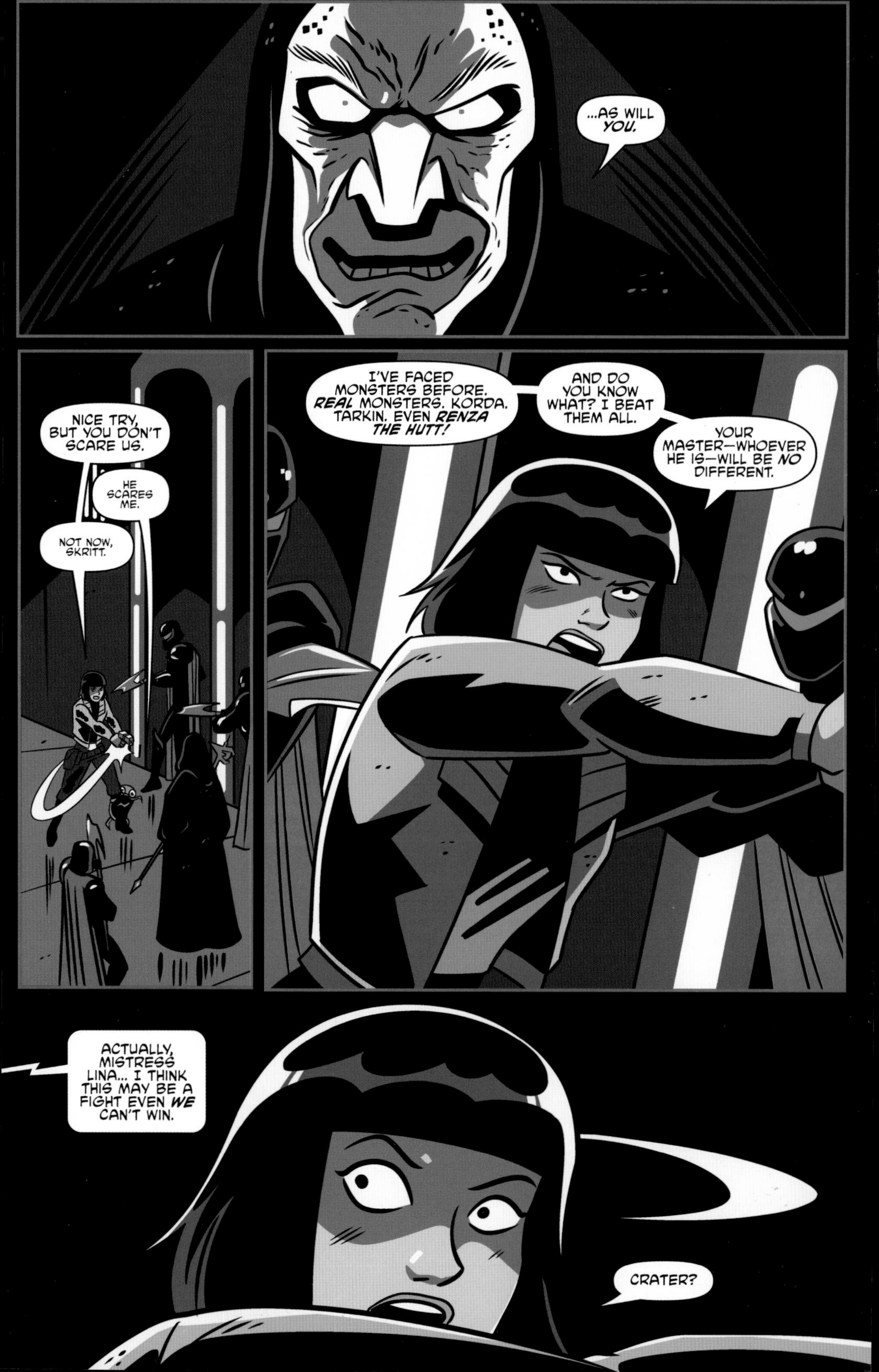
...AS WILL YOU.
NICE TRY, BUT YOU DON'T SCARE US.
HE SCARES ME.
NOT NOW, SKRITT.
I'VE FACED MONSTERS BEFORE. REAL MONSTERS. KORDA. TARKIN. EVEN RENZA THE HUTT!
AND DO YOU KNOW WHAT? I BEAT THEM ALL.
YOUR MASTER—WHOEVER HE IS—WILL BE NO DIFFERENT.
ACTUALLY, MISTRESS LINA... I THINK THIS MAY BE A FIGHT EVEN WE CAN'T WIN.
CRATER?

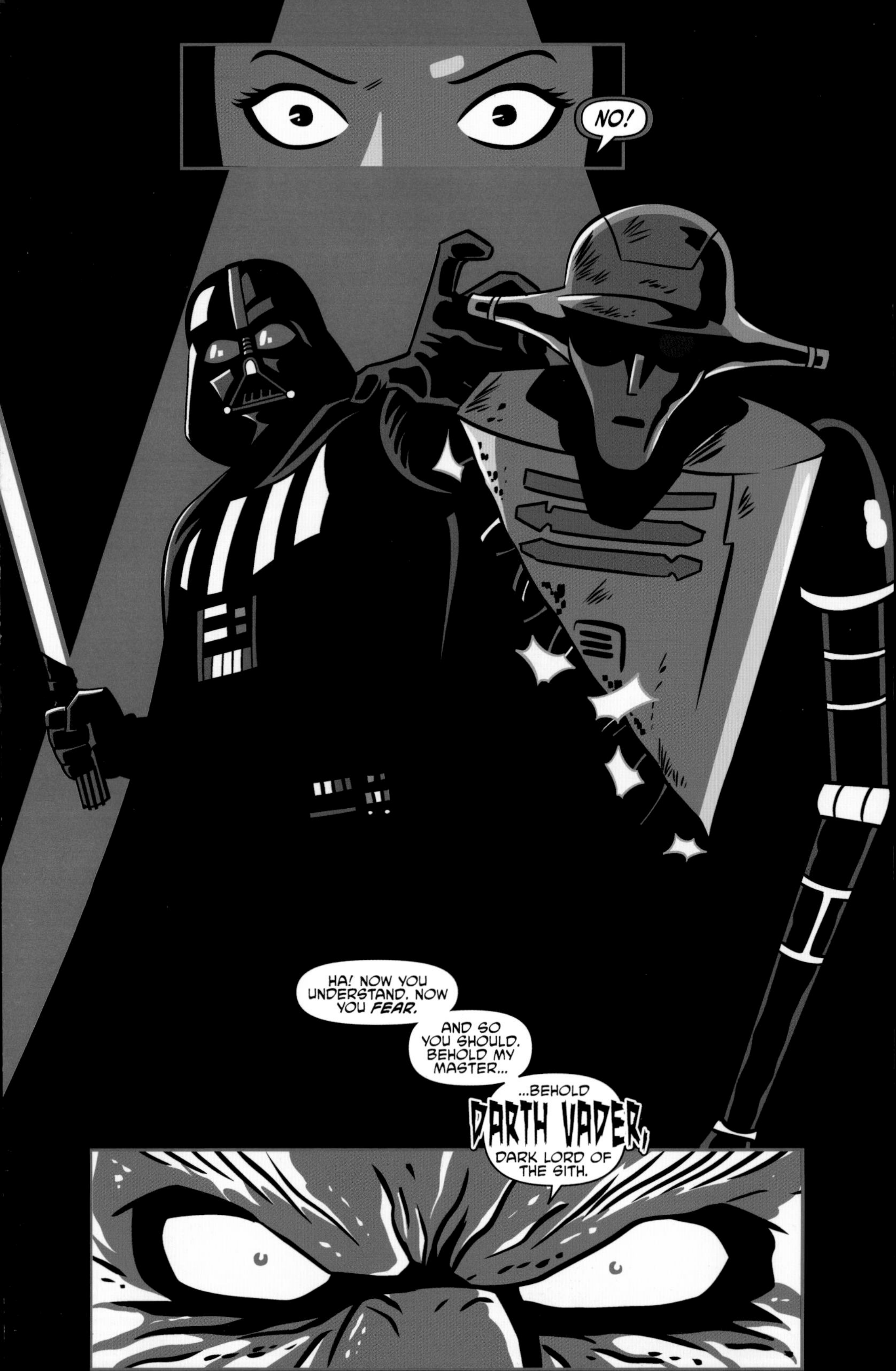
NO!
HA! NOW YOU UNDERSTAND. NOW YOU FEAR.
AND SO YOU SHOULD. BEHOLD MY MASTER...
...BEHOLD DARTH VADER, DARK LORD OF THE SITH.

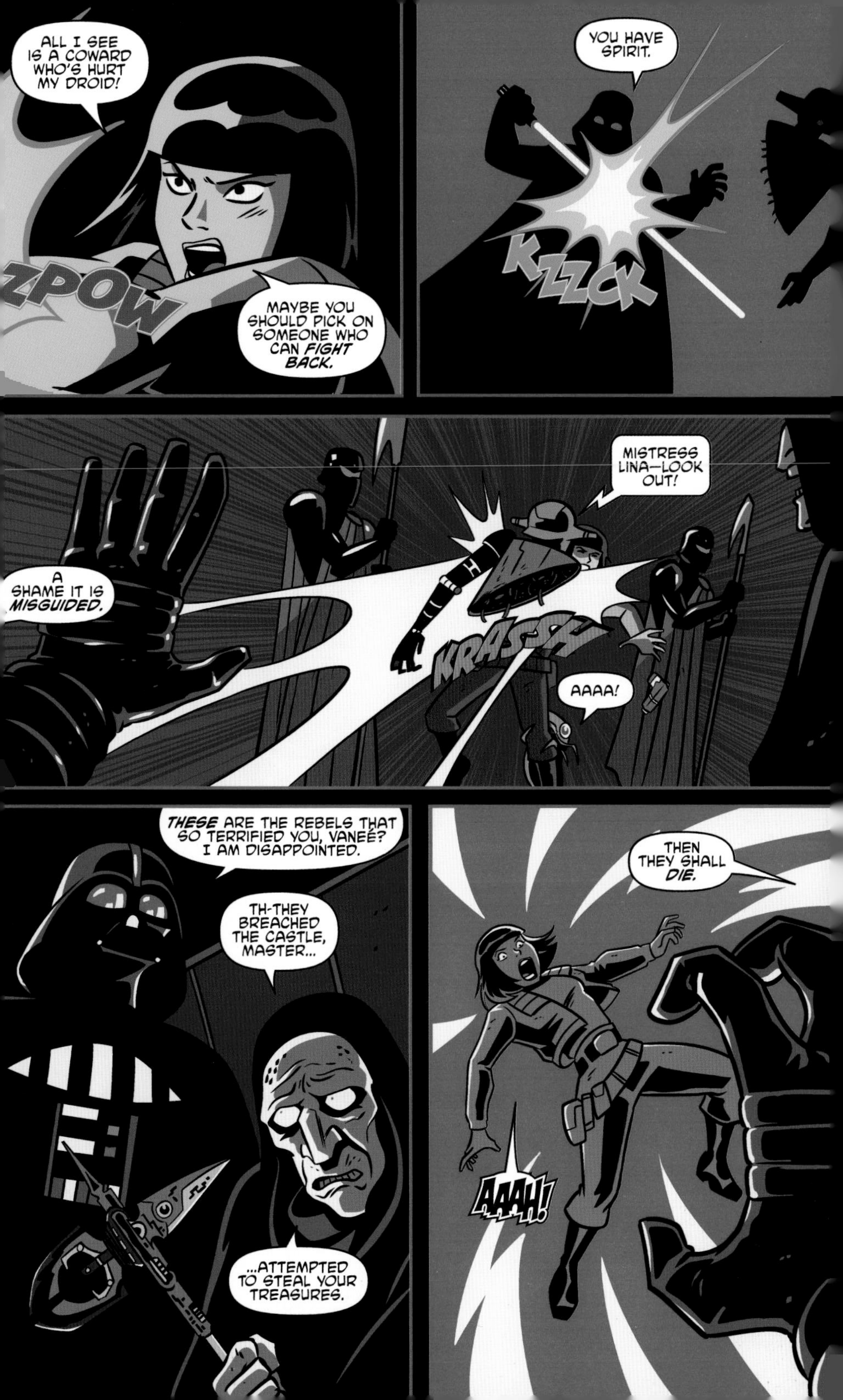
ALL I SEE IS A COWARD WHO'S HURT MY DROID!
ZPOW
MAYBE YOU SHOULD PICK ON SOMEONE WHO CAN FIGHT BACK.
YOU HAVE SPIRIT.
KZZCK
A SHAME IT IS MISGUIDED.
MISTRESS LINA—LOOK OUT!
KRASSH
AAAA!
THESE ARE THE REBELS THAT SO TERRIFIED YOU, VANEÉ? I AM DISAPPOINTED.
TH-THEY BREACHED THE CASTLE, MASTER...
...ATTEMPTED TO STEAL YOUR TREASURES.
THEN THEY SHALL DIE.
AAAH!

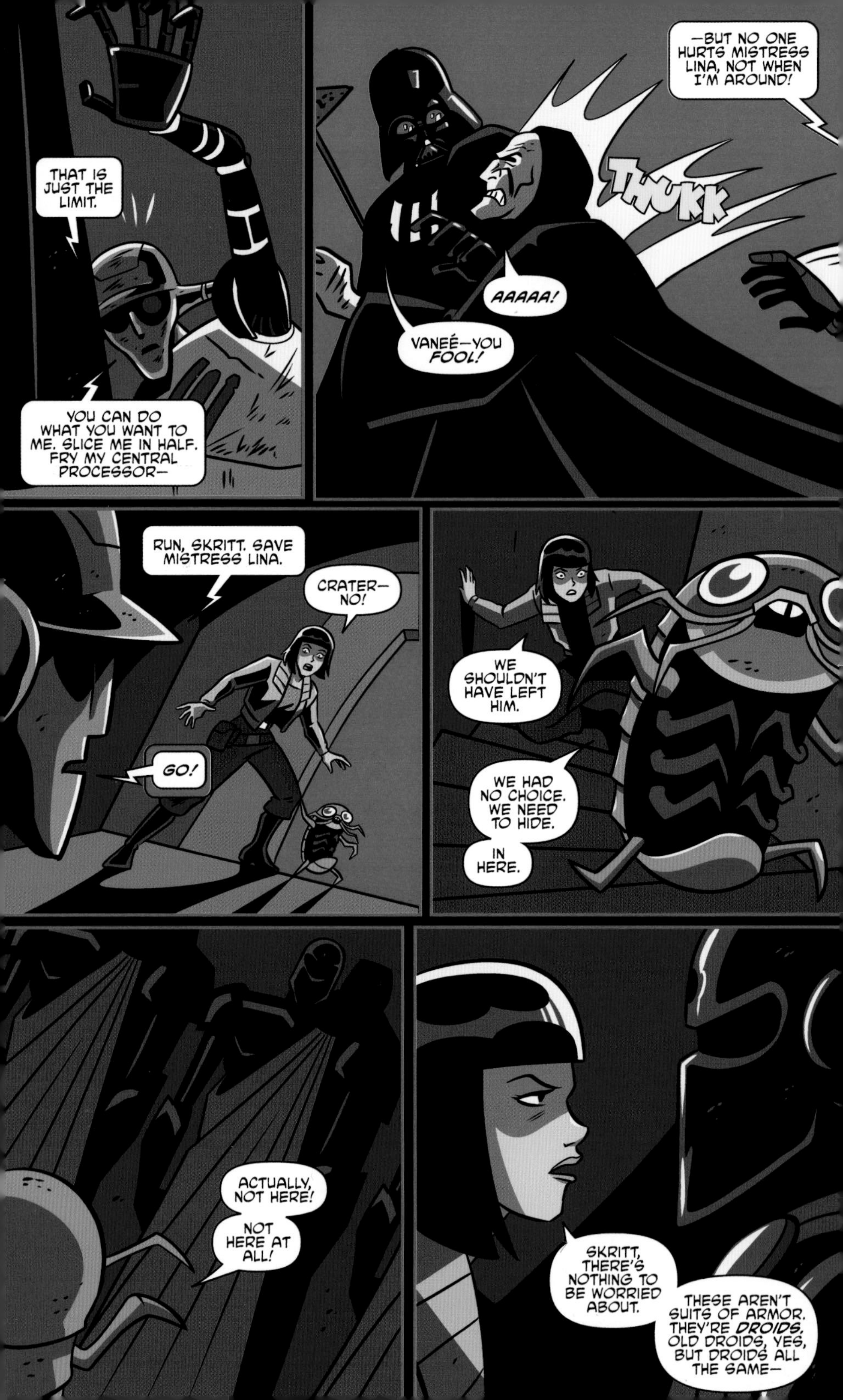
THAT IS JUST THE LIMIT.
YOU CAN DO WHAT YOU WANT TO ME. SLICE ME IN HALF. FRY MY CENTRAL PROCESSOR—
—BUT NO ONE HURTS MISTRESS LINA, NOT WHEN I'M AROUND!
THUKK
AAAAA!
VANEÉ—YOU FOOL!
RUN, SKRITT. SAVE MISTRESS LINA.
CRATER—NO!
GO!
WE SHOULDN'T HAVE LEFT HIM.
WE HAD NO CHOICE. WE NEED TO HIDE.
IN HERE.
ACTUALLY, NOT HERE!
NOT HERE AT ALL!
SKRITT, THERE'S NOTHING TO BE WORRIED ABOUT.
THESE AREN'T SUITS OF ARMOR. THEY'RE DROIDS. OLD DROIDS, YES, BUT DROIDS ALL THE SAME—

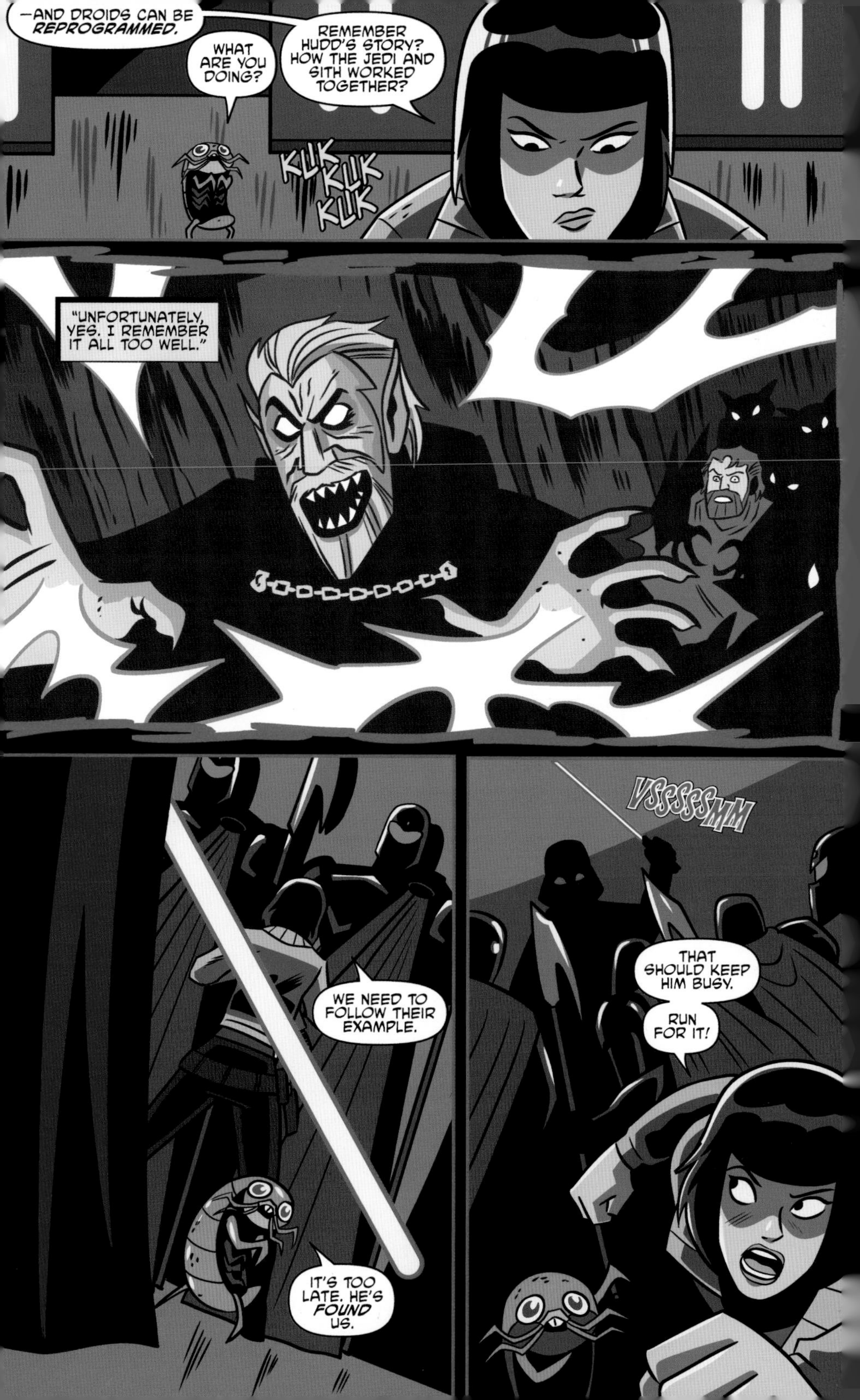
—AND DROIDS CAN BE *REPROGRAMMED.*
WHAT ARE YOU DOING?
REMEMBER HUDD'S STORY? HOW THE JEDI AND SITH WORKED TOGETHER?
KLIK KLIK KLIK
"UNFORTUNATELY, YES. I REMEMBER IT ALL TOO WELL."
WE NEED TO FOLLOW THEIR EXAMPLE.
IT'S TOO LATE. HE'S *FOUND* US.
VSSSSSMM
THAT SHOULD KEEP HIM BUSY.
RUN FOR IT!

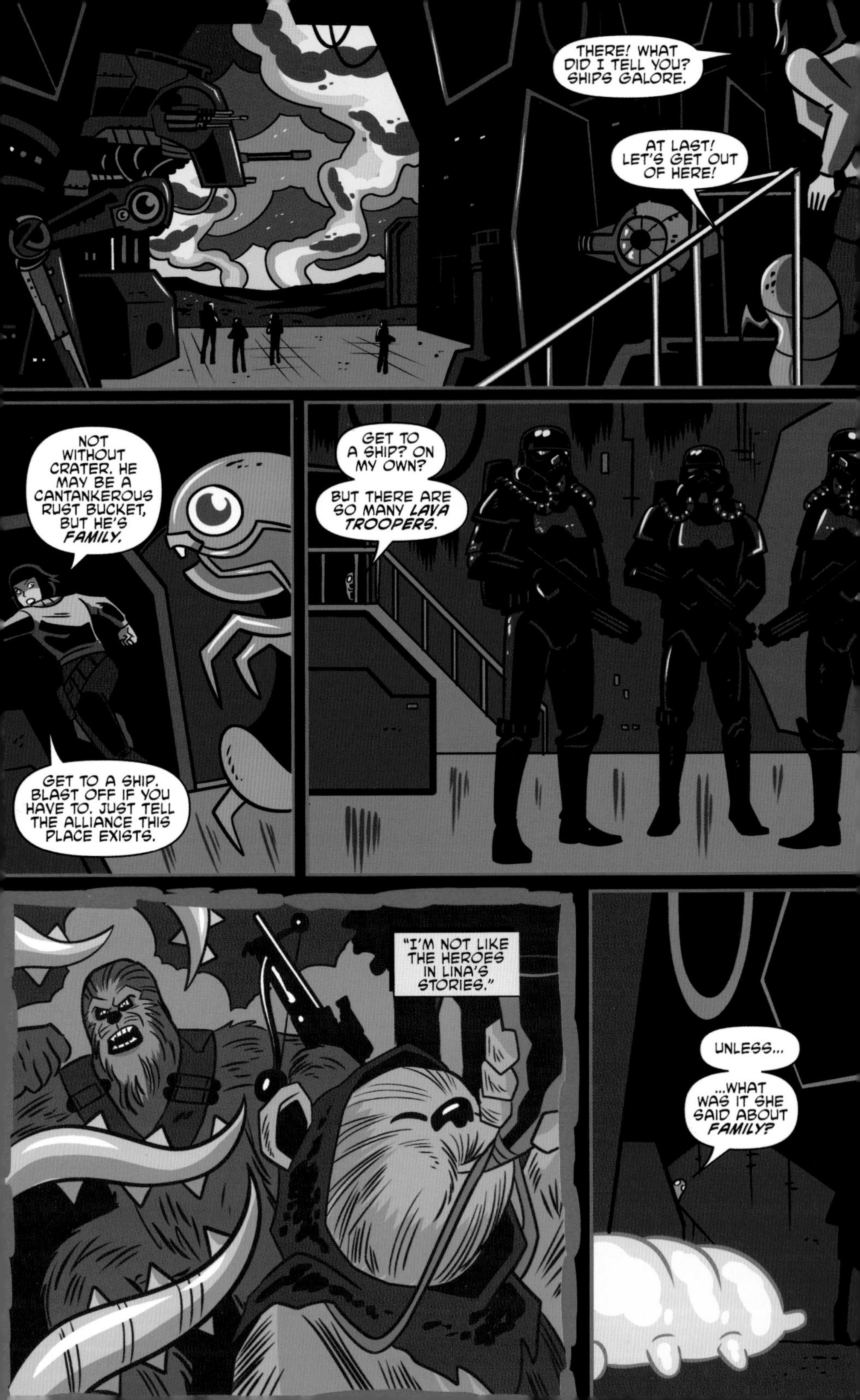
THERE! WHAT DID I TELL YOU? SHIPS GALORE.
AT LAST! LET'S GET OUT OF HERE!
NOT WITHOUT CRATER. HE MAY BE A CANTANKEROUS RUST BUCKET, BUT HE'S *FAMILY.*
GET TO A SHIP. BLAST OFF IF YOU HAVE TO. JUST TELL THE ALLIANCE THIS PLACE EXISTS.
GET TO A SHIP? ON MY OWN?
BUT THERE ARE SO MANY *LAVA TROOPERS*.
"I'M NOT LIKE THE HEROES IN LINA'S STORIES."
UNLESS...
...WHAT WAS IT SHE SAID ABOUT *FAMILY*?

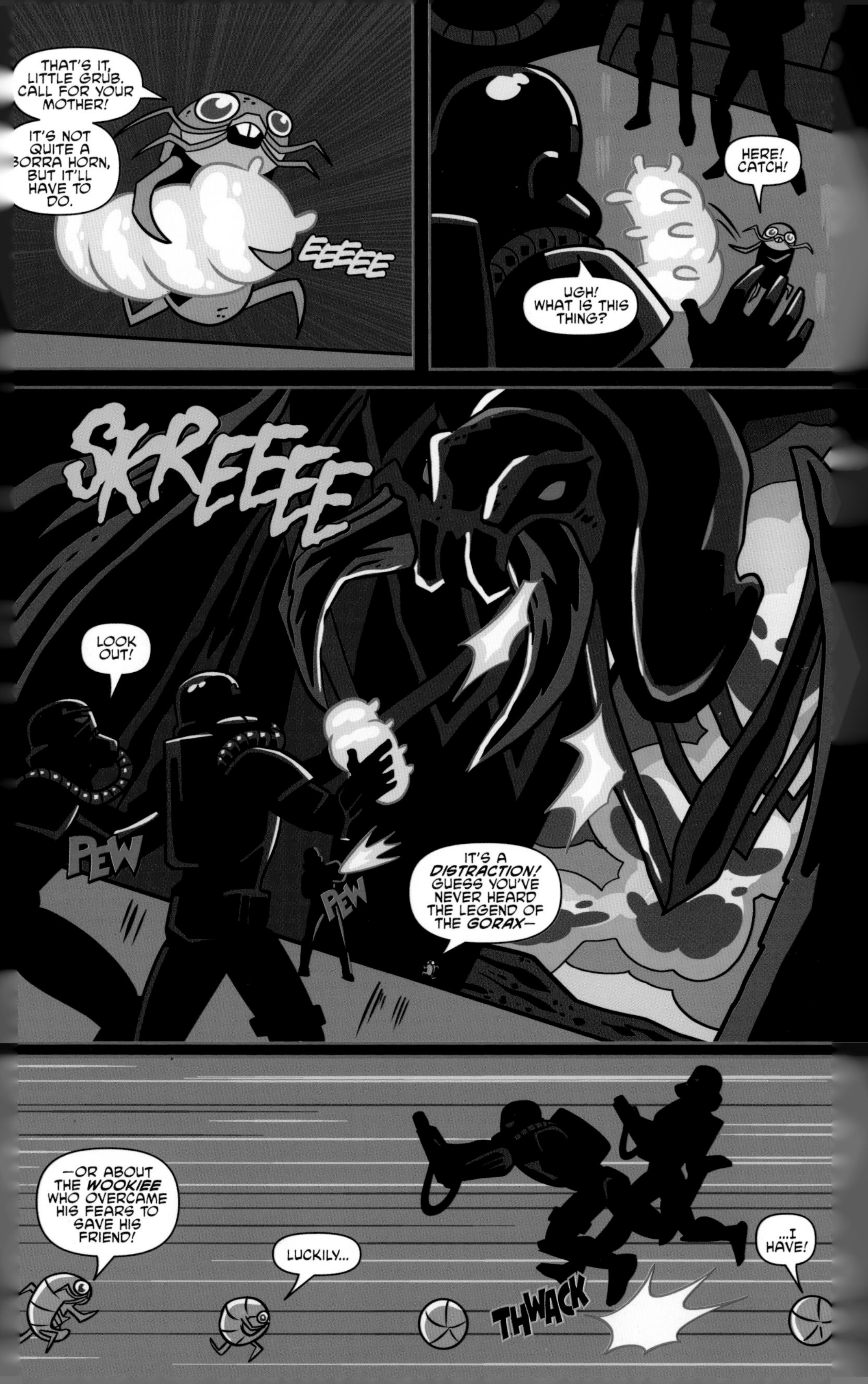
THAT'S IT, LITTLE GRUB. CALL FOR YOUR MOTHER!
IT'S NOT QUITE A BORRA HORN, BUT IT'LL HAVE TO DO.
EEEEE
HERE! CATCH!
UGH! WHAT IS THIS THING?
SKREEEE
LOOK OUT!
PEW
PEW
IT'S A DISTRACTION! GUESS YOU'VE NEVER HEARD THE LEGEND OF THE GORAX—
—OR ABOUT THE WOOKIEE WHO OVERCAME HIS FEARS TO SAVE HIS FRIEND!
LUCKILY...
THWACK
...I HAVE!

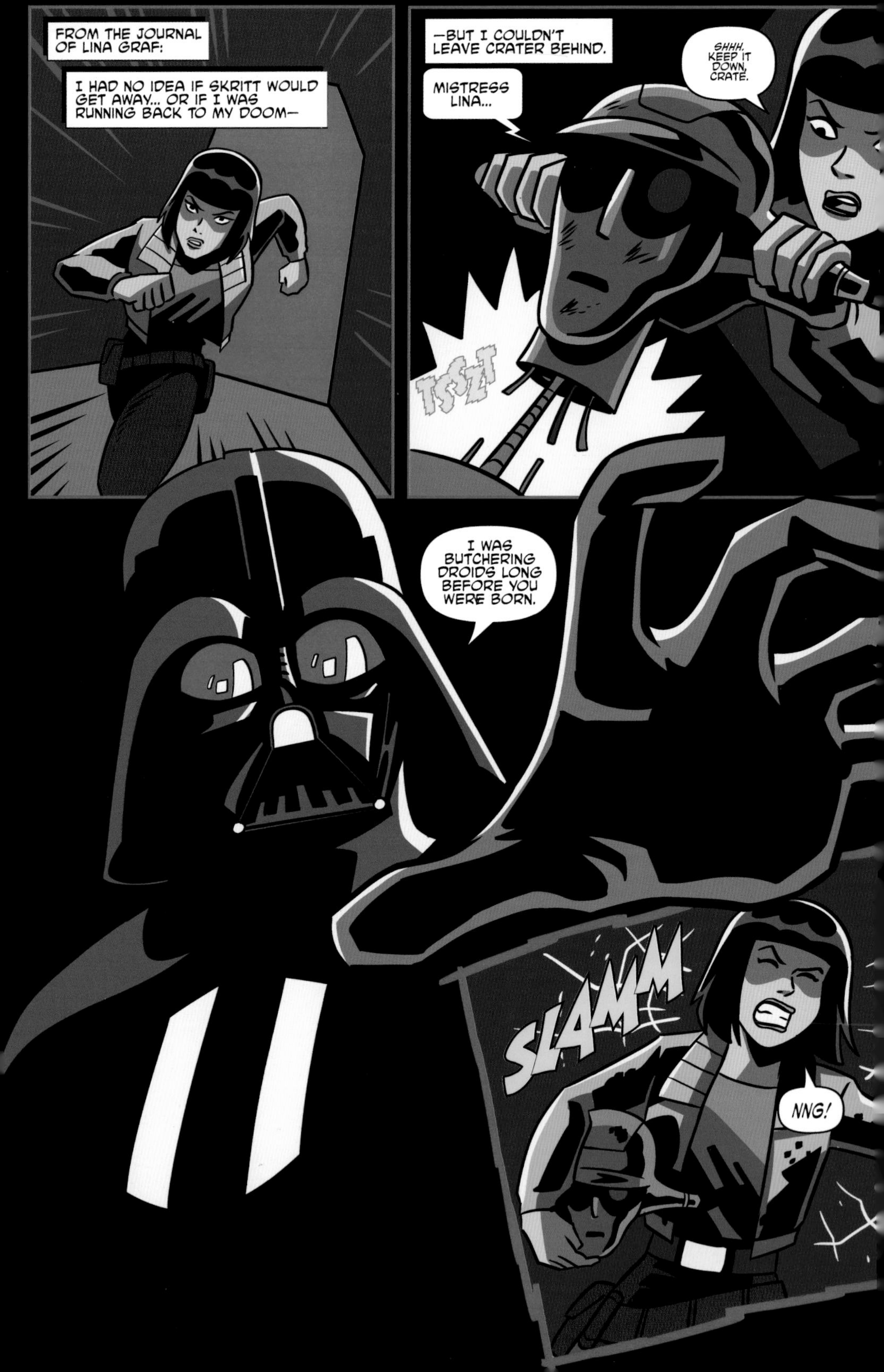
FROM THE JOURNAL OF LINA GRAF:
I HAD NO IDEA IF SKRITT WOULD GET AWAY... OR IF I WAS RUNNING BACK TO MY DOOM—
—BUT I COULDN'T LEAVE CRATER BEHIND.
MISTRESS LINA...
SHHH. KEEP IT DOWN, CRATE.
TSZZT
I WAS BUTCHERING DROIDS LONG BEFORE YOU WERE BORN.
SLAMM
NNG!

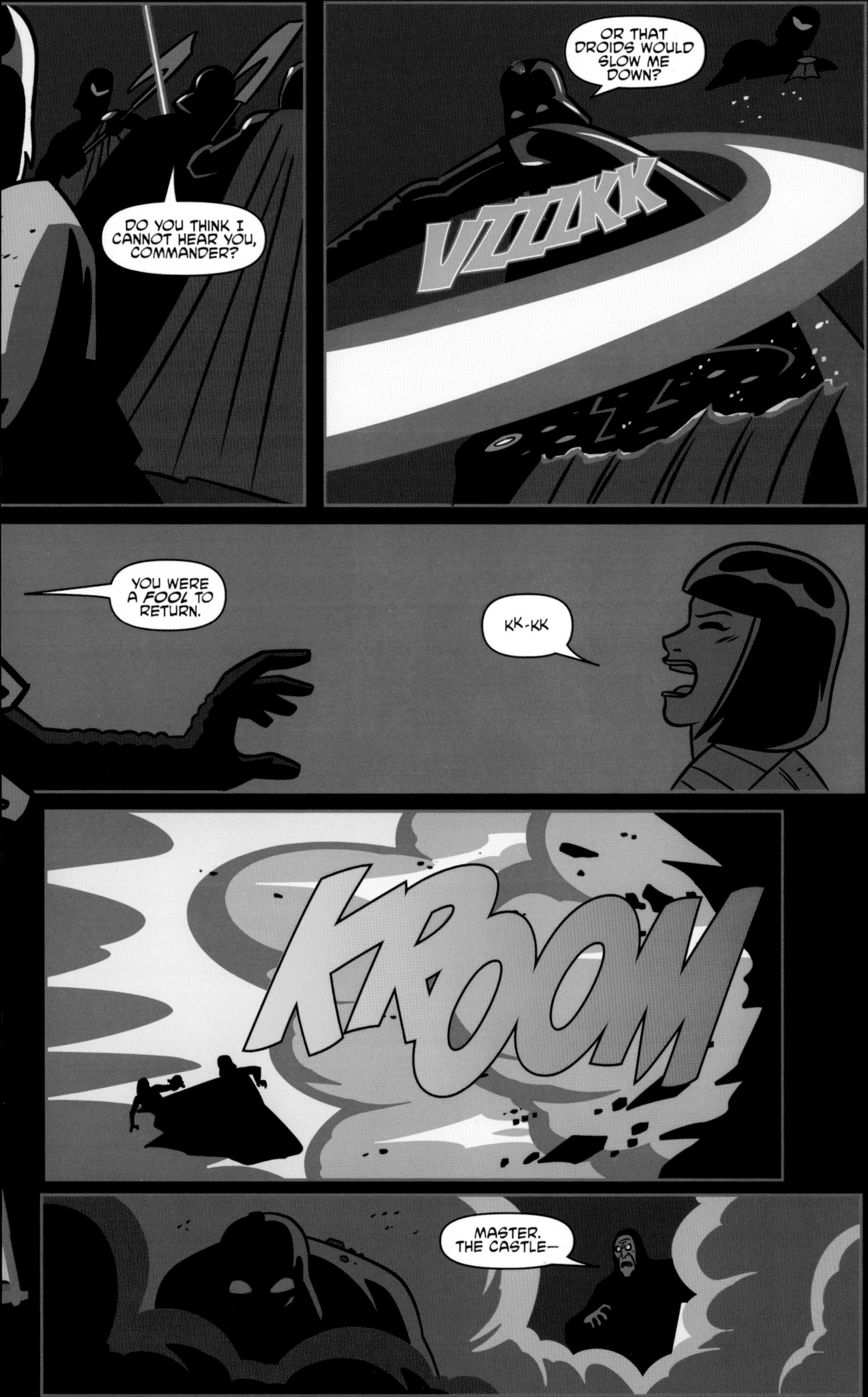
DO YOU THINK I CANNOT HEAR YOU, COMMANDER?
OR THAT DROIDS WOULD SLOW ME DOWN?
VZZZKK
YOU WERE A *FOOL* TO RETURN.
KK-KK
KROOM
MASTER. THE CASTLE—

"—IT'S UNDER ATTACK!"

VZZZW

VZZZW

MY BROTHER HAD ALWAYS BEEN THE ONE FOR STORIES. I USED TO LAUGH AT HIM WHEN WE WERE YOUNG.

"YOU NEED TO GROW UP, MILO," I'D SAY. "GET YOUR HEAD OUT OF THE CLOUDS."

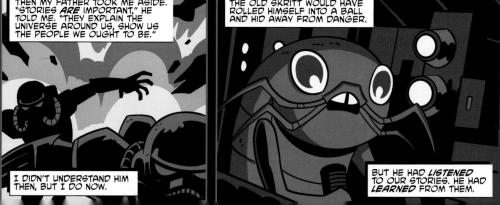

THEN MY FATHER TOOK ME ASIDE. "STORIES *ARE* IMPORTANT," HE TOLD ME. "THEY EXPLAIN THE UNIVERSE AROUND US, SHOW US THE PEOPLE WE OUGHT TO BE."

I DIDN'T UNDERSTAND HIM THEN, BUT I DO NOW.

THE OLD SKRITT WOULD HAVE ROLLED HIMSELF INTO A BALL AND HID AWAY FROM DANGER.

BUT HE HAD *LISTENED* TO OUR STORIES. HE HAD *LEARNED* FROM THEM.

HE SAVED ME...

...BUT AT WHAT COST?

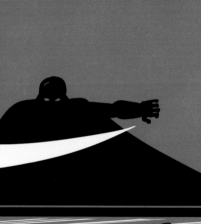

WHSSSH

AAAAAA!

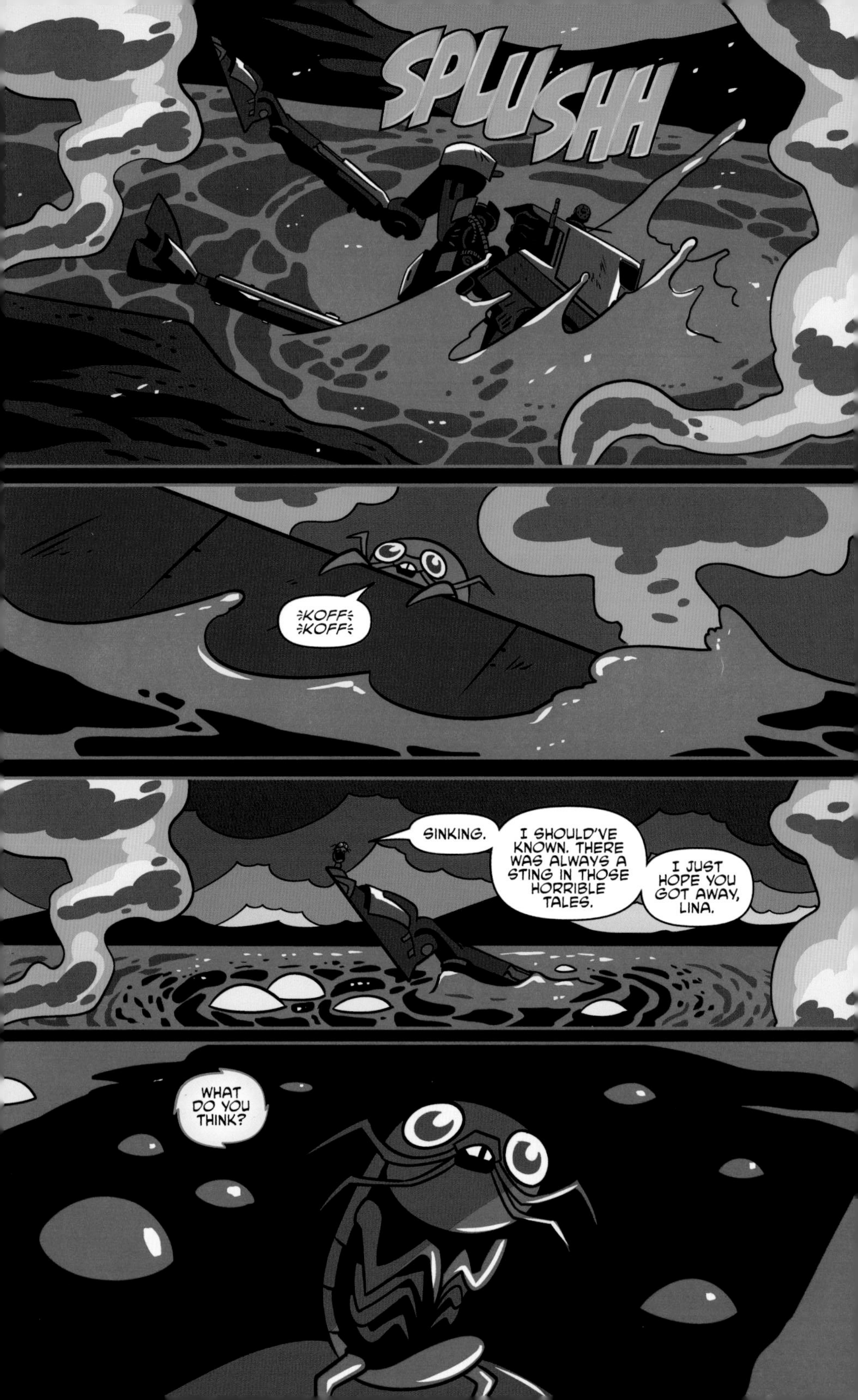
SPLUSHH
KOFF KOFF
SINKING.
I SHOULD'VE KNOWN. THERE WAS ALWAYS A STING IN THOSE HORRIBLE TALES.
I JUST HOPE YOU GOT AWAY, LINA.
WHAT DO YOU THINK?

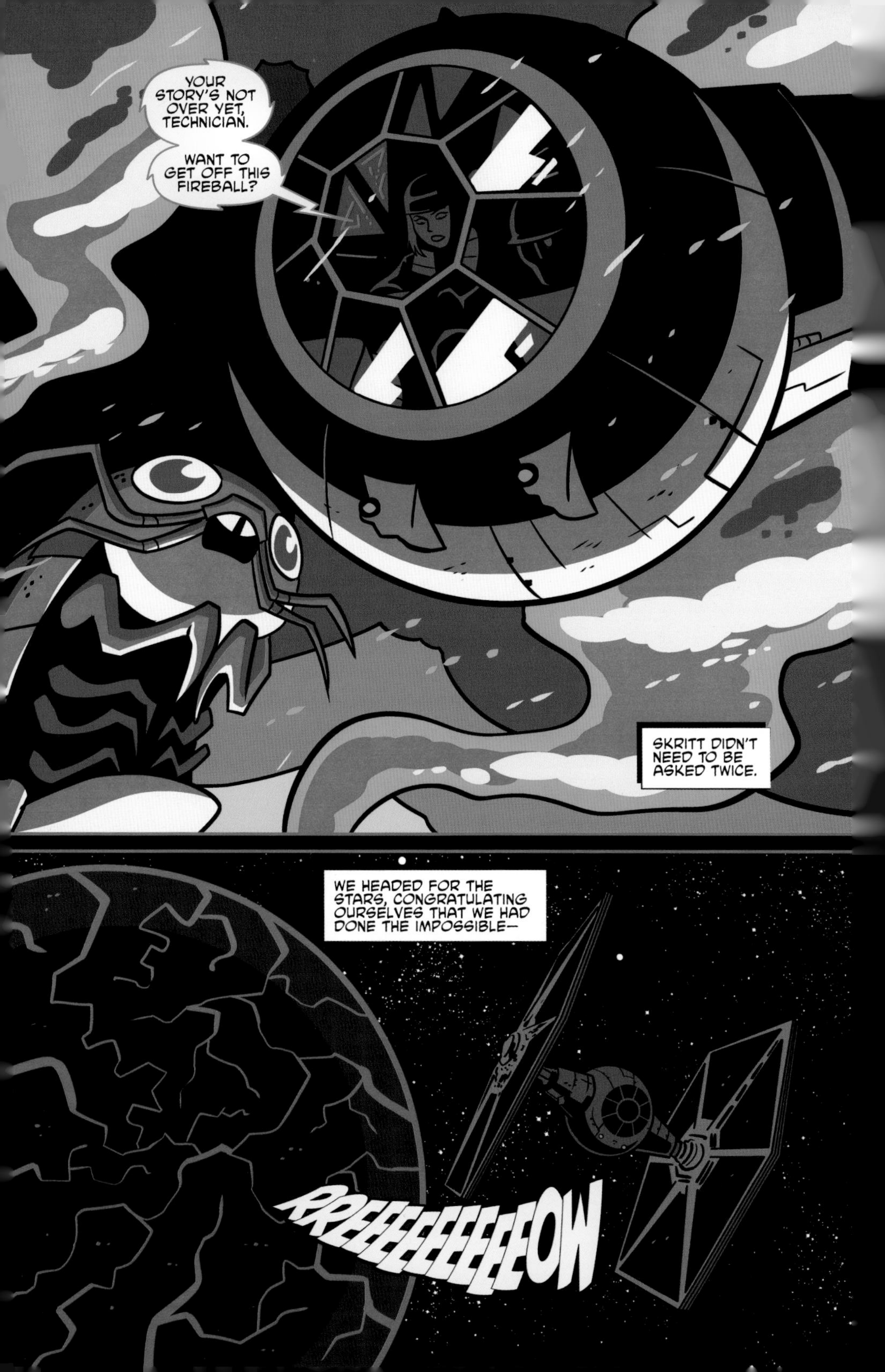
YOUR STORY'S NOT OVER YET, TECHNICIAN.
WANT TO GET OFF THIS FIREBALL?
SKRITT DIDN'T NEED TO BE ASKED TWICE.
WE HEADED FOR THE STARS, CONGRATULATING OURSELVES THAT WE HAD DONE THE IMPOSSIBLE—
RREEEEEEEEEEEOW

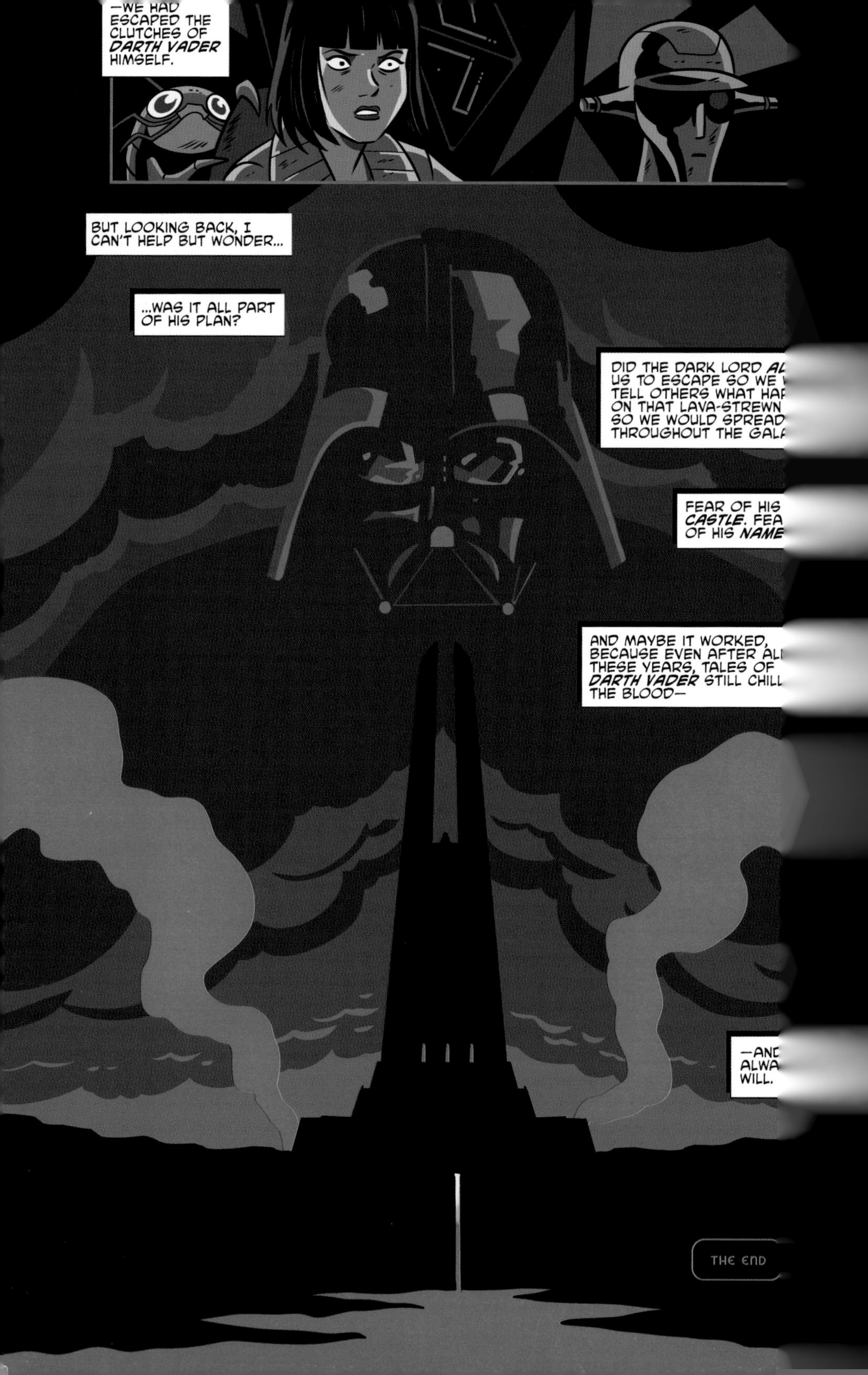

—WE HAD ESCAPED THE CLUTCHES OF *DARTH VADER* HIMSELF.
BUT LOOKING BACK, I CAN'T HELP BUT WONDER...
...WAS IT ALL PART OF HIS PLAN?
DID THE DARK LORD *AL* US TO ESCAPE SO WE TELL OTHERS WHAT HAP ON THAT LAVA-STREWN SO WE WOULD SPREAD THROUGHOUT THE GALA
FEAR OF HIS *CASTLE*. FEA OF HIS *NAME*
AND MAYBE IT WORKED, BECAUSE EVEN AFTER ALL THESE YEARS, TALES OF *DARTH VADER* STILL CHILL THE BLOOD—
—AND ALWA WILL.
THE END

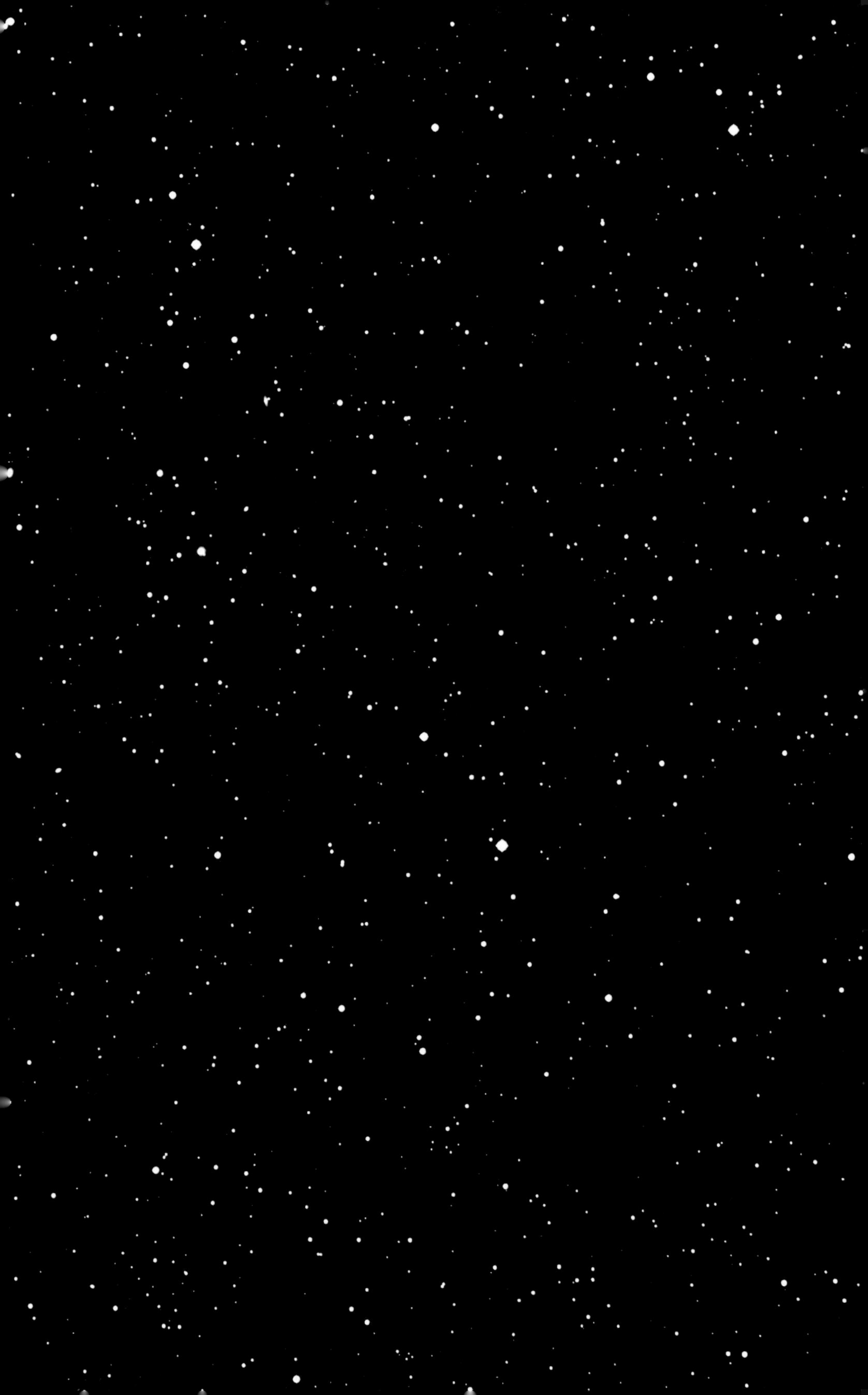

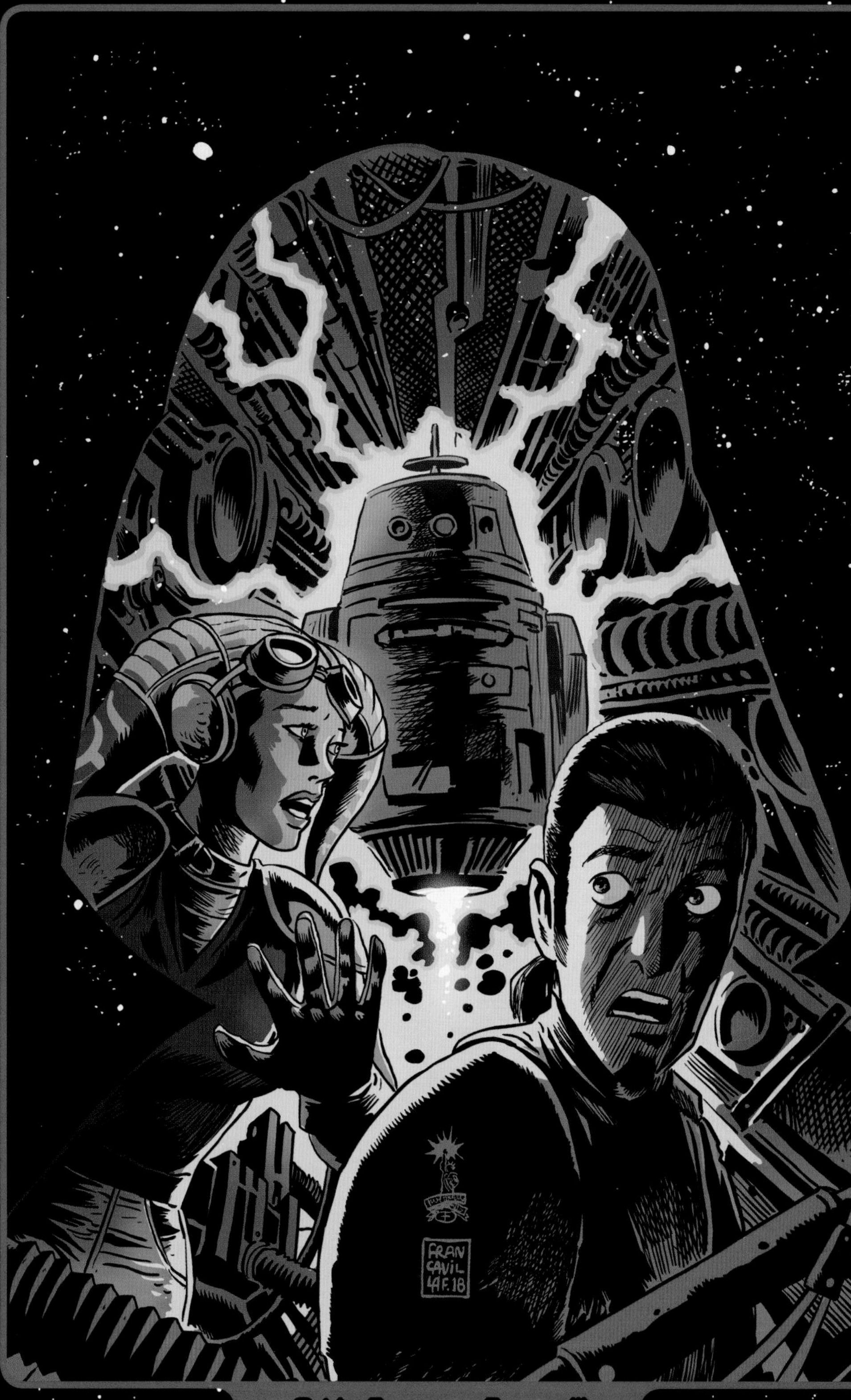

Art by Francesco Francavilla

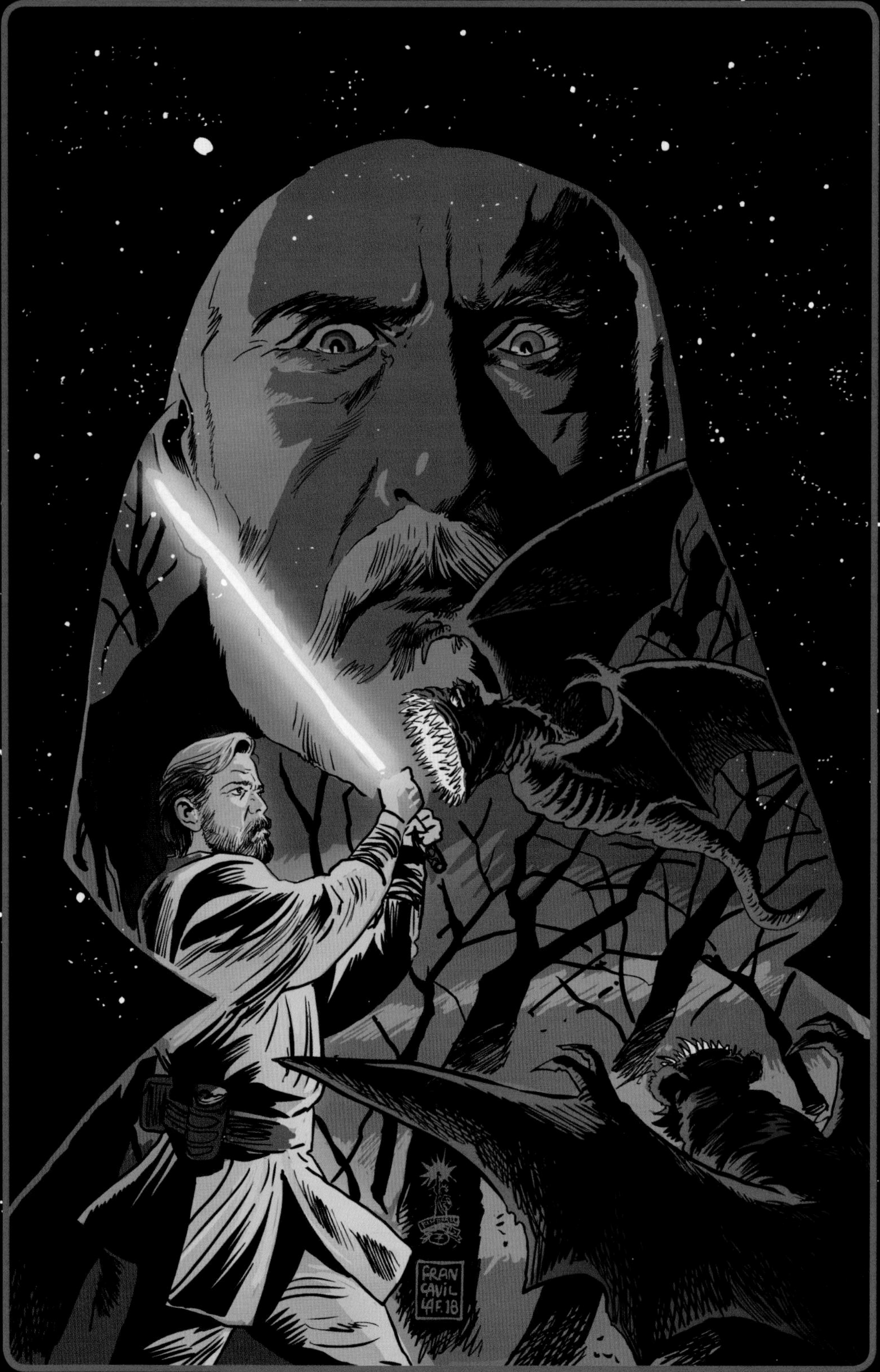
FRAN
CAVIL
LA F. 18

Art by Francesco Francavilla

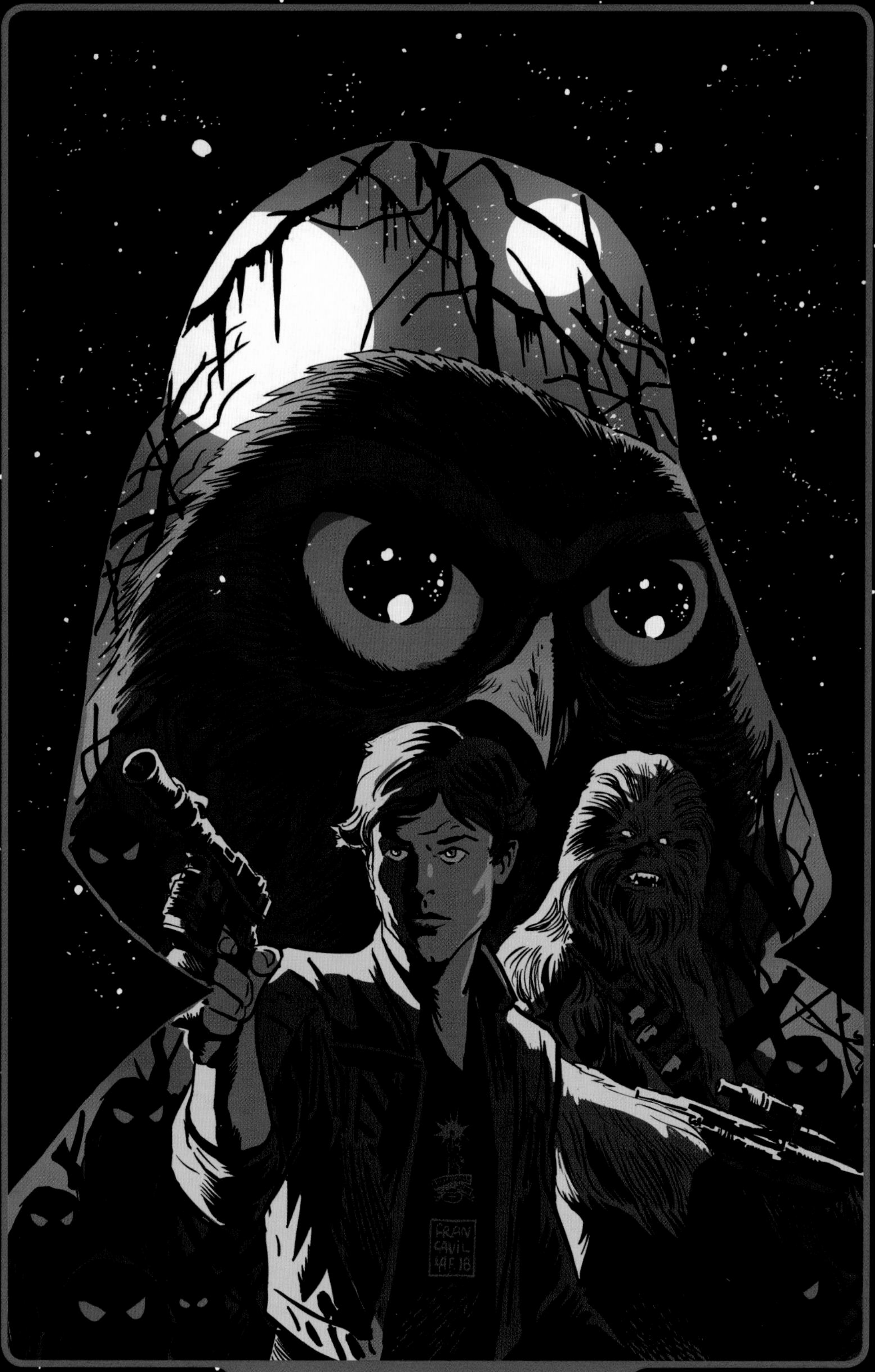
FRAN
CAVIL
LA F. 18

Art by Francesco Francavilla

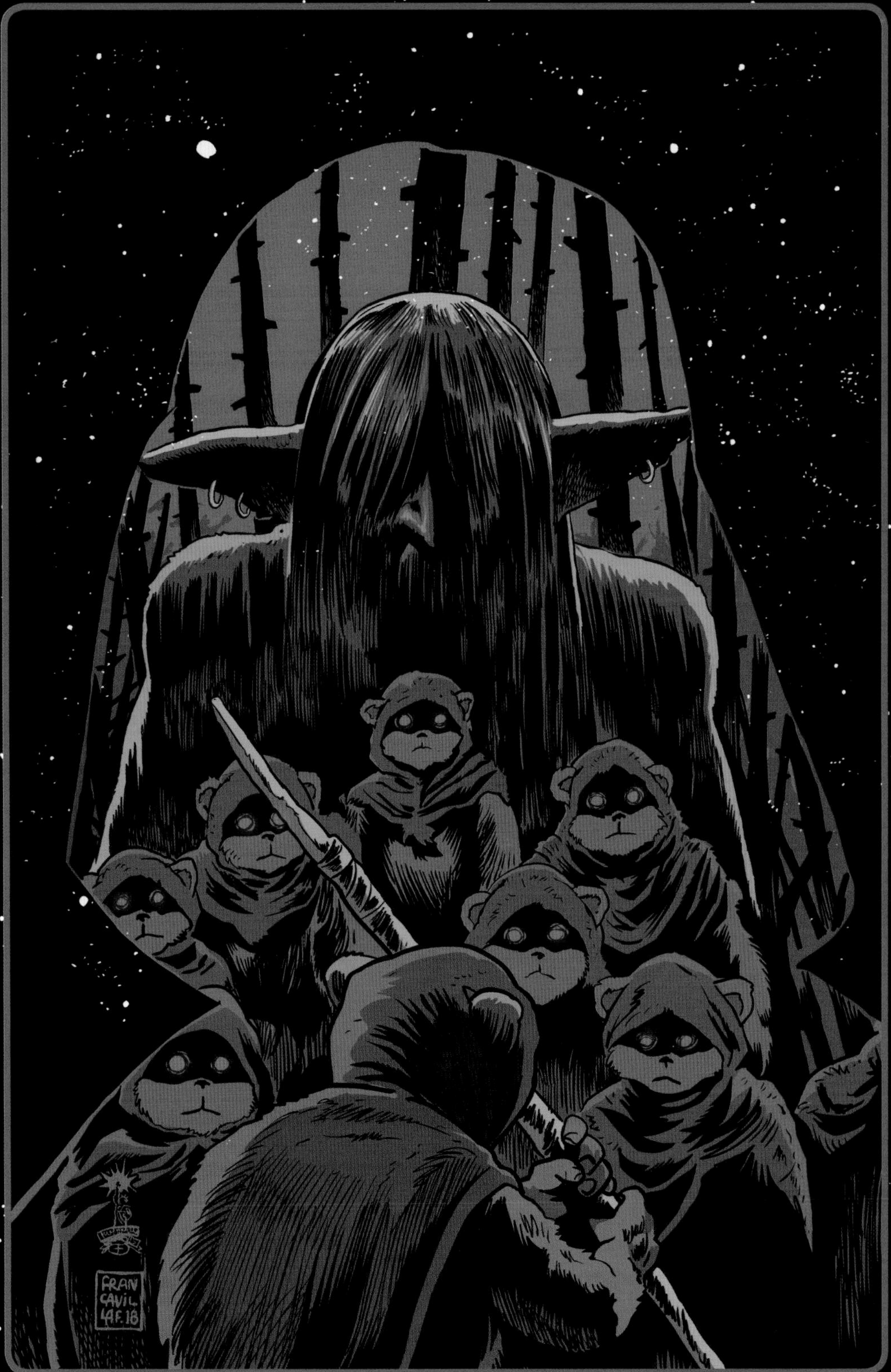
FRAN
CAVIL
LA F. 18

Art by Francesco Francavilla

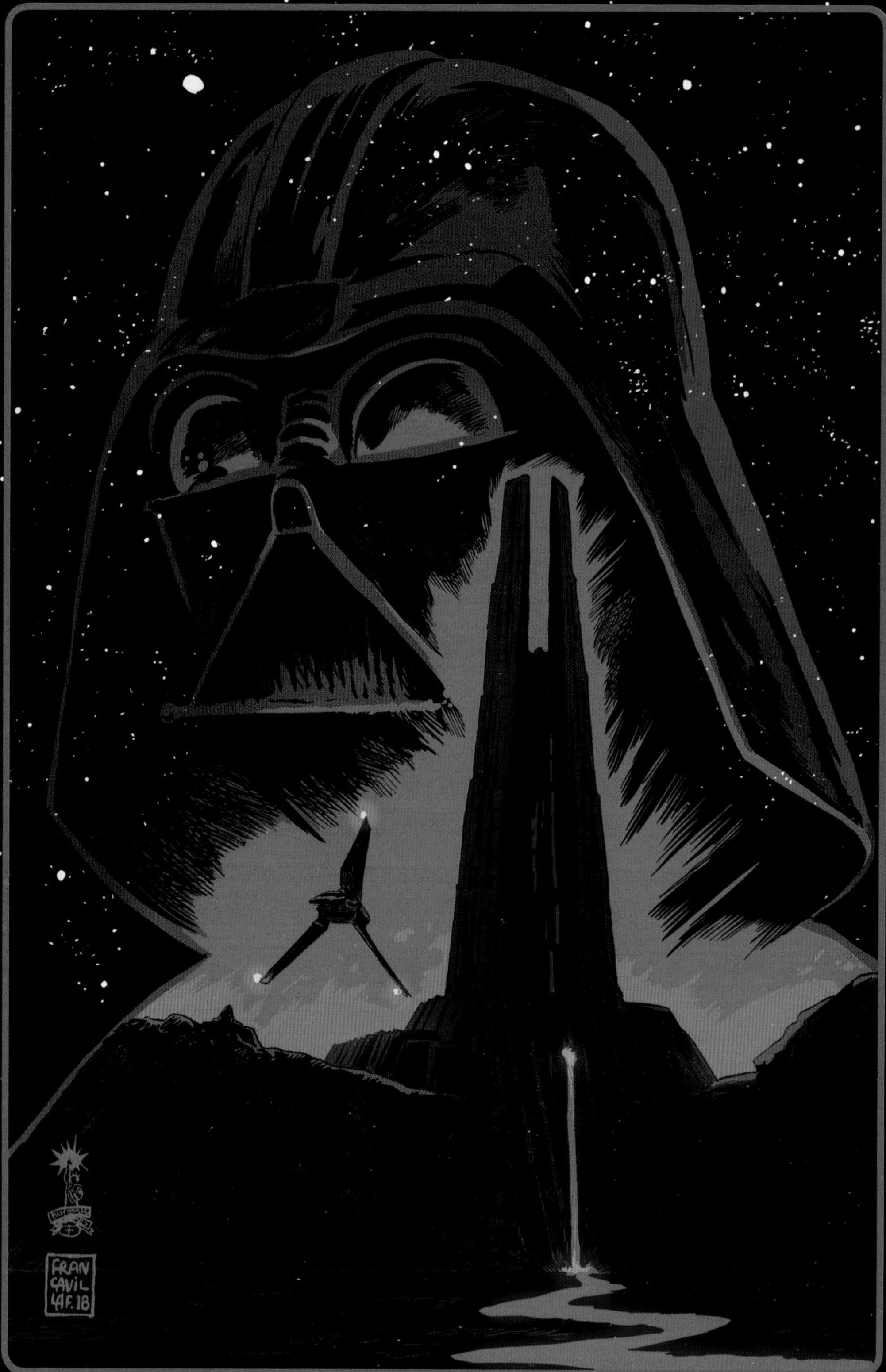
FRAN CAVIL LA F. 18

Art by Francesco Francavilla

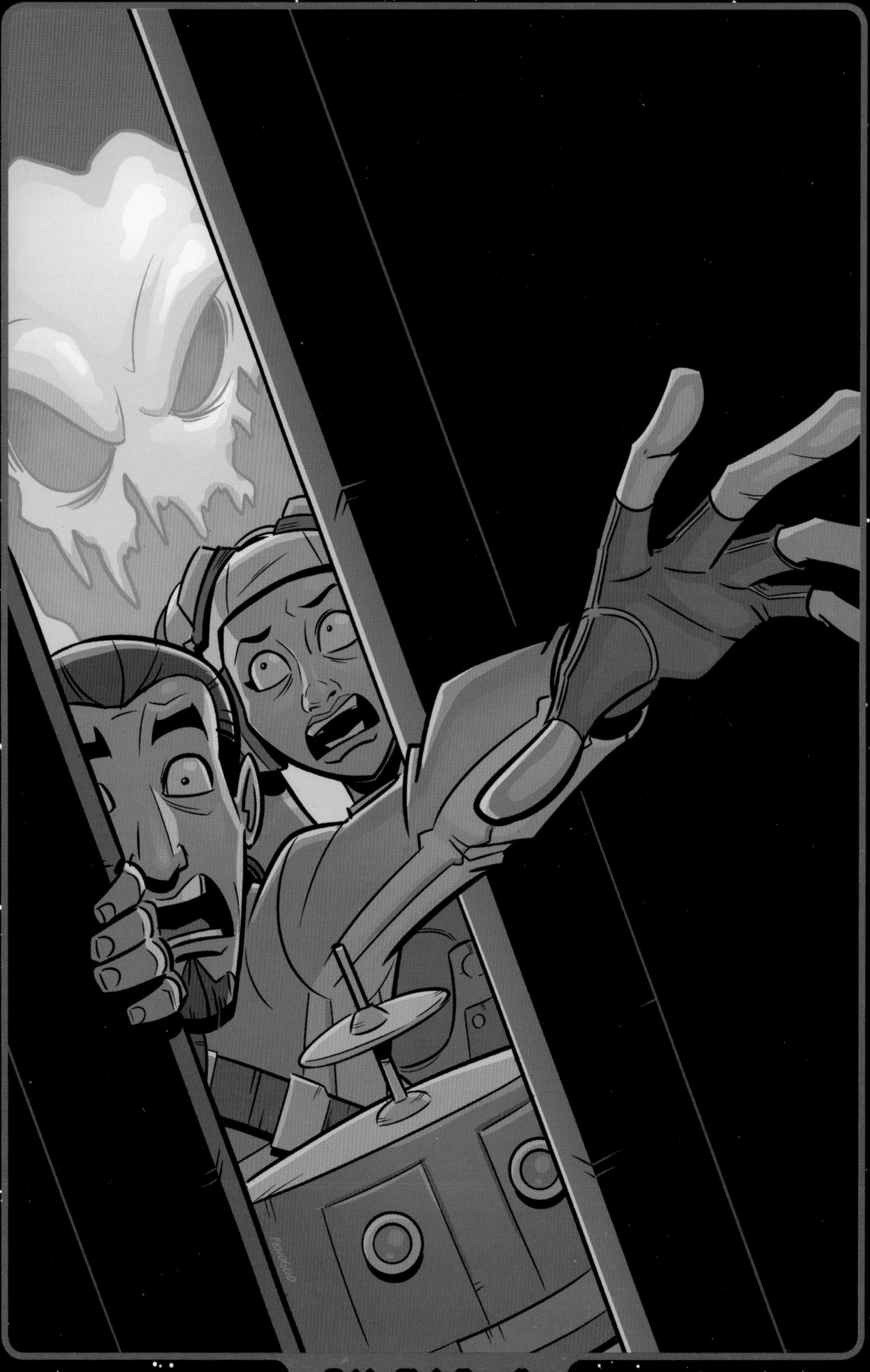

Art by Chris Fenoglio

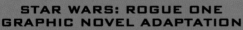